To
Audrey:
I hope you
enjoy reading my
novel.
Love,
Brenda Lee
8/4/2000

WEB OF DECEIT

A METAMORPHOSIS NOVEL

Brenda Sue

Fairmount/Ballou Publishing
Chelmsford, Massachusetts

Library of Congress Cataloging-in-Publication Data
Brenda Sue

PUBLISHING HISTORY
WEB OF DECEIT/Brenda Sue
Publishing date, January, 2000
ISBN: 0-9677124-0-8
Printed in the United States of America
WORDPRO PRESS, Ithaca, New York
Cover illustration and design by: Barbara Wells

For Harvey

When I started writing this book, you were a beautiful memory. Thank you for coming back into my life and making my memories, hopes, and dreams a reality. I'll be forever grateful for your love, inspiration, guidance and encouragement.

Chapter One

Do not imagine that character is determined at birth. We have been given free will. Any person can become as righteous as Moses or as wicked as Jereboam. We ourselves decide whether to make ourselves learned or ignorant, compassionate or cruel, generous or miserly. No one forces us, no one decides for us, no one drags us along one path or the other; we ourselves, by our own volition choose our own way.

Maimonides, 12th century

Stoney Brook, Massachusetts • October 1991 • 5:54 a.m.

The familiar terror gripped her again. She struggled to escape as the tip of the long silver blade glinted above her in the half light. He straddled her body and, leaning downward, pressed his left arm across her chest, pinning both her shoulders to the ground. With his right arm, he lowered the tip of the stiletto downward until it touched her neck. She fought against him when a spasm of pain seized her as the point pierced her skin. A moment later Suzanne felt a warm trickle of blood oozing downward across her slender throat and into her hair splayed out on the ground beneath her.

Feigning surrender, she forced her trembling body to go limp and still beneath him. She waited for the moment when she knew he would pause to catch his breath. When he did, she mustered her strength, twisted to the right beneath him, shoved Brian out of the way with a kick, and rose to her feet.

A narrow, dark hallway loomed ahead and enveloped her as she fled into it. Suddenly, a door opened in front of her and she was blinded by the light outside. As she pushed herself to run as fast as she could, her legs began to tremble. Then, her weak knees gave way momentarily and she stumbled.

Close behind, he needed only that slight lapse. The distance lessened between them, with one vault he sprang at her and pulled her down again. "Suzanne, Suzanne you can't get away" he whispered close to her ear as he pressed himself down on her again. His hands closed around her throat and the wound above them widened. Blood flowed freely from her neck as the life within her began to fade.

The alarm's shrill ring brought Suzanne out of her nightmare. She had difficulty swallowing and her hands went directly to her throat, half expecting to feel the sticky blood.

Reluctantly, she sat up and reached across the foot of the bed to the bureau and pushed in the cruel white knob. Her comfortable bed enticed her to return to its warmth under the large down comforter. Pulling the covers back over her head, she let its protective refuge provide shelter. Last evening's dull headache returned with a vengeance. The throbbing returned every time she thought of the information her client, Mrs. Pearlman, had inadvertently revealed. From the disclosure, Suzanne had surmised that her ex-husband, Brian, was involved in a scheme to take the Pearlmans' family business away from them. Even if her guess was wrong, her intuition told her that no possible good could come of his dealings. Should she use the knowledge and the power she possessed to destroy him and the others involved in this racket? She could quite possibly ruin the man who was the father of her children.

Suzanne asked herself, "What would happen if my daughters find out that I'm responsible for their father's downfall? Will they understand? Shaking her head she told herself, "I could be worrying needlessly."

Suppressing the urge to remain in bed, sheltered from life's cruel blows, Suzanne gradually lifted herself off the mattress and forced herself to emerge from her refuge. If her suspicions were true, Brian would be in deep trouble with the law. Shaking her head, she thought, "He has done many foolish things over the years, but I never thought he was capable of breaking the law."

She wrapped her robe around her and descended the spiral staircase, oblivious to the prattle coming from the early morning talk show on the television in the family room. As she neared the bottom of the stairs, a haunting apparition of Brian appeared before her. His brazen, enticing smile, mocked her, as always. It was a ruse.

She sat at the kitchen table, poured herself a cup of hot tea and opened the morning newspaper. She tried to get involved in the current events, ignoring the queasy feeling in the pit of her stomach. Suzanne hoped that the thunderstorms that were forecast would wait until her plane was safely airborne and well on its way to Bermuda.

Mrs. Walsh, her housekeeper and dear friend, startled Suzanne as she suddenly entered the kitchen to begin washing dishes. Chattering incessantly about Suzanne's upcoming vacation, she advised Suzanne, "Why you chose Bermuda is a puzzle to me and to go alone without a friend - well, I just don't understand."

Suzanne tried to keep the impatience out of her voice. " I know I could have chosen a more intriguing locale, but as I told you before I have my reasons for going back there. Now, enough of this; I'm already tense enough. I hope that this tea settles my nerves. You know how much I *love* flying."

Mrs. Walsh wiped her hands on her apron as she turned away from the sink to look at Suzanne, lovingly, like the daughter she had become. She walked over and hugged her tenderly. "I hope you have a wonderful trip and that you accomplish what you want. It's been a long and hard fifteen years. It seems all you've done is work, work, work, since you opened your first *Metamorphosis* salon. My goodness, you've built so many spas all over the world now; I can't keep up with them all." With a look of remorse she continued, "I'm sorry if I upset you. Have an excellent time and I'll be here waiting for your safe return."

Logan Airport • Boston, Massachusetts • October 1991 • 11:10 a.m.

Suzanne boarded the plane early with one other first-class passenger. She settled in next to the window, removed the latest best seller from her purse and read while she waited for the remaining passengers to board. She was glad no delays were expected and the plane would take off on schedule.

As the aircraft taxied into position on the runway and the engines began to roar, Suzanne noticed the man sitting next to her clasping his hands together and digging his fingernails into his palms. Acknowledging his obvious distress, she asked, "Are you nervous? Does the noise bother you?"

"Well, I try to stay calm, but the noise is unsettling. I find it difficult to relax whenever I fly."

"Before I got used to flying, I felt that way too."

"I'm sure you realize that most accidents happen on take off or landing, though."

Suzanne continued to reassure him. "Well, you're safer here than you would be on a bus or a cab in Manhattan, you know."

"You're right, but I hate not being in control."

"I'm usually in control, too, of my business and most other aspects of my life. I like it like that! Not knowing what's going on in the cockpit drives me crazy, but I've learned to let go and let the pilot handle the job."

As the jet gained altitude, she noticed that he gradually relaxed. She breathed a little easier herself.

Suzanne looked down on the city. As the plane banked, she could identify different areas around Boston that had been the backdrop of her life. As she watched the ground diminish below, she saw the city from a strange new perspective - a curious mosaic of various neighborhoods and people. All had played a part in her life, some good, some bad. As the 757 climbed higher and went into the clouds, the scene disappeared. She was left with her memories - and her dilemma. Forcing herself to suppress the problem that clouded her mind, she returned to her book. Unable to concentrate on the story, her mind returned again and again to her ex-husband, Brian.

"Brian, Brian, how could you be so witless and misguided? You've really outdone yourself this time," she thought.

As the plane leveled off at cruising altitude, Suzanne put her book away and tried to doze, but she couldn't sleep and her mind wandered back to the earlier years.

Stoney Brook, Massachusetts • 1972

Her three daughters, Hope, Melanie and Taylor, had adjusted well when she and Brian divorced. The girls were young at the time and Suzanne hoped that if she was a stable and well-balanced parent, they would suffer less trauma. After Brian moved out, he saw them regularly. Their home life was as secure and supportive as it could be, but Suzanne was aware of the many problems that could befall the children of divorced parents. The girls were all in their twenties now and they were well-adjusted and happy. Suzanne was proud of her daughters and she was sometimes astounded that everybody survived those unpleasant early years.

An only child herself, Suzanne handled each of them as she had been treated by her doting parents. While the girls were small, Suzanne managed to keep them under control with the help of her parents and her housekeeper, Mrs. Walsh. It had been an arduous task, raising the children alone and developing her business at the same time. When they became teenagers, life changed drastically.

Suzanne always thought that she would be spared the traditional turmoil of the teen years since she had worked so hard to establish a good rapport with her children; but it was not to be. She firmly believed that handling her teenagers had been harder than getting her spa off the ground and establishing herself as a successful member of the business community.

She had come to live in Stoney Brook, there she was, so very young at the teenage year of 18 - - vulnerable, naïve, in a town far from her family, and placing her trust in a person she did not really know. Free finally from her partents' grip and out on her own, there was, nevertheless, an eerie sense of insecurity that rode tandem with her hopes. Raising her daughters in this affluent community, where young people could obtain liquor or drugs easily and many had broken their parents' hearts. She was thankful that her girls had survived those rebellious years and gone on to become lovely young women with successful careers.

Suzanne remembered when she had been in her twenties. It seemed so long ago. At age twenty-three, Suzanne had already been married for five years and had two active little girls. She had little free time for herself. At that age she thought that she knew everything. Looking back now, she realized that she was very wrong. At the time, she never fully understood the complexities of life and could never have anticipated the adversities that would ensue.

The plane hit a patch of turbulence and Suzanne was jolted out of her reverie as the service cart rattled noisily in the aisle beside her. The seat belt sign stayed on, but the stewardess continued to serve drinks. Suzanne ordered a mimosa to calm her nerves.

Hamilton, Bermuda • 1:27 p.m.

She was looking forward to visiting this beautiful island country again and prayed that the vacation here would help her to put some perspective back into her life. She needed to decide what action she should take.

As the plane began its decent to Bermuda, Suzanne watched the land come into focus and remembered her honeymoon twenty-seven years ago. A lot had happened since then. After her divorce, she had worked arduously to develop her worldwide chain of successful salons. She had to admit she had become a workaholic at the age of forty-six. In her efforts to manage each of her establishments, she spent much of her time flying from one to the other. She made it mandatory that Hope and Taylor also visit each spa regularly. Suzanne had many personal clients that came to her in every salon and she loved working directly with them.

Suzanne checked into the secluded beach front resort. Her private bungalow on the shore had a breathtaking panoramic view of pink sand and sparkling turquoise water. "Why would anyone ever want to leave a spot like this?" she thought to herself as she unpacked. The air itself was heady and relaxing and Suzanne could feel herself beginning to unwind. "I'll just lay down for a while and then I'll look around the rest of the hotel." In less than five minutes she was fast asleep.

When she opened her eyes it was already three-thirty in the afternoon. For the first time in ages she didn't care what time it was. Usually, her very demanding and tight schedule ran her life. She was determined to be as carefree as humanly possible on this vacation. She realized that one week would not completely restore her emotional well-being, but it was a good start and she hoped she would find the strength she needed to sort out the perplexing web of deceit that she found herself caught in.

Suzanne stepped through her door directly onto the beach and found her way through the abundant hibiscus plants to the shore. As the water lapped at her bare feet, she watched the snorkelers diving and bobbing in the clear waters.

She settled into a lounge chair and ordered a rum swizzle from the waiter. Slowly sipping her exotic drink, she gazed out at the clear, blue waters and let the sun's warmth beat down on her body. Luxuriating in the fine weather and the island's casual atmosphere, Suzanne closed her eyes. She remembered the events leading up to her first trip to Bermuda twenty-seven years ago.

His name was Brian Morse. He was older than most of the boys she knew. She caught herself staring at him when they were first introduced. Not the rugged, handsome type that usually attracted her, he wore black, horned-rimmed glasses, was good looking in a studious sort of way with almond-shaped, hazel eyes, and dark brown hair. He wore clothes that were just a bit more formal than that of the other young men she knew. If the others wore chinos and an open shirt, he added a necktie and sport jacket. He made up for his somewhat short stature with an exuberant personality and a great sense of humor. He spent the whole evening making Suzanne laugh.

Suzanne couldn't help noting how different he was from her first love, Stephen LeVigne. Thinking of Stephen's six-foot-one, muscular frame and his large dreamy, azure eyes made her heart miss a beat. Stephen had strong, Roman features and a determined square jaw. Suzanne loved to run her fingers through his dark, wavy hair. He had a slight lisp that crept into his speech when he was excited about something. Once when he arrived to pick her up for a date, Suzanne had to laugh at the outfit he had on. He simply had no color sense. It was as if nobody had ever taught him how to coordinate clothes. After that, he made it a point to ask her advice beforehand about what he should wear.

Massachusetts • *1963*

When his father died unexpectedly, Stephen had to take over his father's role. Everyone now looked to him as the head of the household. On the day of the funeral, Stephen, in a daze, listened to Rabbi Solomon deliver his father's eulogy to the friends and family who had come to pay their last respects to Max LeVigne. The rabbi spoke of the wonderful husband and father who had been taken in the prime of his life by a heart attack.

At the graveside, Stephen was surrounded by many friends and relatives, as he gathered his younger sisters and brothers close to him. When he and his siblings climbed into the limousine together to head home, he spotted Suzanne, but he couldn't catch her attention. He hoped she would come back to the house while he and the rest of his family sat Shiva.

Their own plans must wait now. He must explain his new responsibilities to her and his need to finish college before they could go on with their life together. He had a feeling she might not understand, but she deserved to know what was happening, since they had been dating and loved each other since childhood. He was the first child in the family to have the chance of a college education. He remembered his parents' financial difficulties and their determination to ensure a college degree for their children; a chance that hadn't been afforded them. Stephen shuddered as he remembered the many evenings his parents had come home exhausted after working their tedious second and third jobs.

Suzanne was talking to his cousin Esther as Stephen entered the kitchen. She kissed him on the cheek and extended her sympathy to him.

"She smells so good," he thought. He wanted to hold her, kiss the small of her neck and tell her how much he needed and wanted her, especially now.

After the week of sitting Shiva at his house Stephen had a substantial amount of studying to do. During many of the following evenings his head fell onto his books as he dozed off at the kitchen table. He woke up dazed, forgetting for a moment where he was. Suzanne was never far from his thoughts. He wanted to call her but realized by the time he got home from work and finished studying for the evening, it was too late for the phone call he desperately wanted to make.

When he finally saw her, things weren't the same and he couldn't understand why. Stephen was totally shattered after Suzanne deliberately started a quarrel that led to the end of their relationship. "She's such a brat," he often thought, as he forced himself to focus his mind on his studies rather than on Suzanne, whom he felt didn't understand his position. "Doesn't she see that I'm working for our future together?" He forced himself to go on with his life. "I'll give it a little time. Someday soon she'll come to her senses and appreciate what I'm doing."

Suzanne was heartbroken when she and Stephen separated. She realized it was a foolish argument that preceded the end of their bond. The petty quarrel was over the fact that he hadn't called her during the week of his final examinations and Suzanne wanted him to devote more time to her. She felt disconnected and alone without Stephen. He meant everything to her, like a best friend, brother and lover. She missed their endless hours of conversation on the telephone. She looked to him as a mentor, helping her with school work and more. When playing hooky from school, instead of carousing with her friends, she would attend Stephen's college classes with him. She learned the word UTOPIA on one of those days - - all at once her idealistic hopes and dreams vanished. When she met Brian after the split from Stephen, she wondered if she could ever learn to love again, but she soon found herself engaged.

Suzanne started having serious doubts two months before the actual wedding. Besides being ten years older than her, Brian was not Jewish. Brian's parents themselves were of different Christian faiths and practiced neither. It didn't seem to her that they had given their children any religious training, convictions or values. She tried to discuss her concerns with Dorothy, but her mother dismissed her notions and said, "Every bride-to-be has some doubts. Brian is well-educated, makes lots of money and his parents are rich. As long as you bring up your children in the Jewish faith and he attends temple with you, it'll work out." Suzanne didn't want to hurt her parents and have them lose hard earned deposit monies - - she didn't know what else to do except go through with the wedding.

Even up to the day of her wedding to Brian she missed Stephen and wondered if she was making the right decision. She realized she was marrying Brian on the rebound, but his constant attention and devotion to her kept her unbalanced and unable to sort through it all. Young and highly disraught over the termination of her ties to her first love, Suzanne was vulnerable to the intervention and pressures from her parents. They saw Brian as a person of some wealth and misread his ten years older than Suzanne to represent stability. They were superficial in their assessment and inaccurate. They had browbeaten Suzanne into submission to sever the relationship she had yearned to sustain and were again imposing their will with unrelenting zeal. Alone, with no siblings to comfort her and with her true love now gone, Suzanne knew not where to turn. All appeared hopeless with youthful dreams now shattered.

Ignoring her doubts, Suzanne married Brian. In later years she came to realize that she should have paid more attention to that little voice in her head.

Suzanne did not understand how Brian's parents had raised him, but that upbringing would make a big difference in years to come. In their own way they did love him, but had a hard time displaying their feelings. They criticized his every move. Consequently, he constantly strove to win their approval. Invariably, every friend or girlfriend he brought home was ridiculed. Then came Suzanne.

Stephen found them hard to believe when he heard rumors about Suzanne's impending marriage. "How could she marry someone else?" he asked himself. On the day of the wedding, he restrained his frustration and tears and drove recklessly to the reception hall where "his Suzanne" would be married to another. "She should be walking down that aisle to pledge her loyalty and love to me," he thought. He parked his car a few blocks away and entered a darkened doorway across the street. He watched as Suzanne emerged from the limousine. "My God, she's beautiful," he thought. After the guests were seated, Stephen stepped into the hall, staying far to the rear, concealed by the large flowering trees adorning the room. He mustered all his strength not to grab the love of his life and carry her far away from the place. When the rabbi asked if anyone would come forth if these two should not be joined as one, Stephen left disheartened, tears visibly running down his face. He wanted to step forward and tell everyone in attendance that she really loved him and she was the only woman he could ever love. But, he didn't want to embarrass or hurt Suzanne in any way. "What if she really loves this guy?" he asked himself. "She must," he reasoned, "Why is she doing this?" he kept thinking. Discretely Stephen walked out of the hall and out of her life.

Everyone's eyes were focused on the beautiful young woman as she walked down the aisle in her mother's wedding gown. A petite five feet four inches tall, she had inherited her mother's large, dark brown eyes and high cheekbones. Her fair skin, like her father's, radiated with happiness. Her natural, dark blonde hair had been highlighted to a becoming light blonde. The guests who had attended her parents' wedding were reminded of that occasion as they watched Suzanne keep the slow pace to the music as she met her future husband.

Underneath the chupah that was adorned with beautiful orchids, French tulips, lilies, peonies and greenery, the rabbi evoked their rapt attention as his resounding voice echoed the traditional sermon and religious marriage ceremony. The first cup of wine - representing their betrothal - was sipped at the beginning of the ceremony, reminding them of joy and their common destiny, for henceforth their lives would be inseparable. Brian slipped the plain marriage band on Suzanne's finger, a simple ring, unadorned, a circle without beginning or end. Suzanne then placed Brian's ring on his finger. Suzanne's voice was barely audible as she repeated the rabbi's words.

The couple shared the second cup of wine after the actual marriage. This gesture symbolized shared sacrifices of husband and wife and burdens that would be lighter falling upon two deeply devoted people, each bearing equal measure. The rabbi then placed the glass in a cloth, and Brian, accepting his traditional role, broke the glass with his left foot, climaxing the service. People clapped and cheered as they heard the noise of the breaking of the glass. To many, it symbolized the frightening away of evil spirits that were jealous of human happiness. To others more pious, it recalled the destruction of the temple, a symbol of the sorrows of Israel. Brian kissed Suzanne tenderly when her best friend, Beverly, lifted her veil.

The evening flew by, and soon the couple was off to spend their first night together as husband and wife. They spent that evening at a hotel near the airport. The flight for Bermuda was leaving at seven o'clock the following morning.

Suzanne was apprehensive about her wedding night. Although Brian and she had done some very heavy petting while they were engaged, they both wanted to wait until their wedding night to actually make love. Brian turned the radio to romantic music and opened the chilled champagne, as Suzanne changed into her white, lace, chiffon negligee set. He couldn't wait to hold her in his arms and make passionate love to her. Realizing that Suzanne had never had sexual intercourse, he was prepared to be gentle.

He was in awe when she finally came out and walked across the room to him. He thought she looked sumptuous. The lights were dim, and, as she slowly strode toward him, he could see her nakedness under her gown. She went to him with apprehension. Their lips touched, their wet, moist mouths hungering for more closeness. His tongue probed her partially opened mouth, guiding her tongue to explore his. His hands moved down and caressed her body, while their passionate kisses inspired more exploration of their fervid bodies.

He slowly slipped the straps from her nightgown and she let it fall to the floor. He gently moved her to the bed and started to kiss her body with his wet lips. Starting at her neck, taking her firm large breasts into his mouth, gently sucking her erect, pink nipples till she moaned with passion. His hands were now massaging her buttocks and finally his fingers felt the moist wetness between her thighs. His head went down to her groin and his lips and tongue now explored her moist crevice, enjoying the pleasures that she was experiencing for the first time while she moaned for more.

Suzanne was wild with sexual excitement. She had never experienced anything like this before. The quivering of her body was uncontrollable; she felt exhilaration. She wanted to give him as much pleasure as she was having. She responded to his kisses with caresses and cravings of her own. Her kissing and probing tongue started at his lips and moved down to his toes, while she softly rubbed his body. Suddenly, Suzanne hesitated. Although her own body ached to be fulfilled, she felt unsure of what she was doing. Was she performing like the other woman she read about in those true romance magazines? She felt inadequate. Brian was eager for her to continue as he guided her. She then embraced his solid erection with her mouth, until he groaned with desire. She loved his reaction and the taste of his manhood in her mouth. Gently, putting her on her back he entered her. His thrusts penetrated deeply within her and they moved in unison, consummating their sexual appetites as they climaxed together.

She had been afraid, and now realized that she shouldn't have been. He was a gentle and, at the same time, a great lover. She had heard many horror stories of honeymoon nights and was glad that hers was a good one. They fell asleep in each other's arms.

Chapter Two

Hamilton, Bermuda • October, 1991

Suzanne couldn't believe what her ex-husband, Brian had gotten himself into this time. He was usually an astute businessman, but he sure lacked common sense. "Brian, how could you be so stupid and misguided?" she thought as she lay on the lounge chair enjoying the quiet solitude of her vacation. Suddenly she realized there was something she could do. She signaled the waiter for a telephone, then called the one person she knew she could rely on - Nancy.

"Hi. I hope I'm not disturbing you."

"What are you, Crazy? You're supposed to be on vacation. Why are you calling me? The business hasn't collapsed because you took a few days off, you know. Is everything OK? Did you hurt yourself on one of those mopeds?"

Laughing at her friend and business partner, Suzanne explained the reason for her call.

"I'm fine; really, but I have a favor to ask you. I came to Bermuda to decide what to do about a problem I have. And, don't jump to conclusions; it has nothing to do with the spa or our relationship, but I'm calling you because of our relationship. I feel I can tell you anything and you'll be able to keep your mouth shut." She took a deep breath before continuing. "I need your support Nancy and it's dangerous. Don't say anything 'til I'm done, then, you can ask me anything you want or tell me what you think."

"What? Tell me."

"Well, first I'm going to tell you something one of my clients disclosed to me and I think it involves Brian, my ex-husband.   Do you remember my client, Mrs. Pearlman? She and her husband are the ones who survived the death camps in Poland.   Then they eventually came to this country and through ambition and hard work made a good life for themselves here."

"When she came in for her monthly facial two weeks ago, I noticed that she was extremely tense.   The more I tried to put her at ease, the more anxious she became. Usually, clients fall asleep during the massage, but she wouldn't shut up.   She had just found out that her husband has lung cancer and would be undergoing extensive treatments, but something else was bothering her too."

"Although I've never met Mr. Pearlman, I know by the way his wife speaks of him, he must be a very special person.   She never says anything bad about him, only nice things."

"Well, Mr. Pearlman has numerous cash businesses. He has the Midas touch, and everything he owns makes money.   Right now, he owns four laundromats and dry cleaners, three restaurants, two bowling alleys, four cinemas, five lounges, and he just opened two pool halls. The pool halls also have billiards and darts and they encourage woman and couples to play.   They have leagues and lessons for people who want to learn how to play the new 'in' sports."

"Well, this is what she told me."   Feigning a Yiddish accent Suzanne elaborated. 'My husband Harry, he's such a good husband and such a vonderful family man.   Never mind being such a great provider. It's not fair that after all he's been through, he has to go through this torment too. He's been feeling soo ill lately. He can't sleep through an entire night with all his coughing. I'm so nervous. My body is feeling his pain.'

'He was born in Poland, you know, and survived the death camps. After the war there was nothing left of him but skin and bones. When he came over here, kind, but poor relatives in Philadelphia took him in. They cared for him and, after getting him on his feet, they encouraged him to go to college. In those days it was very hard for a poor boy to further his education - and he had nothing.'

'Harry worked hard, had three jobs and went to night school. He has good business sense. He eventually finished his MBA. That was quite an accomplishment.'

Suzanne held her hand up against her forehead, blocking the strong rays of the sun from her face, and continued. "She was pensive for a short while, then she told me the rest of the story." 'Did I tell you Harry is now a millionaire? Not that I'm bragging, but I'm so very proud of him.'

"I told her that was wonderful, but she should relax and enjoy this facial. Mrs. Pearlman let out a heavy sigh and continued, 'I feel better when I'm talking.' So, I decided to let her continue and didn't try to stop her again. I thought maybe she needed to unwind. I don't think she had anyone else she could talk to about this!"

'We came to Boston, and eventually moved to Newton, because of the schools there. My Harry, he wanted our children to have a good education and also we could be with people of our own kind. He didn't want them going away to any private schools. I guess losing his parents and brothers the way he did, he wanted to keep his family close around him. Even though our children are grown and away at college now, my Harry and I wouldn't leave Newton. No, we've made many friends through the years. I just hope that they can find a cure for my Harry.' "

"Then she rambled on about his businesses. You know, I frequently hear about personal problems or confidential business deals from my clients, and I've kept many secrets and confidences, so it didn't surprise me when she started talking about the businesses. Sometimes I take my clients' troubles home with me and, without being too obvious about it, I'll give them advice at their next visit. But what Mrs. Pearlman told me that day was a real shock. It sounds as if Brian is involved in something illegal that's going on at the Pearlmans' main office."

Clearing her throat while she looked carefully around to make sure no one was watching or listening, Suzanne continued. " 'Suzanne,' she went on, 'I'll tell you, my Harry, he's sick, but it's not only from the cancer. It's from the nogoodnicks that he's gotten involved with in some of his business deals.'

'I'm telling you, Suzanne, there are some very bad people in this world.'

"I told her 'You don't have to tell me that, I've known a few of them myself.'"

'There is a business venture that my Harry got involved with, that the owners should only croak. They take over the management of a company and make investments with other people's money. I tell you, something isn't kosher. When Harry questions them, they nicely tell him to keep his eyes and ears closed, and find something else to do. And, it's his business. I don't think that Morse Associates is an ethical company.'

"Nancy, I'm not kidding. I almost lost it as I continued Mrs. Pearlman's massage. I kept thinking - could Mrs. Pearlman be talking about Brian's corporation? Mrs. Pearlman doesn't know my last name. Most of my clients only know me as the owner of the *Metamorphosis Spa*."

"I had to find out. I mean, how many Morse Associates could there be? In a roundabout way I asked Mrs. Pearlman some questions indirectly, trying to figure out if Brian was involved. Where was the business located? Did she ever meet with the men involved? What did they look like? I don't think she realized what I was doing."

"As I listened to her answers, I realized it had to be Brian's firm that she was talking about. It sounded as if he was involved with some kind of money laundering, but I can't be sure without more information. I feel sorry for the Pearlmans and, this is where you come in. I hope with your help we can discover the truth, one way or another. You know, Brian has done many cruel things over the years, but I never thought he would be stupid enough to do something illegal."

"Well, that's the end of the story, or maybe it's the beginning. I don't know; call it a sense of duty or principle, whatever, but I've got to get to the bottom of this. It's been on my mind constantly since she told me. Will you help me? You don't have to answer right now, but think about it and when I see you, tell me what you've decided."

"Of course, I'll do whatever I can for you. Call me as soon as you get back, okay?"

Returning the phone to the waiter Suzanne settled back into the chaise and again tried to relax as thoughts of her early married life reentered her mind.

Stoney Brook, Massachusetts • 1965

Daily life, bills, struggling at work, and going to school nights had a grim effect on Brian. He was striving to attain the highest rank in his class. Anything less would be unacceptable. In addition, he was teaching, going to graduate school and lining up business opportunities for his future advertising and marketing agency. His sense of humor completely disappeared and the irritability he displayed to Suzanne was a side of his personality that she had not seen before.

Suzanne also worked hard at her job and maintained a luxurious home for Brian. After working a strenuous day, she came home, made dinner and while he studied, she did the dishes and cleaned the house. On weekends she ironed his shirts and her clothes. Always meticulous about his clothing, Brian insisted that she iron his socks and underwear, as his mother used to do. She did it, but did not like it.

If the house was not cleaned to his satisfaction, he would instruct her to scrub it again. Suzanne didn't think he was serious at first, but she came to realize that he was quite earnest. At times he would give her the white glove test, running his hand over the counter tops, and making sure there was no dust on the furniture or under the bed. If the silverware holder had crumbs in it, he would dump the whole container on the floor and insist that she wash it. Suzanne was brought up to be neat and clean, "but this is ridiculous," she thought as she knelt on the floor wiping up crumbs. She knew why he was imposing irrational pressures on himself and her, but understanding it didn't make her life any easier.

She hoped that after his graduation, the pressures on him would lessen and he would return to being the man she had dated, married and learned to love. She realized, all too late, that she had married Brian on the rebound from Stephen, but she was determined to be a good wife. After graduation, the old Brian did return. He opened Morse Associates with another student, Carl DiBonna. Carl was also an aggressive young man and together they developed wonderful ideas for their company. Life fell into a routine. Suzanne loved her work and took pleasure in decorating their new home, although Brian still insisted on an immaculate house.

On weekends they socialized with neighbors and old friends, and, of course, their relatives. Suzanne loved entertaining, and delighted in serving the many ethnic recipes her Grandmother Pessa had taught her. Morse Associates landed two prime accounts, and had bids in for others as well.

Brian and Carl worked hard and frequently brainstormed until midnight or later at Brian's insistence. At times they asked Suzanne's opinions on publicity projects and advertising copy. She loved being involved with the business and readily accepted the challenges. Though Brian was less irritable, he now had different pressures. Suzanne tried to take some of the load off his shoulders and suggested she handle their personal finances and bills. For some strange reason, Brian wouldn't hear of it. "I'll pay all of the bills and don't ask me again, I won't discuss it" an angry Brian retorted. Although Suzanne was disappointed, she kept her feelings to herself. She thought it was strange that she didn't even know what their monthly expenses were, or if any of their money was invested. She decided not to pressure him right now, but resolved to try again later.

A year after they were married Suzanne found herself pregnant. With delight, she prepared a lovely steak dinner. With candlelight and romantic music in the background, she told him the good news. Brian was ecstatic. After the pregnancy was announced to Brian's family, some comments were made that didn't make sense to Suzanne.

Suzanne and Brian were in the habit of visiting his family one Sunday a month. As an only child, Suzanne was delighted to become part of Brian's larger family. On many of these occasions, card games would take place, and inevitably, arguments ensued. Sometimes as much as two-hundred dollars would be lost at polka, rummy, whist or blackjack. Suzanne could not understand how relatives would take hard earned money from one another.

When Suzanne's family got together, there was plenty of friendly chatter, and the young children entertained the adults. Very rarely did altercations occur in the "Pollack Family Circle Club." When the adults gathered they would play pokeeno, fish or whist. During warm weather, all her aunts, uncles, first and second cousins would get together at Norembega Park or another large area to play softball and picnic. In the winter months they would meet in a large hall, drink, dance and have an old-fashioned good time.

Occasionally Brian's father would grab his mother by her dress collar and pinch her arm if she played the wrong card that would make them lose a round. The people playing with them paid little attention to this mean and cruel act. They were used to this behavior. Suzanne couldn't believe some of the stories that were brought up in these conversations.

There was always painful fun being made of someone. The children were made to compete with each other, rather than be best friends. The adults were like mean adolescents who had never grown up. They would snicker at and ridicule each other. The closeness that Suzanne shared with her family was missing among these misguided people.

At one of these gatherings Suzanne heard some comments that gave her goose bumps. It seemed Brian's father had a terrible temper. When he was younger he had often kicked and beaten Brian. His siblings and parents now laughed about these stories.

Before they were married, Suzanne and Brian had spent very little time with his family. If they had, Suzanne realized she would have seen the unhealthy atmosphere Brian had grown up in. She wondered what psychological effects this abusive background might have had on her husband.

When Suzanne was five months pregnant, feeling wonderful, and the exhaustion of her first trimester had passed, she was looking forward to the birth of their first child.   She and Brian wallpapered the smallest bedroom and picked out baby furniture.

One Sunday afternoon after they had attended an informal dance performance at the Dorothy Quincy Suite in Boston given by one of Brian's clients, an incident happened that was to set the stage for the remainder of their life together. Brian had always been an aggressive driver. He used the horn and swore at other motorists to express displeasure if he felt that person had cut him off or was driving too close to him.

As they were heading home on Route 2 in Cambridge, another driver drove extremely close to the rear of their car. "Who the hell does he think he is? I'll show him!" Brian sped up and then, purposely, decreased his speed and drove very slowly. He then pumped his brake. Suzanne asked him to please stop acting that way and ignore the other auto.   The situation escalated when the other man cut in front of them, stopped, and got out of his vehicle. He was a rather large person, and Suzanne knew he could beat the living daylights out of Brian, if given half a chance.

"Here I'm pregnant, and Brian's acting like a jerk," she thought as her own anger built. As the man headed for the sedan, Brian took off. By the time the other guy got back into his hatchback, Brian had run two red lights and was driving very fast.

Suzanne was raving. Why he would deliberately do something so stupid that could injure her and their unborn child, was incomprehensible to her. She huddled in her seat the rest of the way home. She didn't dare say anything while they were driving for fear of his reaction. She waited until they got into the house, then she told him exactly what she thought.

"Listen to her. Who does she think she's talking to? I know that jerk in the car wouldn't catch up to me. She has one hell of a nerve overreacting. He could feel his face getting red and he clasped his hands repeatedly until his palms hurt. I'm not some pip-squeak she can speak to like that!"

In an instant, he was on her, punching, slapping, and kicking her legs and back. She could feel her nose bleeding and tried to get away from this maniac she happened to be married to. It was futile. Suzanne wound up on the floor trying to head off the brutal kicks. All she could think of was protecting the baby inside her.

Lifting herself up off the floor, she tried hard to fight him off. She kicked back at him and tried to push him away from her. He was still trying to grab her and punch her while she fought to get free. Releasing herself from his hold, she blindly ran into the bathroom and locked the door. He yelled at her and tried forcing the door open. Suzanne watched the door bulge with each of his shoves and prayed that it would stay closed. Her knees buckled and she prayed that her baby would be all right.

She didn't know what else to do. She had never been through anything like this in her life. Her whole body was aching and she could feel the blood dripping from her nose. Her head was pounding and the nausea was not to be stopped.

After a while, he gave up trying to get into the bathroom and all was quiet. Suzanne was afraid to look into the mirror. Her mind was in a turmoil. She was afraid to come out, not knowing what to expect next from him. Should she pack her clothes tomorrow and leave him? Could she? Where could she go? What alternatives did she have? Would it be fair to saddle Dorothy and Morris with their adult daughter and a baby? In all her life, she had never been exposed to this kind of violence.

Too numb to think clearly, she cautiously opened the bathroom door. He didn't seem to be around as he didn't come after her again. Relieved, she headed for their bedroom. She heard the television playing in the family room as she slipped under the bed covers. Lying on her side in a fetal position, she let her exhaustion take over and, in spite of her pain, she fell fast asleep.

Brian sat in the family room watching the game, but his mind wasn't on it. Sighing, he continued staring at the television, oblivious to what was on. "I hope Suzanne's okay. I didn't mean to react like that but, God, she never lets up. She should know by now I won't stand for her lip. She better be aware not to provoke me like that again. She has to learn to keep her mouth shut. I don't understand what comes over me sometimes, but I guess I didn't really hurt her or the baby. If she was hurt she'd be leaving by now or calling an ambulance. She'll be okay. I'll tell her

I'm sorry, that I over reacted a little and she'll forgive me. Where would she go anyway? She wouldn't dare go home to Mommy and Daddy after having it so good here. I give her everything; a good home, money to shop with, and we have great sex. What else does she need?" he asked himself as he fell asleep on the sofa.

The next morning she got up before Brian. The deep cup above her right eye ached and she saw bruises on her arms and legs. She called her boss and told him she was not feeling well and would not be in. He told her to take it easy and said he hoped she'd be okay by tomorrow.

Brian acted as if nothing had happened, gave her a kiss on the cheek and started talking about his plans for the day. Suzanne was amazed. If she brought up the incident, would it enrage him again, or could he talk about what happened like a civilized human being? She didn't want to look at him, let alone talk to him.

Summoning her courage she said, "Brian, we have to talk."

"Oh, honey, I just got mad at you for opening your mouth up to me. Nothing much happened, and I love you, so let's forget it." Laughing he said, "Did you see the way that big jamoka looked when I peeled away in the car?"

Suzanne couldn't believe what she was hearing. He was like Dr. Jekyll and Mr. Hyde, laughing and joking, ignoring the ugly scene of the night before. By the time he left for work, she was emotionally drained. Remembering the terrible spectacle of last night and his callous lack of remorse this morning, she went into the bathroom and threw up.

She went back to bed and thought, "What options do I have? How can I support a baby and myself?" She was scared but didn't know what she could do.

As time went on, Suzanne tried to act normally, functioning as she did before, but the events of that horrible day played over and over in her mind - with no resolution. The days merged into weeks.

The first time Brian tried to make love to her after the beating, she was actually sickened. She pretended to have a headache, but knew she couldn't feign an imaginary illness forever. After a while, the loving and tender Brian reappeared. Suzanne tried to put the unpleasant incident out of her mind. She realized she had no options and she had to accept her situation. Their life returned to its usual routine.

Brian was obsessed with having a son. The offices at Morse Associates were being repainted and Brian insisted on doing his office in pale blue. "I'm telling you, Carl, I'll teach my son to pitch and hit a ball. I can't wait to do father and son things. My dad was away most of my childhood, but I'll be there for my son. What boys names go good with Morse?" he asked.

Carl rolled his eyes with boredom. "Enough, let's get back to work. Stop this mania about your future son. It could be a girl you know," laughed Carl.

Brian threw the list of names, now rolled into a ball, at him. "Never, I always hit home runs!"

Suzanne didn't care what sex the baby was as long as it was healthy, although she would love a girl whom she could pamper and dress in pretty clothes.

The nine months flew by. Suzanne gained only twenty-two pounds. Both Suzanne and Brian agreed that she should be a full-time housewife and mother.

Ten days before her due date, Suzanne's water broke. She was visiting her mother's house and chatting with her Grandmother Pessa. "Mama, Mama, I just went to the bathroom and I'm still leaking. What's wrong?"

"Oye, it's your vater, and you'd better call your doctor, and then Brian. Here's a pad; go put it on and you'll be all right."

Brian was at a client's office when his secretary called to tell him to get to his in-laws home as soon as possible. Suzanne was going into labor. He arrived to find Suzanne under the portable hair dryer. "I drove like a madman, and you're doing your God damned hair. What are you, crazy?"

"Brian, relax. I spoke to the doctor, and he said I'd have plenty of time since this is my first baby. Mama and I are timing the contractions. When they are seven minutes apart we can leave. Mama will make you a cup of coffee. Please, try to relax."

The contractions became stronger and quicker, and after pinning her hair up in a French twist, they left for the hospital. Suzanne was really nervous, but tried to put on a brave front. The nurses prepped her and told her to take all the hairpins out of her hair. "What a waste of time for me to have put it up," she told herself.

When the doctor arrived, she was glad to see him as her pains were intense. She wanted to scream, but restrained herself, even though it was considered normal behavior in the labor room. The doctor explained what he would be doing, and told her she'd be out of pain soon. He stuck a needle into her arm, and told her to count backwards from one hundred. She got to eighty, then everything faded.

The doctor called from the hospital. "Congradulations Dorothy, you are now a grandmother. Suzanne and the little girl are doing fine. She weighs 6 lbs. 4 oz. and came out sucking her thumb." "It's a beautiful baby girl." Dorothy yelled to her husband and son-in-law from the kitchen.

"It can't be!" Brian thought as he heard his mother-in-law calling their relatives. It had to be a son. My son. After all, I was the first born in my family." Swallowing his disappointment he went to the nearby florist and had a lovely bouquet of flowers sent to Suzanne's room.

As soon as Suzanne held the baby in her arms, she knew unconditional love. Her heart was filled with joy. Her features were like a doll's, and her thumb was in her mouth. The nurses told Suzanne that at delivery the baby was sucking her thumb, emphasizing two big dimples on her cheeks. "She has two large dimples, just like Mama Pessa's," Suzanne thought as she caressed her little daughter. She rocked her in her arms observing that the baby's hair and skin were light like her father, Morris'.

The next morning Brian stood in the doorway holding another bouquet of roses. Hesitant to enter his wife's room, he knew he had to mask his frustration. With a fixed smile on his face, he went into the room and told Suzanne he was happy that she and the baby were fine.

"I don't care what you name her. Really."

Suzanne suggested the name 'Hope' for their daughter. She had always liked the name and was delighted that Brian had no objections. Suzanne felt that by naming the baby Hope, all the baby's aspirations and desires would be fulfilled. Hope's Hebrew name would be Aviva, after her Grandfather Abe. Papa Jake and her father went to the synagogue and named the baby at the same place where her father and uncles had been named.

After a week in the hospital, mother and baby headed home. Mama Pessa, would come out for a couple of days to help because Suzanne was a little apprehensive about taking care of Hope by herself.

Brian's mother came over the next day and made known her child-raising philosophy. "Holding the baby will spoil her, so hold Hope only when you need to. Put her to bed by five o'clock, six at the latest, and don't put up with any nonsense. You'll be tired, so prop the bottle. That way, you'll be able to clean the house, and not waste time." Suzanne could not believe what she was hearing. Suzanne had her own thoughts on these matters, but allowed the woman to ramble on.

Brian, on the other hand, revered his mother, and believed everything she said. He was constantly looking for her approval, which, unfortunately, was never forthcoming. Because of his mother's advice, Suzanne and Brian had many arguments on how they should raise Hope.

To make matters worse, Brian was determined to establish his business as a leader in the field within ten years. He worked tirelessly at it and would frequently not come home until late in the evening.

"Brian, do you think you can try to come home a little earlier once or twice a week? I miss talking to you and it would be nice if you saw Hope after dinner and play with her before I put her to sleep."

"For Christ sake, give me a break. I'm working my ass off to provide for you and the kid, and all you do is bitch and complain. Get the fuck off my back." Slamming the bedroom door he went into the family room to watch television. As the weeks and months flew by, Suzanne busied herself by taking care of her daughter.

One day Brian came storming home after a particularly frustrating day. Suzanne was surprised by his early arrival. "Where the hell is my dinner?"

"Brian, I didn't expect you. Why didn't you call to tell me you'd be home early?"

"I shouldn't have to call my own wife to tell her I'll be home. You should automatically have dinner waiting for me. My mother always had dinner waiting for my father. What the hell have you been doing all day long? Sitting on your fat ass watching the soaps and taking care of the kid. What the hell do you know about pressure? Make me something to eat."

Suzanne knew better than to answer him back when he was in a bad mood. Biting her tongue, she quietly started the dinner. The silence while they ate was unnerving. Clearing the dishes Suzanne hoped he would just go into the family room and watch television. Coming up behind her, he spun her around abruptly, then unzipped his pants.

"Brian, Hope is still up. Let's wait until later."

"Hope's in her room playing and she won't know what the fuck is going on." His hands went directly to her breasts and he commanded Suzanne on what he wanted done. His gyrating movements and moans of delight both stimulated yet repulsed Suzanne.

Suzanne was disgusted by his behavior. Too embarrassed to ask her closest friends about sexual matters, she wondered, "Do other wives have to go through this humiliation or is it just me?" These questions obsessed her as she tried to maintain the illusion of a happy married wife.

As the months passed, Suzanne enjoyed spending time with Hope and the other young mothers and children in the neighborhood. On pleasant days, they walked the children and engaged in small talk about the babies and community gossip. She loved being at home and watching Hope's progress.

Things got no worse, but they didn't get better either. When Brian did manage to come home early, he usually sat in front of the television, in his own little world, and not pay any attention to anything happening or being said around him.

"Is this it? Is this going to be my life? Is this all there is?" Suzanne frequently wondered.

Chapter Three

Stoney Brook, Massachusetts • January, 1968

Nothing ever, ever happened in their perfectly Lilly-white neighborhood.

Although Suzanne enjoyed her routine with Hope, she found life in the suburbs boring beyond belief. Her mind was never stimulated, although her life with Brian and the baby consumed all her physical energy. When Brian came home at night, she had nothing of interest to contribute to their conversations, except whatever Hope had accomplished that day.

One day while she was feeding Hope, Suzanne turned on the midday news and realized she had no idea what the newscasters were talking about. As she put the lunch dishes into the dishwasher, she saw that the floor needed mopping - again, and she promised herself that this endless stream of mopping, cleaning, running the house would not be her whole existence. She was determined to do something more. While the baby napped that afternoon, she spent the time trying to figure out how she could put some dimension back into her life without creating an adverse effect on Brian and the baby. She wrote down six things she was interested in doing or knowing about. By the time Hope woke up, Suzanne had determined that she would make the time again for her art-work. She decided to go one evening a week to the library and read about subjects that interested her.

That evening when Brian came home from work, Suzanne approached him with an idea. "Brian, I'd love to take art lessons in the evening at the DeCordova Museum in Lincoln. What do you think? Would we be able to afford that?" Continuing, Suzanne said, "When I was a youngster I spent many hours drawing. I guess I take after my Uncle Herman. He's such a good artist."

"Brian, did you hear what I said?"

"No. What did you say?"

Repeating her thoughts, she waited for his reply, ready with responses to objections she expected him to make.

To her surprise, he seemed to welcome the idea. "That sounds good to me. It'll give you something to do besides cleaning the house and taking care of Hope. How much will it cost?" Then, with an edge to his voice, he cautioned her, "But don't let the housework fall behind. Who will you get to mind Hope?"

She had already solved the first problem. As far as the house work went, she was determined to hire one of the teenagers in the neighborhood to come in right after school to help with the daily housework and mind Hope so she would have time to paint. She planned to ask for double the amount of money that she would need for the cost of the art courses so that she could cover the expense of the housekeeper and leave her enough free time to do what she felt she had to do to maintain her sanity.

"Well, I haven't really figured it all out yet. First, I'll find out when the courses are held and how much they are. If I can get into a course in the afternoon that'll help me decide who will baby-sit. Maybe one of Kay's girls would like the job or another teenager in the neighborhood."

She was at the museum when it opened the next day. After reviewing the available classes, she selected an 'introduction to oil painting' class that was held on Thursday evenings and was starting the following week. Brian attended Rotary Club meetings on Thursday nights and usually was not in until after midnight. Things were falling into place perfectly.

Brian told her to write a check for the amount she needed and never questioned her about the cost. She wrote the check, cashed it, and opened an account of her own in a small bank in the next town. She had enough to pay for her class and supplies with enough left over to cover the expenses of both a baby-sitter and household help for the next three months.

Suzanne arrived exhilarated for the first night of class. She had forgotten how much she loved doing this. When the evening was over she was positive she had taken the right step for herself.

She was fascinated blending the colors and mastering the different palette knives and brushes to attain the various effects on the canvas. Suzanne had a vivid imagination, and she frequently incorporated various objects and gadgets in the art itself. Sometimes she used sand and shells, other times she used mesh on the canvass, covering them with the oils. She loved the smell of the paints and fabrics, but Brian complained bitterly about the odor. He insisted he could detect it on his clothes when he was at work, so Suzanne set up her studio in the garage.

While Hope napped in the mornings or after Jeanine came by in the afternoon to mind her and do some light housekeeping, Suzanne worked diligently at her canvas. The arrangement left her evenings free for Brian and kept things between them on an even keel.

Sometimes if Brian was out of town, she would return to her easel after she put Hope to bed at night. She would get so absorbed in her work that often she wouldn't get to bed till two or three o'clock in the morning.

When Hope got older, Suzanne bought her a small easel and encouraged her to draw. They hung all of Hope's artwork on the wall. Suzanne enjoyed teaching her, especially since Brian was more and more intent on hard work and frequently didn't get home until very late at night.

On one occasion Brian came home in a particularly good mood. His firm had finally landed a contract that they had been after for a long time. With flowers in hand he grabbed Suzanne around the waist and danced around the kitchen. After Hope was asleep, they sat down to a romantic dinner Suzanne had prepared for the two of them. "The flowers are beautiful. I really like it when you come home early like this. Thank you."

Brian laughed and said, "Well it's the least I could do for my beautiful, accomplished wife."

After dinner they relaxed in front of the fire. Suzanne again broached the subject of their finances and suggested she take on the role to free Brian up to go after more clients for his agency.

Abruptly, Brian's whole personality changed. He became defensive and irritable. "Jesus, Suzanne. Do you have to take over everything? First, you wanted to pick out all my clothes. Then you had to have this house. Don't you have enough to do with the home, baby and now this art stuff?" Suzanne was outraged by his tone and ugly disposition. Unfortunately for her, she could not contain her own anger and frustration any longer.

"Brian, for God's sake, what's wrong? Where did this come from? I thought you liked the clothes I picked out for you. And, you wanted this house as much as I did. I'm a grown woman, capable of handling the money matters. Why don't you let me do it? It'll take some pressure off you and you'll be free to bring in more business for your firm. Are you afraid of giving up some of the authority? Let me know what's going on."

Without a warning Brian rose from the sofa and grabbed her by the collar of her dress. "You just don't know when to shut up, do you Suzanne?" Dragging her into the kitchen he threw her backwards onto the kitchen table and slapped her repeatedly across the face with one hand as he held her down on the table with the other.

Stunned by the intensity of his rage and the hideous turn of events, she struggled for release. "Get your hands off me," she screamed, but she couldn't escape his grip.

"Who the fuck do you think you're talking to, you son of a bitch whore?"

Still in shock by his bizarre behavior, she forced herself to think. Suddenly she realized he had relaxed his grip and was trying to catch his breath. With one quick twisting motion she managed to free herself and slipped down to the right and out of his grasp. Chasing her, he renewed his hold on her and threw her down again. Unexpectedly he reached for the silverware drawer. As he turned Suzanne freed herself and tried to run away. As fast as she thought she was, he easily caught up to her.

"Let go of me. Get away."

"I'm the boss. And don't you ever forget it."

He pulled the large carving knife from the drawer and brandished it in front of her face. "I'll cut you to pieces if you open your big mouth up about money again. Shut the fuck up, you cunt." He lowered the knife towards her neck.

Suzanne wanted to murder him but she could feel the tip of the blade pressing in onto her neck and she dared not move. She wanted to scream but again she forced herself to think. She realized that in his state of mind, he probably wouldn't hesitate to kill her. She didn't know why, but she knew when she was licked. Forcing herself to hold back, she controlled the rage seething within her. Suzanne could feel the cold metal on her bare throat.

Through clenched teeth, he angrily asked, "Are you ever going to ask me to take care of the money and bills again? Tell me, are you?"

Suzanne could only barely voice a mumbled "No."

"If I let you up I don't want any more of your crap or lip, do you understand?" His eyes glowed with fire as he released her and tossed the knife onto the counter.

Once free of immediate peril, hysteria set in. She ran sobbing to their bedroom and locked the door behind her. She went into the master bathroom, and, afraid to look in the mirror, she dampened the washcloth under the cold water tap and gently pressed the compress to her face. "He's a lunatic. What am I going to do? I have to get away from him, but how?" she questioned. She was frantic.

She lay down on the soft bed, and tried to quell the heart-wrenching sobs that were escaping from the depths of her soul. Her whole body shook uncontrollably. Her head felt as if it would explode from the persistent pounding within it. After a few minutes, she struggled up from the bed and stumbled back into the bathroom. She returned the washcloth, now warm, to the cold water and again pressed the cool relief it provided to her forehead. The room spun while she struggled to figure out what she had done that was so wrong. An empty helplessness set in as she fell asleep.

Brian tried to forget the unfortunate incident that had just occurred. Pulling an Izod over his undershirt he, too, felt depressed. "What the hell is her problem? Damn her. She knows just the right buttons to push. I don't want to hurt her, but I just loose my temper. When she starts in on me, I can't help it." He tried to figure it out, but couldn't.

He squeezed his eyes shut tightly and thought back to his childhood. "Yes I remember many evenings of yelling, screaming and finally the violence that he, my wonderful father, inflicted on my mom. I remember pulling the blanket over myself so I wouldn't hear the fights. How I hated to hear the awful abuse my father gave her. "Why does she make him hit her and get him mad?" I would wonder as I cried myself to sleep.

He shuddered. He remembered how, as he got older, he felt he had to shelter his mother. Many an evening he would become the clown for the matador to divert the ragging bull.

The next day, Suzanne tried to figure out what to do. She was not one to air dirty laundry in public, and she certainly wasn't about to worry her parents with her problem. Thank God Hope had been asleep and not awakened during the commotion. She determined that she would not be a victim and thought, "Somehow and someday I'll get out of this crazy marriage. I must find a way."

As the months went by and winter turned into spring, Suzanne was careful not to set Brian off again. She made a point not to bring up the finances and she was sure to have everything, as he liked it, when he arrived home at night. One afternoon she found herself in front of her easel looking at an empty canvas. She realized that two hours had gone by and she had done nothing but look at the blank canvas, thinking about Brian and their dismal marriage. She prayed that he would change, but she was convinced, more than ever, that he had a definite psychological problem. The more she thought about it, she realized that she probably should not have married Brian, especially being so young. Had she been more mature when they met she would not have married him and, most likely, called Stephen up to make amends.

Brian never mentioned the incident and their life returned to its routine. He was still a fanatic about the house. He wanted everything neat and clean when he came home at night. Suzanne kept a tight rein on her temper, fearing he would lose his and beat her again. When Hope was just over one and a half, Suzanne found she was again pregnant. As an only child herself, she was happy that this would not be Hope's fate. Brian was thrilled, and counted on having his son this time.

The pregnancy progressed well. Suzanne found she could frequently sleep while Hope napped. Jeanine continued to take care of the routine housekeeping chores so Suzanne could paint whenever she felt up to it.

Since Suzanne had delivered Hope early, as her due date approached, her obstetrician wanted her to stay at her parent's house. One evening after dinner, Suzanne called the doctor complaining of cramps. He sent her directly to the hospital. After the examination, he told her she was in early labor and wanted to admit her. Soon, the pains began to progress rapidly. She didn't remember a thing afterward.

When Suzanne woke she asked the nurse if she could see her baby. "Why of course, Suzanne, she's beautiful." As she cuddled her new daughter in her arms, she thanked God she had another healthy infant. She had dark brown hair, and very long fingers. Brian came into the room the next day and again tried to mask his disappointment. They named the baby Melanie and gave her the Hebrew name Devoida after one of her maternal great grandmothers.

A light knock on the door woke her from her nap. Expecting to see a relative or friend, she was shocked to see Stephen LeVigne poke his head into the room. Suzanne had not seen him in years, and was caught totally off guard. Her face lit up with joy. She chuckled to herself, but kept a straight face as she noted the argument between his checkered shirt and his plaid jacket.

"Hi, I hope I'm not disturbing you. Are you up for some company?"

Speechless, she motioned him to come in. "Thank God I've taken a shower and did my hair and make up," she thought to herself.

Gathering her wits about her she said, "Stephen, hello stranger. I'm stunned. How'd you know I was here?"

He hugged her and put a vase of yellow tea roses on the bureau. "Remember how my mother always worked that third job on weekends? Well she's still working here at the hospital every Saturday, so she keeps up with everything that's going on. She told me that you had another baby girl." Concerned for his former sweetheart, he continued, "How's everything going for you? Are you happy? How's the baby? Do you think I could see her?"

She watched him discretely, examining every feature and gesture. She had to admit, "He hasn't changed much. He's as gorgeous as ever."

"Sure, we can walk down to the nursery to see her." She stepped into the white slippers and he helped her into a pink robe. As they stood at the nursery window watching the baby sleep, she told Stephen briefly about her life, omitting her true feelings about Brian. Articulating, "Life is perfect, now that I have two lovely daughters, a solicitous husband, a home in the suburbs, and an evolving art career. What else could I ever want?" Knowing in her heart that what she stated was untrue – life was a sham. She put on a smile, hoping he didn't see through the concocted story.

When she felt tired, they walked back to her room. "I should probably leave, you must be exhausted," Stephen suggested.

She wanted him to stay and held firmly to his arm. "No, no, don't go just yet. I get fatigued, especially when I'm on my feet too long. Now tell me about yourself. What have you been doing and is there a woman in your life? Are you still living around this area?"

"Well, I'm working on my doctorate in Mechanical Engineering at the moment."

He seated himself on the edge of her bed. The tips of their fingers touched lightly. Suzanne held her breath momentarily. He spoke aloud but softly, as if to himself "I wish we hadn't drifted apart the way we did. We could've at least kept in touch. You have to realize, I was young and if I could turn back the clock, I'd do a lot of things differently. I was such a fool. Please forgive me for the hurt I've caused you." Taking her hand into his as he looked intently into her eyes, he said, "I wish things had turned out differently for us, but I'm glad that you're happy. You deserve the best in life."

They talked for hours, and, when the nurse reminded Suzanne that it was feeding time, she thanked him for coming. They hugged again and she wished him success and love. She took a long, last look at him as he turned and waved from the door. She wanted to remember his face always, as it was now.

Stephen closed the door and leaned against the wall outside her room, oblivious to the sideways glance he received from the nurse rushing by. "She's as beautiful as always," he thought. "Boy is her husband lucky. I hope she's really as happy as she says. Maybe I shouldn't have gone in there and visited her. Am I stupid thinking she'd be so glad to see me. I wanted her to tell me she's miserable and that she married the wrong guy." Disappointed, he shook his head then slowly walked down the corridor, out of the hospital, and away from her again. He now realized that any hope of a life with Suzanne was definitely out of the question.

As she fed Melanie, tears welled up in Suzanne's eyes. All her repressed longings for Stephen and for a life with him were now coming to the surface. As the tears fell freely down her cheeks, she wished that Stephen had fathered her children and, yet, she felt guilty thinking those thoughts. Why hadn't she told him how miserable she was with Brian? Was her pride so deep, that she couldn't reveal her true feelings? She was doing what Stephen had learned not to do: keep one's true feelings inside. Looking at Melanie she thought, "It's hopeless." When Brian came in that evening, she didn't mention her visitor.

To strangers and acquaintances Suzanne and Brian had an ideal relationship and marriage. Brian's business was flourishing thanks to his hard work. He bragged to colleagues, friends, and neighbors, what a beautiful family he had. "When I come home, even if it's late, a hot meal is always there for me." My wife is an excellent gourmet cook, and she keeps the house spotless. I love my family, and I spend every spare moment with the children." His true character was never revealed to his clients.

"If only the truth were known," Suzanne thought.

Suzanne really did like cooking, but kept their meals simple. Weight was always a concern to her. While pregnant, she gained no more than twenty-five pounds. Even though Suzanne was now a perfect size eight, Brian was always on her case. His constant criticism ate away at her self-esteem. No matter what she did, it wasn't good enough.

"Boy, are you fat. What happened to you?" He was always on her back. "What's wrong with your hair, your skin looks terrible, why is your face always breaking out?"

She never told anyone how Brian berated her and stripped her of her dignity. Suzanne still wanted a more active roll in the house finances, but Brian told her she did not have the brains for math. He wanted her to be there for him when he needed her. He invited businessmen and their wives for formal dinner parties and expected Suzanne to entertain them lavishly.

Often, Suzanne would be at the other end of the house when Brian called for her. Putting down what she was doing, she would go to him.

"Oh honey, would you change the television channel for me?" Thinking now of her subservient behavior turned her stomach.

He told his mother everything that went on in their household. If Suzanne criticized a member of his family, the comment inevitably got back to the individual. She learned, all too late, to keep her opinions to herself. Brian was continually looking for his parent's approval, at her expense. He still threw tantrums, but not as often. Occasionally before dinner guests would arrive, he would inspect the ice cube trays and the silverware drawer. If the ice didn't appear fresh enough or there were crumbs in the drawer, he would empty the contents on the kitchen floor and demand that she clean it up. She felt she was his personal slave.

Walking through his property, picking up one of the many toys scattered in his path, he would think, "I need a clean house and everything should have its place. Why the hell can't she just clean up this mess before I get home?"

Dorothy and Morris were regular visitors for Sunday dinner. Late one Sunday afternoon, while they were in the middle of eating, Hope wanted the ketchup bottle and reached in front of Brian. Out of the blue, Brian yanked her out of her seat and dragged her across the room. He started slapping and yelling. "You're a little brat, I'll teach you not to reach in front of me."

Everyone else at the table was in shock. The incident happened so fast that Suzanne was taken by surprise. She got up from the table and ran to the hallway where Brian was hitting Hope. She shook as she screamed at him to stop.

"Stop it, stop it! What're you doing?" yelled Suzanne. As she struggled to separate Hope from his grip she thought she would collapse. Hope was bleeding from the cut on the side of her head.

"I'll show her who's boss," Brian raged.

Suzanne shouted, "You're crazy, leave her alone, she's only a baby, leave her alone."

Morris was out of his seat, coming down the corridor, and Suzanne didn't want to alarm him. "Everything is under control, Daddy, just go back to the kitchen. We're all right." Morris was not a young man and Suzanne did not want a confrontation between the two men. Suzanne brought Hope into her bathroom. Hope was hysterical. She had no idea why her daddy hit her. Suzanne didn't understand it either.

Dorothy was so upset she was in the main bathroom throwing up her dinner. Never excessively fond of Brian, she had long suspected that something was wrong. Now she knew what it was.

Suzanne calmed Hope, washed her and put pajamas on for her. "Come on honey, Mommy will read you a story. Daddy didn't mean to hurt you. He's sorry and I promise you, that will never happen again. I promise!"

Dorothy came into Hope's bedroom. A deeply concerned Dorothy proclaimed, with a determined voice

"You don't have to put up with this behavior. How long has this been going on?"

"Mom, could you put Melanie to bed? Then we'll talk." When Hope was asleep, Suzanne went to her mother. Suzanne had never told Dorothy about Brian's rages. She was cognizant her parents would want to help, but they were not wealthy and could not help her financially if she left Brian.

Dorothy knew that Suzanne was not telling her the whole truth, but she let her finish, then said, "If you ever need me or your father, you have to realize that we love you, and we'll do anything we can for you. Do you want to move in with us?"

Shivering, Suzanne answered, "Mom, I don't know what I want to do right now. I never thought I'd be in a situation like this."

Tears welling up in her eyes, she hugged her daughter, and said, "Remember, we'll always be here for you. Don't ever hesitate to call us."

Brian was in the kitchen finishing his dinner, not understanding what all the fuss was about.

After her parents left, Suzanne checked on Hope and Melanie. They were sleeping, but Suzanne could tell from the way Hope was quivering in her sleep that she was having a bad dream. "Rightfully so," Suzanne thought.

Not wanting to start another fight, Suzanne approached Brian with trepidation.

"Brian, we have to talk."

"There's nothing to talk about."

"Brian, it's not normal to go into a rage over little things that annoy you, or if someone doesn't agree with you. I think you need counseling." Lying, she told him she loved him and if he wanted to continue in this marriage, he had to go for professional help. "I'll be glad to go with you. Brian, if you don't go, I'm going to take the girls and leave you. I swear to God I will."

"Okay, okay, I'll go to a counselor." He thought to himself, "I don't have a problem, but maybe this will shut her up."

On the way home from work, the following day, Brian stopped at the local jewelry store.

"Close your eyes," he told Suzanne. "Now don't move."

She could feel him fumbling and his hands were around her neck. Afraid to move she didn't know what to expect. "We're not arguing so he's not going to choke me," she thought as he moved his hands down along her sleek neck and then rested them on her bare shoulders under her loose shirt.

Turning her around, he kissed her tenderly. "I'm sorry. I hope this peace offering will help make up for my temper tantrum. Thanks for hanging in there with me, honey." Then, looking down at the floor, afraid to look her in the eyes a contrite Brian continued. "I promise I'll help get everything back to normal."

She looked into the mirror and saw a beautiful diamond heart on a gold chain and realized she honestly couldn't remember what normal life was like. It seemed so long ago.

Later, Brian played with the children instead of watching the television as he usually did. He even helped Suzanne wash the dishes.

They put the girls to bed and Suzanne asked him if he had called a psychologist. He answered somewhat abruptly, "I told you I would and I did. The appointment is for the end of this week." Patting the bed Brian motioned to Suzanne, "Now let's forget about everything and shut off the lights."

Suzanne felt consoled; at least this was progress in the right direction. Brian was full of passion. It was hard for Suzanne to resist him; his expertise made her body yearn for more.

Lying in bed next to him, Suzanne hated herself. "How could I have let him make love to me. And, how could I enjoy it? I must be as sick as he is. First, letting him abuse me the way he does and now letting him hurt the children. I can't go on living like this." She vowed to find a way out, that she would never allow him to treat her or the children badly again.

When a local bank manager suggested that Suzanne display some of her artwork at his bank, she was delighted and gladly accepted. With Beverly's help, she placed over one hundred paintings in the various branches of the bank.

Soon she received calls from several prominent citizens asking her to paint pictures for their homes. Using her natural decorating talent, she incorporated their taste and color scheme into the pieces and came up with imaginative objets d'art.

The money she collected for the pieces went into the separate bank account in her name. Brian had no idea how much money she made from her paintings and Suzanne wanted to keep it that way. He'd find out at tax time, but for now he had no idea she had money of her own. Although he was still seeing the psychologist and seemed a lot better, Suzanne still had reservations. A nest egg of her own would come in handy when she figured out what she was going to do.

Brian now had thirteen people working for him, including two secretaries and an accountant. His business was thriving. He strove constantly to make a name for himself in the profession. Not content owning one company, he negotiated the acquisition of another related business. The more dealings and negotiations he implemented, the more he wanted to expand his capital ventures. Prosperity was in sight.

When Brian was home, Suzanne noticed that he was usually preoccupied, home in body, but not attentive to Suzanne or the girls. She usually left him alone to do his own thing. When other people were around or when they had company, he acted like a fun-loving devoted family man.

Suzanne received a phone call from an art gallery in Boston. The owner, Justin Ferris, had seen some of her pictures at a friend's house and wanted to meet with her. Suzanne agreed to get together with him the following week, then almost died when she heard the Newbury Street address.

She called Beverly to tell her about the call and asked to meet her at Filene's after the business appointment for lunch.

"You're taking this matter-of-factly. How come you're not your usual excited self?" asked Beverly.

"Come on I can't take this seriously. With all the talent that is out there, he'd call me? Get real. It's too good to be true."

The charismatic gallery owner extended his hand to Suzanne, completely encompassing her dainty hand with his own. He was an immense man in his early forties with somewhat long brown hair. Looking up at his six feet four inches, she could see his expansive chest expand rhythmically as he talked, as if he were continually out of breath. She never expected such a powerful physique on an art gallery owner. She had to force herself not to stare at him. His chin had a unique cleft that gave him a ruggedly handsome look.

After showing her through his showroom, he got down to business. He was impressed with her work and wanted to see more of it. If he liked her newest paintings, he requested that Suzanne exhibit her art with another upcoming artist. Overwhelmed, but flattered, she arranged to show him additional pieces. With her heart beating so fast that she was sure it could be heard she shook his hand and thanked him for contacting her.

Beverly was anxiously waiting for her at Filene's corner.

"Come on, I'm treating you to lunch at the Ritz," Suzanne informed Beverly.

"Wow! Good thing I'm dressed up," laughed Beverly.

Walking briskly, arm in arm, they enjoyed the aroma of the budding flowers and trees in the Common. The swan boats were filled with cheerful children and adults who were indulging themselves on this delightful spring day. The park benches were filled with men and women feeding pigeons and squirrels during their lunch hours. Music blared from battery operated radios and joggers wove in and out around pedestrians on the paths.

At the Ritz Cafe, they ordered a carafe of rosè and toasted the upcoming exhibit.

Two tables from theirs, Suzanne noticed a man who looked familiar, but she couldn't place him. During their conversation, Suzanne felt his eyes on her. While waiting for their salad, Suzanne excused herself and headed for the rest room.

In the lobby, the familiar-looking gentleman approached her. "Excuse me, but aren't you Mrs. Morse?"

Hesitantly, she answered, "Yes I am. How are you?" She felt foolish not remembering who he was, but didn't want to embarrass herself by admitting it.

"I was disappointed that you couldn't make the appointment I made for you and your husband two months ago. Brian explained you had a very demanding schedule. I hope you can persuade him to come back. I'm not usually this forward, but I felt that when we met for those first few visits we got some matters out in the open. However, quite a few important subjects should be resolved."

It came to her. He was Dr. Steinberg, Brian's psychiatrist. Now, things made more sense. He must have stopped his visits and he had been lying to her about his progress.

"I definitely will call you. I have some questions of my own that need answers. I'll set up an appointment next week," she assured the doctor.

Four months ago, at Dr. Steinberg's request, Suzanne had gone with Brian to see him. Brian had been seeing the psychiatrist for months now, or so she thought. The doctor had impressed her, and though Brian appeared to be better, some aspects of his behavior still worried her.

Suzanne was visibly upset when she went back to the table where Beverly was waiting for her.

"What's wrong?" Beverly asked. "You look like you lost your best friend, and, as you can see, I'm still here."

Beverly was her oldest and closest friend, but Suzanne had never told her how unhappy she really was with Brian. She had been too ashamed and embarrassed. Beverly had sensed it, but didn't pry.

Composing herself, she finally told her everything that had happened in the last six and a half years.

Beverly was quiet and let her friend finish. Then Beverly voiced her unflattering opinion of Brian and continued, "Furthermore, you can come to me if you want to chat, no matter what time of day or night. If you need anything, you know that Louis and I will be there for you."

"Well, it looks like I've talked so long that we won't have time to shop. Sorry about that, but I'll make it up to you," apologized Suzanne.

"Don't be silly; you needed to get these terrible issues off your chest."

When the girls were in bed for the night and Brian was watching television, Suzanne told him about the offer that Justin Ferris made her. Inattentive, his response was half-hearted. Without revealing what she knew, she asked him how his sessions with the doctor were going.

He turned, looked her directly in the eye, and said, "Fine."

She finished telling him about her day, omitting her encounter with Dr. Steinberg.

Two weeks later she was sitting across from the doctor in his office on Marlboro Street. Feeling in control, now that she had taken this step, she readily disclosed her agitation with Brian for lying to her about his treatments. She also informed him of her fears of Brian's temper.

She related the unhappy episodes to him. He listened to her without interruption. He handed her a box of tissues as she related her story. "I feel like a fool," she told him. "Until recently, no one else knew my thoughts. I just kept them to myself."

He pointed out many things to Suzanne that she had been unable to realize. Her torment had clouded her vision. She was very young and on the rebound when she had married Brian; they came from families with completely different backgrounds and values.

Brian had been an abused child, kicked and beaten by his father. His mother had little time for him, always giving in to the demands of his father and the other children. Brian was still trying to gain his mothers love and approval. He overcompensated for his lack of stature by being overbearing and dictatorial. His unhappiness was compounded by the fact that he had not fathered a son.

Suzanne's head was spinning when the two-hour session ended. She left the office a more mature person with a better insight about herself, as well as Brian.

Suzanne knew she had to have a steady income to provide for herself and the girls before she could get out of this unhappy situation. The nest egg she had been able to save was a cushion, but she realized that she would never earn enough money as an unknown artist. Certain that Brian would make her life miserable in any way he possibly could, for he hated rejection - he would make her pay dearly for leaving him.

The summer months flew by. She went through the season with mixed emotions but she began her preparations for her future.

The Jewish New Year was approaching. Rosh Hashanah marks one of the most sacred holy days in the Jewish faith, and ushers in the Ten Days of Penitence when "Mankind passes in judgment before the heavenly throne." Tradition holds, God looks into the hearts of men and examines not only their deeds but their motives as well. It is also the period when Jews sit in judgment over themselves, comparing their conduct during the past year with the hopes and resolutions they had cherished.

Suzanne was no exception. Although the girls were too young to fully understand and appreciate the ethics of the faith, Suzanne took them to the temple for the services.

Suzanne was exhilarated at the sounding of the shofar calling the faithful to worship. An instrument of communication in ancient times, it is said that in the hills of Judaea it was possible to reach the entire country in a matter of moments with shofar calls from the mountain peaks.

The shofar calls upon the faithful to repent for their misdeeds of the past year, to return to God with contrite and humble spirit and to distinguish between the trivial and the important in life, so that the next twelve months may be richer in service to God and man. Suzanne often wished that Brian would come to the services and pray with her, not for anyone other than himself, especially when the rabbi gave a lovely and inspiring sermon. Unfortunately, Brian never attended, pretending to be too busy at work to take time out for this important holiday.

In spite of the solemn nature of the Rosh Hashanah observances, a general air of happy expectation filled their home. Dorothy and Morris regularly worshipped with Suzanne and the girls and afterwards enjoyed the festivities back at Suzanne's house where she served the traditional meal of chicken soup with knadelas, chopped liver, and roasted chicken with tsimis. The round, golden challah symbolizing the continuation of life, was dipped into honey to mark the New Year with sweetness.

Dorothy and Morris slept at Suzanne's house every Jewish holiday to make sure that Suzanne instilled religious beliefs into their grandchildren. The Pollacks visited for the last two High Holy Days of Judaism, Yom Kippur.

As the sun began to set on the Eve of Atonement, the family gathered for the festive meal. The candles were lit and members of the family asked forgiveness of one another for the wrongs they had committed - child of parent, parent of child, and husband and wife of each other, knowing they must enter the sacred day with a clean slate. Everyone made sure that they filled themselves at this meal, for this holiday is marked by twenty-four hours of prayer and fasting.

Kol Nidre is the prayer of people not free to make their own decisions; people forced to say what they do not mean. The Kol Nidre chant, led by the cantor, is the prelude to the Day of Atonement and is a prayer for absolution, asking God to release us from vows undertaken, but not fulfilled. These vows refer only to man's promises to God, not his fellow men. Suzanne constantly felt sorrow

and fear for this holiday.   Whenever the rabbi would lead
them in prayer and silent meditation, tears would well up in
her eyes. Suzanne's mind tried to cleanse itself of the bad
feelings for Brian.

The tears fell on her cheeks as she prayed:

> *For transgressions against God,*
> *the Day of Atonement atones;*
> *but for transgressions of one*
> *human being against another,*
> *the Day of Atonement does not*
> *atone until they have made*
> *peace with one another.*

Suzanne rose as the Ark was opened.   The Scrolls were
taken from the ark. The beautiful words of prayer were
spoken and mixed emotions ran through her.

> *When justice burns within us*
> *like a flaming fire, when love*
> *evokes willing sacrifice from us,*
> *when, to the last full measure of*
> *selfless   devotion,   we*
> *demonstrate our belief in the*
> *ultimate triumph of truth and*
> *righteousness,   then   Your*
> *goodness enters our lives. Then*
> *You live within our hearts, and*
> *we   through   righteousness*
> *behold Your presence.*

All sat down. Suzanne prayed:

You, O God, will set us free from all our faults! We have sinned against You, O God, and against each other. Help us to turn, O God; help us to find forgiveness. Help us to find ourselves; Help us on our way, O God; lead us on our path.

The Ark was opened and the congregation rose. After more meaningful prayers the shofar was sounded. Suzanne and the girls loved to hear the magnificent and magical sound of the shofar. The Ark was closed. When the sun lost its shine and went in for the evening, Suzanne was happy to see an end to the last year. She hoped for a better, healthy, happy, prosperous New Year. She kissed her parents and children and wished them a "Happy New Year." They hurried home, anxiously looking forward to eating their evening meal.

"Well, God willing we will be inscribed in the book of life for another year." Morris spoke as he lifted the glass of wine. Suzanne embraced her personal thoughts. She prayed, "God, please help me. I need you to show me the way to escape from this horrible situation." Sipping the sweet liquid she closed her eyes and again prayed, "Please, please God, hear my plea, let me survive and discover what you want me to do with my life." Tears visibly flowed onto her cheeks.

"Let's have peace, health, and prosperity and hope that we will be healthy enough to fast next year at this time," interjected Dorothy. "The good Lord willing." Everyone raised a glass of wine and drank it without pause.

Braintree, Massachusetts • 1969

Beverly and Suzanne had gone to the South Shore Plaza to buy some fall clothes. The women always had a good time together, laughing and reminiscing about their teenage years. As they passed a make-up counter, Suzanne noticed an older woman being made up. She stopped, suddenly.

"Bev, do you remember when I had a complete make over and it changed my looks and the way I felt about myself?"

"How could I forget? You were pretty before, even though you didn't think so. But after you had it done, you were gorgeous, you bitch."

They both laughed. It was that day, when they were having a cup of tea, that Suzanne told Beverly that she wanted to go back to school and study esthetics. "I'd really love to make my living with my art, but I have to be realistic. My children will need me to provide for them financially. I'm certain I won't be able to depend on Brian. I think I'd be good at helping women to feel better about themselves. I'd teach them how to properly take care of their skin, applying makeup, and improving their self-esteem. What do you think?"

"I think it's a great idea, go for it. Find out where you'd go to school, how long it will take and how much money you'll need. If you need some additional funds to get started, let me know."

"Thanks, but I think I've got to see this through on my own."

"Well, if we can help with anything, don't be too proud to ask."

Beverly was thrilled to find that her friend was finally taking control of her own life. It would take time, but Beverly could see there was a light at the end of Suzanne's tunnel.

Chapter Four

Boston, Massachusetts • 1970

Suzanne was in shock. The doctor continued to talk, but Suzanne barely heard what he was saying.

"It looks like you and Brian will be having that boy you've been looking for," Dr. Greenberg pronounced.

Now she really felt sick. She loved children, and had hoped to have four or five. But, now that she had made up her mind to leave Brian, it was inconceivable that she could be pregnant again.

"Are you all right? I thought you'd be delighted with my news."

"You know I want more children, but I don't want them with Brian. I have every intention of divorcing him. If I have this baby, I'll have to put my plans on hold. I don't know what I'm going to do." She went on to fill him in on some of the details of her life with Brian.

Sitting on the edge of the highly polished cherrywood the doctor rose and walked around the desk to Suzanne. He said, "You and I go back quite a long time, since you were a little girl, and I've got to tell you - I feel terrible about this."

He went on, watching her carefully. "Abortion is a controversial issue that doesn't have a right side or a wrong side, but it shouldn't be taken lightly. Only a few states have legalized termination of pregnancy, but I think you should go home and think seriously about this matter. I wouldn't ordinarily suggest it, but from what you told me and from what I can see of your mental anguish, you'd be an exception. If you decide to have one, the sooner we do it, the better it will be for everyone. Please call me as soon as you decide. And Suzanne, God be with you."

On the way home, Suzanne pondered her choices. She never thought she would have to make a decision like this. "How could it have happened?" she asked herself. She always used precautions, always. Then it hit her. She remembered the one time she was too tired to insert the foolish diaphragm, because Brian had insisted on having sex at two in the morning, when she was sound asleep. "That selfish bastard," she thought to herself.

She walked into her home with the weight of the world on her shoulders. She greeted her girls and knelt down close to them and told them how much she loved them. Suzanne held them tightly to her chest, sobs emanating from the depths of her soul.

She trudged through the next week in a daze as she pondered the complicated moral issues. The problem was a complex one. She knew she was in need of pastoral guidance and made an appointment to talk with her rabbi.

She found him to be the inspiration she needed. He did not look at her with contempt as she voiced the complex issues that bothered her. At the end of the two-and-one-half hour meeting her mind was made up. She already loved this new baby and knew she could not still this being within her. She would put her plans on hold and go through with the pregnancy.

After making the decision, she was surprised to find herself depressed. She behaved as if everything was fine, but it was painfully difficult to feign affection or passion for Brian. She did it because she didn't want anyone to suspect that anything was wrong. The only person she dared confide in was Beverly.

"Suzanne, I don't like the way you look," Dorothy admonished her daughter. "You're not growing correctly. It's not normal to gain only a few pounds. I hope everything is all right with the baby."

"Mom," Suzanne replied, "the doctor isn't concerned about the small weight gain, so don't worry about it. Please, don't look for things to worry about."

Besides her children, Suzanne's only pleasure was painting. With Hope in school, Suzanne would sometimes leave Melanie with one of the neighbors and drive to Chester where she enjoyed the peace of the state forest. Occasionally she would hear the sound of hooves on the trails as a lone rider galloped through the woods. Often she brought her sketchpad and sat on the small, wooden bridge overlooking the clear sparkling water. She enjoyed drawing here and tried to capture the true light and color of the woods.

Weighing in at seven and one half pounds, with a mass of straight, dark hair and a rosy glow on her cheeks, Taylor arrived two weeks early. She was absolutely beautiful. The girls were delighted that they had another sister and couldn't wait until Suzanne brought her home from the hospital.

"I thought it was going to be a boy this time for sure. You carried so much differently. Oh well, there's always the next time," voiced a disappointed Brian.

"Like hell," Suzanne thought to herself.

With Hope in school half days, Suzanne devoted her time to Melanie and Taylor. She persuaded Melanie to lie down next to her in the afternoons and rest while Taylor slept. These late day respites gave Suzanne time to recuperate, because she found herself staying up past midnight, painting. For hours on end she absorbed herself in her art. Her painting was her salvation during this time.

She had inquired about esthetics schools and now examined her options. One part of her wanted to start school as soon as possible. Another part of her reasoned that Taylor was too young to leave with a sitter for such long periods of time. Suzanne felt Taylor deserved the same attention that she had given to both the other girls.

Meanwhile, Brian had no idea how unhappy Suzanne was. She was a good actress. She didn't want to betray Dr. Steinberg so she never told Brian that she knew he was no longer seeing him. She kept the house neat and clean and spent enormous amounts of energy and time just keeping the children out of his way. Nights were the hardest, because even though she never went to bed until way past midnight she found it difficult to sleep soundly beside him.

This preposterous task had a damaging effect on Suzanne's body. She lost ten pounds and developed a drawn, gaunt look. Her parents were worried about her but didn't know how they could help.

"Suzanne," her mother stated, as she took hold of her daughters arm and led her into the living room. "You know I don't like to interfere, but honey, you look like hell. What's the matter with you? I hope you're not pregnant again."

"No Mom, it's nothing like that. I'm a little run down, that's all."

Exasperated, she persisted, "Oh no you don't; a mother knows when something isn't right. Now I'm going to make an appointment with you to see Dr. Schwartz. He'll find out what's wrong. Why Mama Pessa looks better than you do lately."

Suzanne laughed and promised that she would see the doctor soon. She knew all too well that he wouldn't find anything wrong with her. Her only problem was Brian.

After a routine examination by the doctor he told her, "Well, I don't find any serious problems, but you have to take better care of yourself. You must get more rest. Think of your small children. They need their mother."

"Oh, no kidding. Thanks for pointing that out to me," she thought to herself. "A brain surgeon he isn't."

On the ride home from the doctor's office, Suzanne wondered what a future without Brian's constant criticism and overbearing presence would be like. She knew it would be a financial burden, but she had to make a move soon.

One afternoon, she picked up the younger girls from the sitter and took them grocery shopping with her. Brian was supposed to come home early that day. Suzanne didn't rush back from shopping knowing he'd let Hope in when she returned back from school.

As soon as she returned home she sensed something was amiss. Hope, who customarily greeted her at the door, did not appear. Brian's car was parked in its usual spot outside, so she knew he was there.

"Hope, honey, are you in the house?" called out Suzanne. There was no answer.

"Okay Melanie, let's bring in the bundles," directed Suzanne. "I'll put Taylor in the kitchen and she can watch us." While getting the bundles from the car, she saw Brian in the garage.

"Honey, do you think you can help us take in the groceries?"

"Sure," replied Brian.

"Brian, where's Hope? I thought she'd be with you."

"She's in the house somewhere," responded Brian.

A knot formed in the pit of Suzanne's stomach. Stifling her fears, she began to look for Hope by calling out her name. She went through each of the bedrooms and looked in the bathrooms. Then, for some reason she could not comprehend, she went back to the bedrooms and searched the closets. "Maybe she's visiting one of the neighbors or playing with a friend," Suzanne thought to herself. It didn't make sense, though. Hope knew enough to tell either her or Brian, if she was leaving. Suzanne tried not to panic, but she wanted to find Hope and she didn't want to ask Brian for help doing it.

Calls to the neighbors proved fruitless. "Brian, are you sure Hope didn't say she was going anywhere?"

"For God's sake, I'm not an idiot," Brian remarked belligerently. "Even if you treat me like one at times," he muttered sarcastically under his breath.

Her mother's intuition sent Suzanne back to search the bedrooms again. She finally found Hope sound asleep under Melanie's bed, against the far wall with two blankets crumpled on top of her. "This is bizarre," Suzanne thought.

"Honey," she said softly, as she pulled the child out from under the bed. "Mummy's been calling you, and I was worried because I couldn't find you. Don't ever do that again," she scolded gently.

Waking up slowly from a deep sleep, Hope had understood what Suzanne had said and started crying pitifully.

As she brought her out into the light, Suzanne saw at once the bruises on Hope's face and, on examining her further, she found more of them on her arms, legs and abdomen as well. Raging, Suzanne struggled to hold down the bile that rose from her stomach. Her own body was shaking uncontrollably. Restraining herself to remain in control, she placed her daughter in a tub of warm water and gently cleaned her while she continually reassured her that she had done nothing wrong. After she had dried her off, she calmly questioned her daughter.

"Honey, what happened?" Suzanne inquired, as she held Hope in her arms, caressing her.

Hope told Suzanne, "Daddy was home and let me in the house. I was happy to see Daddy, and wanted to play with him." Sobbing and shaking all over again, Hope continued, "I asked Daddy if he would play catch with me."

"He said yes, so I went to my room, and changed, because I know you don't want me dirtying my school clothes." Hope told Suzanne as her little body quivered while she wept.

"Go on honey. Don't be afraid to tell Mommy everything that happened."

"All I did was throw the ball at Daddy. I thought it was funny when it hit him. I didn't mean to hurt him. Honest, I didn't, Mummy, and all of a sudden he started yelling at me and scared me. I ran to my room and all I could remember was when he yells at you, he hits you, and I was scared. He caught me and I told him I was sorry, but it was like he didn't hear me. He had a funny look on his face and he started hitting and kicking me and it hurt and the more he shook me the more I cried and he kept yelling at me to stop, but I couldn't Mummy. I'm sorry I didn't mean to hurt Daddy and scare him."

As she rocked Hope in her arms, Suzanne knew she had finally reached the end. She wasn't sure what else she could say to Hope. She knew she had to reinforce the message that it wasn't Hope's fault, and she repeated that. She also knew she had to get the girls out of this environment. There was no question about it now. And, it must happen soon.

She made a solemn vow, "I'll make everything better. We will get out of this mess. I promise you, Hope. Mommy, will make everything all right, and we'll get away from him soon, I promise, as God is my witness."

Her mind was reeling. She blamed herself because she had not taken action sooner to get out of this horrible situation. One thing was certain; she would never leave any of the children alone with Brian again, ever.

She knew that if she took Hope to the doctor, Brian would be accused of child abuse. Suzanne felt that physically, except for the bruising, Hope was all right; at least it didn't seem as if anything was broken. Emotionally, she wasn't sure about the effects this abusive act would have on the child. With an enormous amount of guilt, she decided against bringing the authorities into this. She had heard some horror stories about the, "so called, professionals", and was convinced that they didn't always know what to do either. What if they took the children away from her? She knew she couldn't bear that. She didn't want Hope to be any more traumatized than she already was. "I've got to find a way to protect them myself," she thought.

She was never able to understand how Brian could go about his business as if nothing had happened. She knew that if she brought it up he'd say she was making a big deal out of something minor. That evening while Brian was at his weekly business meeting, Suzanne finalized her plans.

The next morning, after Hope had left for school and Brian for work, Suzanne first called the esthetics school that had been recommended to her by her dermatologist, Dr. Klein. He had worked with some very talented estheticians there who had helped some of his severely burned patients use the proper type of make up to cover their scars. Suzanne realized that it would be very hard on her and the children if she went back to school now, but she made an appointment to talk to the admissions director anyway.

Next, she placed an advertisement in the local newspaper for a baby-sitter who would mind the children while she attended school. She knew Brian might take phone calls from people responding to the ad, so she had to tell him of her plans and hope he would give her money for school. She had never asked for much and now that she was, he had better say yes. She lied and told him that she was restless and wanted to start a different career. She had a prepared response for each argument he posed. She fielded his questions and when he realized that she was serious about her new endeavor, he relented.

Interviewing the applicants for the sitting position took Suzanne a considerable amount of time. She wanted to find the right person for her children. Suzanne watched for certain traits in the individuals that would help her decide. She wanted an upbeat person with a warm personality. If an applicant had poor listening skills, dressed sloppily or spoke crudely, Suzanne rejected her promptly as a possibility.

After Suzanne had almost exhausted her list of applicants, Mrs. Walsh, an older woman, mother of four and a widow for almost fifteen years, arrived for her interview. A large, robust woman, almost five feet ten inches tall, she toted a large shopping bag into the house with her. The brown pouch contained her references, the newspaper, and two books she was in the middle of reading. Suzanne took to her immediately, liking her sincerity, warm smile, and the twinkle in her brown eyes. As she spoke, Suzanne detected the remains of a brogue. She drove her own late model car, which was a big plus. She would be able to chauffeur the children when the need arose. Suzanne quickly settled on Mrs. Walsh for the position.

Mrs. Walsh loved children and had seven grandchildren of her own. Unfortunately, they all lived out-of-state. Her only child living nearby was unmarried. When she was in her early twenties, Mrs. Walsh had come over from County Cork in Ireland and, although she had only a grade school education, she had years of experience with children and an uncommon amount of common sense. She had worked as a cook in a diner for years but lost her job when the establishment closed. She wanted to work but wasn't trained for a "professional" career. This job would give her "bingo" money plus something extra to put aside for her future. They agreed that Suzanne would pay her extra if she did the wash and cleaned the house.

Finally, Suzanne joined a carpool with a neighbor, Bob. Suzanne was delighted that someone else would drive, as this would give her some extra time to study while she was a passenger and it would save her nerves from the strain of the city traffic.

With her preliminary plans in effect, Suzanne was able to start school early in December.

The parking lot Bob used was close to his office near the Boston Tea Party Ship. Suzanne's school was located at the other end of Boston. It took her almost twenty-five minutes of brisk walking to get to her school from the car. She had to pass South Station, which was famous for its very strong wind currents. She made it a point to listen to the weather forecast and dressed accordingly. In adverse weather, the stinging winds ripped through her clothes. On rainy days, especially if the wind was blowing, it was doubly hard, but Suzanne refused to spend money on the subway. She was saving everything she could so that she could rid herself of her dependence on Brian.

From the first day of class, Suzanne loved school. She attacked her studies with enthusiasm. She found herself fascinated with the dermatology course and especially loved the practical aspects of esthetics - makeup applications and facials.

On beautiful spring days Suzanne and some of the other students often walked to the Boston Common for lunch. There they would eat their sandwiches while sitting on a park bench or upon blankets spread on the grass. Someone was always performing on the Common. She enjoyed the mimes and the jugglers the best. Young musicians played guitars and in one section religious fanatics stood on soapboxes and preached, predicting the end of the earth - - doom for all who did not "believe."

As spring drew near and she looked forward to graduation, she began to formulate her next course of action. She would need money to start her own business. If she could sell a few of her art pieces, the money would be the answer to her prayers. The excitement she felt stimulated her desire to forge ahead with her plans to separate from Brian. She owed a phone call to Justin Ferris.

The receptionist answered the telephone, "Justin Ferris, Art Gallery, can I help you?"

"Yes, is Mr. Ferris in? This is Suzanne Morse."

"One moment please, Ms. Morse."

After waiting for what seemed five minutes, Mr. Ferris picked up the receiver. "Suzanne, I'm glad you called," he said. "What can I do for you?"

She hoped he still wanted her paintings, but she braced herself for a letdown. "I've been busy and must apologize for not getting back to you since our meeting in January. I'd still like to meet with you to discuss an exhibit," replied Suzanne.

"Good, good. Let's set up an appointment now. I'm anxious to arrange this showing. Can you come in next Saturday about 11 a.m.?"

As she put the phone down, Suzanne emitted an audible sigh of relief.

The week dragged slowly by. Suzanne prepared for the meeting by gathering all the pieces from her house and picking up many that she had lent out to friends. Placing aside some of her earlier work, she organized the remaining pieces of art in groupings of landscapes and abstracts.

Brian was busy flying to various states visiting clients and was to be in Ohio on Saturday. Suzanne carefully loaded all the paintings into her station wagon. While she was arranging the paintings, her mind was full of unkind thoughts about her husband. He left everything up to her. She felt as if she were both mother and father to the girls. At times she resented that she had to handle so much by herself without help from him. She would have loved to have someone share in the excitement she felt.

She speculated about the years ahead and dreaded having to assist in mathematics, algebra, geometry, and calculus homework. For some reason, math never came easily to her, people who knew of her 'math anxiety,' though, laughed, pointing out that she never had difficulty when it came to counting money.

Suzanne arrived at the gallery at 10:30 a.m. and was helped by Frank, Justin's aide. After the paintings had been set on stands against the wall and the lighting had been adjusted for each of them, Justin entered the room. He wore a dark blue pin stripe suit that must have been custom-tailored for him. He quietly walked back and forth, examining each piece thoroughly. Three or four times he stopped and adjusted the light for a particular canvas. His walk was deliberately slow, with his left hand under his right elbow, and his right thumb under his chin. He took his time - scrutinizing, inspecting, and making notes in a small black leather notebook. Occasionally, he picked one up and held it close to his face, peering into it.

Suzanne's heart beat rapidly. For once her instinct about people failed her for she could not interpret the expression on Mr. Ferris' face. After what seemed like hours, but was, in reality only forty-five minutes, Mr. Ferris turned to her, and playfully said, "Relax, we'll go over my notes in a few minutes and I'll tell you what I have in mind."

He spoke into the intercom, "Tricia, have Frank bring two chairs down here. I want to sit in front of the canvases while I talk with Ms. Morse."

He took Suzanne to the far end of the room while they waited for the chairs. "We are going to be here for a while longer. I'm sending Frank out for lunch. What would you like?"

Suzanne's stomach was in a knot, and she was not the least bit hungry. "Nothing to eat, thanks, but I'd love a cup of tea."

"Okay, tea for Mrs. Morse, and my regular Trish, he pronounced over the two way radio. Are you sure you don't want anything to eat?"

"No, thanks, Mr. Ferris. I couldn't eat a thing."

"First of all, you must call me Justin, if we're going to do business together. Okay?"

Suzanne laughed relieved by the direction the discussion was taking. "Okay, but then you'll have to call me Suzanne."

Justin chuckled, "Deal."

Taking her hand into his, he weighed his next words carefully. "Suzanne, I don't pull punches or say anything I don't mean. I'm in business to make money, so I don't take on an artist or art that I don't think will profit me. I don't mean to be crass, but that's the truth of the matter."

Frank arrived with the chairs and gave Suzanne a quick wink. She relaxed even more. Until then, Suzanne thought that Justin might be preparing her for a gentle letdown.

"When I first met you I thought to myself; 'This woman has control of herself and her art.' I believe, with the right guidance you can become a pacesetter in the art world. All your paintings are strong, unusually so, if you'll forgive me, for a woman. You show a unique imagination and creativity, it comes through in your work beautifully in graceful, well-proportioned, and well-executed pieces. I love your use of rich, vivid colors. They're fresh. Your work is unique. I would like to exhibit your seascapes, still- life and abstracts."

Suzanne could not contain her astonishment. She was taken by surprise at this eloquent appraisal of her work. She broke into a delighted, joyous smile. Words stuck in her throat, but she forced herself to respond and thanked him.

"Don't thank me my dear, for it's you who should be thanked. Let's get down to business. We'll finalize matters such as commissions and the dates for an exhibit. Before we settle on a final date, I want to talk with another young artist who I may exhibit at the same time. Would that be agreeable to you?"

"Sure," replied Suzanne. "That's great."

Justin continued, "I'll have to talk to him and then I'll let you know what we decide. Now, let's look at possible dates." They chose a tentative date of the Saturday before Mother's Day.

Suzanne was on cloud nine when she left the gallery. She couldn't believe her good fortune and she smiled all the way home. She couldn't wait to tell her parents, Beverly, and even, Brian. Over the years Brian had not encouraged her artistic endeavors. He dismissed her work as her "hobby." When she honestly thought he might be right, Justin Ferris was giving back some of her self-esteem.

Her mind was in turmoil. Finals were approaching and she knew she should become more organized if she was going to run her own business. She was nervous. A different world was opening up for her. Suzanne regained her zest for life and looked forward to waking each day. The constant demands and criticism that Brian imposed on her didn't anger or frustrate her as they used to.

Would she be up to the challenges that lay ahead?

Chapter Five

Suzanne awoke to a Bermuda sky ablaze with sunshine. Without a set schedule she could do whatever she wanted, whenever she wanted to do it. After breakfast she planned to pick up the moped and drive to Hamilton to visit a perfume factory. At the dining room Suzanne ordered a lunch to take with her on the excursion. Greeting the people at her table she listened to Mike narrate last evening's adventure.

"Now Suzanne, we won't take any excuses tonight," Ruth said. "You're coming out with us!"

"Well, I'm off to Hamilton this afternoon on the moped. I'm sure I'll be back in time. Okay, I'll go with you tonight."

"Suzanne, don't go breaking any bones. I've heard about terrible accidents with those things."

Suzanne chuckled to herself. With everything she had handled in the past few years, she was sure she could handle a piece of machinery. "I'm sure I'll be fine. Thanks for the concern, though. I'll see you all at dinner. Have a good day."

A warm breeze cooled her as she cycled along the main road to Hamilton. She forced her mind to stay focused, especially at the rotaries, which got very confusing since she was driving on the "wrong" side of the road. She couldn't resist turning in at the beach at Horseshoe Bay.

The pink sand felt good beneath her feet as she walked to the secluded coves at the far end. The azure water cooled her as she submerged her body in the ocean surrounded by the cavernous rocks. Suzanne struggled to keep her mind free from clutter, as she revitalized herself in this momentary haven.

She stopped at Devonshire Bay for lunch. She removed her sneakers and let the warm soft sand envelop her feet. Again she stripped down to her bathing suit and stretched out on a large towel. The beach was fairly deserted. Only a handful of tourists had ventured away from their hotels to enjoy the clear, blue water of this secluded inlet.

Nibbling on cheese and crackers, she puzzled over what she could do to help Mr. and Mrs. Pearlman. "I hope Nancy will be able to help me find a way to get into the company books." She again thought of the Pearlmans as the tepid water touched her toes.

"The Pearlmans worked hard to build their companies, but they are still vulnerable to these unscrupulous characters. They've already been through more pain and hardship in the prison camps than anyone should have to face in a lifetime."

"Whatever Brian is doing to them, I'm sure it's illegal." She had to question her motives. "Am I trying to help the Pearlmans, or am I really trying to get even with him for all the pain he has caused me?" She knew she had a bias when it came to Brian, but she still held out a faint hope that she might be mistaken and that her assumption was wrong. "If my worst fears are confirmed, I'll have to go to the authorities. There will be no other choice."

"How will the girls react to the news and publicity if their father is involved in something illegal and I'm the one who put the rope around his neck? Will the girls forgive me if they find out I'm responsible? Will it be worth it?" she asked herself.

Her lunch lay like a knot in her stomach as she wandered into the sea. The cool water felt good on her body. She wished the ocean's wetness could take away the fiery pain that Brian was causing her again, after all these years. She emerged from the water and lay on the towel to dry.

"I need someone like Nancy to help me find out about Brian's business dealings; someone he doesn't know, with intelligence and business savvy, one who, once made aware of the danger involved, will be willing to help anyway. It's going to take an extraordinary person to take on this dangerous assignment. I think Nancy can handle this. I bet she'd be good at it, too."

It was very important that Brian not recognize Nancy or anyone who would help her as being a friend of Suzanne's. She was aware that he might have met Nancy at the art exhibit, but there were so many people there that night, that he probably wouldn't remember her.

When she was dry, Suzanne went on to Hamilton and found the perfume factory she was looking for. The manager greeted her and they discussed her requirements over tea. What she wanted was a particular scent that would become identified with the chain of *Metamorphosis Spas*. Once he understood what she wanted he took her through the factory so that she could see how their scents are produced from the natural flora of the island. She sampled a wide selection of bouquets that were available to the general public. The manager then suggested a dozen different combinations of fragrances, some of which were produced for private customers. He had recently created a unique combination of gardenia and nightsage. The aroma was an unusual blend of floral and spice. It was the perfect formula for her spa.

Suzanne placed an order to be sent to her Dallas salon where she would run a trial sale. If the perfume was successful there, she would continue its distribution in her other spas.

She arrived back at the hotel at five-thirty with plenty of time left until dinner. She changed her clothes, relaxed a bit and went downstairs just before eight o'clock for the evening meal. Her table companions were already seated when Suzanne arrived. Everyone gave a narrative of their day's activities. The newlyweds, Jennifer and Todd, had gone snorkeling. Ruth and Mike had gone to a swizzle party and afterwards took a glass bottomed boat ride.

Ruth and Mike were meeting some business friends in Hamilton for a few drinks after dinner. They asked Suzanne, Jennifer and Todd to join them. The group piled into a taxi and went into Hamilton to a local nightspot. Leaving behind her worry and anxiety, Suzanne danced and enjoyed the local music and the congenial people. She spent part of the evening dancing with Raymond Leach, a native Bermudian and a friend of Mike's.

When she arrived back at her hotel room, she glanced at the clock and couldn't believe it was two o'clock in the morning. She hadn't been out this late since her teenage years. Too tired to remove her make up, she fell fast asleep, with not a care in the world.

The following morning, Suzanne arose early and had breakfast before most of the other guests. She wanted to be alone to walk the beach and catch up on her reading. Remembering that Devonshire Bay had been fairly deserted the day before she retrieved her moped and ventured back to the secluded inlet. Enjoying the solitude, she was surprised to see Raymond Leach approaching.

"I thought I recognized you when we met last night. I saw you here yesterday, didn't I?"

"Raymond," said Suzanne, "how nice to see you again! Do you live near here?"

He pointed to the magnificent pink, stucco mansion jutting out over the water on the cliffs above them and continued, "I'm on holiday myself right now. I usually spend most of my time abroad attending to my businesses, but I'm meeting some of my associates and we decided to meet here and kill two birds with one stone, as you Americans would say."

The articulate Mr. Leach mesmerized Suzanne. She found his clipped, British accent entrancing. He told Suzanne his family's fascinating ancestry. He was a descendant of a famous Portuguese pirate, John Silva, who had married a wealthy British woman. Through his inheritance Raymond now controlled a vast amount of land throughout Bermuda.

Raymond also owned companies in Europe and the United States. He had a large communications company based in New England. "In fact, the reason I'm here this particular weekend is that some of my engineers and managers are flying in late this afternoon to discuss some acquisitions we're about to make. But enough of my rhetoric, tell me all about yourself. Are there other people in your party?"

Suzanne did not go into detail on the reason for her solitary vacation. She told him enough to satisfy his curiosity, mentioning that this was the first vacation that she had ever taken alone and she was truly enjoying herself. Sifting the finely granulated sand between her fingers, she tried changing the subject. "The first time I came to Bermuda I was a young girl of eighteen. I fell in love with the beautiful land, people and flowers. In all my travels, I've never experienced people who are so polite and proud of their country. When I paint various pictures I find

95

myself visualizing the lovely homes and their colorful exteriors. Raymond, I can't tell you how lucky you are to have been born in such a special place. Whenever I visit I feel as if I've come home."

"Suzanne, I'm having a dinner party tomorrow evening for my associates. Do you think you could join us? I can have my chauffeur pick you up at your hotel, if you'll be able to attend."

Suzanne was delighted. "Thanks, Raymond. I'd love it."

The following evening she wore a long, stunning dress in shades of purple and turquoise. A simple pair of amethyst earrings completed her outfit.

While she waited for the driver to pick her up, she put a phone call through to the States. "Mrs. Walsh, how are you? Any news?"

"Everyone's fine here. Are you having a good time?" asked Mrs. Walsh.

Suzanne related the happenings thus far. "I'm having a great time. I found the perfume I wanted in no time flat so I can rest for the remainder of the week." She told Mrs. Walsh that she would keep in touch with her and said good-bye.

As soon as she got off the telephone, the manager rang to tell her that Raymond's driver was waiting for her.

A short ride along the shore brought them to the house. A gracious Bermudian woman answered the door and led her into the living room. What she saw on her way to the parlor was a spacious home with a bright airy decor. Raymond greeted her and introduced her to the other guests.

"We're waiting for one more gentleman. His flight from Texas was delayed but he should be here momentarily."

Suzanne accepted a glass of wine. Ten executives from Raymond's companies were in attendance along with their wives or husbands. The couples were all from the United States or Japan. Suzanne enjoyed meeting them. She heard Raymond again expound on the beauty and history of this lovely island.

About twenty minutes later the doorbell rang and the latecomer arrived. As he entered the foyer he handed the bags to the maid. "Thanks, Marion, could you put this briefcase where I can see it? I have some papers Raymond should sign before I leave tonight."

Suzanne was in the middle of a spirited political conversation with some of the guests as the newcomer greeted Raymond and nodded to the other people.

"Well, finally," said someone in Suzanne's immediate circle. "The big executive, always a stickler for promptness? How late is he?" Everyone laughed at the good-natured banter aimed at the late arrival.

The women were eager to see if he had brought anyone with him. One of the females in the small group whispered to Suzanne "Boy, is he fine. I love working with him. It's one of those 'fringe benefits' I get working for Raymond. "The women in the group nodded in agreement. Exuding confidence, the handsome gentleman walked over to the bar and mixed himself a scotch and water. "Okay, okay, give me a hard time will you? You'll be singing a different tune, when you see the new contract I've worked out with the Tandler Corporation."

Raymond took Suzanne's arm. Bringing her to the long, oak and brass counter to introduce her to the newcomer, Suzanne was taken by surprise and a sense of déjà vu overtook her. Conversation faded around them as their eyes met. She hadn't forgotten those azure eyes that were like pools of deep blue water. His smile was still warm and sincere but now a bit of gray streaked his dark, wavy hair. As Raymond made the introduction, they both smiled from ear to ear.

"There's no need for introduction. Suzanne and I go way back, don't we?" Looking at her with a twinkle in his eyes he explained, "Actually, Raymond, we went to the same high school."

Suzanne interjected, "Of course, I'm quite a bit younger than he is." Both of them laughed. Suzanne felt herself blushing. "I can't believe that of all people, Stephen LeVigne would come walking through the door," she thought. Never in a million years, would she have dreamt of a chance meeting like this. She could feel the pounding of her heart and she was intensely aware of his nearness.

The old feelings engulfed her as she took all of him in - his eyes, the cleft in his chin, his masculinity - every feature that had been engraved in her heart and kept suppressed for so long. With a relief that surprised her, she noted that he wore a tone-on-tone shirt that went well with the vivid pattern of his necktie. Intense emotions welled up from the depths of her soul. She had never forgotten him. Declining a second glass of wine, lest she betray her feelings, she struggled desperately to maintain her composure.

A piano played in the background as they sat down at the antique Spanish dining room table. The good-natured joking continued throughout the meal. These people certainly had great personalities. They weren't stuffy at all. Suzanne was surprised at how relaxed and welcome everyone made her feel.

After dinner they settled into the library for cordials. The conversation was kept light and entertaining with no mention of the dealings that had brought them to this vacation/business meeting. The rest of the evening went by much too fast. It was well past midnight when most of the guests departed for their hotels.

"Ray, I'll drive Suzanne back to her hotel." Stephen turned towards Suzanne, "If that's okay with you?"

"That would be nice," said Suzanne, taking another look at her surroundings, so that everything about this evening would be ingrained in her memory forever. She memorized the elegant yet comfortable furniture and the distinguishing character of this home and it's owner, the chance encounter with Raymond Leach that had subsequently led to her seeing Stephen again. She wanted to remember it all - - forever.

Taking Raymond's hand, Suzanne spoke sincerely, "Thanks so much for a wonderful evening. The next time you're in the States, you'll have to let me reciprocate."

Stephen led the way as they left the house. He took her arm, embracing it, guiding them down the narrow walkway to the car. The old emotions came rushing back. She never wanted him to let go of her.

Alone in the car with Stephen, Suzanne didn't know where to begin. With her heart pounding, she was about to speak, but before she had a chance Stephen said, "You haven't changed one bit. If anything, you've gotten more beautiful. I can't believe that we bumped into each other like this. Have you known Raymond long?"

"No, I only met him a couple of days ago," Suzanne responded.

"What an incredible surprise. I just can't believe it."

She was glad that it was dark, because her face was crimson, Suzanne spoke.   "The years have been good to you, too, Stephen. You don't look too bad yourself. I like your clothes, by the way!" Both of them laughed.

"Seriously Suzanne, what brings you to Bermuda? You have to tell me what's been going on in your life." He stopped the car outside the resort and shut off the engine.

Determined to see him again, but needing to hold him at arm's length until she had a chance to reflect on the unexpected turn of events, Suzanne ventured, "I'd love to ask you in, but I have an early appointment. Why don't we have dinner tomorrow night?"

"Great idea. I'll look forward to it. Pick you up at eight?" He winked and gave her a hug. She returned the embrace and waved back to him as she entered the lobby.

The fragrance of her perfume lingered in the car. He wanted to bottle it, so he would never forget her scent. "God I've prayed many times in my life for a second chance and I hope this is your answer. Let this be mine. Please let her be free." Aware that the request might be in vain, he started the engine and headed back to the hotel. It took all his strength not to follow her, barge into her room and confess his true feelings.

She had a hard time falling asleep knowing she was headed for deep water. "It could only be fate that had brought us together like this," she thought. "Am I going to get another chance?"

As she tossed and turned, she listened to the waves breaking against the reefs outside her window. Uneasy thoughts raced through her mind. I can't let Stephen distract me from solving my dilemma. It took a long time but finally Morpheus took over. In her restless dreams, Stephen's face was intermingled with the Pearlmans' and Brian's.

The laughter of people outside her window broke into Suzanne's slumber. Still feeling sleepy, as if she had been through a long, tedious ordeal, she took a long hot shower, hoping it would sharpen her senses. On edge, she could not eat the French toast that the waiter put in front of her. When the others asked her to join them for a day of sightseeing she explained, "I've met an old friend and will probably be busy for the next couple of days." "You hope," she thought to herself.

In Hamilton, she found a great little boutique that had a perfect dress - feminine but not too dressy. Determined to keep occupied, she returned to the hotel and went directly to the front desk. "Any tennis games going on? Does anyone need a partner for doubles?" she asked the clerk.

"Mrs. Morse, of course. Someone was just here looking for another player. I'll let the group know you're available. The game starts in an hour."

Suzanne could hold her own on the tennis courts. She enjoyed the game with the others who were from New

York. They played for about two hours, then went to the lounge for refreshments.

One of the women, Cheryl, knew of Suzanne's New York spa and had been going there for about three years. "It's sure a small world isn't it?" the two women said at once. After some inconsequential talk, Suzanne thanked them for the game and returned to her suite.

She changed into her bathing suit and settled into a lounge chair beside the pool. The hours couldn't go by fast enough. She felt like a schoolgirl before her first date. She wanted to call Beverly back home in the States but thought better of it.

"This is ridiculous. I run my own business. I'm supposed to be in total control. How can I let my emotions get the best of me?" she said to herself.

The message light was flashing when she got back to her room. Suzanne returned the call to Miko Takahashi, one of the executives whom she had met the previous night. During their conversation, Suzanne asked Miko if she would like to join her for a game of golf. Hanging up the phone, Suzanne called the lobby and made reservations at the adjacent course for the following day.

She returned a call from Peter. As soon as he heard her voice he said, "I called to let you know that everything is fine and no one misses you. Are you having a good time?" Before she could reply he said, "You know I'm only kidding. The phones have been ringing off the hook. Do you want me to pick you up at the airport when you get back or are you going to take a limo home?" he asked.

"I'm having a great time, thanks. Let's play it by ear. I'll call you before I leave and let you know. Send my love to everyone, and, oh, tell Nancy I have some interesting news."

Suzanne drew a hot, steamy bath and loaded the water with bath oils in the scent of her new perfume. She settled back in the tub, closed her eyes and visualized Stephen's face and muscular body. She felt completely relaxed when she dressed for her date. She wore her new outfit and no jewelry except for a simple pair of pearl earrings.

Impeccably attired, Stephen was waiting in the lobby and spotted her immediately as she came through the swinging doors. He rose to meet her. "Hi, you look beautiful this evening. My car is right outside. I've made reservations at Lantana, in Somerset for eight thirty. It's my favorite."

In the car their conversation was amicable. "Do you come to Bermuda often?" Suzanne asked.

"Maybe every three months or so, whenever Raymond feels that a few of his key people from the various offices should converge. We usually manage to take a few days to relax when we get here."

"How long have you worked for him? And, tell me what you've been doing all these years. I was so surprised when you came walking into the room last evening."

"We have a lot to talk about. We have so many things to find out about each other. Is this the first time you've been to Bermuda?" Stephen asked Suzanne.

"No, I was here years ago. The unspoiled beauty of the land and the warmth of the people have always held a special place in my heart. I've been to many places since then, mostly on business, but I've wanted to come back to Bermuda for a long time and I'm glad I did."

They sat by a window overlooking the ocean. A local band played, making a truly picturesque and enchanting setting. Stephen proposed the toast. "May we get to know one another all over again."

His eyes, so deep and sincere, looked directly into Suzanne's large dark brown ones. "I want to know everything, Suzanne. What's been going on in your life? How are your children? How's that adorable little girl I saw in the hospital that day? I tried keeping track of you through the years. The Jewish community in Quincy is small and my mother kept me informed of how well you're doing in your business. Your parents are quite proud of you. Are you still married?" He closed his eyes momentarily and silently prayed her answer would be the one he wanted to hear.

Suzanne tried to describe her marriage. It was difficult to describe her life with Brian, without making him look like a complete ogre or herself like a complete fool for staying with him, so she focused on the children and her business. She couldn't admit to Stephen that she probably married Brian on the rebound from him. She took out the girls' pictures from her wallet and vividly described each one. Then she told him, "When you saw me that day in the hospital, things were already very bad, but I didn't know what I was going to do about it." She felt it best not to elaborate any further on her marriage, so she left it at that.

She went on to recount the first difficult years of her business. "There was a time when my favorite appliance was a crock pot, you know, a slow cooker? For the entire time I went to school all the meals tasted exactly the same. I couldn't afford expensive cuts of meat, so I bought the cheapest. I found if you cook the meat slowly in plenty of sauce, the meal was usually quite tasty. I prepared the next night's meal the evening before and then plugged it in before I left for school in the morning. By the time I came home the aroma filled the house and the children couldn't wait to sit down and eat." Chuckling, she added, "It didn't matter if the meat was chicken, beef, or lamb. Everything tasted the same."

She continued, "When I finally graduated and we didn't need the slow cooker, one of the children dropped it and its ceramic dish shattered into a thousand pieces. They all shouted with glee that it was broken and that particular part of our life was over."

Stephen laughed at her amusing narrative.

She was not usually this open but felt she could be honest with Stephen and that he would appreciate her sincerity. When the story ended, he took her hand nearest to him and brought it to his lips. This act of compassion told her what she needed to know and realized that she had done the right thing.

Speaking in a relaxed manner she continued, "What I missed most, was not being with my children. Although I left them in capable hands with Mrs. Walsh, I know they resented my being away so much. One never knows how things would've turned out, if I 'd stayed in my marriage. I still think I made the right decision. Occasionally the children would try to lay a guilt trip on me, but as they matured, they realized I did what I had to do."

"If I'd stayed in that marriage, it would've been disastrous for everyone concerned." Shrugging her shoulders she continued, "Many an evening I missed the companionship of an adult who I could converse with and share hopes and dreams. It hasn't been easy for me, but when I look around and see the tragedies that happen every day, I thank God for my blessings. But enough of my long-winded self, now that I've bared my soul, you have to tell me how things have been for you." _

Chortling, Stephen told Suzanne that his life wasn't anything as glamorous and exciting as hers. He winked at her and was about to speak when their dinner was served. They kept the conversation light during the main course.

The discussion of Stephen's life came during their dessert and coffee. In reality, Stephen's life had undergone as much turmoil as Suzanne's had.

"After graduating from college, a startup company hired me as one of their research and development engineers. That company was, and still is, owned by Raymond Leach. He's a very generous man. He gave us the leeway to do what we wanted and encouraged us to be creative. The company grew rapidly and consequently we were able to produce many innovative products."

"When I'd been with the company for a few years, Raymond sent me to Texas to run a subsidiary. While living in Texas I met and married a 'southern belle.' At first our marriage was ideal. She was lovely to look at but later became a bitch to live with. I'm sorry to be so blunt, but that's the only way I can describe it. Her family had a history of alcoholism and, unfortunately, Lou Anne had already progressed to an advanced stage in her addiction by the time we married. I didn't realize that her drinking was more than social. It was a complete shock to me when I finally recognized it. You see growing up I never had a drinker in my family. When did you ever hear of a Jewish alcoholic? It's virtually unheard of."

"Her family's wealth was enormous. One side had money from the oil fields, the other side, from cattle. Her father used his vast holdings to get into banking. He wanted me to leave engineering and take a position at one of their banks. I told them, 'Thanks, but no thanks.' I wanted no part of it. I didn't study engineering all those years just to drop it for a spot in the family business."

Squeezing Suzanne's hand, he added "I'd given up many important things in my life and I had learned something from my mistakes. I wasn't about to make another big one."

"Lou Anne and her family couldn't understand my attitude. They loved to entertain, and their type of socializing was very different from what I knew. It upset me that they didn't care about social issues. It was hard to have an intelligent conversation with them on matters of concern to the rest of the world."

"I tried, Oh God, I tried desperately to get help for Lou Anne. It was one of the most difficult tasks I ever undertook. I thought that if we had children, she would change. We tried for over four years to conceive and finally we had twin boys. I truly believed that after the birth of the twins that she'd settle down."

Pushing a few crumbs out of the way, he twisted his linen napkin. "I realized she was having an affair when the twins were about two years old. I was devastated and my ego was shattered. Suzanne, it's so hard for me to trust anymore. Emotionally, I was drained. I put all my energy into my work and my boys. They were my life."

"Desperate, I tried everything I could to stop her from destroying herself. Nothing helped. I didn't want to leave her because of the boys. I loved them so."

Suzanne could see him choking on the words. There were tears brimming in his eyes. She let him continue at his own pace.

His voice quivered as he went on. "Yes, I said 'loved.' You see, my sweet innocent boys died in a car crash. It's hard for me to talk about it, even now." He paused, trying to gain his composure, then went on. "But it's important to me that you understand the position I'm in." He let the tears fall freely and Suzanne could see the vivid pain in his face as he tried to relate his unhappy life to her.

After he poured another cup of coffee, he continued. "One day Lou Anne was taking the boys to a friend's house. As usual, she was in a hurry. I surmise she was in a hurry to get rid of the children to meet her current boyfriend. She lost control of the car. The boys were thrown from the automobile and died instantly."

"When the police came to my office I knew immediately that something was terribly wrong. All the way to the hospital I kept praying that I'd find they were okay. When I got there, the doctors took me into a private room and told me that the boys were dead and Lou Anne was in surgery. It was a living nightmare. Nothing made sense. They were talking to me, but I couldn't hear them. Their faces blurred in front of me. Lou Anne teetered between life and death. The alcohol level in her bloodstream was not excessively high, but God, Suzanne, why would any normal mother even think of driving, with a buzz on, especially with her children in the car? I wanted her to die. When she didn't, I wanted to kill her myself."

"Sometimes I lie awake at night and blame myself for not leaving her earlier and taking the boys with me. But, more anguish was to come. You see Lou Anne didn't die. She suffered a fate worse than death. She's paralyzed as a result of the accident. I really think that God took care of her in His own way. Who am I to say, but I feel she got what she deserved. I know it's wrong, but I hope you can understand why I feel the way I do."

Pausing briefly, he inhaled and began again, his voice now stronger. "After two years in rehabilitation, she came home. She has nurses who care for her, both day and night. I never divorced her. My heart was aching for my children. Their loss left such a void within me that I thought I'd never care or have feelings for anyone again. I put all my energy into my work."

Giving a little chuckle he said, "Raymond Leach benefited enormously from all the late evenings I devoted to the business."

"Seriously though, we still live in our home in Dallas and we do manage to communicate with one another. It took this terrible destructive blow to change Lou Anne. At times she lapses into depression, but most of the time she really tries to be decent."

This time Suzanne took his hands into hers as he spoke. She had a lump in her throat. She simply could not

111

fathom the loss of a child. She wondered how he had ever handled the despair of losing both of them. She looked directly into his eyes and with appreciable understanding nodded for his continuance.

"It's hard for me to explain, but I'll try. I was in therapy for years. I now recognize I was wrong to wish her dead. It's not that I've forgotten what happened, but I've learned to forgive and in so doing I've helped myself also. It's like when Yom Kippur comes and the Rabbi tells us we must forgive others for their sins against us. Unless you do, your heart can never be free. I still mourn my boys and pray for their soul. I better stop this talk or you'll think I've become very religious. I guess in a way as I got older, I did."

"Suzanne, many times I wanted to get in touch with you. I can't believe that we met like this."

Both of them were drained emotionally. They had shared their unhappy pasts. As a result there was a feeling of intimacy and a sense of relief. They knew they could not go back in time, but a renewal of their affection for each other was obvious.

Stirring her tea, Suzanne couldn't help but think how natural it felt being here and talking openly with Stephen. It didn't feel as if much time had elapsed since they last saw each other, as if it were just yesterday.

"But, enough of this melancholy. Do you like this place?"

"Suzanne, are you alright?"

"Of course, I was thinking about how quickly time passes and how true friendship never wanes."

It was difficult for Suzanne to maintain her self-control, but she answered, "I see why this is your favorite restaurant in Bermuda. I've thoroughly enjoyed it."

When the waiter brought the bill, Suzanne automatically reached for it. Stephen insisted that he would pay. "Stephen, don't be silly, I invited you. Besides I can probably write this off as business. I'm down here looking for a signature perfume."

"I could probably write it off too, but this isn't business. You know it and I know it," he said as he looked directly into her eyes. "Are you up for a nightcap back at the lounge at the Reefs?" Stephen asked Suzanne.

"Sure."

There were about fifteen couples seated in the lounge. Max, the Bermudian bar tender, was as usual, behind the cherry bar. The large, six footer, had a mass of long black hair, was in his thirties. He was pouring drinks and singing songs of the past in his wonderful baritone voice. His wide, beaming, smile was accentuated by his white teeth. The large gap between his two front teeth made it easy for him to whistle. He winked at Suzanne and Stephen as they entered the lounge.

As Max finished, the piano player began a medley of old tunes. Stephen led Suzanne onto the small dance floor. Effortlessly their movements became one. Suzanne felt secure in his arms, remembering how nice it was. She rested her head on his chest and wished that the night would not end. She wanted to stay in his arms always. When the music was over Stephen guided Suzanne back to their small table.

They finished their drinks and Stephen walked Suzanne back to her room. Outside her door, he asked for the key. After placing it in the door, he drew her to him. His warm, fervent lips found Suzanne's full eager mouth that responded quickly to his kiss. The impassioned kisses let loose in them a desire neither one had envisaged. Suzanne stopped him. "Stephen, wait a minute. What are we doing? Do we *know* what we're doing?"

Not answering, he again drew her close to him.

She forced herself to stop him. "Stephen, no. I'm not ready for this. Too much is going on in my life right now and I can't allow myself to be hurt again. I'm so sorry."

Stephen said, "I know I hurt you before. Please tell me I'll have another chance." She was astounded to hear the return of the lisp that she hadn't heard in twenty years.

He refused to leave until they made plans for dinner the next night. Stephen assured her that he would be thinking of her all day long.

She was perplexed by conflicting emotions and determined not to let Stephen's sudden entry into her life deter her from her goal. Suzanne closed the door behind her and set the latch. Pressing her back against the door, she was completely drained. "You fool," she said to herself, realizing that the old feelings had come back. She recognized that the butterflies in the pit of her stomach that she used to experience every time she kissed Stephen, when they were teenagers, had returned.

As she hovered between wakefulness and sleep, Stephen's image constantly reappeared before her. A restless night ensued as she dreamt of her earlier life.

Chapter Six

Stoney Brook, Massachusetts • February, 1972

"My God, Mrs. Walsh. You scared the daylights out of me. Are you all right?" Suzanne found her friend sitting in the darkened family room. Dried tears stained her beautiful milky white complexion.

Embarrassed by being discovered in a state of despair, Mrs. Walsh tried to distract Suzanne. Quickly leaving her favorite chair she took a cloth from her apron pocket and began to polish the already glossy furniture.

Authoritatively she instructed Mrs. Walsh, "Please sit down." Standing in front of the obviously frenzied housekeeper, Suzanne stood her ground and without raising her voice, directed Mrs. Walsh to the couch where she sat down beside her.

Taking Mrs. Walsh's hands into her own and looking directly into her dear friend's eyes, she asked with genuine concern, "Catherine please will you tell me what's going on? You're not acting like yourself. Don't I confide in you when I have a problem? You know that's what friends are for - to stand by each other in the bad times as well as the good. What's wrong? What can I do?"

Mrs. Walsh withdrew her hands from Suzanne's and let out a heavy sigh. Wringing her hands in her lap and wiping her eyes with the edge of her apron, she deliberately avoided eye contact. Suzanne was beside herself with worry. Everything bad imaginable ran through her mind. A vision of Mrs. Walsh lying on her deathbed interrupted her train of thought. "Are you sick? Are you having those dizzy spells again?"

"No, no," assured Mrs. Walsh as she waved her hands in the empty air. "I wish it were that simple."

"No, it's just...." Even though Mrs. Walsh loved her children and grandchildren, Suzanne could usually tell whenever her dear friend had spoken to one of her offspring. Her usual cheerful nature gave way to the sullen and morose disposition that she exhibited now.

Woefully she went on, "Well, yesterday, Carol called to complain about her finances. As always, she wanted me to send her money. It seems, every time I speak to her she wants me to send her some. It's not that I begrudge anything, but Suzanne, enough is enough. I told her 'No.' She's a grown woman. Let her get ambitious. I told her, 'Either go back to school for something that will enable you to earn a decent income or get a second job.' I swear I must have done something wrong bringing her up. Being the youngest, I naturally tried giving her everything. When her father died I felt so alone and sorry for her because she wouldn't know him like the other children had. I probably over indulged her."

"You can't keep berating yourself over the past. I think you did the right thing."

With a cry of despair she continued, "Then Tricia called and I feel so helpless." Again she kneaded her hands while she spoke. "Tricia's third son, Christopher, who is only 14. Well, they found him unconscious on the garage floor. Apparently he's been experimenting with drugs or fumes or something. I don't know. Tricia was talking so fast I got kind of confused. Anyway, they took him to a hospital. Then this morning, Moira called and told me how she and Francis are probably getting a divorce. Can you believe it? They've been married for over twenty-five years and suddenly they want to find themselves? I tell you, Suzanne, people are going crazy. What is this world coming to? I feel so helpless. It's not that I'm a selfish woman. I'd give my life and soul for my children and grandkids, but...." She could not go on.

Suzanne held Mrs. Walsh and let her sob. She reassuringly patted her. "Now, now, it just seems that everything is turning topsy-turvy." After letting her cry for a time, Suzanne said to her, "Stay right here. I'm going to make you a cup of tea. You'll see after a good night's sleep, things will look better."

As soon as Suzanne had gotten Mrs. Walsh to compose herself and made her see the lighter side of the situations, she went upstairs to get into comfortable clothing. Lying on her bed, she let her mind wander, trying to figure her next plan of action.

Suzanne had numerous ideas but couldn't decide how to implement them. She used Beverly as a sounding board.

"It's going to be hard getting this business off the ground. How am I ever going to open a salon? There are so many issues that have to be dealt with, sometimes I don't know where to begin."

"Look Suzanne, you've come this far. I know you can do it. You're not the first person to start a business, you know, and you won't be the last. I hate to bring up a sore subject but how is dear Brian doing?"

"He's doing fine I guess. I rarely get a chance to see him with my busy schedule.   I worry about the girls, though. I hope that someday they understand why I don't have much time to spend with them. But, I've got to get this school work finished."

Her faith in God helped Suzanne get through many perplexing issues. She prayed often and asked God to give her the strength to handle her problems. She trusted that He would, indeed, help her find a way to overcome the obstacles.

In New England the weather in April is predictable. It rains. The sun was rarely seen that April. The days that Suzanne disliked most were ones that combined winds, damp, cold and rain.

When Suzanne got home from school on this particular day she was soaking wet. The gusty winds had driven the raging, pouring rain straight through the region. By the time Suzanne walked from the school to the parking garage, she looked and felt as if she had taken a shower with her clothes on. In her foyer, she carefully removed her outer garments, discarding the rest of her clothes in the hamper. She put on a clean, dry robe and was thankful to be home with the children.

"Mrs. Morse, I got a really strange phone call from Mr. Morse's secretary this morning," announced Mrs. Walsh. "I normally wouldn't mention it to you, but I thought you might understand it better than I did. When I picked up the telephone, she asked for Mr. Morse. I remembered you telling me that he'd gone to New York on a business trip over the weekend, so he wouldn't be home. Well, I told her 'Being his secretary you should know that he's in New York on business and won't be home 'til this evening!' Then she told me his trip had been canceled as of last Thursday and she had to get in touch with him to discuss some important business matters."

Suzanne's head was spinning. She did not want to let Mrs. Walsh know that she was upset. "Oh, don't worry. Brian probably had a change of plans and forgot to tell his secretary," replied Suzanne. "Now, you be careful going home. It's hard seeing with the pelting rain, so drive carefully, and I'll see you tomorrow morning."

"Don't worry about me, I've driven through much worse weather than this in my time," laughed Mrs. Walsh as she opened her umbrella and stepped out into the torrent.

It was a chore for Suzanne to get dinner ready without showing her distress to the girls. She was sick to her stomach from the thoughts that raced through her mind.

She was furious at the possibility that Brian had lied to her and that she did not know where he was in case she needed him in an emergency.

While the girls cleaned up after dinner, Suzanne made a few phone calls of her own. Not letting on that anything was suspect, she talked to Carl, Brian's partner.

"Hi Carl. How are you? We're all fine here, but the reason I'm calling is crazy. Brian must have told you how busy I've been lately with going to school, and the upcoming exhibit. Well, I must have got some wires crossed, because I thought Brian was going with you to New York and I need to reach him."

Carl sounded flustered or was it Suzanne's imagination? "Well, no, no, Suzanne. Bill, the guy we were supposed to meet there, had to cancel because his mother-in-law died, so we're going to New York later."

Suzanne thanked him for clearing up the misunderstanding. She was through deceiving herself. For years she had stood his physical and mental abuse. She had made excuses for his abnormal behavior. But she was not going to tolerate lying and cheating.

Many nights Brian would not get home till one or two o'clock in the morning and he would make excuses about late meetings, or car troubles. "I must have been stupid to believe him every time," she thought. If, indeed, her perceptions were correct, this was the final straw. "I put up with many things," she thought. "I'm not going to put up with cheating. I'm going to get him out of the house once and for all."

Brian got home shortly after eight o'clock that night. "Hi honey, I'm home," shouted Brian from the front entrance.

"Daddy, Daddy," yelled the girls in unison.

"How are my little darlings?" asked Brian.

"Fine, Daddy. What did you bring us from New York?"

"Let's see how he gets out of this one," Suzanne thought to herself as she finished washing the dishes.

"Nothing much, just some pads of paper. Daddy was busy, and didn't have time to go shopping. The next time I'll bring you home some tee shirts." After kissing Suzanne on the cheek, he sat down and played with the girls.

Suzanne was fuming, but maintained her composure. Knowing Suzanne as well as he did, Brian knew something was amiss. "What's wrong, Honey?" he asked.

"Nothing," she replied. "How was your trip? I hope you got a lot accomplished."

"Oh I did. We got a lot of work done and Carl came up with some exceptional ideas," Brian announced.

"Well, that's good," Suzanne uttered, leaving the room for fear she would start screaming at him right there in front of the children.

"Girls, it's past your bedtime. Say goodnight to Daddy, and let's get to sleep," commanded Suzanne. After tucking the girls into bed, and kissing them goodnight, Suzanne went back into the kitchen. She cleaned the counter tops and prepared herself for what she was about to say.

"I'm glad you had a productive meeting in New York."

Sensing that something was drastically wrong, Brian got up off the couch and headed for the kitchen. "What's the matter with you?" asked Brian.

As she threw her wedding band at him she shouted, "I hate you, and I know you're lying."

"What are you talking about? Are you crazy? You're talking like a nut," Brian yelled back.

"I know you didn't go to New York. I know the meeting was called off," roared Suzanne.

"You're talking like a madwoman. Of course I've been to New York. Where'd you get such foolish ideas?"

Controlling her rage, she told him she knew that he was lying and fooling around on her. Sweat broke out on Brian's forehead as he vehemently denied her accusations. He felt his heart beating rapidly. "How'd she find out?" he wondered to himself. "I'll call her bluff." She wouldn't dare call and make a fool of herself.

"Go ahead. Call Carl if you're so sure! He'll set you straight."

"Look, I've already talked to Carl and Bill, too. They both confirmed my suspicions."

Brian was furious, "The stupid bitch! Who does she think she is? Now try to stay calm," he told himself.

"How could you call these men? Do you realize how it makes me look? Let alone, what kind of a fool you are, not knowing where your husband is?" His voice rose three levels. Shoving her aside, he left the room angrily yelling, "You're a nut. Get out of my way!"

The tactic didn't work. Suzanne had never been so angry with anyone in her entire life. She wasn't sure how he was going to react, but at this point, she really didn't care. If he hit her again, she would be angry enough to kill him, but she didn't want to wind up in jail.

"Now," shouted Suzanne, "you're going to tell me where you really where and who you were with!" She had never seen Brian so upset.

Brian was shaking visibly as he tried to calm her down. "I don't know where you got such a half-witted notion that I've been cheating on you, but I haven't. I love you and the children, I'd never do anything like that," proclaimed Brian.

Suzanne knew Brian better than he knew himself. She kept after him to tell her where he had been and with whom. "You know I'll find out eventually, so tell me who she is. Is she one of your secretaries, or someone you met at another office? I know you were with some woman, so let's save ourselves the aggravation. Just for once, be honest with me."

They argued until Brian was exhausted. "I'm going to bed. You're crazy. Maybe you'll come to your senses in the morning."

Suzanne knew she was right, so she followed him into the bedroom and continued the offensive. Finally worn down, Brian confessed. "Okay, already, okay! I didn't go to New York. Are you happy? I went to New Hampshire to a motel along the coast." Angrily admonishing her, he continued his onslaught, wanting her to feel guilty. "I feel at times I have to get away from you and everyone else. I need to be alone to sort out my feelings. Sometimes I do my most creative work when the telephones can't get to me and everyone leaves me alone. Okay. Are you happy now?" He turned his back to her and shut off the light.

Not believing for a minute that he had been alone, Suzanne was grateful that he at last admitted that he had lied. Turning the light back on and trying not to raise her voice, she continued the assault. "Don't think for a moment you're fooling me. I know you all too well. But, let's not get into that this second. First of all, don't you realize that if I needed you for an emergency, I wouldn't have known where the hell you were? I've also had a lot on my mind, but I'd never leave you or the children, and not tell you where I was going. Somehow, though, I still feel you're not telling me the truth. Tell me who you're having an affair with."

Brian vehemently denied fooling around. Again, Suzanne felt if she pestered him long enough, he'd come clean. The harassment paid off, at long last. He admitted that he had sex with several different women when he was out of town on business but denied having anyone in particular.

"Honey, I love you, I don't see anything wrong with a little quick romp in the sack with some whore who I don't give a damn about." Suzanne knew he was lying, but felt that she finally had what he called the truth.

"Thank you," she retorted with sarcasm. "You could have brought me home some real rice presents, like gonorrhea or syphilis. I want to thank you very much." After ten years with this man, giving him all she had, emotionally and physically, Suzanne felt completely betrayed and outraged. Now she had something solid to go on.

She sat down on the edge of the bed. Her head was pounding and she felt as if she were going to throw up. Wracked with emotion, she shook visibly as she tried to compose herself and said, "We have serious problems. I want you to look for an apartment, so that we can both have our own space to sort out our feelings."

Taking a deep breath, she proclaimed, "I've taken a lot of physical and mental abuse from you over the years. I know you've gotten better as you've matured, and I've overlooked some things. The Lord knows we all have faults. I don't know if I can ever trust you again, and you haven't even said you're sorry. Your values are all messed up, and even if you asked me to forgive you, I don't know if I can. I've told you, many times, that if I ever found you cheating on me, I'd kill you. Well, you'd better watch out while you're in the house."

Brian was dumbfounded. "Suzanne you're overwrought." He was crying. "I'm sorry, Suzanne, I never meant to hurt you or the girls. I do love you with all my heart. Please forgive me, and I promise I'll never do anything like this again, as long as I live."

"Don't do this," cried Brian.

Physically and emotionally exhausted, Suzanne told him, "I'm going to sleep in the family room tonight. We can talk again in the morning."

Despite what she thought was a good nights sleep, Suzanne was still tired when she woke up. She sat at the kitchen table and chose her words carefully. They would convey her decisive thoughts to Brian. The way he had betrayed her trust kept returning to her mind. "When you loose trust in a person you have loved and wanted to believe in, you can never get that trust back," she thought as her shaky hands poured the hot water for a cup of tea.

She called her school and said she would not be in. She then called Mrs. Walsh asking her if she'd mind taking the day off and that she would take care of Taylor herself. She woke the girls and got them ready for school. "I'm taking the day off from school, and I'll be home when you get back this afternoon," Suzanne told them as they were having breakfast.

"Oh good," replied Hope and Melanie in unison. "Maybe we can make cookies when we get home, Mummy?" asked Hope.

"And the cottage cheese turnovers with the strawberry jam inside?" asked Melanie.

"We'll see," Suzanne answered back, trying to sound and act cheerful. Seeing them off on the school bus, Suzanne kissed them good-bye. "Have a good day kids. I love you."

Taylor was just waking up, and Suzanne wanted to take care of the baby's needs before she confronted Brian. She tiptoed into their bedroom and shut off the alarm so it would not arouse Brian before she was ready. She fed, changed and dressed Taylor. When everything was in order, she put Taylor into the playpen and gently shook Brian.

Seeing things clearly in the new light of day, she was ready to finish what she had started last night. She knew that Brian's admission was her way out of the marriage. Now that all the pieces of the puzzle were in place, she was ready to go on with her own life without him.

As he finished dressing, she started coffee for him. She wanted to poison it. Brian came into the kitchen, sat down, and waited for his breakfast. Knowing that this would be one of the last times she would have to wait on him, she gladly served him. "I hope you slept as poorly as I did," she said.

"In fact, I was exhausted, and had a good night's sleep. I feel better now that I told you about my little indiscretions. I know that we can work things out and have a better marriage," Brian said confidently.

"I don't understand how you can sleep soundly after what you've done. And for you to call your affairs little indiscretions is incredible: I don't want to continue arguing like this. Obviously your values and ideas aren't the same as mine." Taking a deep breath she struggled to gain her composure.

She poured herself another cup of tea and sat opposite him. "I've done a lot of thinking, and I want you to leave. I really feel that we should separate for a while."

Shaking his head in disbelief he chided, "Suzanne, I can't believe that after all these years and having three beautiful children together, you'd ask me to leave." He got up from the chair and walked over to Suzanne's chair. Putting his arms around her shoulders from behind and hugging her he proclaimed with a breaking voice, "I love you, and I'll do anything for you. Just forgive me and love me as you once did," begged Brian.

Suzanne had to get him out. Even if she lied, she knew she just wanted him to leave. Once out of the house she would never let him back in. This was the excuse she needed to finally rid herself of this disgusting pretense of a man.

"Brian, I did love you, but now I don't know, and I really need time to think," answered Suzanne. "Please just leave and find an apartment. Let me sort things out," pleaded Suzanne.

Brian rambled for a while before he realized that Suzanne was determined. He again went to her and hugged her. Visibly shaking and with tears in his eyes, he kissed her tenderly on her head, neck and then on her lips. Suzanne was also crying, but she refused to respond to his gestures. She sat rigidly in the chair.

When Brian left for work, Suzanne cleaned the dishes and played with Taylor. It seemed as if years had passed since she had the luxury of being home during the week. Her tears mixed with the water as she scrubbed the dishes. "This is the pretext I need to ask him to leave," she thought as she vigorously wiped the dishes dry. "Why do I feel so sad and frightened when I should be feeling jubilant?"

It took Brian a month to find the right apartment. The girls acclimated to the idea of Brian being away. For the month before he left, Suzanne slept on the living room sofa. She knew how physically attractive she still was to him and she didn't want to take a chance that he would somehow divert her plans for a divorce. When she told her parents about the separation, they told her that they would help her in any way that they could.

The day of departure came all too soon for Brian. He did not want to leave his wife and children, to say nothing of his home. He attempted one last time to convince Suzanne that she was acting too hastily. Before loading his car with the many boxes of his personal belongings and clothes, he hesitantly approached his wife. The inflection in his voice told it all. "Suzanne," putting his arms around her, he tried to draw her to him. Her head was pounding.

"Can't we try one more time? I promise I'll be different. I've learned a lot in this month. I've done a lot of reflecting and I realize I was wrong in many ways. I love you and the girls from the depth of my soul. Can't you find it in your heart to change your mind? Forgive me this one last time."

Disconcerted and confused, vacillating only a second, she refused to budge. "I'm just as upset as you are, but I want you to leave and give me time to think things over. In my own way I love you too, but so much has happened that I had no control over. Just go and let me think things out." Her voice began to crack.

With tears now shamelessly running down his cheeks, Brian forced himself to complete the heartbreaking task of packing his belongings into his car. He blanched at the thought of leaving permanently and loosing the only person who had made him feel whole.

Backing out of the driveway, many thoughts crossed his mind. As in the past month, he kept asking himself what went wrong. "Why did I fuck up the only good thing that ever happened to me? Maybe I should go back to Dr. Steinberg and try to get my life together. I can't keep punishing myself for my parent's mistakes. I wish I treated Suzanne better, but what does she expect? No one is perfect. I'll try to see the girls often. Who knows? Maybe we'll even become closer when I bring them to my apartment. Suzanne won't be there to interfere. Someday she'll be sorry she asked me to leave. I'll show her. I'll get a life without her."

The weeks passed quickly. If there was any iota of a doubt in Suzanne's mind that she had done the right thing by asking Brian to leave, it disappeared every evening when she returned home. Gone were the anxiety, strife, and arguments that often occurred when Brian was in one of his antagonistic moods. Gone was the fear of reprisal by Brian when he was in a bad mood, or an infraction of his rules by the children. For the first time in years Suzanne looked forward to coming home. Whenever insecurities crept into her thoughts she consciously remembered how life used to be, and was thankful for the change.

~~~~~~~~~~~~~~~~~~~

The next day's golf game went well, and Suzanne thoroughly enjoyed her pleasant conversation with Miko. After playing, the women continued their discussion over drinks at the clubhouse. Suzanne enthusiastically described her work. Miko was an amiable woman and was very interested in visiting the spa. "Suzanne, do you think you could help me? I don't know how to put on makeup, and I've been so busy with the business, I'm afraid I've let myself go completely."

Miko and her husband visited his business in Florida every month and it was located not far from Suzanne's West Palm Beach spa. She promised to make an appointment for her next visit to Florida.

Suzanne cautioned Miko, "I love helping a person change her image, but it doesn't happen overnight. It takes time to lose weight and get into the right exercise program. The next time I go to the spa, I promise I'll personally go over your file with Gloria, my manager."

The women hugged each other and departed with the knowledge that they would become good friends.

As Suzanne lay on her bed, Stephen's face passed before her eyes. Warm thoughts of their evening together put her in a mellow frame of mind. Suddenly she remembered the main reason she had come to Bermuda and hoped that this interlude with Stephen would not impede her progress toward her goal.

Stephen called to tell her he was on his way.

It seemed like a mirage. Although the food was superb, the restaurant beautiful, and Stephen a great conversationalist, Suzanne only toyed with her food. Stephen asked if everything was all right. Suzanne's stomach was in a knot. She knew that she was falling again for this man. Most of their unburdening and serious conversation had taken place last evening. They found themselves laughing and discussing what had happened during the day.

After dinner they took off their shoes and walked hand-in-hand along a beach near the resort.

"Suzanne," Stephen began, "I couldn't get you off my mind all day. "We can't take this lightly. I want you to know that I think I've always loved you. This time, I don't want to lose you." He paused briefly, then added, "If you want me to, I can stay for the weekend." Stephen held his breath, hoping her response was what he wanted to hear.

Suzanne's heart leapt with joy. "That would be wonderful. I didn't want to see you leave so soon."

"Raymond has a guest cottage that we can use for the weekend if that's all right with you?"

"It's more than all right, it's incredible."

This time when Stephen took the key from Suzanne she let him unlock the door, then invited him in. "Would you like a nightcap? Help yourself."

Moving slowly toward the bed, with only the moonlight to guide them, he again enveloped her in his strong arms. Pausing for but a moment, Stephen whispered to Suzanne, "You have no idea how many nights I lay awake, just thinking of this." Embracing her, his lips kissed her neck, moving to her shoulders, then back to her neck, lingering there. He sent shivers down Suzanne's spine. They slowly undressed one another, and, delaying the inevitable, their fingers caressed and explored their fevered bodies.

His low husky voice whispered endearments in her ear. "I want you, Suzanne. I want to make passionate love to you." Hovering over her, his sexual excitement could not be constrained. Suzanne was wild with craving. All modesty was gone. Their kisses, so intense, were like hot coals that could not be extinguished.

"Stephen, now!" Her legs wrapped around his body; he entered her quickly. His long, hard penis penetrated her with fervid movements. Their bodies moved in unison. Suzanne quivered with excitement and lust. Her nails dug into his back as she reached intense multiple orgasms.

Stephen was unrestrained. He felt Suzanne's body tremble, and knew when he had taken her to immeasurable heights. Now he could release his own pent-up ecstasy. His swollen hardness escalated to a pinnacle of climax that he had not known possible. Securely holding Suzanne in his arms he kissed her both tenderly and sensuously at the same time.

Suzanne lay for a long while enfolded in his arms. It felt so natural and good lying beside this man who she thought was gone from her life forever. Resting next to him, her long fingers again caressed his arms, shoulders, and stomach. She tried not to think of the years that had been lost to them. The tips of her fingers gently stroked his warm body and, she could feel him respond to her touch moving over his skin.

Stephen moaned with anticipation as Suzanne lifted herself from his side and slid down beside his erect organ. Gently taking his now throbbing hardness into her moist warm mouth, she tenderly kissed his manliness while her fingers still caressed his thighs and buttocks. She then gently licked his manhood, slightly flicking the very top, enjoying his obvious pleasure. He asked her to mount his well-muscled body. Her own anticipation grew as she felt his hardness within her.

With deliberate slow movements their lovemaking reached the height of ecstasy. Once again after their climax, Suzanne settled next to Stephen, his strong, muscular arms enfolding her body, protecting her from the world. They fell asleep, lost in slumber.

"Good morning," Stephen whispered into Suzanne's ear as she awoke.

"I hope you slept as well as I did," Suzanne replied. "What time is it? When do you have to meet Raymond?"

"It doesn't matter. For now, you're the only person or thing that's on my mind."

During breakfast they discussed the day's agenda. Neither of them wanted to leave.

Later that night, they walked along the darkened beach with the luminescence guiding them until they found a secluded cove. Lying down beside each other, looking at the calm darkened water, enjoying the solitude of the moment, each was engrossed in their own thoughts.

Stephen was happy that he had once again found this woman whom he had so carelessly lost before. He drew her towards him.

The swift and electric enthusiasm of making love of the previous evening had given way to a more deliberate leisurely foreplay. One by one, he undid the buttons on her blouse. His fingers deftly undid her undergarments exposing her breasts. Stephen explored Suzanne's body, fondling and caressing every inch with his light touch that sent shivers throughout her body.

Undoing his belt buckle, and removing his clothes, she lovingly stroked his hairy chest. Then, kissing him from head to toe, she could feel herself getting aroused by watching his pleasure. She wanted to consume every part of him. He entered her slowly and consciously, moving with a deliberate effort to control himself from exploding within her. He ached to show her his love, and wanted to hear and feel her reach a climax.

Suzanne's spasms of delight imprisoned Stephen's mind and body. He increased the thrusts of his movements and they simultaneously reached the ultimate boundaries of pleasure.

Later, back at the cottage, wrapped in each other's arms, they waited for slumber.

"Are you asleep yet?" whispered Stephen quietly.

"No, are you restless, too?"

He continued. "I know we've both been through hell and back and if we have a chance to finally find love, I'm not going to back away from it. I've tried to live a moral life, but God knows I'm not a saint. I can't go through life camouflaging my feelings any longer." Hugging Suzanne to him, he again declared his love for her.

"I understand, and I want you to know that I love you too. I'm entering this relationship with my eyes open. If our bond can't be sanctioned by matrimony, then I accept that as the price I have to pay." Suzanne lifted her face to his and kissed him tenderly. Sleep no longer eluded them.

When it was time to leave, Stephen's plane departed first. Declaring their love once again, they made plans to see one another soon. Stephen took Suzanne into his arms, and kissed her with enough affection and passion to last till they saw each other again.

Chapter Seven

Stoney Brook, Massachusetts • November, 1991

Once Suzanne returned home, her life resumed its hectic pace. Her business took up most of her time as one dilemma followed another at the busy spas. Hope and Taylor were studying business management at night school, and they hoped to take over that part of the corporation eventually. Suzanne didn't want the girls to overextend themselves, but she appreciated what they were doing.

She made plans to have dinner with Nancy the week after she returned. They met at a restaurant located midway between their homes. Over drinks, Suzanne told Nancy about Stephen and her wonderful vacation.

Nancy was happy for her friend. "It's too good to be true. Well, you deserve this happiness" she added.

Suzanne then went on to discuss the main reason for their meeting. "As I told you over the phone in Bermuda, it's not because of Brian that I'm doing this. It's because I really like Mrs. Pearlman. It's a shame that this is happening after all their hard work and everything else they've been through. I must find out what's going on. I have to learn if a crime is being committed. I realize that what I'm asking you to do is serious. And I don't know if I have the right to get you involved in something that is potentially dangerous."

As Nancy grasped the situation, Suzanne noticed an expression that came over her friend's face. It was unlike anything she'd ever seen before. Nancy's eyes burned with excitement.

With an eager grin, Nancy responded. "Are you kidding? I'm an avid fan of Jane Marple!" She quickly became serious again. "I'd love to help. I have the qualifications to apply for a position in the accounting department. Maybe Mrs. Pearlman can help me get a job without the new partners' knowledge. Do you want the Pearlman's to know what we're doing?"

"Not yet, no," answered Suzanne.

Two weeks passed by before Mrs. Pearlman's next visit. Suzanne inquired about Mr. Pearlman's health and encouraged Mrs. Pearlman to talk. At a pause in the conversation, Suzanne spoke, "Mrs. Pearlman, a friend of mine is down on her luck and needs a job badly. She's a very hard worker and has four children. Her husband drinks so much I'll call him a drunk. Well, she finally kicked him out last week and now she needs employment. She's a very good accountant, and if Mr. Pearlman can find it in his heart to hire her, I'd sure appreciate it." Suzanne knew the Pearlman's were nice people, and she was positive that within a few days one of them would contact Suzanne about using her friend's services.

Clucking her tongue, Mrs. Pearlman acknowledged the problem. "Oy, I've heard of people like that shika before. I'll see what I can do for your friend."

Sure enough, three days later, Suzanne received the phone call she was waiting for. "Suzanne, your friend, the one with four pitsala children, she still needs a job?" inquired Mrs. Pearlman.

Suzanne confirmed Nancy's desire and need to work. Mrs. Pearlman went on to say that Mr. Pearlman had various businesses, but a woman in the accounting department in Burlington is going on short-term disability. "Do you think your friend would be interested in a temporary position? She would have to start right away." Suzanne assured her that Nancy would definitely be interested and she'd be there the following morning at nine o'clock.

"Hello, may I speak to the sleuth of the house?" Suzanne joked, when Nancy answered her telephone. She went on to explain her conversations with Mrs. Pearlman. "Are you sure you still want to go through with this?" asked Suzanne, holding her breath.

"Are you kidding? This is going to be more excitement than I've had in the past ten years. I couldn't wait till I received your phone call. I'll dress conservatively and I'll bring references. I'll be 'in like Flynn.' Wait and see."

Nancy, true to her word, was conservatively dressed and looked the part of a bookkeeper. Mr. Pearlman introduced Nancy to Brian, telling Brian that Nancy was a friend of his wife's. Brian conducted the interview, and more than once, starred at Nancy. "I know this is a corny line, but have we met before?"

"I don't think so, I've been doing bookkeeping out of my home for the past eight years. I have four small children, and I felt that I couldn't leave them. Unfortunately, my circumstances have changed and I now need a more permanent job. I realize this position is temporary, but it'll get me back into the work force. Hopefully I'll be able to get another position when this one ends." Nancy got the job and agreed to start immediately.

Suzanne maintained her busy schedule, working at each of her spas for a week at a time. She varied her routine, making sure that she practiced on her personal clients at least once a month. *Metamorphosis Spas* were now located in six states. After a long day in the salon, she routinely phoned her daughters, Mrs. Walsh, Peter, Nancy, and Stephen. Nancy kept Suzanne abreast of her progress. Stephen knew Suzanne's calendar and they made plans to meet when Suzanne next worked at her Dallas spa.

After traveling for a month, Suzanne finally returned home. On a nasty, cold, and rainy evening the partners met at a restaurant not far from Nancy's home. Not many people ventured out on an evening such as this, especially on a weekday. Nancy arrived first, ordered a drink and waited for Suzanne. She spotted Suzanne as she entered. Shaking off the excess rainwater that covered her raincoat, she sat down across from her friend.

"It seems like ages since I've seen you. You look great, a little wet, but good," Nancy teased Suzanne.

"I'm dying to find out what's happening."

"I've become rather chummy with Mr. Pearlman, and a few of the other women in the accounting department. They're decent people, used to running the company the way Mr. Pearlman had trained them to. They don't like the changes that have been made. Getting the lowdown on Morse and Associates and how they got hooked up with Mr. Pearlman wasn't a very difficult task. When Mr. Pearlman became ill with cancer, he needed a management company to help him, especially since he expected to be out for a long time."

"As far as I can see, his children weren't, and still aren't, interested in working at the business, they're only inspired by reaping the benefits from it. Mr. Pearlman had interviewed a number of management firms before selecting one. For some reason he took a liking to Brian and chose Morse Associates. He hadn't met Brian's partners or associates before making the decision."

Motioning to the waiter, Nancy ordered another round of drinks. Twisting her drink around on the table, she heard the ice cubes striking the sides of the tall frosty glass. Absorbed in the movement, she slowly forced herself out of her hypnotic state. Clearing her throat, she continued, "When he was finished with most of the treatments and returned to his office on a part-time basis, Mr. Pearlman was shocked to find how strong a hold

Brian's firm had on his company. I think Morse Associates really thought he was going to die and they would face no opposition when they took over the management of all Mr. Pearlman's companies. They were quite surprised when he beat the odds and came back to work."

"Suzanne, I really think you were on the right track when you mentioned money laundering. I've been around a while and I'm sure something isn't kosher. I've met some of Brian's so-called business partners, and they are a sleazy bunch. They talk fast and you can tell just by speaking to them, that they're not your Mr. Nice Guys. I wouldn't trust any of them as far as I could throw them. I can't put my finger on it but I know illegal activities are going on. I've never seen drugs on the premises, so I don't think they're dealing, at least not out of the building. I've done some research into it, and most of this type of crime started in 1985 and 1986. These men have to get the dirty money cleaned. When I say money Suzanne, I mean BIG MONEY. I can't find a second set of books, yet, but they exist, for sure. I can smell it!"

They ordered their meal and Nancy continued, "When I first started to work there I noticed many invoices arriving for materials that had never been received. Now, similar invoices are cropping up in every one of his other businesses. And, I'm not talking a few thousand dollars worth, either. The partners recently broadened the businesses to include real estate, which I think they got into because you can hide a lot of cash there. I've noticed a few deposits made to offshore banks. That's my next project.

When the skuzzes are out of the office, I'll snoop around some more."

"By the way, that ex-husband of yours, Brian, is trying to put the make on me. Can you believe it?"

"I always knew he had good taste in women. Too bad he's lacking common sense," Suzanne said.

"Suzanne, do you know where they're getting all this money? It's got to be either drug dealers or the Mafia, or maybe both. I'm not sure yet, but if I keep probing, I'm bound to find out."

"This is beginning to sound as if we're getting in over our heads. I want to help the Pearlman's, but maybe we should contact the police or the FBI."

"Let's hold off on contacting anyone else for a while. I want to search for that other set of books. It has to be there, somewhere. I just know it. I'll get a miniature low-light camera and go back there late at night when no one is around."

"I hope we're doing the right thing. This is beginning to sound like something you'd see in the movies."

They laughed nervously as their dinner was being served. "I'm leaving for the Dallas Spa tomorrow morning. Please be careful. Peter will kill me if anything happens to you. You haven't told him what we're up to, have you?"

"No, he thinks I'm volunteering at the hospital because they're understaffed. I don't want him to worry needlessly. By the way, you wouldn't by chance seize the opportunity to see Stephen while you're at the Dallas spa?" Nancy said as she winked at Suzanne.

"I just might run into him." Suzanne smiled as she answered her friend.

The next day on the flight to Dallas she thought of Stephen and wondered if their feelings would be the same when they saw each other again for the first time since Bermuda.

Suzanne felt lost, as usual, in the Dallas/Ft. Worth International Airport and was relieved when the limo driver fetched her bags and escorted her to the waiting vehicle. They drove directly downtown to the Adolphus where she always stayed when she was in town. Settled into her regular corner room overlooking Bell Plaza, she called the spa to find the time of her first appointment.

The trial shipment of perfume had arrived from Bermuda and sold out in two weeks. While talking to Nancy, on one of their numerous telephone conversations, Suzanne enthusiastically stated, "I just love working at our Dallas spa. The clients are always willing to try a new product."

"Peter mentioned that Newbury St. is also sold out. The staff and customers can't wait until the next order of our 'signature perfume' arrives, so don't go around expounding the way you usually do on how you love the southern ladies because they're always pampering themselves.

As Nancy defended her northern comrades, Suzanne cut in, "Aren't we a bit testy? What's wrong, Nancy?"

"I'm sorry if I seem a bit uptight. I guess all this investigation is a bit tiring and draining me of my energy. I'll be okay."

"Are you sure?" questioned Suzanne.

"Yes. Call me when you get back home. I'm sure I'll have more to report by then." Nancy hung up the phone and stared out the window. She had not turned on the outside lights. She shivered in the unfolding darkness.

Suzanne had warned her of Brian's charismatic personality and sexual magnetism. Since the day they met, Brian had repeatedly asked Nancy to join him for lunch or an evening out. Her rejections only made her more desirable to him. "Sure I'm flattered, but so what? I'm married and no matter what the pretense for accepting his invitation, I'd only be fooling myself. Yes, he's sexy in a cute way." Admonishing herself she thought, "What am I doing? Besides my being married, Suzanne is my best friend; like the sister I never had. I couldn't hurt her or Peter. I'd hate myself." With these thoughts, she retired to her bedroom, hoping that she'd have a full night's sleep, something she had been deprived of lately.

Stephen contacted Suzanne around noon and they made plans to meet for dinner at eight o'clock that evening. She couldn't wait to see him.

As she hesitated at the doorway before entering the mahogany paneled billiard room that was the bar of the restaurant, she could see Stephen joking with the bartender as he waited for her.

They sat across from each other and chatted about superficial subjects, while ordering their dinner. Suzanne did not tell Stephen about Brian and the Pearlmans. She wasn't quite sure why, but for some reason she believed he would disapprove of what she was doing. Since they hardly saw each other, Suzanne decided to keep things upbeat and avoided that particular topic. They talked about business, children, politics, and of old friends that they had known. Stephen answered her questions about what was happening back home in Quincy.

When dinner was over, they skipped dessert. "You'll be my dessert," Stephen whispered to Suzanne.

Since Stephen was a well-known citizen of Dallas, Suzanne entered the elevator alone and Stephen left to retrieve a package from his car. "I'll be there in a moment," he told her.

When she answered his knock a few minutes later, he brought in two beautiful hand-cut crystal champagne glasses and a bottle of Dom Perignon. They raised their glasses. "To more happy times for us. I love you Suzanne. I hope we'll be able to be with each other more often."

Suzanne kissed him willingly. Undoing the bed, they slipped under the covers. Their lingering, passionate kisses sent quivers of wanton desire between her legs. Stephen gently caressed her firm, breasts, sending shivers through her body. He kissed the brown nipples causing them to become hard and erect as he gingerly nibbled first one until it was aroused and then the other. He could feel the warm liquid as his able fingers fondled her smooth thighs and deep crevice and he found her wetness arousing. Suzanne wanted to feel his hardness moving inside her, satisfying her hunger. She expertly guided his swollen and wet penis to bring her pleasure. They made love late into the night, and finally fell asleep in the wee hours of the morning.

The alarm rudely disturbed their reverie. "I don't know how we're going to function properly today, but I really don't care." Suzanne told Stephen.

"I'll be fine. Don't worry about me."

Stephen had lied to Lou Anne, telling her that he was going to be working or meeting clients. "I don't like being deceitful" he told Suzanne when they saw each other for dinner the next evening, "but I really want to be with you while you're here. I know I may be spotted, but it's a chance I'm willing to take."

They had a glorious week, working during the day and relaxing together in the evening. They didn't venture out to many places because they both wanted to be as discreet as possible. They did go to the Routh Street Cafe one night for some southwestern cooking. Suzanne's heart ached when she realized that their time together was almost over.

On the final evening, they made passionate love all night long, and vowed that they would be together again soon. Stephen would meet Suzanne in Florida when she was in West Palm Beach. She insisted she go alone to the airport. With feelings of joy and sorrow, she waved goodby as she entered the limo.

It was the kind of morning one wants to stay in bed. The rain drummed incessantly on the skylight above Suzanne's bed. Laboriously, she forced herself to get up. For the next few weeks she was to work out of her Newbury St. spa and then she would commute from Stoney Brook to the Newport, Rhode Island salon for a week.

Suzanne left for work at nine o'clock, after the rush hour traffic. If she left any earlier she would be caught in the morning madness in which people acted like maniacs under the pressure to be to work on time. She didn't mind working late into the evening for, again, there were fewer cars on the road after the commuting hours.

Looking over her appointments for the day, she noticed that Madeline Mason was coming in at 11 o'clock. Suzanne usually saw Madeline at her Beverly Hills spa. She had always liked this actress, and was glad that she would be seeing and working on her again. Suzanne remembered when she first became very friendly with Madeline. On one of Madeline's trips east, she brought her only child, Kyle, with her. Kyle's nanny became ill and she brought Kyle with her to the spa. Suzanne truly enjoyed the young, shy, handsome child. Suzanne invited Madeline and him to visit her family in Stoney Brook the following weekend. Kyle and her girls got along extremely well. Her daughters acted like his big sisters and enjoyed entertaining and playing with him. Since then, Kyle would accompany his mother whenever she returned to the east. He thought of Suzanne and her girls as an extension of his own small family. Although Kyle was now grown and a very successful photographer, he and Madeline still kept in touch with "Aunt Suzanne" and his cousins.

Madeline was as charming as ever. Suzanne had always loved working on celebrities, especially Madeline. She thought that she must have inherited her mother's genes when it came to show business. Dorothy, although she never made it to Broadway, was still active in local theater productions. Dorothy was still a ham and enjoyed the applause and the footlights.

The first day back went by quickly. Before leaving for the evening, she called Nancy to see how things were going. They made plans for a late dinner at Suzanne's.

Mrs. Walsh prepared a simple but tasty dinner. Both Nancy and Suzanne loved baked salmon with dill and butter. A large baked potato and green beans were served with the salmon steaks.

As they finished eating and Mrs. Walsh cleared the dishes, they got down to business. Nancy informed Suzanne of her progress. "The only thing that bothers me is Brian's refusal to take no for an answer. He's determined to date me. I'm afraid that Peter will find out what we're up to and he'll kill us, literally. I think it's time I tell Peter what we're doing."

"Could you hold off telling Peter for now. Let's see what else develops, okay?" responded Suzanne.

"I don't believe it. He's putting the make on my best friend, the little bastard. Not that I should be jealous, for God's sake," laughing to herself and then pausing for a moment, she quickly gave her full attention to Nancy's appraisal. "He is single and free to see anyone he wants, just not my best friend."

Nancy described what was going on at Mr. Pearlman's office. "I made photo-static copies of the phony invoices and bank receipts from the offshore banks. One of them is in Montserrat, an island that is part of the Leeward Islands."

"I know that place," interjected Suzanne. "One of my old clients met his wife there. The last time he was in the city, he mentioned some of the unscrupulous businesses and banks that have applied for charters in the past few years. They're really only storefronts. Drug money is deposited at a bank and then the bank sends a cashier's check for deposit here."

Thoughts of Brian distracted her. Nancy got up and poured herself a cup of coffee, then continued. "It's a small world, isn't it? I think this illegal money is being transferred from one business to another. They're moving into money lending now. Mr. Pearlman is beside himself with worry. He doesn't have a hold on his business any more, and he feels useless. The girls in the office pointed out the differences in him to me. He was once a vibrant and confident businessman, and now he's sorrowful and troubled. Of course, the illness must have contributed to his mental state too, but from what I understand, he's furious and has already confronted Brian and his partners about terminating their contract. They are determined not to let him out of it. I overheard Mr. Pearlman say that he was going to go to the authorities if they didn't leave. One of the partners closed the office door and I assume he told him that he was just as involved with their illegal dealings as they were and threatened to kill him or members of his family if he didn't cooperate. He was ashen when he came out of his office."

Concerned, Suzanne asked, "Did you get copies of all the invoices?"

"Yes, but I still can't get at that second set of books. I know it's there, though. I know it," Nancy said with conviction.

Suzanne thought for a moment and poured herself a cup of tea, oblivious to her friend's quandary. She then confided, "I think this situation is considerably larger than we ever dreamed of. I'm going to contact either the police or FBI tomorrow."

"Well, count the police out. You never know who might be on the Mob's payroll. If you insist on doing something, go to the FBI."

"I just remembered something. A friend of Taylor's, Jill Cassidy - her father works for the FBI. I think in the drug unit. I'll give him a call and ask him his advice."

Suzanne called Mr. Cassidy at his house in Stoney Brook. He suggested he meet with her and Nancy the next day at his office in Boston. Suzanne rescheduled some of her clients and walked from Newbury Street to City Hall Plaza. The day was clear and the jaunt invigorated her. When she arrived at his room, Nancy was already there, waiting with the agent.

Timothy Cassidy was a burly gentleman with a ruddy complexion and twinkling blue eyes. He had a strong handshake and exuded fearlessness when he spoke. He listened intently, sometimes taking notes, and, only when Suzanne and Nancy had finished their story, did he speak again. He explained that he worked strictly as an undercover agent dealing with drug enforcement, but he could help them. He wanted them to meet with Kevin Halloran, another FBI agent, who dealt directly with money laundering and offshore banks. Between the two of them, they would assist the women. He walked Suzanne and Nancy down the hall to Kevin Halloran's office.

Kevin Halloran was a man in his thirties, about ten years younger than Tim was. His well-proportioned body looked like he worked out at the gym every day. His wavy, sandy colored hair was unruly, adding to his boyish appearance.

Tim related the story to Kevin, while Suzanne and Nancy listened. They responded to questions from the agents and asked some of their own. Kevin and Tim suggested that the two women wait while they conferred with one another. "Would you like some coffee? I can have one of the guys get you some." "No Thanks," Suzanne answered, assuming Nancy didn't want any either." It seemed like hours until Tim came out of his office and asked Nancy and Suzanne to rejoin them.

Kevin started the conversation by explaining that it was very difficult to get a conviction for this type of criminal offense. After reviewing their notes, they credited the women for their persistence in obtaining incriminating evidence that could, in all probability, send the "gentlemen" to jail.

"I don't want you to think that this is going to be easy. It isn't." Tim said.

"We'll want Nancy to continue gathering as much evidence as possible, while we find out how and with whom these men are working with. We have a feeling they're alone, though not connected to the Mafia. They won't be so hard to incriminate, and it'll be safer for the two of you," continued Tim.

"That's not to say that you won't be in danger if they find out you're onto them."

"We'll see that you'll get protection. We'll get started right away to place some of our people at the business. I don't want to frighten you, but you have to realize the gravity of the situation you've placed yourselves in. You don't have to do this, you know. We could infiltrate the operation with undercover agents."

Suzanne asked dryly, "And, how long would that take?"

"You're right," Kevin said. "It would take some time. But I want you to understand that these men will stop at nothing to ensure that they can continue their work."

Kevin arranged their next meeting and outlined a plan of action, reinforcing his concern for their safety. "I'm giving you both our office and private home telephone numbers. Don't hesitate to call either of us at any time, if you should find out any more important information or feel you need us for anything, no matter how inconsequential or trivial."

As Suzanne and Nancy were leaving, Kevin stopped them and, in all seriousness said, "I wish more citizens would come to us like this. Most people just don't want to get involved if the circumstances don't affect them directly. We'll do everything in our power to help your friends, the Pearlman's. Play it cool, ladies, and we'll see you soon."

Stoney Brook, Massachusetts • November, 1991

Suzanne imagined the worst. "How could I live with myself if Brian and his business are ruined?" she asked herself.

She again questioned her own motives. Was she really trying to help the Pearlman's, or was she hoping to get even with Brian for the pain he had caused her over the years? He hadn't been the best of fathers, but Suzanne knew that his daughters loved him. How would they react if they found out Suzanne was involved in his downfall? She weighed what evidence she had and realized it was difficult to see any way that he could be vindicated. If the girls discover that she was instrumental in his downfall, would they ever forgive her?

Suzanne reacted by putting all her energy into her work. A few favorable events made the remainder of the week hopeful. As she prepared to spend the next working week in New York, Larry called.

"It's so nice to hear your voice again," he said when she answered the phone. What's your schedule like these days? I'm going to be in New York soon and I have some business ideas I'd like to discuss with you."

They arranged to dine together at the "Russian Tea Room". Suzanne wondered about his motives, but she liked Larry and was looking forward to seeing him again.

Back in the empty hotel room, enjoying the relaxation that the deep hot tub provided, she closed her eyes and thought of Larry. It seemed like only yesterday when she first met him that summer on Beverly's yacht. Since then he had managed to keep in touch with Suzanne, and he watched as her various business endeavors grew. She had come to regard Larry as a trusted and dear friend. In addition he was an astute businessman. He was adept at closing deals and knew people of importance in the financial communities all over the world. It seemed as if the terrible incident that led up to her meeting Lawrence VanDer Hyde and the start of her *Metamorphosis Spas* happened only yesterday.

Stoney Brook, Massachusetts • April, 1972

On a bright clear day, Suzanne dashed speedily about town, trying to get all her errands done in time to pick up Melanie. She knew she had just enough time to pick up her second daughter and then she could spend the rest of the evening at home studying. Admiring some early tulips in a flowerbed near the supermarket, she finished packing her bundles into her station wagon.

She turned onto the main street and was too late to avoid stopping at the red light. When the light turned green, she moved out like a race driver at the Grand Prix. Out of the blue her wonderful car stopped dead. The unfortunate person in the blue Mustang behind her didn't have a chance. His car crashed into Suzanne's, ramming hers into the auto ahead of her. Suzanne was slammed against the steering wheel.

For a second she thought she was in an amusement park riding the bumper cars. In an instant her whole life passed before her.

Boston General Hospital, Boston, Massachusetts • April, 1972 • 7:30 p.m.

"I guess the person didn't stop me for my 'For Sale' sign. Does anyone want a slightly banged up station wagon? I'll sell it real cheap."

"Honey," one of the nurses above her replied, "you're one lucky young woman. You won't have to worry about selling that car. How are you feeling? It's been a few hours since you lost consciousness. Do you know where you are, Suzanne?"

Suzanne tried to joke. "Um, Jamaica?" She tried to lift her head from the pillow, but the pain in her neck, ribs and abdomen was overpowering. "What time is it?"

"Time to come in out of the sun, I'd say," the nurse laughed. "No, really, it's about seven-thirty in the evening and you missed your dinner."

"Has anyone called my house. I was supposed to have picked up my little girls this afternoon."

"Your daughters are fine and your parents are outside in the waiting area. They'll be happy to know you're conscious again. Wait right here, and I'll send them in."

"Don't worry, I'm not going anywhere."

"You're just another Phyllis Diller. Hey Cindy," she called to another nurse, "we have a comedian here."

Dorothy and Morris came running in. Suzanne could tell her mother had been crying. "Suzanne, thank God you came to. We've been worried out of our minds. Now don't fret about the children. We called Mrs. Walsh and she came right over and has taken charge. We'll call the kids pretty soon and tell them you're okay. Everyone is worried sick. How are you feeling honey?"

"To tell you the truth, I really can't tell. I can vaguely remember what happened. How are the other drivers? Were they seriously injured?"

"No, they had a few bruises but they were sent home after films were taken. From what I gather, you're one lucky lady." Morris came over to the other side of her bed and kissed her bandaged forehead. "You took ten years off my life. I hope nothing like this ever happens again."

"I'll try to make sure it doesn't. I'm pretty achy. Have you spoken to any doctor yet?"

At that moment, a distinguished looking physician entered the room and introduced himself to Suzanne. He told her, "When someone's hurt the way you were, we like to keep you up, conscious for at least twenty-four hours in case of a concussion. Your parents can take you home, but I want to see you in two days, sooner if you begin to feel worse. You have a few broken ribs. You're lucky that's all that happened to you. We were afraid of internal bleeding. I would really like to keep you overnight."

"No, I'd rather go home. My children are there, and I'd feel better resting in my own bed. I'll call you if I run into any trouble. Who taped up my body? I feel like I'm in a body cast."

"You're going to be one sore young woman for a while. Try not to cough and be very careful when you start walking. You'll be all right in a month or two." Addressing Morris and Dorothy the doctor instructed the two worried parents, "Make sure you keep Suzanne awake for the next 24 hours. If she starts dozing, you don't let her fall asleep."   Her diligent folks took their assignment seriously.

Morris drove Suzanne home. The girls were delighted that she was back and Mrs. Walsh promised to stay at the house as long as she was needed. "Should I call Mr. Morse and tell him what's happened?"

"No, please don't. Brian will know about it soon enough from the insurance agency. I'll just stay in bed and get my rest." Suzanne stated, "Mrs. Walsh, thank you. It seems I'm always thanking you these days."

It suddenly occurred to her as she was lying in bed trying to piece things together that the exhibit was coming up shortly. She realized that she had no means of transportation. The old car that she had relied on for so long had finally gone to the great junkyard in the sky.

When Morris and Dorothy offered her the use of their auto until she was back on her feet financially, she was grateful. "Well, I don't know what to say," she pronounced, as she thanked them. "Once I sell some of my paintings or start work, I'll give you back your car and buy my own. Thanks for letting me borrow it."

The broken ribs took longer to heal than she thought they would, but she refused to succumb to the pain. At times she had to force herself to move about.

Suzanne was just finishing the evening dishes when the telephone rang. "Hi." She recognized Brian's voice. "The girls told me what happened and the insurance company notified me. How are you? How come you didn't call me to come over and help? You know I'd be glad to."

"Thanks for the concern. I'm doing fine. My ribs are healing. They've always gotten the brunt of your punches so I guess they were weak to begin with."

"That was a low blow and not called for."

"Well, thanks for worrying about me but as you can tell I'm doing just fine. I have a lot to do, so if you don't mind, I'll let you go."

"I'm not going to help you get another car while you're being so stubborn and headstrong. I don't understand why you won't even try a reconciliation."

"Don't worry. I never expect you to help me. I'll get along fine without you." Appalled by his attitude, she hung up the phone in disgust.

She was a bit shaky the first time she took the car out. Fatigued by the strain that even the slightest movement caused, she slowed the green Dodge at every intersection or cross street, cautious of any possible oncoming traffic. When she turned back into her driveway she was totally exhausted. "I ought to keep moving, so I'm not worn out every time I exert myself. I must go out again soon. I have to get over this uneasiness."

As she went into her house, an idea came to her. She called her friend, Beverly. "Bev, I'm glad I caught you at home. How would you like to come up to Stoney Brook and meet me early tomorrow morning? It's been so lovely out, I thought you'd enjoy taking a walk with me through the woods at Chester State Forest."

"What a nice idea. I'll leave as soon as the children get on the bus."

The two women, busily chatting away, didn't notice the late model car tailing theirs. Nor did they pay attention when that same vehicle backtracked and parked at the state forest's parking lot a few minutes later.

The aroma of the new grass and the sweet smell of the woods, now coming to life, was the medicine Suzanne needed.

"I'm so glad you suggested I drive up. What a pleasant place," Bev said.

"I come here often. Quite a few of my paintings were inspired by my many hikes through this forest."

"Do you remember when we were in high school? We used to climb the Blue Hills in Milton and view the world from the top of the mountain."

"Sure I remember those treks. It was a different world up there. The air was so clean and fresh. Maybe that's when I developed a love for the secluded places."

"How are your ribs? Are you going to be up to walking through these woods?"

"Sure, I'm healthy as a horse," laughed Suzanne. "I'm very happy you could come here with me today. It's not often we can get together without the children. Tell me, how are you and Louis doing?"

"Thank God, we're fine. He's working as long and hard as ever, but very soon we're sure it'll pay off. I don't think I could keep up your pace."

"I do it because I have no other choice. I can either persevere or give up. And, I won't give anyone the satisfaction of seeing me quit. With your tenacity, you'd be the same way. Don't kid yourself."

"When I finish school and the art exhibit is over, I think we should play hooky for a day and go up to the Quabbin Reservoir. I know you'll love it. The massive area is surrounded by trails and the land around it is crisscrossed with hiking paths and beautiful trees. You can go there on a Saturday or Sunday and never see another human."

The sounds of galloping horses interrupted their conversation. "Aren't you scared walking these woods by yourself?" inquired Beverly. "I know I'd be a little apprehensive coming into these woods alone."

Suzanne made light of her friend's concern. "At first all the varied noises did unnerve me. But then I got used to them and realized that they're the normal sounds of the forest. Trees began to creak as a gust of wind disturbed the still air. The friends thought the crackling of the acorns underfoot and the indirect sounds of the rustling leaves beyond were from a hunter's dog running wild or from one of the various wild creatures scurrying about. Little did they realize that they were being spied upon - by an unseen observer.

As they continued to walk, Suzanne suddenly felt uneasy. A shiver went down her back. "Are you cold?" asked Beverly.

"No. Well, I guess so. I just got a strange feeling that we're not alone. It must be the breeze. It's a little chilly."

"Yes, or your meaningful chatter about walking through the woods alone frightened me a bit." Laughing off her apprehension, she took Beverly by the hand and led her to a babbling, rocky brook where they sat down at its bank.

"You know Suzanne, it's weird. We're the best of friends, but we're such opposites. I'd never think of going out there on my own. It's a wonder we're so compatible."

Suzanne thought about her friend's remark. "I know. You're so quiet, but still waters run deep. I've learned a lot from you. Maybe I'm a little more outgoing and a bit more forceful, but when push comes to shove we have the same values, likes and dislikes. We just complement one another perfectly."

Chipmunks bounded down the hill, chattering away and, ignoring the two intruders, they went about their business. The afternoon sun was now at its peak.

"Do you remember when I thought I'd never live beyond age thirty-two? I thought it was so far away and when a person reached their thirtieth year they'd be old."

"Yes. I remember when and where you made that astounding remark. You'd come with me to visit my Mama Pessa in Dorchester. We were sitting on the stairs by the wooden landing of the third floor apartment. You'd just received your license and you managed to get the car from your mother. You loved Dorchester and never missed an opportunity to take me back and visit my grandmother."

A warm breeze stirred the air and a few old, brown leaves, remnants of last fall's foliage, blew briskly around them. Suzanne picked an old leaf up, twirling it around between her fingers. The crisp-edged leaf, punctured and worn, in a way looked like one of her grandmother's lace doilies. "There's beauty in everything, if you want to see it."

"You're such a dreamer."

"I have to be." Looking directly at her friend, Beverly asked aloud. "I often wonder about young girls of today. These kids live in such a different world than the one we grew up in."

"What do you mean?"

"Like the abortion issue. We're fortunate in this day and age to be able to choose whether to carry a baby to term or not. It's a heavy issue but we're lucky to have a choice."

"Yes we are. I know women sometimes became sterile from a botched-up abortion or never lived through it.

It scares me to think what some young girls have to go through. I'm glad I went through with my last pregnancy, but if I were to become pregnant again, God forbid, I honestly don't know what I'd do. I think the best method is the right birth control technique so that the decision doesn't have to be made."

"Yes, but there's always the chance of rape, incest, or an accident."

"I know, but I hope I never have to worry about pregnancy again. I think I'll become celibate."

Beverly laughed aloud. "Are you kidding? You like sex too much. I can't envision you never making love again."

With an exaggerated facial expression, Suzanne continued. "Well I'm going to focus my attention on my career and the children now. I won't have time for any men in my life for quite a while. I might sound as if I'm feeling a bit sorry for myself, but I'm not. I'm happy with my life, well except for the aches and pains!"

"You're funny, but one of these days, a man will come into your life, and then we'll see how celibate you are."

"Maybe. We'll see. A friend once told me a very funny story. She had been widowed for many years and, before her husband died, he'd been too ill to make love for years. She finally met a gentleman. She was in her sixties by this time. They started dating and she was all worried and upset. She said to me that she felt she had cob webs 'you know where' and she might have forgotten how to do it."

"That's a riot, but it's just like riding a bicycle. One never forgets. You just go with the flow and it all will come back to you."

As the two friends moved on, leaving the tranquillity of the forest, they paid no attention to the crackling branches stirring behind them. The unknown intruder watched their every move and followed close behind, staying just far enough back to remain continually out of sight.

Chapter Eight

Boston, Massachusetts • April, 1972

If you passed Alan Tremblay on the street, you might give him a second glance. Not that he was handsome or homely, for that matter, but that he had androgynous features: A slight frame, blond hair, hazel eyes, a small pointed nose, and thin lips. Justin Ferris was exhibiting Alan's artwork along with Suzanne's.

Justin's substantial proportions towered over Alan's five feet, ten inches. When Justin introduced them, Suzanne extended her hand, "I'm glad to finally meet you. I've heard great things about your art."

Alan seemed very much an introvert. Although pleasant, he was quiet and taciturn. His demeanor gave him a somewhat superior, detached air. His blasé manner continually puzzled Suzanne as they made plans for the exhibit.

Suzanne attempted to break the ice since she and Alan would be working many hours together preparing for the exhibit. She preferred that their meetings be harmonious and productive. At first her efforts were futile, but eventually she got through to him by encouraging him to talk about himself. After a while she found that he was very pleasant and intelligent - not snobbish, but shy. As the date of the show approached, she enthusiastically anticipated the time she shared with Justin and Alan.

One afternoon, a few weeks before the exhibit, the phone rang. "Hi Suzanne, this is Alan. I hope I'm not disturbing you."

"Of course not, how are you? What's up?"

"I'm calling to see if you'd like to take some time off and have a night out on the town, my treat of course."

"You're so sweet. Normally I wouldn't be able to get away, but today I finished studying for my upcoming tests in the car on the way home. If Mrs. Walsh doesn't have any plans for this evening, maybe she'll mind the girls while we go out. Is there any place particular you'd like to go?"

"Yes, I thought we'd walk around Quincy Market and then go to a restaurant in the North End, if that's all right with you."

"That sounds great. What time and where should we meet?"

As she drove into Boston, Suzanne smiled to herself thinking how pleasant it would be to go out with a male "friend" and not worry about the usual pressures of dating. She had been so busy since her separation with school and the children that she hadn't allowed herself any diversion. The change of pace was something she looked forward to.

The square was crowded, but Suzanne managed to find Alan at the flower store at the edge of the market where they had agreed to meet.

The marketplace was bustling with people, providing him with a perfect cover. He was confident that Suzanne hadn't spotted him in the parking lot as he maneuvered his car into a slot five rows behind hers, but he deliberately stayed in the vehicle until she was about a hundred yards away. As she neared the street, he got out of his black Cadillac and followed her, being careful to stay out of sight.

Stalking was not his usual evening's entertainment. He would have preferred being home watching the Celtics on TV, a cold beer in his hand, but he had wondered for a long time if there was a new man in her life. It seemed his hunch was right. Weeks of following her were finally paying off. This guy didn't look like her type. "But sometimes people's tastes change," he thought to himself. When she stopped to look in a store window, he quickly ducked into a specialty shop before he was seen.

Walking through the emporium he managed to come out at the opposite end of the mall, quickly blending again with the crowd.

"Do you come to the market often?" Suzanne asked.

"Not as often as I'd like to." Alan studied a cart with a display of shirts. "I'm taking a few night courses at Harvard Business School and sometimes I come by after class to unwind. I hope one day to open a gallery like Justin's. It's been a dream of mine for awhile."

"Well, I'm sure you'll do it. I don't think you let many things get in your way, once you make up your mind that you want something. Right?"

He laughed, "When I was growing up I was never encouraged to play sports like most young boys. My parents were educators and drummed into my head the importance of books and learning. Their main emphasis for me was education. Athletic diversion was for those who didn't excel scholastically, as far as my parents were concerned. My brother, Peter, was the athlete in the family. You'll meet him and his wife, Nancy, at our exhibit. Anyway, he hated school, and, as hard as my parents tried to get him interested in academics, their attempts were in vain. I was the quiet and shy one who wouldn't go against their wishes. Sometimes I wish I 'd been a little more combative and put up at least some resistance!"

The crowd thinned out and Alan suggested that they walk over to Durgin Park for dinner. Stars illuminated the sky above them as they strolled through the rows of pushcarts.

In an instant Suzanne's lighthearted mood changed drastically. "My, My, what a pensive look. Are you all right?" asked a concerned Alan.

"Oh, I'm okay. I thought I saw my ex-husband a few stores up looking into one of the windows. I must be getting paranoid. My imagination must be working overtime."

Trying to make light of the situation, Alan related, "I always am being mistaken for someone's brother or friend. They say everyone has a twin."

"I know you're right. Besides, I'm sure he wouldn't be here alone, especially on a Saturday night. Someday I'll get over my suspicious nature where Brian is concerned."

Taking Suzanne's hand, Alan led her through more rows of pushcarts filled with wares. Some merchants were engrossed in their own doings, whether reading a book or knitting, while other vendors enthusiastically described their goods to potential buyers.

When Alan took hold of her hand, Suzanne was reminded of her grandfather, Papa Abe, who worked at the original market when it was known as Haymarket Square.

When Suzanne was a youngster, Papa Abe often took her into this clamorous marketplace in the North End of Boston. In those days the square housed fruit and vegetable stalls as well as meat markets. Paper wrappings and discarded lettuce and cabbage leaves lay strewn all over the streets. Vendors lured potential customers with samples of their goods. Papa Abe showed off Suzanne, then, while he visited with his cronies, she was allowed to wander among the various booths and stalls. Enticed by the appealing aromas from the breads and pastries, Suzanne looked forward to visiting the Italian bakeries and specialty shops that surrounded the square.

After visiting with his friends, Papa Abe would take Suzanne to the Durgin Park restaurant for an early lunch. The atmosphere and character of this establishment had never changed. Patrons from all walks of life sat in close proximity to each other. The elongated building with very dim lighting housed long wooden tables on wide-planked wooden floors covered with heel marks from its thousands of customers. A banker talking high finance could be seated next to a housewife or shopkeeper enjoying an afternoon out. Papa Abe always ordered his favorite Indian Pudding for dessert while Suzanne tried a different sweet each time and was never able to decide which one was her favorite.

Returning to the present, ending her reverie, she selected from an assortment of hors d'oeuvres. Alan continued to describe his youth. "I wasn't a lady's man like Peter. Sometimes I would lie awake, the bed covers tucked beneath my feet with imaginary forms dancing on the white ceiling above me; figures of young, beautiful women coaxing me to join them. I had a vivid imagination and often concocted conversations with my hypothetical women. These females appear in my paintings today."

"Your paintings are so creative and dramatic. I've often wondered where you came up with your ideas. Do you mean that you can actually remember those images from your childhood? That's amazing."

Suzanne continued, "I must admit that when I first met you, you seemed quite shy, but once you relaxed, your true personality emerged."

Blushing, Alan ordered coffee and tea. When dinner was over, he insisted on walking Suzanne back to her car. "I hope we can do this again. I had a great time. Thanks for coming."

"Thanks for inviting me. It was a pleasant change."

As she drove home, Suzanne wondered if Alan ever had a serious relationship with a woman, or if he preferred someone of his own gender. "Well, that's none of my business. If we become good friends, he may confide in me," she thought.

Driving cautiously, she watched the rear view mirror, her eyes constantly going back and forth from the road to the mirror and back to the traffic again. She knew she had an overactive suspicious imagination, but she could have sworn that she had observed the same car when she left Boston thirty-five minutes ago. She felt relieved when that car turned off at Route 62.

Suzanne graduated from esthetics school and was preparing for the state boards. She thought that after the exhibit she would be able to spend some time deciding exactly what to do. She knew she couldn't open a business yet. The state required that she work two years for a licensed esthetician before she opened her own salon. Since no skin care salons existed in her immediate area, she would probably have to find employment in Boston at first. Suzanne planned to ask Mrs. Walsh to stay on as housekeeper and baby-sitter when she went to work full time.

She hadn't felt it necessary to tell anyone outside her immediate family about her separation from Brian. She did want to tell her neighbor, Kay, and she caught up with Kay one day at the mailbox, inviting her over for a cup of tea. Over their steaming cups of orange pekoe, Suzanne said, "I don't know if you noticed that Brian hasn't been around lately, but I want you to know that we've separated. It'll probably become common knowledge sooner or later around the neighborhood, but right now I can't deal with a lot of questions."

Kay was speechless at first. "I'm shocked. Of course, you know I won't say anything to anyone if you don't want me to. You can come over and talk with me any time, if things get rough. Do you need help with the children? How are they taking this?"

Suzanne assured her that she had things under control and if she did need help, she wouldn't hesitate to call. Suzanne felt truly blessed that she had a friend like this. The two women continued to talk and when Kay left four hours later, Suzanne called Beverly.

Beverly had already surmised that Suzanne would have to do something drastic. "To tell you the truth, I'm relieved. I mean it, Suzanne. I realize your marriage wasn't all bad; you have three beautiful daughters, but I've seen the way he treats you. I remember him calling you to change the TV channels when you were at the other end of the house." They chuckled at the absurdity of it, then Beverly went on, more seriously, "I've seen worse than that, too, Suzanne, and I never knew what to say or do. I'm just glad you recognized him for what he is and got yourself and the girls out before he did any real damage."

"Thank God, they're okay," Suzanne said.

"Honestly, in a very weird way, I'm happy for you. You're in control now, not Brian. Believe me, you're better off."

"I know. My mother always told me that things happen for a reason, and I have to believe it. But, I just want only those close to me to be aware of my situation for now. Okay?"

"I just want you to be happy. You deserve it."

The art exhibit was scheduled for the weekend before Mother's day. Suzanne was charged with exhilaration. She had sent invitations to her family and friends. She also sent one to Brian. She was deciding what to wear to the event when Brian called.

"Hi, I got your invitation, and I'm glad you sent me one. I'd love to go. Can I pick you up?"

"I'm glad you're going to be there, thanks, but I'll meet you at the gallery." They talked for a couple of minutes and arranged for him to visit the girls the following week. "Thanks for calling. I'll see you at the exhibit."

Boston, Massachusetts • May, 1972

The days flew by and before she knew it, the big event had arrived. The girls giggled with excitement as they watched their mother getting ready. Mrs. Walsh was going to sleep over, so that Suzanne would not have to rush home. Suzanne had invited Mrs. Walsh to the exhibit, but she opted to spend the evening with the children. "Besides, I've seen all your paintings. If you want, we can go into Boston later in the week and the two of us can enjoy them all over again. I know you'll tell me all about it in the morning, so go and have a marvelous time. I'll be there in spirit."

Suzanne wanted to get to the gallery early and meet with Alan and Justin before the seven o'clock opening. She declined Alan and Justin's offer to transport her to Boston. With blues music playing on the radio, Suzanne found the drive into Boston relaxing.

She met Alan as she entered the front door and they headed to Justin's office together. Suzanne refused the champagne Justin offered her. "I'm so excited, I just can't," she exclaimed.

Exceedingly conscious of his vast dimensions, Justin humorously padded his rather substantial stomach. "I wish I could say the same, but as you can see, I don't let anything get in the way of my gastronomic enjoyment."

He continued more earnestly, "I want you both to relax and enjoy yourselves tonight. Mix with the people, of course. Most of them will want to meet and talk to you. Many of them are very wealthy, but don't feel you have to impress anyone. Just relax and be yourselves. That's your job for this evening, okay?"

"We expect approximately three hundred people. If all goes well, many of them will purchase some of your pieces. If anyone tries to talk to you about the cost or attempts to bargain with you over a piece, just refer them to Frank, Michelle, or me. That's our job. One of us will be on the floor at all times. It doesn't happen often, but it does happen."

People started to arrive just before seven. Suzanne's relatives were first, followed closely by Alan's family. Over the years, Justin had amassed an impressive list of clients made up of both older established patrons of the arts and the nouveau riche.

The evening was a dream come true for Suzanne. Many of the attendees were impressed with her works. The guests left with thirty nine of Suzanne's paintings and thirty three of Alan's. She knew this would provide the nest egg she needed to establish her business. Two other guests had requested that Suzanne custom-design pieces for their homes.

Justin assured Alan and Suzanne, "Believe me, this has been a very successful exhibit, and it is only the beginning."

By eleven o'clock only a handful of the people remained. Suzanne felt the pressure lifting, and she could now relax with the few remaining friends. Beverly, Kay, and Suzanne kicked off their heels and sat joking on the broad stairway leading to the second floor, finishing the remainder of the rosè and shrimp. Alan walked over with his brother, Peter, and Peter's wife, Nancy. They joined the three women on the stairs. Peter stretched out on one of the stairs, feigning boredom.

It was Peter who had introduced Alan to Justin Ferris. Peter owned a very successful hair salon on Newbury Street. Suzanne took a liking to Nancy and Peter immediately. She was amazed to discover that it was one in the morning. She had lost track of the time and knew it would be advisable to head home.

Before she left, Peter said, "Nancy and I would love to have you and Alan over to our house for dinner. Nancy's a great cook and I concoct some pretty good dishes myself. If it's okay with you, how about a week from Saturday?"

"I'd love it. I'm, sure the date will be fine. Can I bring the salad or a desert?"

"Thanks, but all we want you to bring is yourself."

"Thanks for the invitation. I'll make arrangements with Alan. Kissing Justin and Alan good-bye, she headed home.

Early the next morning, unable to sleep, Suzanne described the exhibit and recounted all the events to Mrs. Walsh.

Suzanne was delighted when Mrs. Walsh agreed to stay on permanently as housekeeper. She genuinely loved Suzanne and the three little girls, thinking of them as an extension of her own family.

"As long as the good Lord sees fit to keep me going, I'll be here for you. So don't you worry. Work as hard as you want, because the girl's will get the best care possible. I'll treat them as if they were mine."

Suzanne felt profound gratitude to her devoted confidante. It was as if she had two mothers and would always be grateful for this dear and wonderful person she could depend on. The two women talked about the exhibit, Brian, the girls, and Suzanne's future. Suzanne placed another single bed in Taylor's room so that Mrs. Walsh could stay over on evenings when Suzanne worked late. She didn't want Mrs. Walsh traveling home late at night to her apartment in Waltham, only to get up early and head back to Suzanne's house in time for work the next morning. With the arrangements made, it was now Suzanne's responsibility to find a job that could support them all.

Suzanne managed to put the girls to bed early that night. A storm was brewing and she debated whether to start another painting or to study for the upcoming state boards. She admitted she would rather paint than read, so she sat down at the easel. As the rain intensified, she got up and checked to see that all the windows were closed. Once back at her canvas, she became engrossed in blending the oils. She thought she heard a strange noise outside the studio. Thinking that one of the children had wakened, she got up to investigate. Moving cautiously from the workshop through the dim lit back hallway and kitchen, she peeked into the bedrooms to see who it was.

All three girls were sound asleep. She heard the same noise again. Alarmed now, a variety of thoughts went through her head as she moved quietly towards the front of the house. "Is it a burglar who thinks everyone is asleep? I should call Kay or the police. I don't remember if I locked the windows when I checked them." Slowly pulling the living room curtain back, she looked out and saw the shadow of a man trying to open the front door with a key that obviously wouldn't fit. "Now would be a really good time to stay cool and not panic," she told herself.

Going to the telephone she picked up the receiver to call the police. At the very same time, the perpetrator started banging on the door and shouting Suzanne's name. Acting quickly, so that the commotion would not waken the girls, she dropped the phone and ran to the door. Grabbing an umbrella with a very sharp point from the stand, she looked out the sidelights.

"Oh my God, it's Brian," she uttered aloud. She opened the door cautiously. Barely able to understand his slurred speech, she ushered him in, unaware of his frame of mind.

"What in God's name is going on? You almost scared the life out of me. Why are you here?" As he stumbled into the kitchen, Suzanne became aware of his inebriated state. She could smell the stale odor of liquor on his breath. "Sit down and let me make you a cup of coffee. How did you manage to drive here without killing yourself or some innocent bystander?" she asked.

With slurred speech he tried to answer, but it was obvious he had something else on his mind.

Suzanne continued with her annoyance beginning to show, "In all the years we were married, I never saw you drunk."

"Well sweetheart, remember we're still married. Tell me who you've been sleeping with since I left. I know an attractive woman like you won't go too long without a good lay. Who is he? Do I know him?" he demanded.

"Brian, stop talking like that. It's disgusting and it's none of your business anyway. To be honest with you, I haven't had time to date."

Too late she realized that she had triggered one of his rages as he staggered up from his chair with a sinister look on his face. Moving uncomfortably close to her, he took hold of her shoulders.

"You're a God dam liar. I saw you at Faneuil Hall with a tall, skinny guy. You were laughing and it looked like you were having yourself a real good time. Tell me I

185

was imagining that," he yelled as he shoved her against the counter.

Suzanne perspired profusely as she realized Brian must have been watching her for some time or having her watched. Her nerves were shot to pieces. "How would you know that?"

"I followed you. How else? It's a free country."

"Don't you have better things to do than follow me around?" she questioned. A thought flashed quickly through her mind. It was almost humorous: she thought Alan was gay; Brian concluded Alan was his rival.

Then, Suzanne's anger began to swell within her. "How dare you track me like some animal. You don't own me?" she shouted.

Putting his arm around her shoulder, he shamelessly grumbled, "Honey, I've missed you. Come and give me a kiss. You can't tell me you haven't missed me. Just remember all the good times we had together. We could still have a great time in the sack." He suddenly reached forward and grabbed her. He kissed her hungrily.

His alcoholic breath was both disgusting, but in a way sickeningly erotic. "Oh, God, I must be as deranged as he is," she thought as she recognized her instinctive reaction. Trying to free herself from his tight grasp, she pushed herself away while she tried to compose herself and pacify him at the same time. "Let go of me. You're drunk.

You don't know what you're saying or doing. Let me give you some coffee."

"Not until you feel my stiff prick. You know how big and hard it gets." Again he lunged for her and caught her around the ankles as she ran toward the stairway. As she tumbled forward onto the floor he dragged her backwards onto the kitchen floor, quickly lifted up her nightdress, and wrangled himself on top of her, pinning her down with the weight of his body. With deft and manipulative fingers he tried to arouse his struggling wife.

"Don't fight me Suzanne, I'm much stronger than you. Just relax and enjoy it." With a mocking tone, he dared her, "Keep fighting me Suzanne, my prick is bulging. I love it when you fight me. It gets me hotter."

With adrenaline pumping through her veins Suzanne shouted, "Get off me. You don't know what you're doing." Trying to free herself from his heavy handed grip and oppressive weight, she strained to strike her knee to his groin, to no avail. She couldn't summon the strength to scream. Even if she could, she didn't want any of the children to walk in and see this vicious attack. Appealing to him as a father, she cautioned him about the girls.

"Then let me make love to you. Just this once." He persisted on putting his hungry lips onto her tight-lipped, resistant mouth. Forcing her lips open he thrust his wet tongue into her mouth. She tried to bite him, but with his other hand he pinched her cheeks hard enough to prevent any serious damage. Unzipping his pants, he buckled her down and thrust his now wet, hard penis into her.

"Stop this insanity," sobbed Suzanne. Desperately resisting his movements she tried to close her legs, but he only spread them apart again effortlessly. She could feel his sweaty shirt as she tried to claw and dig her fingers into his torso. It only excited him more. She didn't know what else to do. She couldn't think beyond the moment.

"Enjoy the hammering, honey. Oh. Yeah, it feels good."

His hands were all over her wet clammy body. Pinching her nipples and squeezing her heavy breasts, he made her cry out in pain. In what seemed hours, only minutes had elapsed. A brute and triumphant Brian culminated his vicious attack by frenetically reaching his fierce pleasure. "I can get it up again. Keep fighting me and I'll show you, you bitch."

As he climaxed, his body relaxed. He reached for her again and Suzanne seized the opportunity to catch her breath while she mustered all her strength and kneed him. As he recoiled in pain, she scurried away and hid inside the locked bathroom. He lay squirming on the kitchen floor, holding his organs.

Waves of nausea struck her abdomen. Her retching was uncontrollable and vomit sporadically erupted from the pit of her stomach. Even when nothing was left, the involuntary spasms continued. Her whole body was wracked by uncontrollable shaking. She realized her eyes weren't focusing. Behind the securely locked bathroom door, she finally gave up and dropped to the floor.

It might have been five minutes or it might have been five hours. Unaware of how long she had been unconscious, she came to and felt the cool white tiles beneath her. The house was quiet and still. She lay there for a long time allowing the coolness of the tiles to soothe her bruised and aching body.

When she came to again she still had no idea how much time had elapsed. Afraid to leave the bathroom, fearing that Brian might still be in the house, she lay there listening to the stillness. Then she had a horrible thought. "Oh God, what if he's hurt the girls?" She panicked and felt the bile rising in her throat once again. She forced herself to her feet and cautiously opened the bathroom door. Hoping that the coast was clear, she ran first to the older girls' room, then to Taylor's. The three slept blissfully, not a care in the world.

Instinctively she retreated to the security of her bedroom and locked the door behind her. She looked at the clock and saw that it was only three o'clock. Her pounding head was nothing compared to the throbbing of her body. Slowly sitting down on the side of the bed, she dared herself to look in the mirror and examine every part of her face and body.

She couldn't believe what she saw. Ugly red welts covered her face and legs. Her torn and bloodied nightdress hung off her shoulder revealing her bruised upper torso. She once again felt bile rising to her throat as she saw the remains of his dried semen over her reddened flesh.

She went into the bathroom and pulled the shower door open so fast, it hit the wall. Turning on the hot water full force, she stepped inside. She left the shower door open, letting the water splatter over the floor as she tried to purify herself. Scrubbing repeatedly she felt the harshness of the rough washcloth acting as an abrasive against her skin. After soaping repeatedly, she still couldn't wash away the filth she felt, both inside and out. The shame of violation did not leave.

The water ran cold and brought her back to reality. Opening her eyes, she looked down and saw her own blood swirling slowly down the drain. She quickly stepped out of the shower, away from the cool moisture. Grabbing a large towel she wrapped it gingerly around her body and stepped from the stall.

Confusion clouded her judgment. Should she call a doctor or the police? "What if I press charges against Brian? He's still my husband, can I say he raped me if we are still legally husband and wife?" With these frustrated thoughts she drifted off to a troubled sleep.

She awoke to the sound of Melissa pounding on her door. "Mommy, Mommy, wake up. Open the door."

With a start, Suzanne remembered what happened. Jumping out of bed she unlocked the bedroom entry to a scared little girl.

"You never close your door, Mommy. Are you okay? What's that mark on your face. It looks like blue paint." Running down the hall Melissa teasingly sang out, "Mommy went to bed without washing paint off her face."

Looking into the mirror, Suzanne saw the now telltale visible signs of Brian's heavy hands on her cheeks. She'd have to cover the deep discoloration with extra makeup to conceal them.

She sat down to compose herself while she slowly sipped her hot tangy tea. She hoped she'd be able to study but she very much doubted it. Conflicting thoughts ran through to her mind. What should or could she do? She knew one thing. She'd call an attorney this morning and start divorce proceedings immediately.

After giving the girls their breakfast, she dialed Mrs. Walsh's number with trembling fingers, hoping she'd caught her before she left for work.

"Mrs. Walsh, something has come up and I won't be going to classes today. Can you come over later, say about two o'clock? I have a meeting to go to and I'd appreciate it if you'd show up then."

Concerned, Mrs. Walsh asked, "Are you all right? You sound peculiar."

Trying not to exhibit her frayed nerves and delicate emotional state, Suzanne reassured her trusted friend and housekeeper that all was well.

As soon as the older two girls were put on the school bus, Suzanne busied herself. She found it difficult to attend to Taylor and her needs. Disheartened and depressed, she couldn't focus on anything. The hours seemed to drag as Suzanne waited impatiently for the lawyer's office to open. She was hopeful that her attorney would be able to see her later in the day.

Sensing that something was wrong with Suzanne, Mrs. Walsh made sure she arrived at the house earlier than she was expected.

Unaware that her friend and confidant would arrive early, Suzanne was startled when Mrs. Walsh walked through the kitchen door at twelve forty-five. She found Suzanne disheveled and crying as she lay on the sofa trying to take her mind off the terrible defilement that had happened to her.

Not wanting to alarm her trusted friend and second mother, Suzanne tried making light of the situation that Mrs. Walsh came upon.

"I'm glad you managed to come early. Now I can go upstairs and get ready for my meeting."

"You know, you're not a good actress. I've known you too long now not to know when something is wrong.

Look at you. You're pallid, and just look at those bruises. Sit right back down and tell me what's been going on," commanded Mrs. Walsh, as Suzanne was about to leave the room. She patted the couch and held Suzanne tightly as she let her beloved "adopted daughter" shed more tears as she related last night's horror.

"If I had the son of a bitch in front of me, I'd strangle him with my bare hands, I swear," Mrs. Walsh declared, as her anger brought out her deep Irish brogue.

Attempting to compose herself, Suzanne calmed an angry Mrs. Walsh. "Why don't you make us a cup of tea while I get dressed. I'll try to cover up these bruises with some makeup and make myself presentable."

Getting ready for her late afternoon appointment with the attorney, she looked into the mirror and turned away in disgust, not able to face herself. She felt violated and dirty. All at once tears flowed from her eyes. She had taken three showers since her appalling experience, trying to erase the feeling of his hands on her. Still feeling unclean, she couldn't obliterate the feeling of contamination and wondered how long it would take for her to get over this pain.

She left the house at three-thirty, allowing ample time to get to her meeting. Joseph Balan's office was located on Waltham Street, near Lexington Center. Suzanne had first met the Balan family when she joined the temple years ago. Their congregation was made up of people who were new to the area and many made lasting friendships with their fellow members. At first she felt uneasy about seeking help from a friend. Then she realized that she had to talk to someone knowledgeable and he was known to be a very good lawyer.

Joseph Balan emerged from the office and greeted Suzanne warmly, shaking her hand. "I'm glad to see you again. I sincerely appreciate your thinking of our firm for your legal matters."

He led her into his conference room and motioned to her to sit down. As he closed the door, he continued. "It's been a while since we saw each other. When was it? Oh yes, at the Jewish holidays. How is the family and what have you been doing?" Without waiting for her reply, he continued, "Every year Phyllis and I say we'll go to temple every Friday evening, but usually something comes up. Enough of this. You've come here for a reason. Tell me what I can do for you."

Suzanne began, "Not many people from the temple know this, but Brian and I have separated. He's been out of the house for some time now and I'd like a divorce from him as soon as possible."

"I'm truly sorry to hear that Suzanne. I never would have guessed that the two of you had any problems. You've always seemed like such a happy couple."

"Most people are shocked to hear it. Yes, I asked him to leave a few months back and thankfully he's now out of the house."

"How are the girls?"

"I think they're somewhat confused. But we're managing." With a nervous laugh she continued, "I've never been through anything like this before. Is there a lot involved?"

"It depends on the situation. Every case is different. Sometimes, when children and real estate aren't an issue, it can go very smoothly. Other times, when matters are complicated, it can go on for years. If there are hard feelings on either side, it makes it worse. What is the situation between you and Brian? If I'm to represent you, I must know all the facts."

Somehow that question triggered a valve in Suzanne. She couldn't hold the tears of hurt, anger and frustration that came pouring out. Unable to look him in the eye, she took a tissue from the box he held in front of her. He listened to the entire story including the unfortunate incident of the previous night.

Trying to make light of the situation Suzanne said, "So many years and it didn't take that long to tell the story."

"From what you've told me, it looks as if you can claim cruel and abusive treatment. I doubt if any judge in his right mind would deny you a divorce. Of course, it's not as easy as it used to be. Along with equal rights comes equal responsibility. Some judges give women a difficult time about keeping their homes. But if we play our cards right, I don't think we'll have a problem."

With a wavering voice she went on, "I know Brian; he'll fight me tooth and nail."

"Well, there are a few options opened to you. You may be able to file assault and battery charges. There's such a thing as rape by a husband, but, unfortunately, no judge in this state has heard a case of this type yet. I doubt very much if we'd win if we attempt to use those grounds. Society is led to believe that husbands have certain rights."

Still waiting, he went on; "We could have filed a criminal complaint if you had a legal separation or if he had gained forcible entry. Without either of those two infractions, I'm afraid we don't have much to work with. The only thing we have for sure is cruel and abusive treatment. Let's go with that."

"Tell me, did you change the locks?"

"Yes, I had the locks changed the day after he moved out. Boy was I stupid to let him in last night. I feel like such a fool."

"I assume you didn't see another lawyer to arrange for a legal separation?"

"No, the only other time I've been in a lawyer's office was when Brian and I signed the papers to buy our home. I'm so naive. It never occurred to me to obtain a legal separation."

"I wish you'd called the police or gone to the hospital after the incident last night. It would have corroborated your story and his semen would be another piece of evidence. Unfortunately, we can't cry about spilt milk. If you agree though, I can have my secretary, Phyllis, take some Polaroid pictures of your bruises now. That may be helpful when we go to court. How's he doing with his financial obligations to you and the girls?"

"So far there hasn't been a problem. After last night, I don't know what to expect."

"Let me get this paperwork prepared while Phyllis takes the photos. We'll make an appointment for another meeting in, let's say, one month. Meanwhile if you have any questions, feel free to call me any time."

"And, if he makes any attempt to get into the house again, call the police immediately. If he does anything that makes you uncomfortable, call me right away. That's what you're paying me for."

When she left his office she couldn't help thinking how quickly time passes. It seemed like only yesterday that she and Brian had been married. Now, she thought, the pledge of "till death do we part," was an empty, meaningless vow.

A deep emptiness engulfed her as she drove home. She thought with irony that nothing in life is ever guaranteed. "Who would have thought that the charming man I married was really a Jekyll and Hyde? I hope my daughters will use more sense than I did when picking out a husband. I'll discourage them from marrying so young, that's for sure."

Summer, 1972

Suzanne was hoping for a peaceful summer. She looked forward to take some time off and join Beverly for a week of sailing at the Cape, but her plans were still indefinite.

When she arrived home, the telephone was ringing. She ran through the living room, carefully avoiding the toys that were strewn all over the floor. Breathless, she answered on the fifth ring. "Well, I was just about to hang up. How are you doing?"

"It must be mental telepathy. You were on my mind while I was driving home." Suzanne told Beverly everything that had occurred since she had last spoken to her, including the terrible incident with Brian and her visit with the lawyer.

"I didn't think I'd be able to get away with you and your friends for a vacation, but after what happened, I think I really need to escape from everything. So, if you and Louis still want me to come, I'll be glad to go sailing with you. I'm warning you though; I won't be much company. Most likely I'll be studying during the day, not that I won't help you if you need me."

"I'm delighted you can come." They talked for a while longer and Beverly gave Suzanne a list of what to bring.

The *Sea Quest* was a beautiful, seventy-five foot sailboat that made an impressive sight as they approached the dock.

"I can't believe it's all yours. When did you get it?"

"I pinch myself every time I go on board" Beverly enthusiastically verbalized as they walked to the yacht to deposit their belongings. "Louis finally traded in his thirty-foot sailboat at the beginning of the year and it took some time to furnish it the way I wanted. Aren't you surprised?"

"My God, I have rich friends," Suzanne teased.

"Of course it cost more than the mortgage on my house," interjected Louis, who, as he gingerly walked up behind them, was like a proud father showing off his offspring for the very first time.

Suzanne couldn't remember a more relaxing holiday. Besides Beverly, Louis, and Suzanne, there were two couples plus a single man who was a client of Louis's accounting firm. The weather was perfect for sailing and cooperated for most of the week.

One day when the others had gone onto Nantucket Island to browse and do some serious shopping, Suzanne remained on board to study. Beverly stayed behind also, waiting to talk privately with her best friend. A group of men on a yacht docked beside them cast admiring glances at the two women lying on the deck in their bikinis.

"Look at the way those men are giving you the eye. You could have any man you desired, just with the twirl of your finger."

"You're dreaming. Like I want one. They're probably all married and away with the guys for a week. You know I've lost the ability to trust." Visibly shaking and making a disdainful face, she continued, "I don't want a man's hands touching my body. It repulses me."

"When the right man comes along, you'll feel differently."

"Maybe," Suzanne gave Beverly a knowing look. "Did you purposely bring along a single gentleman for me?"

"To tell you the truth, no. Lawrence is one of Louis' clients. His wife died quite suddenly, just under a year ago, leaving Larry with two young sons and an infant daughter. He's a very dynamic and powerful businessman, always on the go. Louis felt he needed a rest almost as much as you did."

"I'm sorry to hear that. How does he ever manage raising his children and running such a successful business?"

"Suzanne, wake up. Hello! Did you catch his name or did it go completely over your head? He's the Lawrence VanDer Hyde of the world famous VanDer Hyde Jewelers. His great-grandfather and grandfather built an empire with their famous diamond mines in Africa. They cut the jewels in their native Belgium. Larry's father has diversified, but he still owns all the diamond mines, and the jewelry firms. He now owns other corporations like men's clothing, cologne and toiletries, plus a dozen other businesses."

"So getting back to your basic question as to 'How can he do it?' He has hired staff and nannies to mind his children. And with his kind of money he doesn't have to worry about getting *good* help. He is rather interesting though, you have to admit. I love to listen to him talk. His accent is oh, so European."

"Yes, he is intriguing, but don't forget I'm just coming out of a terrible marriage. To be honest with you, I have no desire to even think of dating. It's too early for me. The timing is completely off."

Beverly, continuing her own train of thought, wondered aloud, "He really is a handsome man. I wonder why he hasn't been snatched up by some conniving woman?"

"Who knows? It hasn't been a year yet. The businesses certainly must keep him busy. Or, maybe his kids are brats and scare all the women away."

"Isn't that the truth," laughed Beverly.

Suzanne reminded Beverly, "Don't make me laugh too much, my ribs still ache."

During the rest of the trip they spent quiet evenings anchored in the still water with stars glimmering overhead. Listening to classical music, the would-be sailors sat around the big table in the dining room, enjoying wine, refreshments and gourmet food, that was cooked by the on-board chef. After dinner, they played backgammon till they couldn't keep their eyes open any longer.

One day when the wind had died down, Louis suggested they motor to a deserted island he had found years ago. "It's not far from here. Let's go there for the afternoon."

"Sounds good to me," Lawrence said. The rest of the group agreed.

Two hours later they lay anchor by the small island, and rowed the smaller boats to shore. They brought their picnic lunches in wicker baskets and settled on a bluff above the beach that provided a magnificent panoramic view of the neighboring islands.

After consuming a meal of fresh fruits and cheeses, Suzanne felt an urge to walk off her lunch and decided to go down to the beach. Completely absorbed by the island's loveliness, she was startled when Larry caught up and tapped her on the shoulder.

"Can I share the shore with you? You look like you were deep in thought, I hope I didn't scare you."

"I was mulling over some issues. I hope no one was worried about me. I love walking along the secluded beach. Isn't this a lovely island?"

Suzanne continued, "I can remember when my children were very young and I would help them build sand castles. We would toil for hours and hours, only to come back to the same spot the very next day and see no trace of our hard and diligent work."

"I can't say that I spend much time with my children. They're very young. For that matter, I'm usually so busy I can seldom enjoy them," spoke a pensive Lawrence. "I realize I should, but when I think of it, they're either napping or the nanny has taken them out to play. I'm consistently flying from one country to another, attending to my businesses. Though, these formative years are so very important, I must make a point of being with them more often."

"It's too bad you can't be with them frequently. They grow up too quickly, you miss soo much. Even little things mean a lot, like their first step, or when they lose their baby teeth, or say their first word. I'm glad I can say that I know my children well, although I've been rather preoccupied for this past year myself. But, seriously, it's important to be close to your children as they grow and mature. But who am I to tell you how to raise your children? Ignore me, I've a tendency to ramble on."

"No, what you say makes sense. When my children reach school age I intend to send them to private boarding schools. I feel the proper education is essential, and at the right schools they'll get vital training, direction, and guidance. In addition, they'll make contacts that will benefit them their entire lives."

"That's true enough, but don't forget that parents play a significant role in a child's education. The basic values always come from the home." Suzanne turned red and felt embarrassed. "What an idiot I am. I forgot he just lost his wife," she chided herself.

He abruptly changed the subject. "When my wife and I vacationed we would often go to Paris and London. Monte Carlo is delightful and the Riviera is an exceptional place to visit. It's easy to travel from one country to another when you are in Europe. Tell me Suzanne, have you traveled much?"

Seeing Larry for the first time from a different perspective she observed him closely, trying not to be too obvious. She saw a sadness in his large green eyes that were not visible at first glance. She noted that he wore expensive, coordinated clothes.

"I did some traveling with my husband when I was married. My favorite place is Bermuda. Have you ever been there?"

"I'm sorry to say that I haven't."

"Well, I've never been to Europe. Maybe someday, but right now I've other things on my mind."

With a smile on his rugged, yet handsome face, he went on, "Yes, you seem to be enjoying this vacation, but I can tell your mind is on other matters. I look at you and it seems as if you are a million miles away. Do you want to talk about it?"

"You're very perceptive. But, no, it's not something I want to discuss."

"I guess my insight comes automatically. When you run businesses like I do, it gets to be second nature. Care to explore the rest of the island with me?"

"Sure, I'd love to."

They wandered across the island, through trees and underbrush, keeping their conversation superficial. He stood tall next to Suzanne, his six feet casting a shadow and protecting her against the rays of the hot sun. His curly, brown hair streaked with strands of gold from this week's exposure to the light fell onto his forehead.

"Suzanne, you intrigue me. But, I suppose you're used to men admiring you."

With a hint of laughter in her voice, she replied, "You flatter me. Thanks, but no. I haven't dated anyone for a long time. To be honest with you, I'm not ready yet. As I told you, I'm starting a new career and I want to devote my time to that and my three lovely daughters who need me."

Looking directly into Suzanne's eyes, Lawrence said, "I'm a very patient man."

Suzanne quelled her laugh and turned the conversation in another direction. "It's getting late; let's start walking back."

Larry wasn't dissuaded easily. "I was thinking," confessed Larry. "When you start your new business, I'll be more than happy to help you with any issues that may arise. You probably don't need advice right now, but for future reference, remember that I'll be there for you if you want financial guidance."

"Thanks for your offer; let's hope the business gets off the ground real soon. If it does, I'll be more than happy to listen to any suggestions you have." They skimmed flat stones out onto the water as they slowly walked back to the others.

Back on board the yacht, Suzanne avoided any sort of intimacy with Larry. He didn't push her, but he was not to be deterred. Taking his friend Louis aside, he asked about Suzanne.

"Louis, I want to be kept informed of Suzanne's progress with her business. I admire her and I think she's going to make a go of it. I realize she's not ready for any type of romantic involvement right now, but in time she'll change her mind. I want to be there when she does. And, I want you to keep this conversation in the strictest confidence."

"Larry, this isn't like you. You can have any woman you want, and yet you deliberately zero in on someone who's not interested. Are you sure you know what you're doing old pal?"

"All I know is I'm very attracted to her. If she doesn't want a social involvement, then I can help in a commercial venture for sure."

His hands clasped behind his head, Larry stared at the wood above his bed as the water's motion rocked him like a baby in a cradle. Suzanne's face appeared before him. He could not get her out of his mind. "Now, she's the type of woman I could fall for. She seems genuine. If I take my time and play my cards right, some day soon, I'll have her eating out of my hands. She has just the type of qualities that I've been looking for since I lost my beloved Carolyn."

For the rest of the cruise, Larry kept his distance, but he promised himself this was not going to be the last he saw of Suzanne Morse.

Chapter Nine

Ipswich, Massachusetts • May, 1973

Suzanne thought she surely must have taken a wrong turn for she found herself in front of a small mansion overlooking a vast expanse of blue water. The view was so staggering that it dwarfed the house. Alan's car was parked in the circular driveway and she realized that this must be the place. She had no idea that Peter and Nancy had this kind of money; they were so down-to-earth.

Nancy opened the double oak doors and greeted Suzanne warmly. After taking her coat, she gave her a grand tour of the home, which she had completely renovated. She told Suzanne that she had refused to hire an interior decorator and wanted to handle all the decorating herself. She showed Suzanne through the spacious first floor that included an atrium then she led the way up the front staircase to the second floor. After admiring the exquisite workmanship in the bedrooms that wrapped around the atrium, Suzanne followed Nancy and they descended the back staircase that led directly into the kitchen. As they moved through the home, Suzanne noticed many pieces of Alan's art, along with those of other artists, displayed throughout the eighteen-rooms. Nancy admitted to Suzanne that she did have a cleaning woman because of the sheer enormity of the house. Entering the kitchen from the back of the mansion, they joined Alan and Peter at the table where Peter was pouring the wine.

"How long have the two of you been married?" Suzanne asked her hosts.

"For twelve wonderful, fun-filled years," the couple said in unison.

"Alan tells us you have three beautiful young daughters. You're very fortunate.   Growing up as an only child, I wanted a dozen children of my own. Regrettably, we haven't been blessed yet," continued Nancy.

"Honey, as long as we have each other, that's enough for me," declared Peter.

With a petulant tone in her voice, Nancy replied, "It might be enough for you, but please don't speak for me."

Suzanne felt the tension immediately and tried to change the subject by talking about the exquisite workmanship that had been done on the house. She thought it was a shame for these two people to be irritable with each other, for she could also sense the love and warmth exchanged between them.   In addition, they exhibited an ease towards one another that can only exist between best friends.

Nancy explained she had no desire for a career, but she frequently helped Peter at his salon. She also liked working with older people and volunteered at the local nursing home. "You'd be surprised at the number of elderly people who have no one to care about them and never have any visitors at all. If I can make someone happy for a few hours, that makes me feel good."

"A funny incident happened last week to one of our teenage volunteers who donates her time doing laundry." She gesticulated with her hands as she described the scene. "Well, the girl was putting some laundry away for this feisty old lady. Try to picture this happening. The young girl opens the closet and proceeds to hang up the clothes. She doesn't see that a strip of flypaper is hanging from the top of the closet. The flypaper gets caught in her hair. She doesn't know what it is, but thinks something is attacking her, and starts swinging her arms, trying to rid herself of whatever it is. It only makes matters worse. The clothes fall to the bottom of the closet, the old lady screams 'Help! Someone is stealing my clothes.' The poor girl is grossed out when she realizes that dead bugs are now firmly enmeshed in her beautiful long hair."

The four of them roared with laughter as Nancy imitated the young girl flailing her arms about. "I'll give you one more funny episode, then dinner should be ready."

"Another person frequently comes by to play the piano during recreation hour at the home. She plays beautifully and spent a lot of time learning the old favorites. Most of the older people love to hear her play and the ones who remember the words often sing along. The same day as the flypaper incident, she is seated at the piano playing a selection of Stephen Foster when one old grouch yells at her to 'stop'. He starts booing her and gets up from his chair and tries to extract her from the piano bench. The poor woman gets very upset and tells him to go away. The other patients are getting confused and a few start crying loudly, while some are still singing, and others are yelling at this ill-tempered man to sit down and leave the dark haired lady alone. I think it will be some time before that young person comes back to play a concert for our elderly folks! Whew, what a day that was!"

When she was ready to serve dinner, Nancy said, "If you don't mind, we'll eat in the kitchen tonight. We hardly ever use the dining room; only when we have a large number of dinner guests."

The kitchen itself was huge and had its own alcove with a large, rectangular, glass table that could easily seat twelve people. Outside the large oriel window, spotlights illuminated the seascape below. Massive and jagged rocks, silvery and lustrous in the moonlight, were continuously pounded by the frothy green-blue waves. Suzanne had always enjoyed watching the ocean's powerful waves crash against the shore. It had a calming, hypnotic effect upon her.

As a young teenager, she remembered going to Nantasket Beach with her friends. During summer storms they would walk to the bay or out to the very end of the beach where immense boulders jutted out from the shore. The group of adolescents would gather along the retaining wall, near the ocean, and huddle against each other for protection in the face of the cold, hurling, rain. The waves were sometimes so fierce that they could knock people over, and you could surely drown, if you were foolish enough to get too near the water's edge.

That night, Nancy served Rock Cornish game hens, stuffed with wild rice. After dinner, Suzanne helped Nancy clean up and rinse the dishes before stacking the English china into the dishwasher.

Trying to keep the conversation light, Suzanne asked Nancy, "What do you like to do besides volunteering at the nursing home?"

"I love to read romance novels or mysteries with an exciting story line. Sometimes I get so involved in a story that I'll stay up until two or three in the morning, so I can finish the book and find out the ending."

Laughing, Suzanne replied, "I'm the same way. It's a killer the next day, though. Especially by the time I get home and the girls want me to play with them."

At once Suzanne felt uncomfortable for mentioning the children again. "How could I be so insensitive?" she asked herself. Realizing that Nancy would have probably given anything to be bothered by a child of her own, she redirected the conversation once more. "Your home is magnificent. Someday I'd like to own a house near the ocean like this. It seems so peaceful."

"It is. It's majestic when a storm sets in. I sometimes stand at the window and watch the raindrops, from the approaching gray clouds, as it creeps towards me and over the water. On nice days I love to walk along the sand and let the cool water engulf my feet. It's strange, but I never learned to swim. I've taken lessons, but I don't have the confidence to swim by myself. Deep down, I'm scared of the water. I don't even think I could tread water for very long, even if I had to. I love the water, but I can never fully enjoy it because of that."

Suzanne replied, "That's unbelievable. I can't swim either. I think I'm the only person in the world who flunked the Y's swimming lessons three times. I even took instructions from a private coach. I've taken so many lessons that I couldn't begin to count them. Nothing helped. I'm great when I can hold onto a float or when I'm in a pool knowing I can grab onto the edge, but I panic and lose my balance whenever the water begins to come up over my waist. I can't seem to breathe, and I feel as if I'm suffocating. It's unusual that we both love the water but can't overcome our fear of it. When I was a youngster I dreamed of swimming the English Channel, with throngs of people cheering me on from the shore, or, of being one of the performers at Florida's Bush Gardens. My mother used to tease me and call me Esther Williams. I don't know about you, but I always felt awkward when, as a teenager, my friends would gather at the beach for a party. Without fail, I was invariably petrified some wise guy would throw me into the ocean and I'd drown."

"The same thing would happen to me, only it was when my friends had pool parties at their homes," chuckled Nancy.

"None of my friends had parents rich enough to afford pools."

"I guess it depends on your perspective. I can see that we were well off, although I never really thought of it that way. My father was a surgeon with patients from all over the world. My mother was also a physician. I was sent away to a private boarding school at a very early age."

"I suppose it was because it was so unusual for a woman to be a doctor in those days that my mother felt she had to choose her profession over raising a family. To be perfectly blunt, I think I was a mistake. I never remember my mother taking me in her arms and telling me she loved me, for that matter even consoling me if I fell or bruised myself. My father tried but he was not a demonstrative person either. So you see, I wasn't very close to my parents. I never really felt loved by either of them. I was practically raised by the servants, really! Occasionally, if a governess stayed for any length of time, I'd become attached to her and call her mommy."

While Suzanne had come from a lower, middle class, background and her parents were far from economically stable, and Nancy had come from a very affluent family, Suzanne felt sorry for her. Although Nancy had material things and the best education as a child, she had been largely ignored by her parents and still felt the pain and sting of that neglect.

While Nancy talked, Suzanne watched her mannerisms and took note of her looks. Nancy was rather tall and a large-boned woman, but because she knew how to choose the right kind of clothing, she appeared slim. She had an oblong face that was framed by a heavy mane of curly red hair. Her large, green eyes, with flecks of gold, sparkled as she talked. Suzanne was surprised to see that Nancy's teeth were crooked. She was somewhat puzzled and wondered "With all her family's money, why didn't they bother to correct her teeth?" Suzanne remembered her own parents saying that they were thankful that she didn't need braces, but if they were required, she surely would get them.

Suzanne liked Nancy and enjoyed hearing the stories about Europe and her student days at boarding school. After relating a number of episodes, Nancy quietly mentioned, "My parents both died quite unexpectedly." Suzanne looked for sorrow in Nancy's eyes as she related the details of their deaths, but found them strangely vacant.

"They had flown to Portugal for a medical conference, where my father was a guest speaker. After the conference they were to take a private plane to Africa to another symposium. They never made it. The small, single engine airplane crashed in the Ahaggar Mountains in Algeria. It took the authorities a while to find them, then another whole week to locate and tell me about their accident."

"I met Peter a few months later while I was vacationing on the Riviera with a couple of my girlfriends. He'd gone to France with some of his pals to see what Europe was all about."

"Peter was from a very different background than I was. His parents were both educators and had the two boys. Peter always had an artistic flair about him, but unlike his brother, who painted, he performed his artistry on people. Although he graduated from a very good school for hair design they were disappointed, and would have preferred to see their son go on to college and become a *professional*."

Peter cut in on their conversation, "Hey Nancy, what's keeping the two of you? Stop monopolizing Suzanne. Did you fall into the sink? Come on out here and keep us company. I haven't seen my beautiful wife all week!"

"I was telling Suzanne my life story if you don't mind. I was just getting into how we met before you so rudely interrupted!"

"Okay, sweetie, I'm sorry. Don't exclude us. Let me tell her my version of the story."

"Be my guest."

Suzanne was relieved to hear Nancy and Peter joking with each other. The annoyances she had noticed earlier seemed to have dissipated and the ease between them returned.

"My parent's loved Nancy. She had education, a college degree from Brown, no less, and she was rich," related Peter.

"Don't forget, pretty, interjected Alan."

"Well, that's a given."

"Before I was rudely interrupted, where was I, oh yes. While lying on the beach one Thursday afternoon just outside of Cap-Ferrat, enjoying all the beautiful sights and bodies, I spotted these three really nice looking gals. Thinking that they were French, my friends and I went up to them and tried to communicate in a combination of sign language and our rudimentary French. Of course, they pretended not to understand us. For some reason it never occurred to us that they'd be Americans. Of course, since they'd been educated in Europe, they spoke a variety of foreign languages fluently, including French. We finally managed to make dates with them for that evening. We felt rather proud of ourselves since we now had dates with these three very fine, very attractive, very French women."

"Those girls kept us completely snowed for four full days. Can you believe it? Finally, on Sunday in the late afternoon, the six of us were attempting to cross a narrow back street in Cannes and a speeding driver careened around the corner heading directly for us. I jumped out of the way quickly and landed in a grove of palm trees. Why he didn't hit at least one of the others, I'll never know. As he flew by, Nancy forgot herself, and told him what he could do, in what can only be described as a genuine American English curse. The other guys broke out in laughter, but I just laid there speechless, looking at her. I was so mad. She'd fooled me and I had to admit I loved it.

Right then and there I fell in love and wanted her to stay with me forever. I had no idea how rich she was, so Nancy can't ever accuse me of falling for her because of her money!"

As they sipped espresso and enjoyed chocolate raspberry mousse while sitting in front of a fire in the huge marble and stone fireplace, Peter turned serious. "Here we've been bending your ear about ourselves and haven't let you get a word in edgewise. Tell us about yourself."

"There's not that much to tell. I didn't have a very exciting life compared to the two of you." She went on to tell them about her parents and relatives, growing up in Dorchester and moving to Quincy as a teenager. She told them about her children, Mrs. Walsh, and, briefly, about Brian, omitting the abuse she and Hope had suffered at his hands. She was ashamed that she hadn't been able to prevent him from hurting Hope and was embarrassed that she had taken his mistreatment for so long. She felt that the fewer people who knew what she had gone through, the better.

She then went on to tell them of her professional goals and her dreams for a better future for herself and her children. Suzanne told them she loved to imagine how people could improve their image and self esteem with the right clothes and make-up. "I'd love to teach people, from all economic levels, the way to properly take care of themselves. "But, please don't get me started, because I can go on all night about this!"

Turning his attention to Suzanne, Peter said, "I have an ulterior motive for this little dinner. "You've probably already guessed that, though. We wanted to get to know you better and I think we've done that tonight. You and I have the same ambitions. I've always been driven to earn my own money. I can't let everyone think that Nancy is the sole support of this household," Peter laughed and then continued, "Seriously, I think we might be able to reach our goals faster if we pool our energies and resources and combine our businesses. What would you think of an enterprise like that? I think it would be great if the two of us were in business together. We can work out the details as to money and responsibilities later, but it seems that when two energetic people feel as passionately as we do about our professions, that it only makes sense to combine forces. I'd handle the usual rituals of a beauty salon - hair, manicures, pedicures; you'd handle the esthetics end of the business - facials, make-up, massages, spa treatments, electrolysis, and so forth."

With anticipation, Nancy and Peter waited for her response. Suzanne was stunned. She had enjoyed the companionship of her new friends, but was taken completely by surprise by this turn of events. "I'm overwhelmed," Suzanne spoke honestly. "I never expected to hear something like this tonight."

"Don't get me wrong. I think it's a great idea but you must realize that I've no money to speak of. I mean 'nada.' I don't know where I'll stand once the divorce is final since Brian never let me know how much money we had or where it was. I've known for a long time that I can't depend on him. I must do it on my own. But, I'm starting from scratch, I'm afraid." With apprehension, she held her breath and then thought, "What the heck? I might as well go for it." She considered what she had to lose - nothing - and intuitively proceeded.

"All I can say is that if you put up the money I'd need to start the esthetics part of the business, I'd promise to pay you back at the going interest rate. I'm not afraid of hard work, and, thanks to Mrs. Walsh, I don't have to worry about the children. I do want to be honest with you, though. If the girls ever need me in an emergency, I must be there for them."

Suzanne and Peter continued talking about the possibilities of their joint undertaking, and the more they talked, the more excited she became. Suddenly Suzanne realized that it had gotten very late and she had stayed longer than she had planned. Mrs. Walsh would be exhausted. She had been up since five and it was now almost two in the morning. Looking at Peter and Nancy and shaking her head, she continued, "I can't believe this offer. Let me go home and sleep on it. I'll call you tomorrow." Just before leaving she turned, embracing both Nancy and Peter "I can't thank you enough."

Once outside, Suzanne pinched herself to make sure she was not dreaming. She stopped on the brick walkway to take another quick look at the ocean, now glimmering under the full moon. She inhaled deeply. The salt air smelled wonderful. "Someday, I'll own a home like this, maybe not quite as big, but overlooking the ocean for sure."

She had already made up her mind about the business venture.

When she called Peter the next day, they made plans to meet with a general contractor on the following Friday.

The contractor, Tom Donovan, was a large, robust gentleman in his late forties. His blue eyes had a twinkle and, when combined with his Irish wit, he put them at ease immediately. He had expertise in the construction business. Suzanne knew he would recommend the best possible way to redo the shop without breaking the bank, this bank being Nancy's inheritance.

Suzanne told Tom what she had in mind. Taking the number of required stations and treatment areas into consideration, he came up with some unique ideas. He told them he would go home, figure the costs and get back to them in a couple of days. Later, the following week, he presented them with his designs and walked them through the proposed salon - on paper. His concepts were everything that Peter and Suzanne had envisioned.

Suzanne borrowed thirty-five thousand dollars from Nancy and then gave Tom the go ahead to begin the esthetics division. "The only thing that bothers me is that I have to make a rapid move from my present salon to the new one. I've got to keep the old salon open and generating income as long as possible, then immediately have everything ready to move in. Are you sure that you can get this project finished by the date we need? Man, this is scary," Peter told his old high school friend as he paced back and forth, waiting for Tom to finish the measurements.

"I promise I'll get it done as quickly as I can old buddy, but the shop will be messy at times. If I can get my men to work evenings, early mornings, and Sundays, that'll help. When we're here during the day, the banging and drilling will drive you nuts, but just bear with us, okay? I'll even bring a few brewskies for later, when the men are through and you and I can commiserate."

"We don't have much choice, do we? I know you'll do the best you can, and I'll keep my grumbling down to a minimum."

Peter had a difficult time concentrating as he drove home. "I've always been a risk-taker and I've got good vibes about this venture. I've got to prove that I don't need Nancy's money to make it. Our salon will become very big and famous people will come flocking to us. I'll keep Nancy so busy she won't miss having children," he thought as he passed a school bus filled with elementary students coming home from some sort of school activity.

"Kids, who needs them anyway? Sure, they're cute when they're small and cuddly and can't talk, but who needs the headaches when they get older?" He lit a joint and waited in the driveway to mellow out before he went into the house.

When Suzanne got home from their meeting, she sat on the playroom sofa and rested her head between her two hands. She couldn't believe that she had signed a note for thirty-five thousand dollars. She called Beverly, and related in detail, the situation that had led to her borrowing so much money. Then she added, "And, you and I both know that everything always goes over budget. What the hell am I going to do when that happens? I must be out of my mind," she moaned.

"Suzanne, you're a bright, intelligent woman, but you don't have enough confidence in yourself. Wake up. You'll make the money to repay Nancy. You're lucky Nancy could lend it to you. No bank would've ever lent you that kind of money, even if you were having an affair with the president of a financial institution. Well, maybe, if you promised to give him a blow job, every day." They both laughed. Continuing, Beverly said, "Besides, while Brian is still paying for the house and the girls' expenses, take the money that you make on the sale of your paintings and invest it in the business. If you do that, you won't have to borrow any more capitol. I've some cash stashed away, too, and I can lend you some if you go over. Don't worry."

The next few months flew by. Suzanne flew to California, New York, Texas and Ohio, meeting chemists who could supply her with the specialized products she wanted. She spent many hours looking at equipment and supplies. She became friendly with other estheticians that had established their own enterprises and took much of their advice.

One esthetician she particularly liked was Madam Churnick, a Russian woman who had been in the esthetics business for many years. Madam Churnick became attached to Suzanne immediately and enjoyed her unspoiled enthusiasm. This beautiful immigrant taught her pupil many valuable lessons, becoming her mentor.

In a thick, heavy Russian accent she related some amusing incidents to Suzanne. "I was so tired one evening that I dozed off in a comfortable chair in my back room while my patient was under the finishing mask. When I woke up I was disoriented. I had forgotten all about her and went about closing up my shop for the evening. My key was in the door when I suddenly remembered that I had a client in one of my rooms. She must have been under the mask for about forty minutes, when she normally would have been there for about twelve to fifteen minutes. I quietly put back on all the lights and then opened the door to the back room. There she was, totally unaware of the time, her mouth wide open, snoring to beat the band."

"Suzanne, one thing I will tell you. Keep this foremost in your mind, the customer is always right, no matter what. Always remember that when you're dealing with the public you must be a saint. Develop your reputation by doing your best and placing your clients' interests and their welfare first. If a client is unpleasant, go beyond that behavior and continue to treat her courteously. If you can do this, you'll reap many benefits from your business, and they won't all be financial. You'll meet many wonderful people whom you'll cherish."

*A Sidewalk on Newbury Street, Boston, Massachusetts •
June 6, 1973*

After many grueling hours of preparation and hard work, Peter, Nancy, and Suzanne were ready to open their mini spa. One April morning as they stood on the sidewalk outside the front door, with clients, friends, and family beside them, Suzanne pulled on the tassel that loosened the covering that was wrapped around the logo that Alan and Suzanne had designed themselves. As the fabric dropped to the ground, it revealed a brilliantly colored butterfly, just out of its cocoon, resting on top of the mini spa's name - *Metamorphosis Salon.*

The business at their Newbury Street salon took off in no time flat. Word of mouth spread rapidly and many notables frequented the spa once word got out that *Metamorphosis Salon* was the "in place" to go. As he had predicted, Peter and Suzanne worked well as a team. Peter and his staff put the finishing touches to a great number of Suzanne's clients. Suzanne soon hired more estheticians and personally trained them. She was a good boss; she expected loyalty and respect from them. In return she gave her employees the same. Suzanne's patience and guidance paid off, young, area estheticians wanted to work and learn from Suzanne at *Metamorphosis Salon.*

They worked many long, grueling hours that first year. Various affluent clients wanted daytime hours, while the clientele with careers of their own needed to come in after working all day. Suzanne wanted to be available for all possible customers and she soon had so much business that she kept the salon open six days a week, from eight thirty until nine on weekdays and from eight thirty until five on Saturdays. Frequently, by the time her last client left and she was able to take care of the day's receipts, she didn't leave the salon till nine thirty or ten o'clock in the evening.

Suzanne could never have been able to keep those hours if she didn't have Mrs. Walsh with her to take care of the girls. Mrs. Walsh had given up her apartment in Waltham and moved permanently to Suzanne's house. Suzanne hoped that she could get a loan from a bank soon, to add a fourth bedroom for her housekeeper and friend.

The busier she became, the more she missed being with her daughters. Since Mrs. Walsh had Sundays off, Suzanne spent that day religiously with her children. She looked forward to these special days and planned diverse events that would be fun for all of them. When inclement weather forced them to stay indoors, Suzanne taught them how to bake and cook many of the ethnic recipes that had been passed down from her grandmothers.

It wasn't easy being a working mom who was running her own business. On her one day off she would have loved to just let the rest of the world go by and not be bothered by anything or anyone, including parents and children. But, having an ample share of Jewish guilt, she felt she had to be super mom and daughter.

The first five years passed quickly. Suzanne was able to pay off the loan from Nancy faster than she ever thought possible. *Metamorphosis Salon* won an award from Boston Magazine as the best esthetics salon in New England. Just after the fifth anniversary of the opening of the day spa, Peter and Suzanne came to realize that their location was no longer large enough for their operation. They had some space available in the basement of their building that they had been using for storage. However, if they tried to expand the salon in that direction, they would need to find another area for storage space. They finally had to accept reality. They didn't have enough room in their present place for the substantial expansion that they both realized must be accomplished soon, if the spa was to continue to grow.

In the meantime, Brian's business had become successful through his diligent efforts. After they first separated he tried in vain to win Suzanne back. He just wouldn't or couldn't accept that she was serious about the divorce. Eventually, after two full years, he had to accept the fact that there was no hope for reconciliation. He went on with his own life, but became vindictive towards her once that realization set in.

Brian arrived back at his apartment a little after eleven-thirty in the evening. He poured himself a drink and automatically turned on the television, not paying attention to what was on. Swirling the amber liquid in the tumbler, he tried to force the angry thoughts out of his mind. "She thinks she's so high and mighty. She's still the same bitch she was before her stupid salon became successful." Her face appeared, like a mirage, in the alcohol. Trying to erase her vivid reflection, he quickly downed the warm scotch and poured himself another. "Who does she think she is anyway? I hope she's miserable without me. I know she misses me. I see it in her eyes when I pick up the kids. She must be busting her ass and working hard to be able to pay off her bills." Laughing to himself, he thought, "She must shit a brick every time I'm late with my payments. Good. It serves her right. I have a mind to call my attorney and ask for custody of the kids, cause she's never home. That would really shake her up. I wish my mom would let me take them to see her. I don't understand why she's taking this divorce out on the children. It's not their fault we're getting divorced. It's all her fault for not trying it one more time." Tears brimmed around his eyes. "God I miss seeing the girls every day. I guess it'll get worse as they get older. They'll become teenagers, have their own lives and friends, and won't have time for me. I'll be lucky if I see them once every few months." Taking a deep breath, he suddenly felt old and tired. "I guess I have to get on with my life; Suzanne certainly has with hers. Someday I'll find a woman who'll appreciate me, and if Suzanne wants me back, I'd laugh and say 'Sorry. You had your chance.' "

While they were negotiating the divorce settlement, he continued to do whatever he could to make Suzanne's life miserable. At one point he threatened to file a complaint against her as an unfit mother. On what basis, she never found out. When that failed, he played mind games with her. Sometimes, he would promise to pick up the children at a certain time and then would arrive anywhere from one hour to two hours late. Another trick was to bring them home very late on school nights, which made getting them up for school the next morning a frustrating chore. He questioned the girls constantly about Suzanne's schedule and tried to find out if she was dating anyone, not that she was. She was interested in her daughters and the salon. Nothing else could matter if she was going to make a go of it on her own.

To make matters worse, Brian's parents disowned their own granddaughters. All pictures of their granddaughters were removed from their home. They stopped acknowledging the children's birthdays and ignored the holidays. As much as their behavior hurt the girls, Suzanne realized it must have hurt Brian terribly. Knowing him as well as she did, Suzanne waited for the vendetta she knew was inevitable.

Although his company was doing well, he continually strove to make things difficult for Suzanne by being constantly late with his child support payments. When Brian withheld his required obligation, it added to the stress level of her life. It was especially hard on Suzanne when she had first gone into business with Peter. They had invoices to pay weekly and monthly. She couldn't expect Peter, or Nancy, to carry her while she tried to keep up with her bills at home. Many times she wasn't sure if she would have enough money to pay the mortgage or buy groceries.

For years Brian's antics continued to provoke and exasperate Suzanne. After the first five years, his conduct seemed to improve, but occasionally he would do something to stir up trouble. Eventually things took a turn for the better.

Chapter Ten

Massachusetts • April, 1975

Peter was not usually a heavy drinker, and Suzanne thought it odd that he was tipsy tonight. Something else seemed wrong too, but she could not quite put her finger on it. Nancy, Peter, Alan, and Suzanne were dining out and talking about their business. "You know, we really are a good team," Peter said boastfully, after consuming three Manhattans.

Nancy joked to Suzanne, "Wait till I get him home, if we make it, I'll have a good time with him."

Suzanne and Nancy talked about the business. "We should seriously think about expanding soon." Suzanne said to Nancy. "Peter and I have already discussed it, and this is a good night to tell you about our ideas and ask your opinion."

"Will you be able to carry on an intelligent conversation, or should we wait till you've had less to drink?" Suzanne asked Peter.

"No, really, I'm fine. Waiter, would you please bring me a carafe of coffee, black, please. Suzanne, go ahead; shoot."

"Okay. Well, as you know, there's no more room for expansion in our spa, so we've been looking at other options. We think that we could open another salon in another large city, probably New York City. We want New York, because of its location. It's close to Boston and, by plane, travel time is minimal. However, the rent will be astronomical, and we'll have to do heavy advertising and a lot of promotional work as well.

"I have a friend from school, who can manage it for us. She's honest and she's good. Peter mentioned that Michael is ready to leave Boston, and would go to New York. As much as Michael's clients will miss him, he would be more valuable to us in this new location. I also feel that Peter and I should have some special clients at the new salon. It's important to keep in touch with area clients personally. Have I rambled on too much? What do you think?" Suzanne asked of Nancy and Alan.

Alan looked at them, amazed. "When in hell have the two of you had time to discuss all of this?"

"Well, we do have to take a break once in a while you know. Over tea and coffee we often talk about our future salons. Only we never realized that it would come as fast as it did," replied Suzanne as she poured another cup of tea from the hot pot.

"First of all, we'll have to go to New York and find a good location. We want enough space so that we won't have to worry about expansion in another few years."

"I'd like to add a couple of electrologists to our staff to rid people of their hair problems permanently. We'll need separate rooms for waxing and special rooms for bodywork as well. We should hire a holistic health practitioner as well as an aerobics trainer. The laundry facility will be on premises, as it is in our Newbury Street salon. I would like Olga, our massage therapist, help us find and interview other massage therapists."

"You're talking a lot of space, maybe 4000 to 5000 square feet. It's going to cost a fortune," said Alan.

"I know I'm optimistic, but do you honestly feel this large an investment will pay off? Nancy asked.

"If we manage it carefully, I'm sure of it," said Suzanne. "But, we'll have to work our butts off. We'll have to do custom training of the new staff as well. I want the clients to feel pampered. It's very important that they feel that their well-being is our foremost concern."

"Well, are you ready to shop for our new furniture?"

"Let's go to New York next week and start looking for a location. Suzanne, do you think you and Peter can get away for a few days?"

"We'll have to, especially if this comes about, we'll be traveling back and forth for quite a while."

New York City • The Big Apple • August, 1975

As she observed the diverse ethnic groups blending as New Yorkers, she could see why these people had so much vitality. They had to keep moving or they'd be caught in the stampede and be squashed by the hustling masses.

Suzanne, Nancy, and Peter discussed their budget and requirements with Mrs. Cain, a very self-assured and competent realtor. After two hours in her office they left to look at some properties. The day was long and frustrating, as they fought the city traffic, traveling from one possible site to another. All the available places were more than the partners were willing to pay. They were frustrated, but made another appointment for the following day.

At the end of the day Alan surprised them at the hotel when they returned from their expedition.

"I'm so glad you could take some time off from your busy schedule and join us," Suzanne said.

"I've finished my courses and my dream of owning my own gallery isn't far from becoming a reality. Justin may be a silent partner; we still have some details to work out. By the way, he sends his love to you all. I can only stay for a few days, so while you're busy with business arrangements, I'll be visiting some people he suggested I see. They have contacts that might be beneficial to me. Meanwhile where do you want me to put my bags?" he asked as he plopped down on the bed in front of the window.

"Well since there are two large queen size beds in this room, why spend the money on another one? You'll be safe with me!" Suzanne teased.

Over the time that Suzanne had known Alan a bond had developed between them. She regarded him as a trusted friend. She wasn't interested in dating and didn't want any romantic involvement. Alan was the perfect male companion for her. In fact, he had become the brother she never had. She looked over at him, resting peacefully on his bed, and she remembered a significant conversation that had changed their relationship.

One evening after they had gone to dinner and returned to his apartment, Alan confided certain feelings to Suzanne that he couldn't share with anyone else.

"Can I get you an after dinner drink?"

"No thanks, I still have to drive home and I want a clear head, though a cup of tea would be fine." They sat on the living room sofa while the sounds of the city reverberated outside.

Alan blurted out his feelings. "I feel so lonely living here. Sometimes it's so quiet I can hear a pin drop. I wish I could find someone to share my life."

"Alan, I'm in contact with some lovely women who would give anything to meet a man like you. It's hard to find single men these days. If you're not into the bars or the single's scene, it's difficult. What would you say if I tried to fix you up?"

"You've become my best friend, and I should be honest with you. I don't know exactly how to say this, or even where to begin." Clearing his throat, he loosened his tie and pushed his hair back to one side with his hand. He put his feet on the edge of the brass and glass coffee table and began. "Don't say anything until I'm finished, okay?" Suzanne nodded. "I guess as far back as I can remember I always felt an attraction to guys."

"Stay calm and try not to show any emotion," she cautioned herself as he went on.

"When I was younger, I tried to read up on homosexuality, but in those days there was very little written about it, for the lay person that is. As I reached puberty I forced myself to like girls. Whenever I did start going out with one girl rather steadily, I never felt aroused when we kissed. I'd hear Peter talking to his friends about dates and I was more interested listening to the guys than in what they did with the chicks. Peter fixed me up with some nymphs he knew, and if they started to like me, I would discourage them. I felt foolish."

"I guess I was ashamed of my real thoughts and feelings. Rather than acting on my impulses, I ignored them. I didn't want to be one of the 'queers,' (accenting the word as he said it) as Peter and his friends labeled them."

"Rather than give into my emotions, I have resisted dating anyone. You know that I don't consider going out with you dating. I've thought carefully about my situation and to be honest with you, I don't know what to do. One part of me says, 'Screw it and look for a nice guy.' The other part of me doesn't want to hurt my family. I don't want to take the chance of loosing them."

"I know you can't tell me what to do, but I'm being torn apart. Should I take my chances and tell the family my true feelings, or should I try to date a woman again? Maybe I would feel differently if the right female came along. I'd love nothing better than to have children. I see what a great relationship you have with yours." With the heavy burden finally lifted, he looked at Suzanne and a lone tear fell onto his cheek.

Alan had confirmed Suzanne's suspicions. Her heart ached for her dear friend. Putting her arms around him, tenderly hugging this wonderful man, she tried consoling him. "That's such a heavy burden you've had to live with. I can't imagine suppressing your true feelings all these years. Thank you for confiding in me." They both sighed. Suzanne paused for a few seconds.

"Come on, it isn't as bad as you're making it out to be. I know your parents, and they love you very much. I doubt if you spoke to them this way, they'd reject or disown you. It might be hard for them to accept it, but they must want what's best for you. Anyway, if you dated a woman, you have to take her feelings into account. She might come to care strongly for you and if you can't reciprocate, she could be hurt."

"I remember how insecure I felt when Brian was fooling around on me. I can't begin to explain how badly I felt. I thought I wasn't attractive enough. I've had a hard time learning to trust. I still don't think I'll ever be able to depend on a man again. If you were dating someone, she would probably feel terrible if you didn't make sexual advances towards her eventually."

"It's a Catch-22. On the other hand, how do I meet a nice guy, who's not promiscuous?"

She reached for Alan's hands, and squeezed them assuredly. "I really don't know what to say. Have you talked to a professional? It might be helpful and it certainly couldn't hurt. I hope you know that whatever you do, I'll be here for you."

Suzanne drove home under a cloud of confusion. For a while now she had wondered about his sexual preference, but often berated herself. "It's none of my business. He's my friend and his sexuality shouldn't get in the way of my affection for him. My God, the poor guy. I'm so sorry he's going through this turmoil - all these years, never able to be himself. I hope if he tells his family, that they'll be supportive of him. I think Peter and Nancy will be okay with it. I feel honored that I'm the first person he unburdened himself to. I must remember to keep my mouth shut until he decides what to do."

She made a silent prayer. "God, keep an eye on Alan. He's going to need all of your help and guidance."

It seemed like years ago that they had that particular conversation. They had both experienced the hardships and triumphs of life since then. Looking over at Alan, sitting across from her on his bed, she felt nothing but admiration for this gentleman, in every sense of the word.

Three days went by, and still they found nothing. If they saw something that they liked, it was already taken, or the asking price was too high. On the fourth day a breathless Mrs. Cain called them at the hotel. "Mr. Tremblay, something just came onto the market that I thought you and your partner should see right away. The owner of a men's store, a very exclusive one, died suddenly, and their family doesn't want any part of the business. Really, you should see it immediately. The location is supreme, and you might be able to negotiate the price because it would be a takeover on a lease. The store has 4,800 hundred square feet. Do you want to look at it today?"

The store on West 56th street was situated among sensational boutiques and jewelry stores. When they saw the location, Suzanne squeezed Nancy's hand and said, "Can you believe this? It's near all the fine shops and not far from the major hotels."

Mrs. Cain showed them around the building and expounded on the advantages of the location. "Mr. Poughami, God rest his soul, was a fine gentleman, and his store has a wonderful reputation. Unfortunately, neither his wife nor children want to continue in the business. You were fortunate to be here when his untimely death occurred. Well, it was timely for you, though," she said, as a nervous laugh escaped her. He had a long term lease, which is very difficult to get these days. If you can take it over, this may be the answer."

To make use of the entire 4,800 square feet they would have to use the basement level as well as the upper floor. They called Tom Donovan and asked him to fly to New York. Although he was quite busy, he agreed to postpone the work he was doing and meet with them at the prospective location.

The next day they met him at the store and went over the details. "You're lucky I have such a good memory, and remember what you need from working on your other spa. This time it will be easier because the building is empty and I won't have to work around people. I can do what I have to do, without worrying about the noise level or somebody getting injured on the site. I'll try to keep the cost down, and I know you want me to do the work as quickly as possible. Why is it that all my customers want my work to be done yesterday? It will take about a week for me to figure the cost projection. Can you hold them off for that time?"

"We'll try to, and meanwhile, we'll start pricing the equipment and furniture that we'll need. Let's go out for dinner, my treat, you Irish leprechaun," Peter pronounced.

Nancy was very excited about being in New York and she asked Suzanne to go shopping with her.

"I'd love to go with you, but I don't know if we'll have time. I can't believe I'm saying this. No, really, I have to visit the showrooms for the equipment and then I thought you'd help me find furniture for the waiting rooms."

"Are you kidding? I'll help you find and price everything that we'll need and in record time, so that you won't have an excuse to get out of our shopping expedition."

"It's not that I don't want to explore the city, but I honestly don't think we'll be able to do any sightseeing. But, knowing you, you'll have me finish my work in no time, and then you'll be able to show me all of New York. I'd love to see everything, from the Bronx, Brooklyn, Staten Island, The Statue of Liberty, Harlem, Greenwich Village to the trendy boutiques of Manhattan," exclaimed Suzanne.

Suzanne turned pensive. "Seriously, do you think we can afford the rent? The cost of the inside work alone, without the fixtures or furniture will be exorbitant."

"Look, I don't think this place is going to be on the market long. I think we should grab it. As long as my stocks keep their value and I still have my money, we'll be able to survive over the first few months."

While they waited for Tom's figures, Nancy and Suzanne picked out the furniture and wallpaper for the spa. They selected Louis XV antiques with Oriental items scattered throughout the waiting area and the rest of the salon. Soft colors, predominantly mauve tones, were used for the elegant silk flower arrangements as centerpieces for the tables. Glass and brass would dominate the work area with white tile and glass for the working stations. Plants and large oriental prints would be placed throughout the spa.

Suzanne contacted the newspapers for advertising prices and worked that into her projected budget. With most of the preliminary work done, Nancy and Suzanne were ready to do some serious shopping. At least, Nancy was. Suzanne didn't have any money for a buying spree, but she did want to bring back souvenirs for the girls.

As she got ready to go shopping with Nancy, the telephone rang. "Hi" Suzanne answered.

"Suzanne, it's me."

From her mother's tone of voice, Suzanne knew something was very wrong. She hoped it wasn't one of the children. She began to panic, but let her talk.

"I hate to call you like this, but I'm afraid I have some bad news." Suzanne's heart was beating rapidly. "Are you there?"

Losing her patience, "Yes. Just tell me what's wrong."

"It's your Grandmother Pessa. She died sometime last evening. I went to her bedroom to wake her this morning when she didn't come down for breakfast. I thought it was odd since she's usually up before me."

She started crying over the telephone with heart-wrenching sobs contorting her speech. "Oh, what am I going to do? I love her so."

"Mom, try to calm down. Did she suffer? Where's Dad?" asked Suzanne.

"No, no, she went peacefully, I think. She looks very serene. Your father is waiting outside for the authorities."

"Mom, I'll catch the next flight out of here, and be home with you by tomorrow. I'm sorry that she died, but I'm glad she went peacefully, and didn't suffer." Suzanne sobbed into the telephone receiver.

Suzanne got a flight out that evening. Nancy and Peter insisted on driving Suzanne to the airport. They would stay in New York until they finished the business arrangements, sign the necessary papers, once they determined the total cost, and then get back to Boston.

Suzanne was visibly upset, but assured them she would be okay alone on the plane. "Figure out everything and if you think it will work, go ahead and sign. Get everything straightened out here, and I'll see you in the next couple of days."

"We'll call you to find out about the funeral arrangements." They hugged her and didn't leave until she boarded the plane for home.

Suzanne sat numbly by the window staring out at the lights below. Many thoughts passed through her mind. Pessa, her beloved Pessa, was like another mother to her. After Suzanne was born, she and her parents shared the same apartment with her maternal grandparents. How she loved that manipulative old woman. She had to get her own way, and wouldn't stop nudging people until she did. She remembered when she and her parents were leaving Dorchester and moving out of the apartment that they had shared with Mama Pessa and Papa Abe, to move into their own house in Quincy. She recalled the many years of her life before moving. Suzanne's head was spinning and the years came back to her as if they were yesterday.

Dorchester, Massachusetts • 1950

At the time, Dorchester was not considered part of Boston itself. Many Jewish immigrants settled into this tight community after moving from Roxbury, East Boston, and the West End. Suzanne and her parents shared the five-room, third-floor apartment with her maternal grandparents.

The apartment was typical of the area with a large living and dining room. Mama Pessa and Papa Abe turned the dining room into a third bedroom. Beautiful French doors separated these rooms. A front foyer, containing a mahogany hope chest and corner shelves filled with knickknacks, that led to her parent's small bedroom, was the first room one saw when they entered the bright, clean apartment. Suzanne's large bedroom was located at the rear, next to the tiny bathroom. The free standing sink and the enameled, clawed pedestal bathtub took up the whole room. A small frosted window over the tub let in filtered light. The toilet had a pull chain to flush the debris. Suzanne still said 'pull the chain' when referring to flushing the toilet. The big kitchen had a pantry located off towards the back of the building where an icebox and wood stove lined the wall. An oblong maple table in the center of the kitchen was the focal point of many family gatherings.

All the tenements had both front and back porches. Poor Papa Abe could not enjoy his evening cigar in his own apartment. Mama Pessa would not allow the foul smelling cheroot to stink up her immaculate home. In any kind of weather, fair or foul, you could find Papa Abe out on the porch, enjoying his evening smoke. Suzanne watched him many times, pacing back and forth, inhaling the hot gray vapor taking pleasure in his one indulgence. At times he looked as if he were far away - his mind hundreds of miles from this tiny four by ten-foot front porch.

The brown three and six-deck apartment houses were situated very close to one another. On oppressively hot summer days when the windows were opened to let some fresh air into the stuffy rooms, Suzanne could hear her neighbors' conversations as if she were in the same room with them. When Suzanne was in a mischievous mood she would irritate her grandparents by yelling 'God bless you' when one of the neighbors sneezed. It infuriated her Grandmother and Papa Abe that their neighbors would think they were listening to their conversations.

When Suzanne was in a particularly rambunctious mood she would take apple-cores from her secret hiding place and propel them towards her neighbor across the street, Mr. Weinstein. She watched him closely, waiting until she thought he was napping, then aim at his shoes that were resting on the porch railing. Her parents would get so angry with her when Mr. Weinstein yelled at her from across the street and cursed at her in Yiddish. Of course, Suzanne, crouched behind her railing, never knew how Mr. Weinstein figured out who it was.

Suzanne had mixed emotions about moving. She loved the idea of living in Quincy, and meeting new friends, but she was concerned about leaving Mama Pessa and Papa Abe. It would be strange not to see them every day. Not only was she doted on by her parents and grandparents, but by her many aunts and uncles as well. Suzanne was the first grandchild on both sides of the family. Her relatives recalled stories about the "old country" - Lithuania, Poland or Russia - while they sat around the kitchen table. They spoke in Yiddish a good portion of the time, especially when they didn't want Suzanne to know what was being said.

After Dorothy and Morris decided to move, Mama Pessa went to Suzanne. "Suzannala, cume mit me, I vant to give you someting." Taking Suzanne's hand she led her to the bedroom, opened the closet and reaching to the very end pulled out her traveling chest. "I vant you to take this mit you to your new house. Me, I'm getting cold and old. I don't think I'll be moving again except ven God decides to take me, and then I von't be using my trunk. I know how much you enjoy it. You have it Mamala, and pass it on to your children. It will be something to remember your old Mama by."

She presented her with the possession that meant everything to her - the ancient trunk with the arched, copper top. She brought few possessions with her on that long journey from Katringa, Lithuania to Boston, Massachusetts in 1904 when she was 15 years old. The trunk was one of them. Inside it, Pessa's mother had packed a beautiful brass Shabbas candlestick holder for her Friday evening prayers and two pewter serving spoons, which Suzanne remembered using at holiday meals. Also inside were Mama Pessa's cherished photographs of her parents, sisters, and relatives. Apart from recollections of her family life, the pictures and these few belongings were all she had to remember her family by.

Suzanne was overwrought. She remembered the many hours she had studied these pictures looking for features she may have inherited from her distant relatives. It seemed Suzanne's deep set, large brown eyes and joyous smile were the only looks she acquired from seeing and observing pictures of her great grandfather; for Mama Pessa looked very much like him. In most of the pictures the people were very serious, showing no emotion. Suzanne had found two pictures of her great-grandfather smiling, and from these she saw where her own smile had come from.

She loved being able to walk to the specialty shops along Morton Street and Blue Hill Avenue. The Jewish bakery shop, where her mama always stopped to buy the bagels, chula, and dark pumpernickel breads. The bulky rolls were crusty on the outside, yet soft and moist on the inside. For a treat, she would sometimes bring home half moons.

Suzanne remembered helping Mama Pessa make strudel, and special farmer cheese pie with a fancy braided crust. Mama Pessa liked baking her own chula for the holidays. She also had Suzanne help her make mundel bread, kichels, and tagelachs. Suzanne would listen attentively as Mama Pessa reminisced about the farm she grew up on. Mama Pessa's mother was a wonderful pastry cook and owned a bakery where she sold her homemade baked goods. Every time Suzanne saw a goat, it reminded her of mama's stories about the goat milk she enjoyed as a young girl on the farm in Lithuania.

One of her favorite places was the G. & G. Delicatessen, on Blue Hill Avenue. Suzanne went there with her parents when she was young. When she got older she went there with her friends after bowling or the movies. They had a large variety of cold meats, luncheon meats, blintzes, salami, pastrami, smoked fishes, all kinds of pickles in large barrels, lox, knishes, chopped liver, cheeses, and desserts to make your mouth water. Men and women sat around the tables discussing community affairs and exchanging witticisms. Hearing the different dialogues made Suzanne smile.

Once, when Suzanne thought she was really a 'young lady' she ordered a glass of tea, "In a cup, please." Many years later Suzanne still laughed about that incident.

She thought that everyone drank tea from a glass. She would remember seeing her grandfather drinking his tea from a glass, holding a sugar cube in his mouth, between his teeth, so the sweetness would enhance its flavor. When she was older and started dating, a favorite deli would be Jack and Marion's in Brookline, a similar type of deli, only more upscale.

At this time the famous G. & G. was only a memory. The stores of her memories were no longer there, for most of the Jewish population had moved some years later. The storefronts that she remembered vividly were now barred with heavy black metal to keep out intruders.

Holidays would be different now since her grandparents did not drive a car. Her father would have to pick them up if they wanted to spend the day. Walking to the synagogue was easy in the city. There were many places of worship that you could choose. Be it, Reformed, Conservative, or Orthodox. Suzanne looked forward to getting dressed up for the holidays. In those days, girls usually did not attend the services or learn the Hebrew language, unless you were Orthodox and the women either sat upstairs, or on the opposite side of the room. When she was young, while her papa and father were inside the synagogue dovoning {praying}, she played with all the youngsters on the streets between the temples.

The Jewish holidays were usually in September. At that time of year, acorns fell from the oak trees lining the streets. The young boys would wrap them tightly in a handkerchief, and chase the girls, who would run to escape the painful hit. Suzanne, remembering this, could almost feel the sting on her arms and legs. As she got older, she walked the avenue with her friends, up to the long stone wall at Franklin Field. Many young adults would sit along this lengthy wall, socializing and flirting.

For years Suzanne accompanied her mother and grandmother into the city to go shopping. She knew all their favorite stores and would window-shop for hours. The pungent fragrances of the various perfumes, and colognes would make her feel heady. Mannequins dressed in the latest fashioned outfits would have her imagining how she would look in these styles. After viewing the clothes and pricing the various outfits and accessories, they would then be ready to do some serious buying. God forbid, you should pay full price for clothes. Suzanne had been schooled properly on bargain shopping. Off to the bargain basement for everyone.

Filene's Basement was a world in itself. There were no dressing rooms. You either had to have a vivid imagination, or not mind trying the clothes on, on top of your existing apparel. Occasionally, you could get your friends to surround you, undress, put the outfit on, and pray that no one saw you. Some people, who didn't care if anyone saw them, bared it all to make sure that the garments fit them properly. To avoid extreme embarrassment, it was fortunate that men seldom frequented the women's section. Filene's was noted for having very expensive, designer clothes at reasonable prices. If you shopped often enough, and had the patience to wait for a few weeks, you might see a dress come down in price from seventy dollars to five dollars. That's the kind of bargain Mama Pessa really loved.

Many parents eventually allowed their children to take the train into Boston by themselves. At approximately ten years old Suzanne and most of her friends were allowed to venture out into this shopper's delight. Suzanne and Diane Epstein, her next door neighbor, and very best friend, felt both enthusiasm and trepidation on their first outing to the big city. They got the bus at Norfolk Street and it left them off at Ashmont Station. From Ashmont, they descended the metal stairs to the underground station where they were to take a train to Washington Street.

The ride was noisy and the rocking motion of the large green train was fine, if you were lucky enough, to get a seat. Otherwise, you held onto a dirty leather strap or one of the metal poles by the doors and wondered whose dirty, disgusting hands were there before yours. Suzanne would listen to the older Jewish women's conversation, they didn't realize that Suzanne knew Yiddish, and could understand everything they were saying. The opening to Filene's Basement was just a staircase up from the stop at Washington Street Station.

Even though Suzanne was moving, she vowed never to forget her friends. Diane and she would remain close forever. The girls made plans to visit one another frequently.

Boston, Massachusetts • 1975 • 11:37 p.m.

Suzanne opened her eyes and saw the lights of East Boston and Logan airport ahead. "It seems like a different lifetime. So much has changed in my life and the world since those days in Dorchester," she thought as she departed the airplane. With a heavy heart, she headed home to Stoney Brook by cab.

The next morning Suzanne sat the girls down and tried to explain the sudden death of their great-grandmother. Suzanne tried not to cry in front of them, for she didn't want to upset the youngsters anymore than necessary. She was sure that they would see enough people crying and carrying on when they got to her mother's house. Many tears would be shed - not so much for the deceased. The mourners would cry for themselves because they would miss that particular person, Suzanne would be among them. She knew, with all her heart, that Mama Pessa was in a better place, at peace with herself and with God. With fond memories and love she took the girls to Quincy to help with the preparation of the funeral and the week's Shiva.

Only a few people came to her Grandmother's funeral, most of Pessa's close friends had preceded her through the gates of eternity many years ago. Dorothy came from a small family so most of the people who came to the funeral were her parents' friends and a few of her fathers' relatives. Being from a close knit family, relations from one side of the family felt very close their mochetenister's family. Holding her daughters' hands and comforting them, she was glad that they had been lucky enough to have known and loved their great grandmother.

The traditional prayers were said, and, after a short eulogy by her father's good friend and long-term rabbi, they left for the Jewish cemetery in Sharon. Her Mama Pessa would be laid to rest next to her husband, Abe.

Suzanne felt sad, but she knew that Mama was at peace. As she picked up the shovel of dirt and placed it on the top of Mama Pessa's coffin, she realized that she had now replaced her parents in the lineage of generations. The tears she shed were not tears of grief because her grandmother had died. For a person to have lived well over age ninety was truly a blessing. No, her tears were for the memories and love that she could no longer share with her. She'd never again be able to hold this frail woman in her arms and tell her how much she loved her. She looked down at the shoveled dirt and said her final good-by to the feisty lady who had been devoted to her family. Suzanne would miss her.

A shiver went through Suzanne's body as she stood beside her parents and children. She tried to remember how Mama Pessa looked in her younger years. She hoped that her daughters, as they matured, would remain close to the family and one another, and always remember their wonderful ancestors.

Boston, Massachusetts • June, 1976

The New York spa caught on and captured the hearts of many New Yorkers and affluent Connecticut women. The reputation of the spa soared and clients were more than willing to wait extended periods for appointments.

"Suzanne, telephone call. Can you take it?" the receptionist asked over the intercom. "Hi. It's me. I'd love to have you over for dinner next week. I've come up with a great idea and want to discuss it with you," requested Nancy.

"Sure. Name the time and day."

When she sat down at the kitchen table, Nancy wasted little time. "I think we should open another spa. I've given it a lot of thought and if we don't expand now, when?"

"You've got to be kidding. I'm only one person. Granted, I have good help, but I don't want to spread myself too thin."

"Suzanne, you're a great teacher. If you manage your time properly, you'll be able to supervise another spa and still work at all three places."

"And where do you suggest this third spa be located?"

"Where else but Newport? It will be between the other two spas so the commuting won't be disastrous. Doesn't that make sense?"

"It's easy for you to say. But, when you put it that way, no. I'm afraid of the future, though. I have visions, but I don't think we should expand so fast."

"While we're still young, why not?"

It was Nancy's vision and driving force that brought *Metamorphosis Spa* number three into existence.

During those laborious years Suzanne thought she would go crazy, constantly running from spa to spa. As difficult as it was, she continually pushed herself, driving in all types of weather to make it back home to be with the girls whenever possible.

As the girls matured, they saw how hard Suzanne worked, and they appreciated their mother's devotion. Suzanne was proud of her children and their accomplishments both, socially and academically. Whenever the opportunity presented itself, Suzanne expressed her desire for the girls to continue their education. She persistently reminded them that she expected them to make good grades so they would be accepted into a good institute. She wanted them to become professionals, maybe even doctors or lawyers. Unlike her parents, old school frame of mind, she didn't believe that being a female should deter them from any avocation.

It had been one of those long, hard working days that drained Suzanne of her energy. The harsh driving rain was unrelenting, causing her to drive cautiously and slowly. "I can't wait to get home and crash," she thought as the whirring sound of the wipers, threw the water aside. She turned the radio to a rock station hoping the fast paced music would rejuvenate her. It was with great relief that she arrived at her driveway.

Once inside she took off her shoes hurriedly ran up to the bedroom, casting off her clothes and putting on a comfortable lounging robe. In a better and relaxed frame of mind, now that she was finally home, she descended the stairs heading for the great-room to be with her family.

"Hi everyone. It's good to be home and out of this weather. The visibility was poor driving through the storm."

"I'm glad you're home Mom. How was your day?"

"It was good, I didn't stop for a minute."

"Why don't you block some time off for yourself? It's stupid to work straight through."

"Because I never know when a cancellation may occur and I'll be stuck having nothing to do. That's when I allow myself time to eat. It's on days like this when I don't get a break that I'm exhausted."

Suzanne tried to concentrate on a documentary. As she sat there, watching but not really listening to what was being said, Hope asked.

"Mom, can I have a word with you?"

"Sure. What's up? " The mother and daughter sat down on the white sectional sofa to talk.

"I want you to know that I love you very much."

"Well, of course I do, Hope."

"I have a problem, and I don't know what I should do."

All kinds of thoughts ran through Suzanne's mind as she heard her daughter's words. What trouble could she possibly be in? Could she be pregnant? But she doesn't have a steady boyfriend and I don't think she's promiscuous. Or has she gone to a doctor and found she has some rare disease? She told Hope to continue.

"I'm in a quandary. Mom, I know you'd like me to go to college, but I really don't want to. I would love to go to esthetics school and go into business with you."

"My how the pendulum swings," thought Suzanne. "I was in the same predicament when I was graduating and the tables have turned. I would have given anything for encouragement from my parents to attend college. Now I want my daughter to become a professional person, and what does she want? She wants to work with me."

Disheartened, Suzanne replied. "All these years I encouraged you and your sisters to excel in school. It wasn't easy for me to monitor your schoolwork, but I made sure I did. I didn't do it for myself, but for you kids. I want you to be able to hold your head high, be proud of what you become and know that you won't have to depend on anyone but yourself to make a good living."

"Mom," Hope interjected. "You make lots of money. I'm proud to say that my mother owns the "*Metamorphosis Salons*" and I want to be like you."

Suzanne couldn't help but laugh. "Honey, you don't really know all that I've gone through to make sure you girls maintain the lifestyle that I wanted you to have. I've worked many long and hard hours just to be able to pay the bills. I want more for you and your sisters. This is the time in your life to make the right decisions. I thought you'd want to achieve more."

"I want you to know that I would never discourage you from doing anything you really want, but I'm sad to hear this. Maybe you'll keep your options open for awhile. I'll go along with whatever you want. I only hope that you make the right decision."

With optimism, Suzanne prayed that Hope would not be irrational and take her time making up her mind.

Paying little head to her mother's message, Hope jumped up and hugged Suzanne tightly. "Thanks Mom, I knew you'd be cool. Most of my friend's parents would have gone crazy with a decision like this. I can't thank you enough."

Shaking her head in dismay, Suzanne knew that her oldest daughter was now unlikely to attain the level of achievement she had envisioned.

January, 1982

True to form, Nancy was making further plans for expansion.

"It seems only fitting that we should expand into the European Market," Nancy encouraged an already overworked Suzanne and Peter.

"Where do you get your ambition? Why expand when everything is going along smoothly? Why ask for trouble?" Suzanne asked skeptically.

"Come on, don't you have any adventure? This is the perfect time for us to expand into the European market. People over there spend money galore on anything American."

"I know, deep down, that you're right, but there's only the three of us. We can't kill ourselves. I know you're going to tell me to start training Hope and Taylor to take on more responsibilities. I've been thinking the same thing."

"After all, they are family. We're more than partners, we've become like sisters, and besides, you and your family have become mine."

"Okay, okay. Where will our first European spa be located?"

"Where else?"

Paris, France • The City of Lights • Spring, 1982

Paris was beautiful. People told her it would be magnificent and they were right. Suzanne walked along the Seine, looking with awe at the bridges crossing it. She spoke little French and was grateful that Nancy had agreed to accompany her. "Thank God you speak the language. I would never have been able to manage without you."

"Well, I should. I spent enough time in school over here. " Nancy winked and gave Suzanne a hug as she took her hand and pulled her along the rue des Petits Champs, behind the gardens of the Palais Royal.

"Come on. Before we start shopping I'm going to show you the wonderful sights of Paris. I'll contact a few friends from school who still live here. Maybe they'll invite us to their homes. You'll find the Europeans are very different from Americans."

The Pont Neuf was the oldest and most famous of the bridges crossing the Seine. As they passed over it and walked along the cobblestone streets, Suzanne admired the quaint shops and the gorgeous facades of the hotels and other buildings.

"My feet are killing me. Can we stop at one of the cafes and rest awhile?"

"Sure, I'll take you to a favorite place of mine." They walked down the street toward the equestrian statue of Louis XIV on the Place des Victoires. Aux Bons Crus was on their right and the two friends sat down and ordered cheese plates and sandwiches with wine.

As Nancy predicted, her friend, Mimi Brunelle invited them to a dinner party on the weekend. Mimi lived in an apartment on a narrow side street. Suzanne thought, as most people did, that a flat above a small store would be rather cramped. Not so! Mimi greeted them at the door of a suite that was both large and lavishly furnished. Suzanne settled into the overstuffed sofa and accepted the wine offered in a beautiful long stemmed, crystal glass.

As the two old friends became reacquainted, Suzanne had a chance to visit with the other guests who were seated around the massive parlor that overlooked the spires of the 12th century Cathedral of Notre Dame de Paris. Suzanne felt awkward trying to communicate in her smattering of French. Fortunately, most of the people spoke English.

Seated in the high ceilinged, gorgeously adorned dining room, Suzanne couldn't help being impressed by the beautiful old furnishings in this warmly decorated room. Two 16th. Century style chairs and tables, of Venice's Palazzo Cornaro, flanked the beautiful gray marble Renaissance style fireplace. On one side of her sat

Countess Von Fricken, on the other, a Duchess. Countess Von Fricken was, Suzanne guessed, in her late fifties. At first the conversation was both stilted and awkward until the Countess asked what had brought Suzanne to France. Once Suzanne explained her mission and goal, the barrier was broken. The women seated around the mahogany table burned with curiosity as she described her spas. She made many contacts that would bring wealthy and prestigious clients into the spa.

"Suzanne, I want you to see a section of town that I think might be interesting. The shops are both elegant and expensive." It didn't take them long to walk to the Rue Sainte Honore from the Louvre. Women dressed with flair and their make-up was adeptly applied. She did not see anyone with an unkempt appearance or slovenly attire as she had often experienced along the streets back home. The young Parisian woman wore the latest garments with style and flair.

Suzanne could not get over the scents of the people as they walked past. "I know what you're thinking," teased Nancy. "Years ago, pharmacies made personalized scents and placed them in beautiful unique bottles. Today, only remnants of the old craft remain. Now most people buy their perfume at department stores."

"It seems everyone I see has expensive and fashionable apparel. The cost of living must be very high. How can they afford it?"

"It's a matter of priorities. They might own only a few expensive garments, but with different accessories, the look of the entire outfit can change. They might have to wear the same clothes two or three times a week, and we wouldn't know. Does that make sense to you?"

"I think you're right."

"A friend of mine, Countess Von Fricken - I think you talked a while with her at Mimi's party, called and told me of a store that's going out of business. If you like the location, we might be walking to the first of our European establishments."

"I love it. Do you think we can afford it?"

"The countess told me she personally knows the owners of this block of stores.   She'll put in a good word for us and I might be able to bargain with him on the price. His name is Claude Du Bois and I heard from my reliable source, that he's a reasonable man.   A person can talk to him sensibly."

Walking down this exclusive street, Suzanne noticed that one of Lawrence's stores was located a few shops down from the one they were interested in. "Isn't that interesting," she thought.   "I wonder if he visits his establishments when he's in town?"

While Suzanne was busy with her business transactions for the new European spa, Alan arrived in Paris and managed to track her down. They agreed to meet at a popular bistro on the Champs Elysses. Suzanne got there early and sat at the bar chatting with the bartender in her newly acquired French. "Thank you, Countess von Fricken," she thought to herself. Suzanne was determined to conquer French and was spending every spare moment with the Countess, who was helping her master the language.

"Bonjour, mon bon ami," she greeted Alan warmly, when he sat down beside her.

"I'm impressed," he replied, answering her in perfect French. They resumed their conversation until it became too much for Suzanne.

"Okay, okay, let me interrupt. Can we continue this discussion in English, please? I'm only a novice at this and I really want to enjoy our talk," Suzanne pronounced as they both laughed. "You look extremely happy. What brings you to France?"

"You, of course," he teased. "Seriously, I'm here negotiating some acquisitions for our new gallery in New York. Our location after that will probably be Beverly Hills. And then from there, who knows where? Excitedly, he continued. I must tell you, though, something wonderful has happened. Besides the success of the new gallery, there's been a turning point in my personal life. Let me go back to the beginning and tell you all about it." After ordering another glass of wine for each of them, he dramatically recounted his story.

"It was one of those scorching summer days when most people leave the hot city for the refreshing air of the mountains or the exhilarating, gusty, wind at the shore. I was finishing the second phase of modeling in clay, capturing the well-proportioned body and fine features of the beautiful female model posing before me. I was imagining myself navigating a thirty-foot boat, under full sail on the high seas heading for Martha's Vineyard. Bearing down on the swell of the waves, throngs of people cheered me on as I passed the last buoy and sailed in to anchor at the dock."

'Excuse me, but I have a cramp in my leg. Are we almost through, or can I take a minute and massage my muscle?' Sally asked as she broke into my reverie."

"I told her I was sorry and must've been day dreaming. 'Even though we have the air conditioning on, the heat must be getting to me. I think we're through for today. When can you sit for me again? I think I'll need you for one more session."

'My brother is picking me up today. He's in town visiting me for a few days. Can I resume modeling after he leaves? Let's say next week, if that's all right with you?'

'Sure, same day and time. Thanks for hanging around the city during this hot spell. I really appreciate it.'

'That's okay. My brother loves the city, any season of the year. Oh, here he his. Let me introduce you to him, once I get dressed. He hates me to have to do this type of work. But he doesn't pay my bills, does he?'

"Bill told me afterwards that as he opened the door to the ancient building, he felt a strange familiarity as he walked into the old-fashioned but quaint working studio."

"Sally introduced me as one of the most talented painters and sculptors she ever met. Bill firmly shook my hand. Suzanne, I could feel the electricity immediately."

"'It's a pleasure. I've heard nothing but compliments about you from my sister,' Bill said to me."

'Your sister is a sweetheart.'

'I agree. We're going for something to eat. Nothing special, but would you care to join us?'

'Well, I was going home to grab something quick before I left for the Vineyard. I'm really eager to get out of the city. If you don't mind my eating, and running, I'll join you. Sure.'

"Later, we sat at a booth in a small restaurant with scarcely a handful of other lethargic patrons and ordered a light lunch. I felt an odd sensation during our conversation. I tried to ignore the extraordinary attraction I felt for the man seated across from me."

'Too bad you have plans for this weekend. It'd be fun if you could join us and help me show Bill some of the sites of Boston. I'm trying to talk him into transferring to a branch in or around the area. I love it here in New England, but I do miss having family around,' Sally said.

'What kind of work do you do?' I asked Bill.

"He told me he was a software engineer working on his masters in business administration. He didn't think he'd have any trouble getting a job here, besides he had no attachments out in Chicago, where he lived. He also said, 'If my sister plays her cards right, I might be persuaded to make a move.'"

"I asked them to abandon their plans and join me for a few days at the Vineyard." I also asked them if they'd ever been there?"

'No,' they said in unison.

'Well, I hear it's quite lovely,' Sally said.

'Never mind how lovely it is, you'll certainly cool off.'

"Without too much difficulty, I persuaded them to join me for the weekend. It turned out to be a glorious, fun filled, carefree short vacation. The weather cooperated fully. We sailed continuously until our legs could no longer take it. I took them up island to Menemshaw for dinner."

"Driving along the shore road, we were fascinated by the magnificent views and beautiful large homes overlooking the water. I stopped the car and gestured for them to join me. The sun was setting in a blaze of glory in the West."

"'We'll sleep on the boat tonight and you'll see how beautiful it is. After she's anchored, the rocking motion will lull you to sleep. The sun's first appearance is incredible as it rises up out of the sea in the morning. There's nothing as splendid as when you wake up to the sounds and motion of the ocean with salt air filling your lungs.'"

"'Something like being cradled in your mothers arms when you were a baby,' murmured Sally."

"The next evening we ate at the Home Port where we were again enthralled by the resplendence of the spectacular sun set. The last full day and night were spent on board. After anchoring the boat securely, I stretched out watching the stars. The splashing of the waves was the only sound to be heard in the stillness of the lustrous, moonlit night."

"'Mind if I join you?' Bill asked me, as he quietly came up from the quarters below."

"'No, please do.' Intoxicated by the pleasant scent of the salt air, we sat up late into the night. During that evening, vocalizing our hopes and dreams, and talking until sunrise, we realized that the feelings we had for one another were equally shared."

"Bill managed to get transferred to the Boston area two months later. After the initial shock, my parents did accept my life and ultimately welcomed Bill as part of our family. He moved in with me and ever since then we've been inseparable."

~~~~~~~~~~~~~~~~~~~~~~~~~~~~

She shivered, as the water became cool. It brought her back from her reverie.

Thinking about Larry again, he was a friend with whom she could share new business ideas and she respected the priceless information his opinions rendered. Remembering how not too long ago, had it not been for his astute advice and valuable networking contacts, they would have been in deep trouble. At the time when she was negotiating for the land concerning her London spa, Larry had saved her a considerable amount of money and the expense of a potential lawsuit, when he provided her with the invaluable facts that the land was contaminated. Due to his influential contacts in the European business community, he was able to make a phone call to an associate, Mr. Sage, in London. The data provided by his timely intervention saved them both heartache and cash. Luckily, they were able to negate the proposed deal and find an even better location.

"Yes," she thought, "he's become a valuable and trusted friend. I hope someday that he'll find someone with whom he can share his life. She laughed at herself for being a "Jewish matchmaker."

Chapter Eleven

In the facial room of the Newbury St. *Metamorphosis Spa*, new wave music played in the background while Suzanne's client enjoyed her luxurious facial massage. The mesmerizing motions of Suzanne's specialized facial had relaxed the customer who was about to fall asleep. Suzanne moved the steam machine closer to her, then left the room quietly, waiting until it was time to continue with the next procedure.

"Nancy left a message for you to call her as soon as possible," Jane said as Suzanne went out into the reception area. "Oh yes, Stephen called too. He can rearrange his schedule to be in Florida the week you are."

"Hi, what's up?" Suzanne asked when Nancy answered the phone.

"We have to get together, tonight if possible, to discuss something that's come up. Can you do that?"

"Sure, just tell me where and when."

Heathrow Airport • London • England

The co-pilot spoke to Lawrence over the intercom and informed him that the private jet would be clear for take off in about fifteen minutes. "That'll be fine. You can tell Janet that I'll be ready for dinner about an hour after we're airborne. Thanks."

He went back to reading the papers before him, but had a difficult time concentrating. Since his dinner with Suzanne, he could not get her off his mind.

For the first time in the years he had known her he was confident that Suzanne was considering his business offer. "Here I am," he thought, "behaving like a young man smitten for the first time in his life." For years he had patiently waited for this woman who had intoxicated him with her beauty and innocent charm. She had never known how infatuated he was with her. With a complacent smile on his lips, he congratulated himself on the patience he had shown with Suzanne. He was sure his endurance was about to pay off.

He was meeting his children in France and they would fly on to Belgium to be with the rest of his family for the holidays. The thought of his children brought a smile to his lips. They were returning from their private schools in Switzerland.

The children, accompanied by their private guards, anxiously awaited Lawrence's arrival in Paris. With the rash of recent child abductions, Lawrence had hired dedicated and physically able men to escort his children, whenever and wherever they traveled. The children ran to their father when they saw him enter the door of the private club at Orly Airport. Soon they were airborne again, happy to be heading home together to Belgium.

Anderlecht, Belgium • December, 1991

The rain pelted the car and the windshield wipers kept up a steady beat as they swept away the heavy downpour. Home was a small castle of forty-two rooms that stood not far from a forest of beech and oak trees. The light dusting of snow, covering the fields surrounding the property, was a beautiful sight as they approached the home they loved. Three of their faithful staff was standing outside under the portico waiting to greet them.

"Welcome home sir," Charles bowed, as he opened the limousine door.

"I can't wait to see Grandma and Grandpa Maurice" cheerily blurted Carolyn, as she jumped excitedly at the sound of their voices echoing down the corridor. Carolyn, the youngest of their grandchildren, ran past her siblings and father and into the outstretched arms of her grandparents. With a warm embrace, they each bent down and kissed the thirteen-year-old, whom they adored.

"We're glad you had a safe trip," their Grandma said as she walked over to her other grandchildren and hugged them tenderly. "How has school been?" Not waiting for a reply, she continued, "You'll have to tell us everything at dinner."

"Can we go to the Saint Nicholas Day festival this year?" asked Hendrik, the oldest of the children.

"I don't see any reason not to. Of course we'll go," assured Grandpa Maurice.

272

Hubert, the middle child, timid and shy amongst strangers, had more confidence within his family circle and said in an accusing and whining manner, "How can we be sure? We couldn't go to last year's carnival before Lent."

"Hubert, last year was entirely different. Your father had to fly out on an urgent matter the day before. Usually our holidays are not interrupted like that," defended Maurice.

Trying not to scold his introverted son, Lawrence went on to explain, "I told you, that it was an unforeseen crisis. You know I have always tried never to leave during our holidays together. You know that, son."

"I hope not," said a downcast Hubert, "I love the noise making and dancing in the streets."

"And don't forget the bright colored costumes," cut in Hendrik.

"Now enough of this," pronounced Grandma. "Why don't you go upstairs to your rooms and rest a while before dinner. It's been a hectic day for us all. We have some business matters to discuss with your father. Now, away with you until we call you down for dinner."

"Lawrence dear, you look a little peaked. Are you feeling well?" asked his concerned mother.
"I'm fine, really I am. It will feel good to stay at home with the children again. Sometimes I wish I didn't have to travel as I do, and could spend more time with

them." Speaking out loud, essentially talking to himself, he continued, "I wonder how different life would have turned out if Elizabeth hadn't died so young while giving birth to our dear Carolyn," he sighed. When he first lost his wonderful wife in childbirth, he had been devastated. In spite of his wealth and power, for once he was totally helpless.

"Grieving has its place but you can only mourn for so long. You must pick up the pieces and go on with your life. Our businesses rely on your astute judgment. Let's hear some positive news. What happened in the states?" queried Carolyn.

As his eyes turned to his mother, feelings of respect and love filled his heart. A woman of considerable patience, she was courteous and refined, but she was not to be taken lightly. Lawrence knew she was the silent power behind the vast empire his father had built. She was viewed by most who knew her as gracious, charming, and inherently beautiful, but she was a businesswoman at heart. He was grateful for that. Her business interests kept her vibrant and busy. The still graceful and stately lady stood five feet ten inches tall in her stocking feet. Her once blond hair was now snow white.

With discerning eyes he turned toward his father. Maurice was the same height as his wife and, at seventy, was still a prominent businessman. He had retained most of his thick, blond hair, now only a little sparse on top.

"Please enlighten us about the current situation with the takeover of the men's Avalon collection of cosmetics and toiletries," asked a concerned Maurice.

Clearing his throat, Lawrence responded "They're ready to sell their entire division to us with a few stipulations, of course. I'll concede two of them. My instinct is that they'll eventually comply with our original offer. The company is in financial straits and the owners have many obstacles in their way. We have the necessary capital to help them out of their difficulties without loosing their standing in the business world. After the holidays all the essential papers will be ready to sign. However, there's another piece of potential good news that I'd like to discuss with you."

"Go on," a curious Carolyn urged.

"Do you remember my mentioning a woman by the name of Suzanne Morse some years ago?"

"I vaguely remember the name."

"I met her on a vacation with Louis about a year after Elizabeth died. In any event, I found the woman fascinating. It turns out that she now owns the *Metamorphosis Spas*. Have you heard of them?"

"I don't know if your father has, but I've visited the spa in Paris on a few occasions."

"What did you think of it?"

"I was impressed by the services and atmosphere. I regularly use their products. Why do you ask?"

"I have offered to become her financial adviser. Now, before you raise your eyebrows, Mother, I genuinely want to help her. I appreciate the fact that I was born into wealth and social standing. She, on the other hand, came from a poor background, and, through hard work and diligence, now owns nine spas around the world. I feel that we can get her to use our new product line in her spas. Who knows? We might be able to buy her out eventually."

"The idea sounds interesting," said an attentive Maurice. "Keep us informed."

"Now that my curiosity is aroused, why don't you tell me more about Suzanne Morse?" inquired Carolyn.

"Mother, don't read anything into the situation. Suzanne is only interested in my business knowledge, unfortunately. But, who knows," he said, winking at his father, "With the charm and good looks I've inherited, she may be completely overwhelmed and start adoring me."

"Lawrence, you are incorrigible," laughed his proud mother.

Boston, Massachusetts

The Christmas lights were being put up in the Boston Common. The downtown shopping district was lit with ornaments and decorations. "They're rushing the season again," Suzanne thought. Thanksgiving was still two weeks away.

She walked briskly through the Public Gardens and the Boston Common. The white lights strung along the trees reminded Suzanne of the brilliant happy holidays of her youth. People hurried to catch the subways to get home for their dinner. As the masses scurried past her, Suzanne tried to figure out what Nancy had to tell her that was so important. She darted through the city streets, hurrying to the Cafe Marliave located in an alleyway off Tremont Street. She lifted the velvet collar of her coat to protect herself from the bitter cold wind.

Tonio, the handsome, maitre de, welcomed Suzanne. Tonio knew all the regulars and greeted Suzanne warmly. He showed her to one of the best tables in the quaint and charming restaurant.

She ordered a bottle of Chablis. Nancy joined her shortly and when the wine came, Nancy proposed a toast.

"Faithful are the wounds of a friend."

"What is *that* supposed to mean?"

"It comes from the Old Testament, Proverbs. Friends are like fiddle strings. They must not be wound too tight."

"You're really acting strange, "Suzanne said to her

friend. "I've never heard you say anything like that." Suzanne was skeptical. "Please, tell me what's going on," she pleaded with her friend.

"I think I'm in serious trouble."

Nancy explained "Brian's been coming on strong to me and he's been extremely aggressive. I tried to discourage him, right from the start, but to quiet him down, I agreed to have lunch with him last week."

"Unfortunately, instead of helping the situation, it made matters worse. He won't be deterred. Rather than calling you, I took it upon myself to handle it, and I had dinner with him last Friday. If Peter ever finds out, he'll kill me. No, he'll kill us."

"What the hell were you thinking?" demanded Suzanne.

Nancy waved her hand. "Never mind. Anyway, I got to meet with the other members of his so-called company. These men are smooth, believe me. By the way, I've managed to obtain their private home telephone numbers, and their addresses. And, don't ask me how I did it. Sometimes you have to do something, even if you know it's wrong. I believe what I'm doing is justified."

She paused momentarily, then went on. "Now don't say anything, until you hear me out, please. I'm going to have an affair with him."

Suzanne wanted to finish the rest of the wine bottle by herself. Her head was spinning, and she knew she couldn't for she needed a clear head to be objective. "What did I get Nancy into?" she asked herself.

"I'm going to do it to get the son of a bitch, once and for all, for what he's doing to the Pearlman's. I think either he or one of his partners has a second set of books at their house. If I can get friendly with them, I'll have a better chance of getting the records."

Suzanne interrupted, "Who do you think you are, Jessica Fletcher? These are dangerous people we're dealing with. If they find out what we're up to, they'll stop at nothing to have us killed. I'm going to call Timothy and Kevin as soon as I get home."

"Oh no you don't." Nancy spoke with calm authority. Suzanne looked around cautiously. She hoped no one overheard their conversation.

"I think you're getting paranoid. We'll call them in due time, but, I'm telling you this is the only way we can get the goods on them. You heard Kevin tell us how hard it is to get a conviction."

They talked while they ate, but Suzanne was visibly upset and couldn't do justice to the meal. She tried to persuade Nancy to inform the agents about what was going on. It seemed that Nancy was becoming more obsessed with the fight, than Suzanne. Nancy went on to explain that if she became Brian's "girlfriend" she could get information easier and faster. Suzanne started laughing nervously, and jokingly told Nancy "You're acting like Trudy from Miami Vice."

"You can laugh and joke all you want, but we're going to get those bastards, one way or the other. I can be very convincing if I have to, and, even if I say so myself, I'm a very good actress. If I sleep with Brian, and I'm not saying that I will, it will only be to confirm a relationship that he thinks we have."

Suzanne found it useless to argue further. Nancy would not be dissuaded. She knew that once her friend made up her mind, nothing could deter her. She gave up and said, "Okay, tell me what I can do."

They discussed what had to be done next and when they would get in touch with Kevin and Timothy. If they didn't hear from the agents within two weeks, Suzanne would arrange for another meeting.

Suzanne developed a massive headache as she drove back home to Stoney Brook. A variety of scenarios, none good, went through her mind. "I don't believe what I heard tonight. God, please forgive me for getting Nancy involved. I don't know what she's thinking. Although she's already immersed in this business facade, we don't need to aggravate an already messy situation. Peter will kill me. I can see Brian now with his persuasiveness. Nancy ought to be concerned. I have to put a stop to her madness, but how?" Once she got home, she took two aspirins and went straight to bed.

Trying to fall asleep, she heard the unceasing wind howling outside her bedroom window. With the gales came the cold front. "Too early for the second week in November," Suzanne thought as she tucked the blanket tightly under her feet.

After getting up from a restless nights' sleep, Suzanne went through her morning ritual. She enjoyed the sting of the hot water on her naked body knowing that, all too soon, she would be back out in the bitter cold weather that was still raging outside.

When she came out of the shower she wrapped the pink velour bathrobe around herself and walked over to the bureau. She unlocked the top drawer and took out her gun. When she first began working alone in the spa at night, robberies were frequent, and her friend, Tom Donovan had suggested that she apply for a firearm permit. Suzanne had to agree with him as she had worked too hard for her money to let some punk take it away from her. Tom took her to his rod and gun club, taught her the proper way to shoot, care for, and respect the weapon. After a few months of training, Suzanne could hit a target accurately. She carried the small, black 45 for a few years, but had locked it away a number of years ago.

Looking at it now sent a shiver up her spine. Suzanne wondered if she should again carry it with her, "In case Nancy gets into trouble and needs my assistance." Trembling, she thought, "I'm getting as carried away as

Nancy. I can't let this get the better of me," she scolded herself.

"What would a respectable, Jewish woman be doing carrying a loaded pistol, anyway? My parents would be mortified if they found out." Holding the gun in her hand, she remembered the feeling of control and power she felt when she had the piece on her person. If she had it when she was married to Brian, she was sure she would have used it on him. She was grateful now that she didn't have it then. That stage of her life was over, thank God.

After ensuring that the chamber was empty, and that the shells were located in another drawer, she slid the gun back into the bureau and relocked both drawers. She hoped it would never have to be used.

Meanwhile, Nancy's relationship with Brian was escalating rapidly. He was crazy about her, and wanted to meet her 'children.' Nancy had cleverly made excuses and counteracted each of his proposed meetings with her invented family. She had a key to Brian's house and they frequently entertained his business associates there. Nancy had befriended a few of their wives and they all liked her. She was quiet but friendly and made a point of never doing anything that could be construed as making a play for their husbands. Women had a second sense about protecting 'their men' against a single, attractive woman. She knew they had accepted her when they asked her if she had ever played mahjong.

"Many times," she assured them.

"Would you like to join our group. We sometimes have a few tables going at once and we can always use an alternate."

That evening Nancy called Suzanne in a panic. "You have to help me. Do you know anything about mahjong?"

"Just a little. When I was first married a few of the women from the temple asked me to join them. To tell you the truth, I never really caught on. At the time I had tremendous pressures at home and just couldn't enjoy playing. Beverly plays regularly, though. Why don't you call her? I'm sure she'll be glad to teach you."

Peter was working his usual crazy hours, and since he never had any reason to doubt his wife, he believed her when she told him she was either going on a shopping expedition out of town or some other falsified story. Nancy felt awful about the lies but went ahead with her plans, anyway, knowing in her heart that 'the end justifies the means.'

Suzanne spent her workdays traveling between her various spas. After her week at Newport, she went on to her New York spa. She couldn't wait till the week in New York was over for Stephen had called and they made plans to meet in West Palm Beach.

As Suzanne lay in bed, relaxing from her hectic day, Nancy phoned. She picked up the receiver by her bedside and listened intently as Nancy reported the latest episode. She then astounded Suzanne by asking her to join her this coming weekend at the home of Brian's partner, Bernie Rich. The wives of the partners were holding a fund-raising auction of celebrities' possessions. Over one hundred woman attended this annual affair.

Suzanne thought Nancy had gone mad. "No, I won't do it! Are you completely out of your mind? If Brian finds out we know one another, our credibility is shot. How do you propose we do this?"

All at once an idea came to Suzanne. "I know what you're thinking," said Suzanne, "and you're crazy." They laughed aloud in unison. Suzanne was an excellent make-up artist and with her skills she could totally change anyone's appearance including her own. She could make skin tones darker or lighter, change hair color with a wig, and eye color with contact lenses. Suzanne was able to complete the disguise with the clever use of different clothing – from preppy to blowzy.

"You know what? I think we're both nuts," Suzanne pronounced.

Nancy then went on to explain that she had gained the women's friendship and they had invited her to their big yearly charity event. Bernie's wife, Evelyn, already had Nancy over for lunch and showed her the office furnishings that she had custom made for her husband. The red leather, tufted sofa and matching chair represented a mere fraction of the cost of the expensive furnishings. His solid oak desk was massive, as was his matching four-drawer file cabinets.

Nancy went on to explain to Suzanne that she thought the important second set of books was located in that room. "Beautiful bookcases line the walls, and I'm sure there's a safe behind them or somewhere else in that room."

Suzanne told her friend that she would be game, only if they called the two FBI men and told them of their plan. "Who knows? They might be able to help us. I bet they could teach us how to crack a safe or open a locked drawer." Suzanne laughed aloud, surprised at her own daring idea.

Suzanne contacted Timothy Cassidy and arranged for a meeting in Boston on Friday. When they heard Nancy's idea, Timothy and Kevin were against it and feared for the safety of the two women. They tried to persuade them to abandon their plans, but to no avail. Their words fell on deaf ears. The men finally realized that these women were not going to be dissuaded and, against their better judgment, they agreed to give them a crash course on breaking and entering.

"Kevin, would you call Murray and have him come over as soon as possible, preferably within the hour?" Tim asked. Turning to the two women, he explained "Murray is our expert locksmith and resident safecracker. Opening the door and drawers will be easy, but cracking a safe is another matter. Only an expert like Murray could possibly teach you, or try to teach you, how to open one in the time we have. I'll ask him to concentrate on the three most likely ones you may find." He explained that most safes were not at all easy to get into. If they concentrated on the most likely candidates and they found one of those, they'd have a better chance of success.

While they waited for Murray, he brought the women into a laboratory in the sub-basement of the building. A large assortment of safes, tools, weapons, and other paraphernalia was set up. He selected two tools and held them up. "These instruments are called a wrench and a rake. They're made of hard spring steel and are very strong. This one, shaped like a corkscrew with a continuous flattened S, is the rake. These two tools will be the ones you'll use to open locked doors and drawers. It's really easy to do once you get used to handling the instruments and learn how to use them properly. Here, hold them in your hands. Get used to their feel."

Murray arrived almost within the hour. A slightly built man, short, and stooped at the shoulders, he looked older than his fifty-eight years. He had black horn-rimmed glasses that kept falling from the bridge of his flat, misshaped nose. When Suzanne looked directly at him, she saw a wearied, but hardworking, steadfast man. She saw, beyond his obviously fatigued body, a pair of eyes that were keen and alert. His skin was weather-beaten, with the exception of his hands, that were small, but his fingers were long, lean, soft, and nimble.

"His hearing must be remarkable," Suzanne thought. She and Nancy were amazed at the precise reactions of his agile fingers to the inner workings of the safe. He taught the two women to listen for the exact sound of the safe's winding mechanisms. He went on to explain what to do if they heard certain movements from the safe. It was one of the most difficult lessons they ever had. To concentrate on one subject and block out every other bit of noise was exacting work.

To the amazement of the men, the two women were proficient students. They could not become experts in such a short time, but Kevin felt that they were quick learners - - that they could become skillful enough to handle their task. It was dawn before they were finished. Although they were not "professionals," they felt they at least had a shot at getting the job done, - - if they discovered a safe.

Kevin and Timothy wanted to wire the women, but Suzanne and Nancy refused. Kevin tried to make them understand that once they arrived, they would have to play the situation by ear. "This is really a very serious undertaking. Without the wire, we're helpless, unless we can get men into the building. Nancy, give us the address."

Turning to Tim, he said, "Find out who is catering this soiree." Speaking to Suzanne he added, "We'll make sure a couple of our other agents get to help out the caterer. Not that we think there'll be any trouble, but just so you know that someone will be there."

"In any event, we'll have a car nearby if you need us. However, if a problem does develop, one of you will have to get to an agent on location or in touch with us. We'll have no way of knowing about it." The plan was that the women would break away from the auction in the massive combined living and dinning rooms and hoped they wouldn't be missed while they searched the library for a safe.

Before leaving the women unlocked more drawers and opened another safe door. Suzanne and Nancy were virtually exhausted. Twelve hours had gone by without a break.

"Enough already," Suzanne spoke. "I haven't gotten to sleep yet, and I'm a zombie if I don't get my beauty rest."

"Before you go, we've been talking and just for the hell of it, tell Kevin and me why you're taking this risk. It's way out of your league."

Suzanne and Nancy looked at each other and, speaking for both of them, Suzanne began. "Nancy and I had a conversation similar to this when we started this escapade. Our biggest motivation is anger. Most ordinary citizens are enraged and tired of criminals getting away with their crimes. After a while, a person will say 'Wait a second, enough is enough.'"

"The law is on the side of the criminal most of the time. Even if someone is being robbed in his own home, he's supposed to retreat and let the robber do his thing. If he shoots the thief, the homeowner can be tried for felonious assault, attempted manslaughter or even murder if the crook should die. So getting back to your original question, the answer is anger. Besides, you've met the Pearlman's. They're admirable people who have already been through enough. Let the good guy win for a change."

Kevin and Tim stood up from sitting on the edge of their desks and applauded. "I don't want to get into a legal debate, but the laws are made for a reason. Unfortunately, the same laws that protect the innocent can sometimes be manipulated by a clever lawyer," Kevin retorted.

On the day of the auction Suzanne got busy with make-up, clothes, and wigs. She went for a discreet and inconspicuous look, by wearing a short, brown hairpiece and blue contact lenses. She wore a body stocking that minimized her figure and then put on a conservative plum colored, knit dress, accented only by a gold rope chain and leaf-shaped, gold earrings.

Nancy pulled into the driveway. As she chatted with Mrs. Walsh, Nancy paced back and forth across the kitchen floor waiting for Suzanne to make her appearance. "I'm a little tense and uneasy. Don't mind me," Nancy said as she fidgeted with her jewelry. They heard footsteps descending the stairs and were amazed when they saw a strange woman standing before them.

"How do I look?"

"I'd never think it was you," a stunned Mrs. Walsh answered.

"This is an incredible disguise," exclaimed Nancy.

Both Nancy and Suzanne were quiet as they rode to the benefit in Weston, a wealthy town, easily accessible from Route 128. They devised a signal to use when either of them felt the time was right to leave the auction and another one they would employ in case of a problem.

As they drove up to the sprawling, brick colonial, they could see that cars lined the street for several blocks. "I feel like I'm back in Beverly Hills," said Suzanne. "Look at all the Mercedes, Jaguars, BMWs, and Rolls Royces."

"Should I hide my Buick?" Nancy asked.

The long driveway was flanked by two rows of proud oak and maple trees. The expansive colonial was set far back from the road. Suzanne commented that she'd hate to have to shovel or plow the lengthy entrance in the wintertime.

An older woman, wearing a maid's uniform, greeted them at the door and took their coats. A younger woman showed them into the living room. Elegantly attired women of all ages were moving through the massive foyer, living room, and dining room.

After cocktails and hors d'oeuvres, the auction began. Suzanne and Nancy sat on the end of a row, near the aisle, toward the back of the living room. They did not want to be conspicuous when they slipped away.

The committee that had gathered the donations from celebrities and other individuals and companies were introduced, thanked, and applauded. The two women got caught up in the excitement of the auction and found some interesting items that they wanted to bid on. Through clenched teeth, Nancy reproached Suzanne. "Don't get carried away with this."

When everyone was engrossed in the auction of a fur coat that had belonged to Joan Crawford, Suzanne gave Nancy the signal to leave.

Quietly leaving their seats, they nonchalantly walked out to the vestibule. Nancy looked back cautiously to see if anyone had noticed them departing the auction. They satisfied themselves that the coast was clear and moved gingerly down the tiled hall.

When the door to the office was just a few feet away, Suzanne could feel her heart beating rapidly. Surprisingly, they found that the door was unlocked. The women moved inside quickly. The heavily lined draperies were drawn shut, preventing any light from entering the expansive study. They removed their shoes, to avoid making telltale high-heel imprints in the deep pile carpet. Nancy opened her purse and got out her reliable camera and the apparatus needed to ensure the opening of any locked files that they might encounter. With miniature flashlights in hand, they quickly and quietly opened and closed drawers of the desk, looking for any evidence of drug money or drug-related dealings.

Suzanne's hands were visibly shaking as she maneuvered the small metal pin into the opening of the locked drawer. After what seemed minutes the drawer opened and files were exposed. They swiftly searched for and found some papers that looked like a list of instructions with foreign names on it. Included were airplane schedules and itineraries. Nancy photographed the information. Trying not to make any noise at all, they went on to the file cabinets. The drawers were locked. With swift movement, Suzanne skillfully opened them and, as Nancy examined one, Suzanne investigated another. Suzanne was not sure if they should take pictures of all the documents and left that decision to Nancy.

As they were going through the records in the darkened room, they heard rapid footsteps on the marble floor of the hall. The clicking of heels was getting closer. They closed the drawers slowly, and shut off the flashlights. With deadened silence, the two women crouched in back of the desk. They prayed that whoever was coming, would not enter this room.

The footsteps resounded, then suddenly stopped outside the still room. Suzanne's head pounded and her heart beat rapidly. She was filled with apprehension and distress. Muffled voices could be heard and the footsteps recurred, moving down the corridor, away from them.

Beads of sweat trickled down their faces as they resumed their quest.

"I know that second set of books are in this room, and we have to find them," Nancy whispered. "I bet they're hidden somewhere in the bookcases or in a safe that's behind these walls. Suzanne, we just have to find the register.!!"

Carefully exploring the bookcases, they came across a journal written in code. Nancy photographed its pages. Suzanne looked behind the pictures, hoping that a safe would be hidden in the wall. Unfortunately there was none. Crouching beside Nancy, waiting for her to finish her exploration, Suzanne thought she heard a sound again outside the door. She reached over to Nancy and tapped her on the shoulder. "Put that light out. I think someone's out there."

Nancy switched the light off quickly. A moment later the door opened illuminating the room from the hall, silhouetting the figures of a man and woman. Suzanne and Nancy silently backed up and moved behind the heavy draperies. Neither woman had ever felt fear like this before. Had someone heard or seen them enter the office? Their hearts pounded as they held their shaking bodies still and strained to hear what was going on ten feet away.

Soon they heard words of endearment coming from the two people who impulsively took advantage of the red leather couch in front of them. They could hear the rustling movement as the anonymous man lifted the taffeta skirt and made love passionately and quickly to the unknown woman on the couch.

The mysterious female stood up, straightened her skirt, and impulsively hugged the man before her. "I love doing it like this. It's so dangerous. I love the excitement, knowing we're going at it with her in the house."

"I never thought that you'd have enough nerve to show your face at Evelyn's function. You must be crazy. I thought we agreed to keep our affair hidden. Don't you realize she could make big trouble if she finds out what's going on?"

"Didn't you enjoy it, though?" she teased him.

"How did you know I'd be home today, during the auction?"

"I didn't. But I took my chances. Guess it was my lucky day."

"Let me get what I came for. You leave first and I'll follow."

The room was suddenly ablaze with light. Suzanne and Nancy heard the door open and close.

The two concealed women both hoped that they could not be seen in their makeshift hiding place behind the draperies. They could hear the drawers of the desk being opened and closed and listened to the sounds of paper being rustled. The lights went out and the door closed again.

Instinctively, they waited to be certain that the people had really left the room. They remained behind the draperies for what seemed hours but in actuality was only minutes. They dared to come out from behind their shroud of concealment only when the absence of life seemed obvious.

They again resumed their search of the bookcase. Suzanne took one end while Nancy the other. Suzanne lost her balance as she reached for a high shelf. She caught hold of the molding on the woodwork to steady herself. She felt it move and thinking that she had broken it, was disheartened. All at once a separate panel moved and an opening appeared behind the cabinet.

"Son of a bitch," whispered Nancy. "Can you believe our luck?" Among the photos were pornographic pictures of Bernie Rich with some pretty rough looking characters. As Nancy copied them, the women raised their eyebrows. The opening was very deep and Suzanne reached in and took whatever she could lay her hands on. On the second try, she hit what looked like pay dirt and came up with a black and red leather ledger. Nancy squeezed Suzanne's arm, and began taking snapshots as fast as she could. She replaced the film twice as she reproduced all the pages. With emotions running high and their hearts beating rapidly, they finally finished photographing all the material they had found.

Shutting off their flashlights, they tiptoed to the door and stepped back into their shoes. Slowly opening the entry a crack, Suzanne cautiously looked about, making sure that no one would see them coming out of the office. Satisfied that the coast was clear, she signaled Nancy to follow her and they noiselessly left the room. They separately re-entered the living room and slipped into their seats. Nancy bid successfully on a windjammer vacation for two. "I think Peter and I deserve to get away when this is over, wouldn't you agree?"

It seemed like the day would go on forever. Finally the last item was auctioned and the event was concluded. "Beth" shook the hostess' hand and thanked her for her hospitality. "Nancy has told me so many nice things about you. I'm glad to have finally met you. It's been a pleasure." Mrs. Rich was appreciative of the compliments and thanked them all for coming and making this a truly successful benefit.

Suzanne kicked off her shoes in Nancy's car. "I don't know how to thank you. I hope we have enough information for Timothy and Kevin so they can get these people convicted and out of the Pearlman's lives."

"Don't thank me," Nancy retorted. "I only did what any friend would do. Besides sometimes my life is so boring. When would I ever have the chance for excitement like this? I really enjoyed the melodrama. I only regret that I lied to Peter."

"I don't know if I can ever tell Peter what really happened. I have to examine my heart and think what'll be best for our marriage. Do you think Brian might be in this thing over his head without really knowing what's going on?"

I don't know your true feelings about Brian, but you better make up your mind. It's not fair to the three of you. For everyone's sake, please think rationally.

Suzanne spoke slowly. "I've been doing some serious thinking about Brian lately. The girls do love him very much, although I don't know why, and he's been a good father in some ways. I thank God, though, that I went into my own business and I didn't have to rely on him to support them. Maybe he really isn't financially secure; I could never tell. We'll see what the records show when we give them to the FBI. But I definitely agree with you on the point that Brian lacks common sense. The only smart thing that he ever did in his life was to marry me."

"Too bad he screwed that up," she continued. "But he did, and life goes on. You have to do whatever you can with the cards you've been dealt. I have mixed emotions when it comes to Brian." Sighing deeply, Suzanne continued, "I hope matters straighten out quickly, and we can go on with our lives. I'll call Kevin as soon as we get to my house and arrange to get the information to him this evening or early tomorrow morning.

As Nancy dropped her off, she reminded her, "Remember, I have to catch a flight tomorrow morning for

Florida. I'll be there all this week, and I'm looking forward to going to work." Laughing, Suzanne continued, "Compared to this espionage, my work at the spa is a piece of cake."

Chapter Twelve

Boston, Massachusetts • November, 1991

"You won't believe what we went through to get this. I hope it's what you're looking for and that you can decipher it," Suzanne said as she handed the film over to the FBI agent.

"In this business, I'd believe anything. Some day over a couple of drinks Tim and I will tell you some stories that'll make your hair curl. We'll get on with this investigation right away. I can't thank you and Nancy enough. I'll call you as soon as we have something concrete."

As Kevin put out his hand to thank Suzanne, she unexpectedly moved forward and gave him a hug. "Take care of yourself and Timothy, and thank you for believing in us."

"Please feel free to call me anytime."

Later That Morning En Route to Florida

The plane was filled to capacity with people fleeing the cold weather. The flight was smooth, and Suzanne was at the Breakers Hotel before she knew it. She called her West Palm Beach spa and arranged to be there by noon. Although most spas and salons were not opened on Mondays, Suzanne made a point of keeping her establishments accessible six days a week, closing only on Sundays. She did excellent business on Mondays, as many professionals were free to come to the spas then.

The workday passed quickly. She received a phone call from Stephen just after noon and since her last client was scheduled for eight o'clock that night, she arranged to meet him at ten.

After work, she had just enough time to take a quick bath and get ready for their late dinner. Thoughts of Stephen brought a smile to her face. Her hunger was not for food, but for her lover. As usual, he was right on time.

"I would like an appetizer before dinner," he said, his deep voice even sexier than she remembered. In an instant, their clothes were on the floor. Being apart for so long heightened their desire. Hungrily, they fondled and kissed every part of their lover's body. He felt charged with dynamic energy. He responded to her full figure. Towering over Suzanne, Stephen's powerful hands pushed her onto her back. Suzanne adeptly kissed Stephen with ravenous desire. Her body ached with lust, compelling him to consummate their love. Stephen entered her warm, moist opening with insatiable longing. Suzanne let out a moan of delight, and felt her body relax. Later, she cuddled in his arms, gently stroking his body.

"How about ordering room service instead of going out?" Suzanne asked Stephen.

"Great!"

After their appetite for food was satisfied, they went back to bed for dessert. This time their lovemaking was slow and deliberate. It seemed they couldn't get enough of each other.

"I don't know what you do to me, but don't ever stop," Stephen teased Suzanne. Their sleep was sound and undisturbed, and when they woke the following morning, they were ready to conquer the world.

"I certainly don't feel as if I'm going to be forty-nine years old, especially when I'm with you" Stephen pronounced.

She kissed him on the cheek and told him "You're only as old as you feel." Winking at him she joked, "Just keep loving me and I'll keep you young at heart." They left for work after making plans to see each other that evening.

The week went by too quickly. Suzanne and Stephen saw each other every day. On Thursday they managed to grab a fast lunch together at Hamburg Heaven about a block away from the salon. Though it was nothing to look at from the outside, Suzanne loved their homemade relish. Stephen understood why she raved on about it.

As they walked back from their light repast, Stephen said, "I've been thinking about the upcoming holidays. I don't think I can get away from Texas and Lou Anne, but I want to be with you. I'll try to arrange for us to be together for part of the time." As they passed a jewelry store of fine, uniquely designed pieces, he steered her inside, ignoring her protests.

"May I be of assistance to you? Did you see something particular that I can show you?" asked the tastefully dressed salesman.

"Yes, I'd like to see the sapphire and diamond ring in the window, please." He turned to Suzanne; "I'd love to give you this now, just in case I can't be with you on the holidays. I want to get you something to show how much I care for and love you."

Suzanne turned crimson. The breathtaking ring had a two-caret sapphire that was bordered by two one-caret diamonds on either side. Suzanne was speechless as he slid the ring onto her finger.

She spent the rest of the week in her spa during the day and with Stephen at night. Their desire for one another intensified in anticipation of their separation. Their lovemaking took on new dimensions as they became more aware of each other's physical desires. They indulged themselves and each other in their bodies' compulsive needs, satisfying their hunger and passion.

On her last night in Florida, the ring of the phone interrupted the two lovers as they lay in each other's arms.

"Suzanne, this Tim Cassidy. Listen, Kevin and I want to discuss something with you. As soon as you return to Boston, we must talk to you - alone. Please don't mention this to Nancy."

Suzanne was curious about the secrecy, but didn't want to query him over the phone. The questions could wait until she saw him. Stephen inquired about the call, but she told him it was about her business in Boston. She tried to go back to sleep, but found herself too much on edge to do so.

The next morning Stephen drove Suzanne to the airport. She kissed him good-by and promised that she would call him as soon as she got home to Stoney Brook. She was extremely restless on the plane. What could Kevin and Tim possibly want to talk to her about?

Boston, Massachusetts

When she arrived at Logan International Airport, the limousine was waiting for her and drove her directly home. She woke repeatedly during the night with horrifying dreams. Terrifying figures resembling Brian, Nancy, Peter and the Pearlmans floated through dense clouds pursued by some monstrosity. Kevin and Timothy hung from a tree with their eyes gouged out, insects crawling over their lifeless bodies. Sleep continued to elude her, although she realized that soon this awful ordeal would be over.

At daybreak she got up, showered, and dressed. She left for work two hours early. She parked her car and, as she walked down the deserted Newbury Street, pigeons fluttered about the quiet buildings. Abandonment enveloped the usually busy area and an eerie feeling of doom came over her as she unlocked the door of the *Metamorphosis Spa*.

An unusual coolness greeted her as she opened the door. She shivered as she turned on the lights and walked down the narrow hallway. As she moved from room to room, preparing the equipment for the day's clients, she noticed that the lights in Peter's office had been left on.

She knocked lightly on the office door, and, receiving no response cautiously pushed open the door. Observing that the office was empty and Peter was obviously not in, she walked to his desk to turn off the light. She noted that his correspondence and other papers, usually arranged in neat piles, were strewn all over his desk and floor in complete disarray. Picking up a heap of photographs from the floor, she moved to place them on the desk. As she put them down, she noticed a woman in one of them who resembled Evelyn Rich.

On closer examination, she saw Peter posed with some of the people she had seen in the photographs in Bernie Rich's study. A wave of nausea washed over her. With trembling hands, she restored the room to its previous state of disorder so that Peter would not know that she had been there.

Later, sitting in the break room with a hot cup of tea in her shaking hands, she wondered about Peter. How did he know these people?

It suddenly hit her. This had something to do with Timothy's request to meet her without Nancy.

Ipswich, Massachusetts

At daylight, Peter gradually opened his eyes, wishing that the bright light of the morning did not bother him so. He postponed it as long as possible, but finally hoisted himself slowly over the edge of the bed.

He went into the shower. The hot spray of the pulsating water soothed his aching torso. "One would think," he speculated, "that after a night's sleep my body would not be racked with pain."

After he toweled himself dry, he walked to the sauna and sat down on the smooth redwood bench. He weighed his circumstances.

When he first started dealing he vowed he would never use the stuff himself. He just wanted to make some extra money. He hated the sarcastic remarks - cloaked in humor - that people made to him and behind his back.

"Nancy was dazzled by all your wealth."

"Well, of course, he brought a lot of money into the marriage," snicker, snicker.

"Boy, Peter you must have one hell of a wang. Why else would a classy gal like Nancy marry you?"

"You didn't have a pot to pee in."

"You are one lucky guy being married to someone who can take care of you."

Huddling in the corner of the sauna, rocking back and forth, he tried to contain his melancholy and tears. He realized he had to find a way to give it up. He didn't want to become a hophead like some of the mainliners and junkies who were his customers.

He loved the high - like flying through clouds - that he felt whenever he snorted the white powder. It had become a requisite to life itself. Nothing matched the power he had felt when he first began using it. But now it took more and more of the coke and the ecstatic sensations were giving way to depression and pain more and more frequently. He needed it now, not for the high, but to keep from getting sick.

Yes, he had to admit he was addicted. He was at a loss as to how he could retain what was left of his sanity and keep his marriage intact. How could he suppress his hunger and need for coke?

Hating himself for what he had become, his mind went back to his youth. He was never one for book learning, much to his parent's dismay. Sports was his life. He spent long, grueling hours at the local gym, training and exercising so he would be ready if and when a semi-pro team was to offer him a position.

During his senior year when he was presented with an athletic scholarship, he refused it. His parents were furious. He knew the sooner he left school, the happier he would be. He just wanted to play ball.

He envied his brother Alan's intelligence. His parents told anyone who would listen that their son, Alan, who was in the gifted and talented program, always made high honors. Seldom did they attend any of Peter's sporting events. They didn't think of it as anything more than a pastime. Peter didn't fit in with their scholarly crowd.

One day in October, during an exhausting varsity practice session, an incident occurred that would change the course of his life. Peter was playing quarterback, calling the signal. After the play was in motion, he positioned himself to throw the football. He had only a few seconds left before the huge left tackle would sack him, forcing his legs to crumble beneath him.

He never knew who or what hit him. When he woke up in the recovery room in the hospital, he briefly recalled a thump and collision when the massive tackle grabbed him from behind and brought him to the ground.

Three operations later, his hopes for a professional football career came to an abrupt end. His life's ambition of professional or even semi-professional ball would not be fulfilled. He was left in a state of severe depression. Coming to grips with reality was hard, but he had to deal with it. He had to figure out what he could do.

Convinced that he could never get through college, he blamed his parents for not demanding that he pay more attention to his schoolwork. He asked himself why they didn't concern themselves about him as they cared about Alan. He condemned everyone except himself.

He racked his brain to figure out what he could do. He did enjoy creativity so he enrolled himself in hairdressing school. His friends scoffed at the idea when they found out about it. "Hey, you can laugh all you want, but working on gals day and night, I'll be the one scoring with all the good-looking chicks."

When he met Nancy, he had been working for one of the best salons in Boston for three years and was already one of the top hair designers in the East. His female clients would do anything for him - and they frequently did. Money was plentiful; he was riding high and enjoying every minute of it.

Once he and Nancy married, she persuaded him to let her finance a Newbury Street salon. Against his better judgment, he ignored his instincts and took her money.

Opening the sauna's door, he slowly walked back into the stall shower, turned on the cold water and let it close his pores. How in the hell had he let his life become a combination of hypocrisy and mayhem?

What would Nancy do when she found out? He was determined she would not get away from him. They had been married too many years for him to ruin their relationship. His parents adored her. She was bright, intelligent, everything they had wanted for their son. "Well if she's as bright and intelligent as they think, I had to be pretty special for her to fall in love with me," he told himself.

As he was dressing he thought he heard the chimes of the doorbell. When he became aware of a second ring, he ran down the spiral staircase and opened the door.

"It's about time. I've been standing here for ten minutes. Where the hell have you been? You look like shit."

"Come on in. I'm sorry I took so long but I was in the shower. I wasn't paying attention. Usually we don't have visitors so early in the morning. What brings you here at this ungodly hour? Would you like some coffee?" Alan sat at the kitchen table, overlooking the turbulent waters as they splashed against the rocks below.

"Seriously, to what do I owe the honor of your visit?"

"You probably won't believe this, but I had an uneasy feeling all last night, and I still had it when I woke up this morning. I thought something was wrong with you and I wanted to talk."

"So, what's wrong with the phone?"

"I didn't want to talk to a machine. Besides, you don't always call me back. I know something's not right and I want to know what it is."

Peter was now visibly disturbed and said, "Lay off me. You're mistaken."

"Nope. It's not going to be that easy. Look at you. You haven't been yourself for a long time. I've tried to ignore it, but dam it Peter, let me help you. By the way, where's Nancy?"

"I don't know. When I got home early this morning, she wasn't here. We don't keep track of each other, you know."

Peter poured the coffee, then sat down and fell back into the chair. He sipped the slightly bitter brew. He realized he had to speak with someone about his predicament, maybe Alan could find a solution. He summoned his courage and finally said, "I don't know where to begin."

"Just start talking. I'm a very good listener."

Peter unburdened his soul and voiced his fears. After the disclosure he was mentally and physically drained. Putting his arms on the table, he lowered his head and cried out in frustration, "What the hell am I going to do?"

Alan was literally sick to his stomach. Although he thought that Peter was involved with drugs, deep in his heart he hoped it was not true. Now it was confirmed. "How can I help?" he wondered.

Alan rose slowly from the kitchen chair and put his arm on his older brother's shoulder.

"I know you're tormented and you're in deep trouble. If the law finds out that you're a supplier, you can be put away for a long, long time. Besides that, if you want to kick the habit, it's going to be one of the hardest things you've ever done. Do you have the guts to go to hell and back?"

Lifting his brother's face towards him, Alan continued "Look at me, damn you. Stop feeling sorry for yourself. You've got to do something. Deal with it!" Even though Alan was considerably smaller than his brother, he managed to lift him from his slumped position and forced him to sit up.

Despite his confession, Peter was afraid to face reality.

"I know what you're saying is right, but I'm still afraid. These guys that I'm involved with can be pretty tough if you don't go along with them. They'd think nothing of harming Nancy or, for that matter, any member of my family, if push comes to shove."

"If I have to go away to a hospital, it's not going to be easy leaving my business for any length of time. I'll try laying off the stuff, I promise. Hey, haven't I done well so far in my life? I can do it. As God is my witness, I'll do it on my own, you'll see."

"You know when we were growing up I looked up to you. I believed in you. You were my idol. But I'm telling you; you can't do this by yourself. You may go into convulsions. Do you want to put Nancy through that too? Face it. You need professional help. You should be in a hospital where they can take proper care of you. Does Nancy know what's going on or have you been able to fool her like you think you've fooled everyone else?"

"My life has been in such turmoil lately that I don't know if I'm coming or going. I don't know if Nancy realizes the extent of my addiction or even that I have a problem." Perspiration drenched his shirt and he was drained of all energy.

"I'm going to make some calls to find a place for you to get clean. Don't worry about those dealers. I won't let anything happen to Nancy or any of us. I'll call you tomorrow. One way or another, I'll see this through with you."

Peter lifted himself from the chair. He attempted to postpone the inevitable realization that he needed help from others. "Thanks for coming by, old buddy. I'll be okay, don't worry about me any more. What's been going on with you lately?"

He took charge, pushing Peter back into the chair. "Don't change the subject. We're not through with your problem. Even if we have to contact the authorities, I won't let anything happen to you."

Pushing his hair off his forehead Alan ordered, "We have a lot to do. Listen to me for a change."

"I'll be forever grateful. Saying thanks doesn't seem enough. You're the best brother a jerk like me could ever ask for." He hugged him tightly and walked him to the door.

Boston, Massachusetts • December, 1991

Bundled up against the cold, Suzanne found the walk through the Public Garden and Boston Common invigorating. She was apprehensive and wanted to know exactly what Tim and Kevin had to talk to her about. So many pressures weighed heavily on her mind and she hoped that the agents could relieve her anxiety. It was nearly six-thirty in the evening when Suzanne stepped off the elevator onto the nearly deserted fourth floor and stood in front of the open door to Kevin Halloran's office.

The two men heard Suzanne, and Kevin beckoned her in. Suzanne related her latest findings and, perplexed, waited for the two gentlemen to respond to the new discoveries. Evaluating the information, Kevin measured his next statement. Kevin glanced quickly at Timothy, visually searching for his endorsement. Kevin began, "The reason we wanted to speak to you privately, without Nancy, is that we've discovered some troublesome details that, most likely, will have a harmful effect upon her."

"Let me go back a bit. Before we even took on this particular case, we did background checks on you and Nancy. We investigated your personal lives, business associates, obtained pictures of your immediate family members and others close to you as well. Do you follow me so far?"

Sitting in the black standard office chair, Suzanne felt that her life was about to be turned inside out. She nodded her head and told them to continue.

"When we developed the film and deciphered the contents, we noticed that Peter was mentioned in some of the ledger books. He's also in many of the photographs. He's not just a casual acquaintance of these people."

"Maybe Nancy was too busy gathering up the information, that she didn't notice the details of the photographs," Timothy interrupted.

"It was dark in there, and we were working fast, anyway. I certainly didn't notice anyone in particular when we were copying them," Suzanne replied.

"Interpreting the ledger was difficult, but we found out the names of the men who are running this particular business."

"And, let me tell you, this is very big business for them, although it's relatively small time compared to some other organizations."

"We are certain we can convict these scumbags and put them behind bars. The cruel reality is that one of the women who helped us find the offenders is married to one of them."

Despair and anguish were emotions familiar to Suzanne from previous years when she had often felt helpless. Now the old feelings returned with a vengeance as she realized what this would do to Nancy.

"For once in my life I'm at a loss for words," spoke Suzanne, softly. Unsure of herself and the immediate future, she looked to the two men for direction.

"Where do we go from here? I'm still in a state of shock. And, what'll happen to Peter? He's been a wonderful partner and friend. It's still hard to believe. I did notice a change in him. He became moody and irritable, but I attributed it to stress. Do you think he's on drugs himself?"

"We don't know if he actually has a dependency, but it would make sense. Peter will be prosecuted in due time. I know it's a shock to hear this but we're aware that you're a strong woman. It'll take some time to clear this up, and in the meanwhile, we want you to behave as normally as possible. We still need both you and Nancy. We'll keep in touch. We're not letting you out of our sights; not just yet."

As she left the office, Suzanne was emotionally wrought. She could see that she, too, might lose everything. Her fifteen years' of hard work and the stability she had striven to attain might be in real jeopardy. When the scandal broke, would her clients and the business community as a whole think that she was part of it? "Probably," she thought. Would she lose everything?

"God-damn you, Peter. What were you thinking of?" she cursed him under her breath.

At that very moment all she wanted was to be held by Stephen's protective arms. She needed him to seal her from the outside world. It seemed like an eternity before she arrived home and parked her car in the driveway. She sat in the car for ten minutes, still stunned. She ascended the outside stairs slowly, and found, once inside, the quiet and peaceful atmosphere of her home comforting.

She did not want to speak to anyone and was glad to find that the house was empty. She kicked off her black leather boots, leaving them by the door and walked upstairs to her bedroom. When she took off her clothes, she felt she was shedding the burdens of the world. She drew water for the bath and lowered herself into the warmth of the tub. She felt the muscles of her uptight body begin to relax. All at once she felt like a piece of driftwood, flowing with the ocean's tide.

Lying on the bed later, bundled up in her warm robe, she called Stephen at his office. She let his private line ring and was about to hang up when he answered. She had rehearsed what she wanted to say, but when she heard his voice, words escaped her.

After some small talk, she gathered the strength to tell him all that had happened in the last few months. She told him everything, holding nothing back. She asked him if he could understand her reluctance to divulge what had been going on, and if he could forgive her for keeping it a secret from him. Stephen's confidence in Suzanne gave her the support she desperately needed. She declined his offer to fly up to be with her now that her strength was restored. Kissing him over the phone, she thanked him for his understanding, then reluctantly said good-by, relieved that she had finally revealed her problem to Stephen.

She returned to work the next day and eased into her usual routine. She astonished herself at her ability to interact normally with Peter. The spa was very busy, and she thanked God that all of her estheticians were in.

Nancy called and asked Suzanne to go shopping with her. Suzanne knew that she couldn't put off seeing her or Nancy would realize something was awry.

Copley Place was crowded, as usual. The frigid weather had not deterred the busy people from their holiday shopping. Suzanne sat at a black wrought iron table by the frosty window of the Au Bon Pan Restaurant, looking out at the courtyard. She observed the white lights strung on the now bare trees. Nancy arrived and they indulged themselves, ordering cheese and raspberry-filled croissants with their tea.

When they left the cafe, they walked through the large and beautifully maintained mall. Suzanne related stories to Nancy about the old days when she was young and shopped with her mother and grandmother in Filene's basement. Nancy laughed. She told Suzanne that she had never had the pleasure of window-shopping for the sake of it, and never with her mother. Suzanne felt sorry for her and realized this might be one of the last times Nancy would enjoy a relaxed afternoon like this.

Suzanne put her own burdens on hold and enjoyed their little get-together. With shopping bags filled to the top, they returned to the Au Bon Pan. Over hot drinks the conversation became serious. Nancy, who over the years had come to regard Suzanne as a sister, had also let her become her confidante. She felt she could tell Suzanne her innermost thoughts and emotions.

Although Suzanne thought she knew Nancy and Peter well, she was soon to find out that she didn't. Nancy explained, "Our marriage has existed in appearance only for the past ten years. When Peter and I married, I loved him with all my heart. As the years progressed and I was unable to bear children, Peter wouldn't hear of adoption. He told me he didn't intend to raise 'anyone else's child.' God, time went by quickly, and despite my pleading, he wouldn't reconsider."

Nancy continued, "Disappointment, depression, and desperation became my constant companions. I felt alone and helpless. For years I tried to mask my emotions and kept busy by helping others. Now I don't know if I can hide my feelings any longer."

Suzanne handed Nancy some tissues as she saw Nancy's eyes brim with tears. She had never seen Nancy cry before. Nancy had always been the humorous yet dependable person others could rely on. In Nancy's time of need, Suzanne wanted to be there for her. Her heart went out for her dear and wonderful friend. She asked Nancy, "Why haven't you told me about your sadness before?"

Nancy shrugged and could not answer. Her bottom lip quivered as she tried to hold back her emotions. She kept weeping and with trembling hands tried to finish her now cold coffee.

Suzanne empathized with Nancy, for, all too often, she remembered what that sense of helplessness was like. Concerned about her friend's welfare, Suzanne took control of the situation "Nancy, we're going to leave your car here in the garage. You're coming home with me. I'll call Peter from my house and tell him you're sleeping over."

Handing some packages to Nancy, Suzanne led her to the car parked in the garage below the plaza. Nancy was quiet on the ride to Stoney Brook. When they got to her house, Suzanne asked Mrs. Walsh to get the hot tub ready.

It took awhile for Nancy to unwind, but she did so, once Suzanne gave her a massage. After Nancy sat in and relaxed in the Jacuzzi, the two women went to Suzanne's bedroom and talked for the remainder of the evening.

Nancy felt guilty about her new relationship with Brian. "Some nights Peter wouldn't come home and I didn't know where he was." Nancy sarcastically added, "When he did manage to get to our happy haven, it would be very late."

Nancy found it difficult to remember when it first began to change, but she realized that it must have been approximately ten years ago. She never told anyone about her misgivings. She didn't know if he was into drugs, gambling, booze, other women or what. Every time she asked him, he put her off or turned things around to put her on the defensive. She was at her wit's end and didn't think she had anyone to turn to.

Brian was another matter entirely. Suzanne knew she was prejudiced when it came to him. She conceded that he could have changed and admitted that there had been large stretches of time in their life together when he was kind and considerate. She was concerned for her friend's fragile state because she knew Brian had a Jekyll and Hyde personality. She had never been sure what it was that could set him off and often wondered in later years, if it could have been some type of chemical imbalance.

Without betraying her promise to the two FBI agents, Suzanne brought up the drug issue to Nancy. Telling Nancy that she was probably on the right track about substance abuse, she agreed that she also had noticed a change in Peter over the years but thought it was only due to the stress of their business.

"No wonder Nancy was vulnerable and succumbed to Brian's advances. With the bad comes some good," Suzanne speculated. "If Timothy and Kevin were to prosecute Peter and the men from Morse Associates, it wouldn't destroy Nancy because she's not as in love with him as I thought."

She was anxious for this hideous mess to be resolved. Until the FBI was ready to move, Suzanne and Nancy had to wait patiently and keep up the pretense. Suzanne knew that it would be difficult, but believed that everything turns out for the best. I'll contact Kevin tomorrow and tell him about this latest twist."

The perpetual ringing of the telephone alarmed Suzanne and she drowsily reached for the receiver. With a lethargic "hello" she waited for the person on the other end to respond.

"Suzanne, is that you?"

"Yes. Who's this?"

"That old saying, 'Out of sight, out of mind' certainly must apply to you," a pleasant, deep voice replied.

"Who is this?" she asked again, more abruptly.

"This is Lawrence, Larry VanDer Hyde. I hope I didn't wake you. It's four in the afternoon here and I thought or hoped you'd be up by now. It's around ten in the morning there. Isn't it?"

She squinted her eyes to get a look at the alarm clock. "Yes, I must have slept a little later than usual. How are you?"

"Well, I've been on holiday with my children at our home in Belgium. We just had a delightful day today and I kept remembering our conversation about how much you enjoyed your children when they were young. I thought I'd ring you to let you know that you were on my mind."

She opened her eyes fully and with a friendlier tone said, "It's very sweet of you to call me. I'm glad you're enjoying your vacation. How are your parents and children? Do you have special plans for the holidays?"

"We've been having a wonderful time. I took the children to Brussels. They love the Sunday morning flea market there. We went to the Royal Museum for Fine Art in Antwerp, which isn't far from our home. The children cannot start early enough, in my estimation, to learn refinement. They almost talked me into buying a Sheep dog for them, but I'm not quite convinced. I told them they aren't home enough to appreciate the animal, but with their usual persuasion, I might be out voted or won over," he cheerfully acknowledged.

"To change the subject a bit, have you thought anything more about our last conversation?"

"If you're talking about becoming my financial adviser, yes, I have thought about it, and I also mentioned it to my partner. We are interested and want to know more about making a public offering. We're novices in such matters, though, so you're going to have to prove to me that this will be in our best interest."

"When I come back to the States after Christmas, I'll call you. If it's all right, we can discuss the undertaking over dinner. Do you have any special plans for the holidays?" He wanted to ask her to join him and his family for a vacation, but thought better of it. "No," he deliberated. "I can't rush her. I must take one step at a time."

She told him all about her plans and wished him a happy holiday season.

"I must apologize for not getting back to you sooner," Suzanne said, "But an unforeseen circumstance in my personal life has kept me busy."

"I'm sorry to hear that," said a sincere Larry. "Is there anything that I can do to help you?"

"No, the problem really doesn't concern our business and the matter should be cleared up by the New Year. Well, I'd better run. This is the latest I've slept in a long time. I must thank you for waking me, though. I have tons to do and if I don't start now, the tasks will never get done. Larry, thank you again for calling. It was sweet of you to think of me. Please wish your parents and children a Merry Christmas and I hope to see you after the New Year."

"Suzanne, I'll be thinking of you, and, please, have a wonderful holiday season."

As she dressed, Suzanne couldn't help thinking of Larry. A smile crossed her face whenever she spoke with him. "We've known each other over thirteen years and he still puzzles me. If I weren't involved with Stephen, I could easily fall for him. He's a fascinating guy, sometimes a little too gentlemanly. I'm a little curious why he bothers with me. I mean what are his motives? He's never come on to me. He's rich and powerful, so he doesn't need my money." She quickly inspected herself in the large, free-standing mirror and approved of the mature, attractive woman in the reflection. "Oh well, who couldn't fall for me?" she laughed to herself as she walked down the stairs.

Chapter Thirteen

Nancy arose the next morning with the weight of the world off her shoulders. "Mrs. Walsh, thanks so much for that delicious breakfast. If you ever decide to leave Suzanne, you can always live with me."

"It's sweet of you to say that, but you know that Suzanne is like a daughter to me. I'd never leave her."

Nancy turned to Suzanne who was now on her second cup of tea, "And you; I don't know what I'd do without you."

"What are friends for if they can't be there for you?" She drove back to Boston to deliver Nancy to her car.

Nancy arrived home and immediately changed into comfortable clothes. She turned on the television set to let the soap operas drone out the desperate silence of the massive house. She felt relieved that she had finally unburdened her hidden sorrow.

"How can I change the direction of my life after so many years?" she asked herself. "I've denied my real feelings for so long."

She wanted to clear her head and left the empty house to traipse along the deserted beach below. Bundled up against the elements in her alpaca jacket, she heard the crunching of the crusted sand beneath her boots as she walked along the beaches' jagged shoreline. The lengthy coast stretched out ahead of her as she moved slowly along the water's edge. Many thoughts tumbled through her mind. Of one thing she was certain: she wanted to put her desires ahead of her sensibilities, for once, even though it might cause a division between her and the people she loved.

Nancy heard the frothy green water crashing against the cliffs as she neared the end of the beach. The old resentment she once felt against Peter resurfaced as she remembered their bitter arguments about adopting a child. His personality, once happy and even-tempered, now fluctuated between moody and indifferent. His old, warm enthusiasm seldom came through. She would always be devoted to Peter but wondered if her love was enough? What were her real feelings for Brian? She now understood Suzanne's hesitancy to leave Brian after being married for so many years. Could she say good-by to Peter after such a long time? She sat on the flat surface of a mineral speckled rock and let the brisk wind whip across her cold, reddened face.

A few hungry sea gulls circled above her head, finally daring to land near Nancy. Challenging each other for the few fragments of refuse, two courageous gulls boldly ventured closer to her.

Climbing down off the rock, she again stepped onto the hardened seashore, lost in her thoughts. "I don't need Peter's money, so finances will never pose a problem for me, and Peter has become wealthy on his own, so he

326

doesn't need mine," she thought to herself. "Is this what its come down to?" Unable to sort out the mass of confusion, she turned and headed back up the beach towards the stairs leading to her large but empty home.

~~~~~~~~~~~~~~~~~~~~

Kevin was waiting for Suzanne in his office. They talked about the upcoming holiday, then Suzanne related the sorrowful details of Nancy's marriage and her own view of the situation. She rose from her chair, walked to the window, and looked down on the busy street below. A feeling of guilt overtook her as she felt she was betraying her dear friend. Turning slowly around with a determined look on her face she said "Let's forget about Nancy and Peter for now and get back to Brian. Brian might be an unwitting partner and may not know the extent of his associates' dishonesty. Kevin, what would you think if I confronted him with what I know? I could expose the role that his business had in the money laundering."

Kevin waited for Suzanne to finish before he expressed his opinion. "Timothy and I have gone over the journals inch by inch and our decoders have deciphered them. Considering what you told us about his financial problems, we think he might, very well, be another victim. Not to the degree the Pearlmans were. Brian was a different quarry, a man who was looking for a fast buck. The crooks saw a greedy man, a sucker. His company had a good reputation, and they promised him the money that he needed to expand. It looks as if they gave the fish just enough bait. They gave him some substantial sums of cash, but they always dangled the big carrot in front of him. The dough they doled out to him was nothing compared to the bucks they were taking in."

"I don't want you or Nancy to reveal anything to anyone right now. Timothy and I are going to pay Brian Morse a visit this week and we'll explain the situation to him. After he hears his options, I think he'll cooperate. We might be able to offer him a deal. That is, if he comes forward to help us."

Suzanne drove the long way home. Her head was spinning. The satisfaction she craved from seeing Brian squirm was not quite as sweet as she had imagined it would be. The concern she had for her children and Nancy were foremost on her mind. She realized that Nancy had grown very fond of Brian. It might be love, although Nancy hadn't verbalized it as such. She wanted to tell Nancy what was going on, but knew better than to betray Kevin. She might have to wait until after New Years, for this drama to unfold.

A message from Nancy was waiting for Suzanne when she arrived home. "Hi," Suzanne spoke over the phone, trying to remain unruffled when Nancy picked up the receiver. "What can I do for you?"

"I wanted to thank you again for your help. I'll be forever grateful for letting me tell my problems to you." Omitting her meeting with Kevin she related her day and said she was looking forward to seeing Nancy at the Spa's annual Christmas party. The shadows of barren trees reflected on the walls of Suzanne's bedroom as she hung up the phone. A chill ran through her when she speculated on what might happen in the next few weeks. She tried to concentrate on happy events.

Hope was bringing the new boyfriend to *Metamorphosis'* Christmas party, Spencer Bradley from Newport. Hope had not talked much about him, except to say that he was interesting. Suzanne was looking forward to meeting him.

Suzanne knew it was chancy having parties in the wintertime, but that was part of the fun. The Friday before Christmas, a huge storm deposited a foot of snow. The following day was a glorious, crisp day, right out of a Currier and Ives print.

The caterer arrived in the morning and started his preparations. There was a certain flair about him that Suzanne liked. She wasn't sure if he was gay or not, but it didn't matter to her. She and Mrs. Walsh happily relinquished the kitchen to him. The two women relaxed in front of the tree with a glass of raspberry wine and reflected on past Christmas celebrations with family and friends.

"I can remember when I first moved to Quincy, there were only a few Jewish families with which to socialize. Many of my Christian friends invited me to help decorate their Christmas trees. I would string popcorn and cranberries along the branches of the evergreen trees, making sure they didn't get in the way of the multi-colored lights. My Italian girlfriends invited me for their annual

Christmas Eve celebrations where the families enjoyed all sorts of fish dishes. Their mothers spent hours preparing culinary delights. I loved it, and often wished I could have a Christmas tree of my own."

"When Brian first asked me to put up a tree, I found myself looking forward to it. I didn't celebrate Christmas for religious reasons, but rather for the spirit of the holidays and Santa Claus. The Christmas tree itself had been an awful issue when I became a young wife and mother. Brian expected me to carry on his family traditions. Mama Rachel and Papa Jake, of a shalom, expected to celebrate Chanukah at our home. My Dad didn't know how his parents would react when they saw our Holiday spruce at the yearly Chanukah party. We had the traditional lutkies and applesauce, and we exchanged Chanukah gifts and gelt (money). The event turned out even better than I hoped. After their initial surprised reaction, my grandparents came to love opening their Chanukah presents that were under the "Chanukah" tree. My grandparents and parents gave us menorahs and dradles to decorate the evergreen. A large Jewish Star adorned the top of it alongside of an angel that I had for the girls."

Tears fell from her eyes as she thought of her grandparents. God how she missed them. Over the years she appreciated her relatives more, and felt sorry that her friend Nancy had never known the closeness of family.

Dabbing her eyes dry she proposed a toast to Mrs. Walsh. "To the two of us, Mrs. Walsh, and the people we love. May we have health, peace and harmony for this holiday and for the coming New Year."

People began to arrive a little past seven o'clock. The house smelled of fresh pine, and soft Christmas music played in the background lending a festive air to the occasion.

Hope arrived with Spencer and introduced him to the crowd. "He certainly is handsome," Suzanne admitted. They made a fine looking couple. He was very tall, six feet three inches, with wide muscular shoulders and arms. His blond hair was naturally wavy, and he had the palest of blue eyes. He was truly an all-American preppy. His charming smile lit up his whole face. "Oh, too bad he's not Jewish!" Suzanne thought.

Peter seemed to be his old self again. Suzanne noticed that he did disappear for a short time, but she didn't have time to dwell on it. The evening was a smashing success and she was pleased that everyone was having a wonderful time. The last guest left at two thirty in the morning. "Another year is passing," she thought to herself. "Thank you God for another good and prosperous one."

Timothy called in the late afternoon to ask her if they could meet the day after Christmas. Extending holiday cheer and good wishes to both him and Kevin, she confirmed she would definitely be there. Suzanne had made plans to stay around the New England area until after the holidays.

Christmas Eve was spent at Suzanne's house with family and close friends. Dorothy and Morris stayed over for the evening and on Christmas day Suzanne gave an open house for everyone in the neighborhood. Suzanne and Mrs. Walsh prepared the food themselves for this celebration. "Do you think we need all this food? I think we have plenty," Mrs. Walsh admonished. Then she laughed and asked "Don't I ask you this question every year?"

Suzanne's greatest fear was that she would not have enough food for her guests. "I guess it's my ethnic background. I always remember mounds of food at the holidays when my grandparents and parents entertained. I once went to a bar mitzvah where the caterers ran out of hors d'oeuvres. I think it's every hostess' nightmare. I know I go overboard, but humor me." Nothing pleased Suzanne more than preparing her special dishes for her company to enjoy.

With a sigh, Mrs. Walsh went about her business.

"I have one more appetizer to make, and then I'll go to the bakery and pick up the rum cake that I ordered. The children would never forgive me if I didn't serve that. How do the apple pies look, do you think they're done yet?"

"You're so funny. You go through this same big production all the time. You work yourself ragged and then you're exhausted."

"Ah, but I get such satisfaction when people are enjoying the food I've made. Keep in mind that I don't make a large Christmas dinner anymore like I used to. In about an hour, we should be finished. I'll go upstairs and take a shower and then I'll be able to relax and enjoy the company. Remember, I have the next couple of days off."

Pungent aromas of highly spiced seafood permeated the household. Christmas music lent festivity to the happy evening. Beverly, Louis, Alan, Bill, and Justin arrived together, bearing gifts for their adopted family. Justin, his usual jovial self, expressed delight in seeing the family members again and extended an open invitation to visit his gallery again, at any time.

A neighbor who had known the girls since they were young cornered Hope next to the shrimp platter, "Hope, how nice to see you again. What are you doing these days? Is there anyone special in your life yet?"

Dorothy was passing by and heard the question. She moved closer to the shrimp platter and waited to hear her granddaughter's response.

"As a matter of fact, there is. I asked him to join us this evening, but he's spending Christmas Eve with his own family. He'll be here tomorrow to spend at least part of the day with us."

"Is he of the Jewish faith, or a goy like me?" With that remark he slapped Hope jokingly on the back and waited for her reply.

"Let's say he's never celebrated Chanukah." Dorothy was all ears and couldn't wait to tell Morris. Pleasant conversation filled the house from one end to the other. People spent the afternoon catching up with their friends and neighbors.

"It's amazing," Kay said to a neighbor. "We are living in the same neighborhood and we rarely get to see one another. It's a good thing Suzanne has this get-together every year or I'd never see any one."

After their friends and neighbors left, the immediate family sat in front of the crackling fire. Suzanne went upstairs to change into a comfortable lounging outfit. As she was heading downstairs to rejoin the rest of the family, the phone interrupted her.

"It's me," said Stephen, as the grandfather clock in the hall struck midnight. "I wish I could be with you tonight, I'm sorry. I love you and thought of nothing but you all day.

The silence and distance between them seemed unnatural. Stephen felt disheartened. "Don't worry, there will be more holidays for us to be together. I'm glad you called. I've been thinking of you too. I wish I could hold you in my arms tonight." Jokingly, Suzanne remarked, "I could certainly save on the heating bills if I was with you every night."

They talked for a while longer, and then Suzanne had to get back to her family. She was disappointed they couldn't be together, but she was also quietly remorseful. There was no way to get around the fact she was in love with a married man. Who was she to point the finger at Brian?

She composed herself and returned to the living room to watch the family opening their presents. That Chanukah her parents gave Suzanne a piece of Mama Pessa's jewelry, which meant a lot to her. It was a wonderful holiday; spent with all the people she loved, except one.

The week between Christmas and New Years passed quickly. The spas were busy scheduling appointments with clients who had received gift certificates. The pace slackened toward the middle of the week, then picked up again on the day of New Year's Eve for make-up applications.

Suzanne detested New Year's Eve. A void that she could not explain always accompanied it. She disliked the false gaiety people displayed. As a young woman she remembered the disappointment and frustration when not asked out for the holiday. When she was unescorted to a gala celebration, she remembered the awkwardness when the gong struck midnight. As an adult those feelings about New Year's Eve had never left her. Now, with Stephen unable to be with her, the feeling of emptiness resurfaced. This year was no different.

Her parents were going to the annual temple celebration and asked Suzanne to join them. She declined. Beverly and Louis asked her to attend a party and again she begged off. Her daughters were happily anticipating a fun evening. Suzanne would not put a damper on their mood. Mrs. Walsh was off to the Ice Capades with a few of her friends.

Suzanne told the estheticians they could leave early and closed up the spa about eight o'clock that evening. She was looking forward to a quiet night by herself. A late snow was predicted. She disliked driving in the bad weather and tried avoiding going out, when it was inclement, especially on holidays. As she approached her street, the snow slowly started to fall.

Going into the stereo room she put on her favorite tapes. She started a fire, then went upstairs to the Jacuzzi. Looking out of the window she could see that the snow was accumulating rapidly. She thoroughly enjoyed being alone and luxuriated in the warm powerful jets of water. The snowflakes accumulated quickly on the skylight directly over the bathtub, eliminating any possible view of the hazy, gray sky.

After what seemed hours, she slowly got out of the warm spa water. She put on a nightgown and wore the robe that Taylor had given her. She poured herself a glass of wine and settled down by the hypnotic flames of the fire with a book.

Around 11 o'clock, completely absorbed in a new mystery, she realized the doorbell had been ringing repeatedly. Reluctantly, she went to the foyer, looked through the peephole, and was astounded to see Stephen standing there covered in snow. Shaking the flakes off his coat, he took Suzanne in his arms.

Holding her tenderly he said, "Surprise, sweetheart. I never thought we'd be able to land at Logan with this storm. I made arrangements to whisk you away and take you to the Four Seasons this evening, but as you can see there's been a change of plans. My intentions were good. We were the last flight allowed to land. I would have walked to the end of the earth, if I had to, to be with you tonight. I love you Suzanne."

His lips were warm and soft. Flushed with excitement she fervently returned his kiss. She led him into the living room and poured him a glass of wine. In front of the warm fire, contentment overtook her as she lay in his arms. They watched the embers glow and flicker. She felt more love for Stephen than she thought possible.

"How on earth did you manage to get away?"

"Lou Ellen had plans for us to attend an elaborate party with the same obnoxious people we usually see. I was willing to put on my pretense and go, but Lou Ellen got into one of her moods and started drinking heavily yesterday. The holidays are bad for us. I couldn't take any more, and decided I wanted to be with you." Jokingly he teased her. "Of course, I could've found you dancing and in someone else's arms."

"Not a chance," she murmured as she hit him on his arm lovingly, and cuddled closer. As the clock struck midnight, Suzanne couldn't remember a better New Year's Eve. On the first day of the New Year, they would wake up in each other's arms. They shut off the lights and ascended the stairs.

Stephen left for the airport in the late afternoon after Suzanne had indulged him with a scrumptious breakfast of French toast, steak and eggs. Later in the day she telephoned the members of her family to make sure that they were all safe and sound.

January, 1992

New England's economic forecast was not good. Large banking establishments were closing and mortgage foreclosures filled the newspapers. Workers who expected to have secure positions for life worried about their jobs as the large computer firms reported large losses from one quarter to the next. Many others in concerns relating to those also found themselves unemployed. People lost their homes and automobiles. The wealthy, who had old money, held on to it and became more frugal.

The spa on Newbury Street was still reasonably busy and as long as her salons held their own, she was secure. Suzanne could tell that the recession was affecting the clients, though. They still came to *Metamorphosis* because if they looked good, they felt better, but after receiving their treatments they were reluctant to reschedule appointments right away. Rather than rebooking immediately, they preferred to call later for their next appointments.

When Kevin and Timothy called Suzanne to arrange their next meeting, Suzanne knew she had to see them, but she was disinclined to hear any more bad news. Things had gone beyond her control and it scared her.

Suzanne realized that she was luckier than most people, knocking on wood, she was thankful that her health and that of her loved ones was good. Her children had grown up to be thoughtful and delightful young adults. Although her parents complained about aches and pains, they were still able to take care of themselves and their own affairs. They managed to have an active social life.

She had been lucky enough to find a wonderful accountant who had helped her invest her money wisely. Although she had to be careful, she didn't have to worry about becoming destitute. Five years ago, she had invested in a lovely home in South Carolina and frequently flew down there for peace and quiet whenever she could get away. This property was not too far from Charleston, yet it was close enough to the ocean for the tranquillity she yearned for. She could easily dock a boat nearby since the Intracoastal Waterway came right to her back yard. She loved golf and played daily when she was there.

The phone disrupted her reverie. "Hi, Suzanne, this is Bev."

"No kidding. Like I don't know your voice after all these years!"

"Okay, wise guy. Are you busy right now?"

"No, what's up?"

"Louis has a client who owns a beautiful vacation home on Tortola. Have you heard of it?"

"No."

"It's in the British Virgin Islands. Well, anyway, he offered the place to us for a couple of weeks. How about coming with us?"

"Thanks for the invite, but I really can't get away."

"What do you mean you can't get away? Will the spas close down if you take a vacation? For Gods sake, Suzanne, come on. You need some time for yourself. You're working too many long hours." Finally, Suzanne agreed to go, but for only three days.

~~~~~~~~~~~~~~~~~~~~~~~

As they landed on the small runway, the fiery sun scorched the steep, mountainous island. Louis steered their jeep over barren, bumpy roads and up hairpin turns on the sides of the mountains that dropped straight down to the ocean far below them.

"Louis, please be careful. These roads are worse than any roller coaster I've ever seen. I think I'm going to be sick."

"He thinks he's a cowboy. All that is missing is your cowboy hat," laughed Suzanne, seated in the back seat holding on for dear life.

As they rounded a narrow bend, the sprawling stone house built on the cliff overlooking the ocean came into view.

As soon as they unpacked, they walked out onto the patio and watched the many brightly colored sailboats under sail, on the high seas. "Someone told me that this is a haven for sailing enthusiasts. The water and beaches are magnificent. How about going down the path and onto the beach after we unwind and have a few drinks?" Beverly asked.

"Sounds good to me, what about you, Louis?"

"My wife comes up with some wonderful ideas." Enjoying the seclusion and stillness of the private cove, Suzanne was glad that her friend had persuaded her to take the time off. They spent the next two days enjoying the peaceful, resplendent, island that most travelers had never heard of. While Beverly and Louis were out, Suzanne took advantage of the tranquil surroundings. Looking over the vast greenery to the endless blue waters of the ocean made Suzanne forget the ever-present predicament she found herself in. She watched the different color sails of the sleek boats racing one another and it helped Suzanne forget, for a while, the sorry state of affairs that she felt she had put Nancy into. "I can't pretend any longer that Nancy's involvement with Brian doesn't bother me. I don't care what self-denial Nancy tries to fool herself with I'll have to confront her with my feelings. This vacation is just what the doctor ordered. Getting away from the situation will put a new perspective on it. Diplomacy is what I will need when I tell Nancy what is bothering me. It's a chance I have to take. She'll either hate me and I will lose a precious friend and business partner or who knows what? Whatever comes out of this strange development, I'm afraid our lives will never be the same. I hate change and, yes, I'm afraid of the consequence, but I did it to myself. I'm the one who started this whole affair. I'd like nothing more than to bury my head in the sand like an ostrich and let the cruel world pass by without me." A rat ran across the patio in front of her and brought her out of her depression. "Stop feeling sorry for yourself." She went down the stairs and headed for the beach below.

Driving Suzanne back to the airport after her three days in the sun, Louis mentioned that he was looking at property nearby. "How about it Suzanne? Would you be interested in buying the land next to ours? It would be a great place to get away from the maddening crowd. When we get back we'll fill you in on all the details." True to their word, on their return, they gave her all the details that she needed to become their new neighbor. Suzanne's first vacation home abroad became her secret escape. Spontaneously, she would retreat to her special hideaway, a few days at a time. Her very own beach, hidden behind massive trees and shrubs, was completely deserted. The island's proximity to St. Thomas offered her the familiarity of the United States' culture.

Anderlecht, Belgium • January, 1992

The holiday passed much too quickly for the three VanDer Hyde children. Carolyn reveled in the attention bestowed upon her by her adoring grandparents and father.

On their last morning at home, Hubert knocked on Carolyn's bedroom door.

"Come in," she said, as she deliberately loitered, packing the remainder of her clothes into her suitcase as slowly as she could.

"In a way I wish we weren't going back to school," Hubert proclaimed dispiritedly.

"I know what you mean. As much as I love my friends at school, it's not the same as being with your family. Wasn't the festival fun? What presents are you bringing back to school?"

"Most of them, since we won't be back here again until Easter. Hendrik and I were talking the other day, and we're going to get one of those high, plumed hats from one of the Gilles' men dressed in costume. Ever since we were young, we loved to see the fellows dressed in their bright costumes."

"How are you going to do that?" asked his inquiring younger sister.

"I don't know. If they won't sell it, one of us will distract him and the other will swiftly flee with it in his hands." Shrugging his shoulders he replied, "We'll worry about that when the time comes."

Carolyn's eyes widened with anticipation.

"Hey, what are you two doing in there?" asked a curious Hendrik, as he passed the opened door.

"Come in and join us, if you want," spoke Carolyn. "I'm just finishing with my packing. Are you done?"

"No, not quite. I was just going to my room to get started."

"What other unscrupulous exploits are the two of you up to? I'm not doing anything underhanded, do you understand?"

"What do you mean by that?"

"Oh, I heard all about your plans for this coming Lenten festivities."

"Boy you have a big mouth," he turned and accused his brother. "It's just Carolyn I mentioned it to. She won't tell anyone, will you?" he asked his sister.

"Of course not, but I hope you'll let me join in procuring another hat for me," she said with a twinkle in her sparkling blue eyes. Putting the last bit of clothes into her bags she asked Hubert to sit on the over stuffed suitcase enabling her to fasten the lock. "Will you write to me while I'm at school?" she asked them.

"Of course we will," replied Hubert.

"I'll try to," replied Hendrik, "but my classes are pretty hard this year. I intend to do quite a bit of studying so I can prove to Dad and Grand-papa how smart I am so they'll want me to come into the business. After all, I am the first born and everyone knows that the oldest is expected to take over."

"Well I want to come into the business also. It doesn't matter that I'm a girl, does it?" asked a skeptical Carolyn. Turning to Hubert, she inquired, "do you want to come in with us?"

"I don't know what I want. Gee, I'm still young."

"Well, I'm younger than you are, and I know what I want."

"Good for you" Hubert said sarcastically, "but I might want other things out of life. Who knows?" Hubert, usually shy and timid, could speak his mind to his siblings. Looking down at his feet, he mumbled at first, "I wish we could be together more often. Don't you miss everyone when we're away at school?"

"Sure I do," answered Hendrik. "When I was younger I used to feel the same way you do, but now I think of all the good times we'll have when we're united and it gets me through the depressing times."

"I'm only a year younger than you, and I still miss everyone," said Hubert.

"You'll change your mind. Sometimes we all have to take our time to realize certain things. That's all," replied Hendrik.

"Well," getting her two cents in, Carolyn chimed, "I know how Hubert thinks, and I can sympathize with him. I often used to cry myself to sleep while away at school."

"Oh, grow up you two. This is our lot in life. The faster you accept it, the better off you'll be."

"What makes you the authority?" asked a depressed Hubert. Before he could answer, their Grand-mama called from the foyer and asked them if they were ready.

"The driver is waiting downstairs. Hurry up. We don't want to keep your father waiting."

The animated conversation, carried on in the limousine from their home to the airport, disguised their true feelings. Hendrik, being the oldest, recognized his duty, and realized that nothing he said or did would change it. He tried to remember when it was that he had adopted the behavior that was expected of him.

"Hendrik, your mind must be a million miles away. I asked you a question and you didn't reply. Are you all right?" asked a concerned Lawrence.

"I'm fine, Father. I was looking at the land. What did you ask?"

"It was nothing important. I hope you children had a nice vacation. I know I did." As they entered the airport, each of their private guards was waiting for them.

He kissed Carolyn lovingly on her cheeks and hugged her affectionately. He embraced his two sons and not caring if he embarrassed them, kissed them on either side of the face then shook their hands. He watched them embark and afterwards walked slowly to the other end of the airport where his private plane was waiting to whisk him off to the States.

The airplane climbed to its cruising altitude and leveled off. Lawrence was eager to get back to work after spending the month with his family. Although he was officially on vacation, he managed to stay in daily contact with his offices around the world. His secretaries and the executives called routinely between 8 and 11 in the morning and didn't hesitate to disturb him at any other time, if necessary, to keep him informed of any significant or decisive information.

He was thrilled to be back in Boston so that he could see Suzanne. He had his driver drop him off in front of his offices on State Street. A few people greeted him with a nod or smile as he headed through the reception area to his private elevator.

One of his executive secretaries, Mrs. Lily, had arranged his papers according to priority.

He had been working diligently for two hours, when he received the phone call he had been waiting for.

"Mr. VanDer Hyde, a Suzanne Morse is on the telephone. Should I put her through?"

"Yes, very well, I'll call you when I need you to come back Mrs. Lily."

"Hello, what a pleasant surprise. I just arrived back in Boston this morning. How were your holidays?"

"They were wonderful, thank you. I hope yours went well."

"Yes, the children and I had a splendid time. What can I do for you on this lovely morning, Suzanne?"

"I'm very interested in taking my stock public. I gave your number to my accountant and he'll contact you by the end of this week. I know how busy you are so if we can meet with my lawyer and bookkeeper at the same time it will make it easier for both of us. I may be away for a few days, but I can always change my plans if I have to. I realize you travel constantly and it'll probably be easier for me to alter my agenda."

Tilting his chair, putting his feet onto his desk, he had a delighted expression on his face as he asked her out. "Now before you say no, answer my question. Are you at your Newbury Street Spa today?"

"Well, yes," replied Suzanne.

"Splendid. If you have a break in your schedule, I can have my driver pick you up and we can dine at the Bay Tower Room. Just tell me what time is best for you. We can go over some of the details at the restaurant. Does that sound good to you?"

The limousine was waiting for her when her last client left the spa. It was dusk when Suzanne took the elevator to Larry's suite of offices on the top floor of the State Street address.

The receptionist was waiting to show Suzanne to Mr. VanDer Hyde's office. "He told me to expect you around this time. I'll let him know you've arrived, then I'll bring you to his office."

Suzanne couldn't help admiring the exquisite white and brass furniture and the beautiful grandfather clock that served as a focal point in the waiting area. Larry's office was tastefully done, very masculine, modern, and effective. He walked around his desk and kissed her on each cheek, as many Europeans do.

"You look wonderful, Suzanne. I'm glad you could make it on such short notice."

"Thanks Larry. You look very good yourself. The vacation seems to have done wonders for you. You look well rested."

He laughed, "I don't know how much rest I actually had. With three active young children, one tends to get tired out. They had all sorts of adventures and places that they wanted me to take them to. I made reservations for seven o'clock. Shall we go down earlier and have a cocktail?"

"That sounds good to me."

His table was by the windows. They enjoyed the magnificent view of the Custom House clock. With the arrival of darkness, Suzanne could look out and see the lights of approaching planes against the stillness of the dark evening sky. It was a beautiful sight.

The Dom Perignon was brought to the table. Larry toasted the beautiful woman in front of him as he raised his glass to her. "You shine like one of the stars out there, and you brighten any room you're in. How do you keep yourself so beautiful and yet manage to have such an active life? You amaze me."

Suzanne, who had never learned to accept compliments well, quickly changed the subject. "Thank you, but what about the business details you mentioned?" she asked, steering the conversation away from a personal discussion.

"Yes of course. I take it from our talk that you've thought over my proposal of becoming your financial adviser."

"Yes, I spoke to my partners and children and they all agree it would be wise."

"Well then, I must stress that no one, other than the people directly involved with your business must know any of this. It's imperative that no one finds out. Secrecy is of the utmost importance."

"I've spoken to a large stock brokerage firm and one of the vice presidents, who happens to be a personal friend of mine, will help us. An enormous amount of work must be done to get your company ready. First an underwriter must compare your company to similar ones that are already public. He'll go over your books and your records have to be meticulous. The federal rules and regulations must be followed closely. Well, what do you think, Suzanne?"

"All this is new to me. It's like speaking a different language, but one that I want to learn. As far as my records are concerned, I have a wonderful bookkeeper and accountant who keep my books and records up-to-date. The *Metamorphosis Spas* have come a long way from the days when I was just hoping to bring home a good week's salary. I think you'll be impressed when you see the net profit that my partners and I realize. I'm concerned about my children, though. Maybe you can advise me on what to do with their shares and how I'll divide them."

"I'll be more than happy to help you in any way possible Suzanne. If I wasn't, I wouldn't have offered my assistance."

Larry proposed a toast. "To Suzanne, I hope life is good to you and you get all that you desire and deserve."

"Thanks. I can't tell you how much I appreciate what you're doing. But I'm a little concerned. Through the years we haven't seen much of each other. I keep wondering why are you doing this for me? Can you give me an answer?"

"My dear, how long have we been acquaintances? Over thirteen years if I'm correct. Almost fifteen, maybe. I was very attracted to you from the time we first met. If you're not going to let me become close to you in the way I'd like, then I'm determined to at least have a business relationship. Once I make up my mind Suzanne, I don't falter."

They ate in silence, enjoying the quiet atmosphere, lost in their own thoughts. Larry tried hiding his perplexing situation. The more he saw of Suzanne, he realized how much he wanted her. Not for beauty alone, but for her integrity and values as well. He decided not to give up his quest for her to become the next Mrs. VanDer Hyde.

While sipping her after dinner drink, she looked across the table at this handsome, intelligent, sexy man - a man most women would do anything to get to know better. She asked herself what was it that stopped her from getting involved with this eligible, virile gentleman, other than in a business relationship. From all that she had heard and learned about Lawrence VanDer Hyde, he was someone to admire. "Why," she asked herself, "am I in love with a man that I can't have totally when I could have someone who is obviously willing and very available?"

Later, back in his penthouse, Larry looked out the large windows, admiring the Boston skyline - - its charm and beauty enthralled him. He was too wound up to concentrate on business. He closed his eyes and let the sofa replace his comfortable bed. After a while, he fell into a restless slumber. In only a short time, he woke in a cold sweat, frightened and alarmed as he usually did whenever the similar dream occurred. He always remembered these nightmares. He thought that after fifteen years the vision would have stopped, but it hadn't. It seemed so real, as if it were happening all over again.

Everybody envied the beautiful couple - Elizabeth and Lawrence VanDer Hyde. They had it all. Money was plentiful; they never needed to worry. Their parties were talked about for weeks afterwards. People from every walk of life - actors, heads of state, royalty and corporate presidents - hoped they would be invited to the VanDer Hyde's soirees.

They traveled extensively and owned homes all over the world. True philanthropists, they donated money to various worthwhile causes and endowed many colleges and museums. In addition to all this, they were truly in love.

The first child was a son, who would carry on the name of the famous family. Their second child, another son, was just as cute, cuddly and adorable. Elizabeth wanted a daughter she could pamper, dress up, and teach all the social graces to. She knew, deep in her heart, that this third child she was carrying was the daughter she had hoped and longed for. They had the best doctors and private hospital that were available. It never crossed their minds that any problems would occur. Driving to the hospital they were full of hope and anticipation.

"I want you to know darling, that whatever sex this baby is, as long as it's healthy, that's all that really matters," said Elizabeth, as she squirmed in discomfort as the labor pains increased. Patting her hand lovingly, he assured her it didn't matter as long as she and the baby were fine. They kissed and then the nurse wheeled her into the labor room. The private waiting room was empty, except for a terminal that could display information on the patient's conditions. While he waited patiently, Lawrence heard unusual activity going on in one of the rooms down the hall.

The door opened and the doctor walked slowly towards him where he was calmly seated by the window. He had no cause to be concerned or restless. This was their third child and, like before, everything would turn out fine.

"Mr. VanDer Hyde," a look of concern and trouble was on his tired face.

"Yes." At once, Lawrence knew that something terrible had happened. Getting up from the sofa, he walked hurriedly toward the doctor.

Clearing his throat, the doctor continued. "I'm sorry to have to tell you this, but a terrible tragedy has occurred. The baby is fine, but your wife had a very fatal air embolism happen that couldn't be detected or helped until it was too late. We tried everything within our means and power, but nothing worked. We were able to perform an emergency Cesarean and rescue the baby."

The doctor went on explaining what ensued; his words fell on deaf ears. "The baby's amniotic fluid sac ruptured, precipitating air bubbles into the blood cells. Your wife's blood pressure dropped, her blood could not circulate and she went into heart respiratory failure. We did everything we could. At that point it was imperative to save the child. Your new daughter had a bit of trouble also, but she is fine and doing well now. I don't know what I can say except that all of us are so sorry. We struggled for quite some time, but, unfortunately, nothing worked."

Lawrence was in shock. "What are you saying. Isn't there something you can do?"

"Mr. VanDer Hyde," said the doctor guiding Lawrence to the sofa, "You don't seem to understand. Your wife is dead. Do you hear me, Mr. VanDer Hyde? I hate to have to say this to you again, but we tried everything we could. It's a horrible misfortune."

Still shaking his head in disbelief, not able to fully accept what the doctor was saying, Lawrence asked, "Did she suffer doctor?"

"No, she was heavily medicated and wasn't aware of the situation."

"How could this happen? I thought childbirth was safe these days. How?" Lawrence was talking to himself, suffering mental anguish and distress he never thought possible.

The doctor spoke again, "She's a beautiful little baby. Would you like to see her Mr. VanDer Hyde?"

In self-denial, ignoring the doctor, Lawrence spoke again "Can I go to my wife? Please, I want to see her."

"Of course. Come with me."

Elizabeth's body lay still and lifeless. The only noise he heard was his heart throbbing. He stood by the side of the bed caressing her hair, thinking how beautiful it always was. Now it lay damp and tangled on the pillow. He held her still warm, limp hands, taking and holding them in his, hoping his life could will hers back. Tears streamed down his face as the hurt, frustration and anger were released. He sobbed uncontrollably; his body racked with grieving pain.

"We promised we would live until we were old and gray. How could you leave me like this? I need you Elizabeth. The children need you and we love you. Oh darling, I love you so."

He bent over her lifeless body, kissing her lips, for the last time. "I'll cause breath to enter you, that you may live," he kept thinking. "I'll always love you sweetheart. No one will ever take your place in my heart." After a while he regained his composure and walked back towards the nursery to see his new daughter.

Chapter Fourteen

Boston, Massachusetts • February 2, 1992

The once fruitful trees were barren and menacing. Icicles hung like daggers from their frigid limbs. Bundled up in her coat and braced against the harsh, cold winds, Suzanne walked briskly to the FBI offices at the Saltonstall Building to meet Timothy and Kevin. She was one of only a few brave souls dashing through the Public Garden and Boston Common. Engrossed in her own dilemma, she was undaunted by the bitter, weather. She found it invigorating. It helped to clear her mind.

She took the elevator to the sixth floor offices where the two FBI agents were waiting. She accepted the hot tea the agents offered and sat at Kevin's desk, waiting for his news.

"Suzanne, thanks for coming here tonight," Kevin said. "We've deciphered most of the information that you and Nancy found. It seems that you were right about Brian Morse. He's only a pawn in the grand scheme of things."

"Once we apprehend the criminals, the Pearlmans will regain control of their businesses. Our Florida office is checking the names of the drug connections that we obtained from the files you gave us. Let me tell you, Suzanne, these people are professionals. They may be small time, but we must deal quickly and severely with them. They could do a great deal of damage, if they find out that we're on to them. I don't want any more innocent people hurt. We've tapped their phone lines and placed undercover agents in their organization. Our biggest problem now is resolving the borderline illegalities between drug money and capital flight money."

"We've put your information together with the financial records that we helped confiscate along with the Colombian government. We were able to trace the money to accounts in Toronto, Nassau, the Antilles, and Vienna. The dealers constantly move the money from bank to bank, always keeping one step ahead of our agents. One of the dealers called Daniel Miller of Morse and Associates, and told him to move several million dollars to an account in Panama. He warned Miller that if the money didn't move quickly, 'someone' might get hurt or even killed."

"We're hoping that because of the new banking regulations and our recent crackdown on financial institutions, the bank officers will leave the money where it is for a while. It's a Catch 22. On one hand this Colombian has threatened Mr. Miller's life. On the other hand, if the banks don't cooperate, Miller's life is over anyway, because we will nab him for money laundering, income tax evasion, and drug smuggling."

Suzanne sat in awe with her hands wrapped around the untouched cup of tea. She never realized that trying to save the Pearlman's company would thrust her into the middle of an incident like this. The crooks would eventually be punished for their illegal activity and she was glad that she could play a part, even a small one, in seeing justice done. "I can't thank the two of you enough. I hope everything will turn out for the best. If you need me or Nancy for anything, please feel free to call us - any time."

The two men exchanged glances and Tim continued. "Well, we still have to get Brian to help us. I'm sure he'll cooperate, especially when he considers the consequences."

Suzanne walked back across the Common to her car. She felt much better about her decision to go to the authorities and was sure that it was only a matter of time before the Pearlman's situation would be resolved.

Although she was bundled up tightly against the cold, a shiver went through her. She was still worried about Peter. He looked terrible lately, and, to make matters worse, his work had become sloppy. He was moody and irritable. Suzanne was sure it was the drugs. Nancy had not mentioned anything more about him, and Suzanne didn't probe. Suzanne was curious about Nancy's relationship with Brian but she would wait for Nancy to bring it up.

Suzanne tried to put her life back in order, now that she wasn't doing her "Suzy the Sleuth" act. She continued making routine visits to her spas. She saw Stephen when she was in Dallas and he joined her occasionally in West Palm Beach. Every so often he managed to get to Massachusetts for a few days.

Suzanne enjoyed their intimate relationship immensely and, although she did not want a marital commitment, she was engulfed in guilt by her involvement with a married man. She knew the pain of being the wife whose husband was unfaithful. Lou Anne's problems and emotional battles would be compounded if she found out about the affair. Suzanne recognized that nothing could excuse the immoral situation she had placed herself in, although, in her heart she knew that their love for each other was not "an affair." After all, if circumstances were different, she and Stephen would have married like they originally planned. They believed that God brought them back together, it had to be Devine intervention. There were many regrets. The inability to have and enjoy children of their own caused an abundance of tears as they lay in each other's arms, thinking of things that they were denied. A "normal family life," reaping the satisfaction and adoration from grandchildren, could never be attained. So many years of separation that couldn't be made up, little things that people take for granted, and things that could only be imagined but never realized - - they would never take their gift of love for granted.

Stephen looked forward to the times he would be with Suzanne. He hated being apart from her and only wanted to hold her in his arms, kiss her passionately, and tell her how much he loved and needed her. Often times, driving to work his mind would wander and inevitably Suzanne would appear, an apparition before his eyes. He wanted to be with her always. The past burdens of his life weighed heavily upon him. So too, he felt a sense of longing when distance and circumstances would keep them apart. He could not find the ways to bring normalcy to his life and resolve the complexity of his situation. He believed that God brought Suzanne back to him, and he would never let her out of his life again!! He didn't bother wiping the tears as they flowed down his face.

For the first time in her business career she went against the dismal economic forecasts of the experts and instead followed her own instincts. She planned to open another branch in Charleston, South Carolina. Her motives were selfish because she wanted to retire eventually to her home there. She made plans to fly down for a brief rest and find a suitable location for the future spa while she was there.

Charleston, South Carolina • February 6, 1992

After arriving at the airport in Charleston, she picked up her rental car and drove to her home in the plantation at Stono Ferry. The weather was pleasantly mild and the jaunt proved relaxing. The courtesy of the other drivers on the road never ceased to amaze her. She was glad to see that Charleston had recovered from last year's hurricane that had destroyed much of it. She stopped at a local roadside stand and bought a bag of roasted peanuts.

She had met Carl Saunders when his real estate office handled her purchase in Stono Ferry five years ago. They kept in touch and whenever the Charleston Cup was held at the polo fields at Stono Ferry, they dinned at one of the finer restaurants in the beautiful old city of Charleston. Suzanne enjoyed Carl's companionship and loved listening to his Southern drawl.

They met at Garabaldi's. After ordering the renowned diamond cut, apricot flounder, Carl brought Suzanne up to date on the local politics and gossip. During lunch he reviewed the locations that would be appropriate for the proposed spa.

After lunch Carl took her to see the properties. One possible site on King Street was next to an art gallery and an antique shop where Suzanne had found some furnishings when she first came to the city. Suzanne was well acquainted with Mr. Cohen, the elderly Jewish owner of the shop. After being shown several other sites, she went back to the location on King Street to look at it again. Mr. Cohen also owned the entire block of stores that housed the space Suzanne was interested in. "Mrs. Morse, how nice to see you again. How are you and your beautiful daughters doing? It's been a long while since I last saw you."

"I'm fine, and, please, call me Suzanne. I hope you feel as good as you look. My girls are fine, thank you. Tell me, how is the economy affecting business in the area? I understand it isn't half as bad down here as it is in the northeast."

"To be honest with you, we had a terrible time after the last hurricane, but thank God, we have bounced back. You know us southerners; we don't let anything get in our way. We're survivors. I hear you're interested in opening a spa in Charleston."

"As a matter of fact, yes. I really love South Carolina, and if and when I retire, I'd love to live in my house at Stono Ferry. It would be pleasant to have one of my spas here so I could pop in every once in a while and work."

After reviewing his price, Suzanne quickly made a lower offer and, surprisingly, he accepted it immediately. With only a handshake, until the lawyers could arrange the paperwork, the deal was sealed.

Suzanne drove back to her home and opened all the windows to let fresh air into the house that had been closed up for three months. She loved this dwelling that she had bought with the first real profits from her business. It looked like an elegant plantation manor, with windows at the front that covered the entire area from floor to ceiling. A friendship staircase led up to the large white porch that partly encircled the front and sides of the house. The front door was half stained glass and half aged, Italian Oak. The roof was metal, and Suzanne loved listening to the sounds of the rain as it beat against the slate during a storm.

Suzanne rested a while on her chaise by the window overlooking the water. The view was lovely. She watched the yachts and pleasure boats as they cruised along the Intracoastal Waterway. Later she strolled through the neighborhood savoring the enticing aroma of the trees surrounding the area. At one house an elderly lady was weeding her garden and at another, a group of youngsters was selling lemonade to passers-by. Suzanne walked towards the golf course and sauntered through the gardens surrounding it. Even though it was late January, golfers were engrossed in their passion. The weather was mild, nothing like she encountered back home. In about a month people would discard their sweaters and by March they would be in their pools.

Suzanne couldn't wait till she was able to settle down in this lovely community and take full advantage of what if offered. She knew she wouldn't stay during the summer time for she had a hard time coping with the hot, humid weather. Smiling to herself she thought that if this spa did well, her next home would be overlooking the jagged rocks and ocean in Ogunquit, Maine.

Back in the kitchen decorated with beautiful baskets made by the local artisans, Suzanne cooked herself a light dinner. She called Nancy to tell her of the proposed site and discreetly asked about Peter. Suzanne realized that if Peter was to be convicted she and Nancy would have to take over his responsibilities. Nancy was in a very good mood and told Suzanne that Peter was not at home, but matters were coming to a head. She mentioned that she and Brian were still seeing each other and hoped the relationship would not jeopardize their friendship. Suzanne assured Nancy that whatever happened with Brian, she wouldn't let it get in the way.

She went on, "I told you that I met with Lawrence VanDer Hyde, didn't I? In a few weeks we'll meet with our attorneys and accountants. Lawrence will be there with a vice-president from a stock brokerage firm. They'll explain the details to us about selling on the open market."

"That sounds fine to me. I can't wait to meet this Mr. Lawrence VanDer Hyde."

"I'll be back tomorrow evening with the details on the new location."

"I'm sure I'll like it. Have a good flight home. I'll see you in a few days."

As Suzanne hung up the phone a sense of foreboding came over her. She remembered Larry saying, "the records have to be meticulous" and "there can't be any hint of a scandal."

"If Peter is involved in either money laundering or drug dealing," she thought "we're going to be put through the ringer and it might jeopardize any future stock deals."

She tried to sleep. Many complex issues again crowded her mind. Like ghosts appearing, then disappearing, images of Stephen, Larry and Brian surfaced in front of her eyes. Suzanne sat up, propped her pillows against the brass headboard and looked out at the moonless sky. It was the color of blueberries, a dark bluish black, with not a star in the heavens above.

The trouble Brian had caused her was now a thing of the past. If Nancy loved him, then Suzanne would have to live with it. She would never deliberately hurt Nancy's feelings. She didn't want to see Nancy distressed any more. The love she felt for Stephen was increasing, but would her remorse ruin their relationship? Could she ever really give him up?

She didn't understand what motivated Larry and that bothered her greatly. She couldn't figure him out. "Larry is my biggest concern now." Her gut feelings told her to beware. "But beware of what?"

Boston, Massachusetts • February 9, 1992

Daniel Miller called Barry Rich and told him about the threat. "Barry, I'm really frightened. I don't know what to do. Don't forget there are three of us involved in this scheme in addition to the Colombian cartel. If you'd gotten a phone call from this animal, you'd be scared shitless too. Barry, what the hell is going on? In the few years that we've been doing this money laundering, breaking up companies and creating new ones, we've never been threatened. What the fuck am I gonna do?"

"Look, each of us has made millions. Try to stay calm. I'll make some phone calls and try to straighten this mess out."

"Sure, it's easy for you to sit on your ass and tell me to be calm. You weren't the one who was threatened by this goon. I'm really afraid and I don't panic easily. When you're dealing with bankers, it's different. They're out for making money like we are, but these other guys are animals. They don't care about life or who they hurt in the process. They're only interested about money and drugs. I'm telling you, Barry, I'm the one who's terrified. I hope these bankers will move the money quickly. I think the authorities have found out about our friends in Colombia, and I only hope they haven't discovered our involvement in this."

"Dan, will you chill out? Stop being a schmuck. They won't do anything. They need us. Use your head. Cool it for a while and see what happens."

"It's easy for you to say. I'm telling you, this had better turn out in our favor, or we're all in deep shit."

Timothy and Kevin set up an appointment to meet with Brian Morse. Brian was clueless and had no idea who they were or what they wanted from him. "I wonder why they won't divulge what firm they own," thought Brian.

When the two agents met with him at the Cafe Escadrille in Burlington they watched as the tail they had following Brian signaled to them that all was clear. Brian's associates had no idea what the hastily called meeting was about. They had other problems to deal with.

The dark atmosphere caused Brian to be apprehensive as he entered the eating establishment. With a troubled look on his face he found the two men who were waiting for him at a corner table. Extending his hand, Brian introduced himself. With firm handshakes the two FBI men greeted him and asked him to sit down and join them.

After ordering a round of drinks, Timothy and Kevin got directly to the point. "I'm sure you're wondering why we asked you here. Instead of giving you a lot of worthless bullshit and taking up valuable time we're going to be aboveboard and give you the straight facts."

"We don't own any business that you might want to help us run, so you can forget that."

"Mr. Holloran and I - by the way, pronounced as if you're hollering and running at the same time," laughed an amused Tim Cassidy, staring directly into Brian's questioning eyes, "you inadvertently pay our salaries."

"As I was saying," Kevin continued, "we indirectly work for you."

Reaching into his jacket pocket he pulled out his identification and presented it to Brian.

After examining the credentials, Brian sat there and said. "What is this, some kind of sick joke? Am I under arrest because I didn't pay a few parking tickets?"

They came down strong on Brian and left little to his imagination. With a cold watchful eye glaring at Brian intensely, Tim pointed a finger directly at his chin. "First of all, this is not something we go around joking about. What we're about to tell you isn't a laughing matter. I don't see anything funny about working for an organization that gets skuzzballs like you out of society for a while. Okay?"

Brian was stupefied. He felt as if a weighted lead pipe had hit him in the abdomen. Listening attentively, he nodded for them to continue.

"We know that recently you and your so-called partners have taken over a business owned by a Mr. Harry Pearlman. We're acquainted with all your partners and their addresses - - they don't shit without us watching. We know more about you and your slime bucket pals than you can dream of and possess information about your, so called, business. Did you know that your buddies have quite a few business dealings with some banks that let's say, are not kosher. Get my point?"

"Have you ever wondered where your partners get all their money and why you don't seem to be able to make ends meet? Have you ever questioned their motives about certain situations and business dealings that they suggested you do? Buddy, you'd better start talking. If you don't convince us that you don't know what's going on, you're going to be in the slammer along with your good buddies, for a very, very long time, capeesh?"

He attempted to raise his glass, pretending to be cool and collected, but his shaking hands gave him away. He swallowed quickly hoping the warm liquid would give him the courage to break his nervous silence.

Clearing his throat, he began his verbal prattle. "First I want you to know that what you told me leaves me stunned. I'll cooperate with you in any way I can. The last thing I want is to go to jail. In my whole life, I've never dealt in drugs. I may have done other things, but, if what you implied is true, you're talking about drug money and money laundering. Now I'm no saint. Sure, these men became partners and got in touch with me about three years ago." Overwrought, he exaggerated, "They came to me; I never went after them. They paid me some good money to buy into my business. Now I realize that they probably wanted to use my good business name to get involved with firms that would associate with my kind of company's reputation. Sure, I met a few of their other associates. I did think some of them looked a little shady, but as long as I kept getting paid good money, hey, I looked the other way."

The sweat was now visibly rolling down the sides of his face. "Whatever you want from me, I'll be glad to do, I assure you."

"Buddy, you really don't have much choice, do you?"

They never mentioned Suzanne or Nancy's involvement. Brian had no idea how they found out about his partners and their criminal involvement in capital offenses. Brian had never been so scared in his entire life. He realized that he had done things that he was not proud of, but he would never deliberately deal in drugs or go against the U. S. Government. "Please, tell me what you want me to do. I'm upset but I'll do anything you ask me to do at this point."

"Okay, first get your hand on as many documents as you can on all the new real estate holdings they've purchased through the Pearlmans. Get us the names of the men they deal with in foreign banks. That's for starters. When you come back with that information, we'll have more legwork for you to do."

Brian knew that they would get back to him shortly and realized he had better get the data to them quickly.

"I hope this week goes by quickly," Kevin pronounced as he and Timothy walked back to their car. "You always imagine what someone will look like before you see them. Brian surely didn't fit that mold. He's not what I perceived him to be."

"Yeah, I think his priorities are fucked up, but when push comes to shove I think he'll come through for us."

"Suzanne is a great lady. Too bad she married a creep like him. Who knows, he might have been different when she first met him. In this business we deal with such shit bums it restores my opinion of humanity when we meet and work with people like Suzanne and Nancy."

"I hope we can wrap this case up quickly now that we have Brian doing some of the dirty work. I'd love to take a vacation after this is over."

"Sure, you talk a lot, but you'll go crazy like you did on your last vacation and come back to work early. Shirley must have loved you for that one." "Fuck you," Tim sneered as their car reached the Hay Market Square exit ramp off the expressway.

Driving back to the Pearlman's office Brian drove cautiously through the heavy noontime traffic. Looking through the rear view mirror, his pensive thoughts brought back memories of long ago.

With his new therapist, he was able to make headway and, for the first time in his fifty years, he really liked himself. He felt badly about the way that things turned out with Suzanne, realizing all too late that the marriage might have worked if he had behaved differently. But he couldn't go back, and his life, although it didn't turn out as he had hoped, wasn't as bad as it could have been.

Only through intensive psychoanalysis was Brian able to make sense of his life. He loved his parents and siblings and of course his children. Not until he was in therapy for a while did he realize that he had been an abused child. His father demeaned and berated him, making fun of his height. His short stature and his fathers constant criticism and abusive language had a devastating effect on his self-esteem. Brian grew up feeling he would never measure up - in any way.

He loved his children with all his heart. He gave Suzanne credit for raising them as well as she did. He had wanted to give his offspring more financial help, but since he and Suzanne split up it seemed everything he touched had the reverse Midas touch. His personality took a change for the better once he understood himself on a different level. It was not necessary for him to pit the children against each other or make fun of people for their inadequacies. Though life had its ups and downs, he hoped that the rest of his life would be an improvement, now that he had some insight into his early years.

After he met Nancy, his thoughts centered on her constantly. There was something quite different about this unusually beautiful woman. He found her vulnerability and personality appealing. He wanted to love and protect her. Knowing that she was back at the office made him feel better about what actions he had to take against his so called partners.

He wanted them to croak in hell. The two FBI agents had warned him not to disclose any of their conversation and he didn't want to betray their confidence. He only hoped he would be able to keep his thoughts to himself on this particular matter and not let any of it slip when he spoke to Nancy.

London, England • February 12, 1992

The familiar roar of the jet engines served as the backdrop as Lawrence traveled back to Europe to attend to his business matters. He hoped the next two weeks would pass quickly. He couldn't wait to get back to Boston and see Suzanne once again. The first stop on this trip brought him to London's Heathrow airport. From there he went to his London offices located in Mayfair.

Dispensing with all the formalities among his office staff, he sought the necessary refuge his suite provided. Mrs. Healy, his secretary, had all of the essential work placed in order of priority on his spacious, cherry wood desk. Working diligently, he did not stop for a moment until the work was complete. Only then did he allow himself to sit back and relax. Looking at his watch, he rang for his driver to meet him a few minutes early in front of the building complex.

"Sir?"

"You can drive me to my house." He looked out the window of the limousine, admiring the uniformity of the beautiful old homes, reminding him of Beacon Hill in Boston, back in the States. The traffic was not bad as they made the trip past Knight Bridge from Mayfair to South Kensington in approximately fifteen minutes.

"Albert, would you let me off here? I'll walk home from this place. You can take the rest of the day off, I won't be needing you until tomorrow." He walked along Sloane Street, browsing in the windows of all the shops. The fresh air felt good, even though it was a bit nippy.

He passed a linen shop and saw a beautiful lace shawl displayed in the window. It reminded him of the lovely handmade one that he had bought for Suzanne while he was in Antwerp. Lawrence tried to reinforce his memory thinking, "I must not forget to bring it back to the States after visiting home." He remembered placing the shawl in the bottom draw of the bureau in his bedroom. "Yes, Suzanne would appreciate its delicacy."

The damp air chilled him to the bone and he looked forward to the warmth of a fire and a cup of hot tea when he arrived home. He had inherited the beautiful old brick home in Cadogan Square from his grandfather, who used to take him there when he was a boy. He reached into his pocket for the key and opened the door. In an instant the smells associated with the house brought back a flood of memories of his grandfather.

Placing his coat on the old, polished brass coat rack, he walked to the fireplace and started the fire. He had instructed his secretary not to engage the services of Mrs. Wood his housekeeper. Now he wished he had asked her to come into the house, for she would have had the radiant hearth enflamed when he entered. As he stirred the wood with the fire iron, the scent of the heated logs reminded him of the many walks he shared and took pleasure in with his grandfather in the forest near their home.

When he was young, he hid in the heavily wooded forests, urging his stately grandfather to find him. And, as a young man, holding his beloved Elizabeth's hand, he saw the forests in a different light. The forest was romantic, not menacing. Breathing in the wonderful aromatic trees, savoring the hibiscus, eucalyptus and evergreens made him appreciate the various scents of the many species that lived in the woods. As a grown man he now enjoyed the fragrance of the sandalwood and balm, bringing back the memories of youth. He sat down with a cup of tea and flavored it with a few ounces of whiskey, making notes in the book in front of him.

Whenever he entered this house, it brought back many mental images, and visions of the past. He didn't remember his paternal grandmother. She had died still in the prime of her life when Lawrence was only a few months old. His grandfather never remarried, preferring the company of a selected few family members and devoting most of his time to his business. On a few occasions he would incorporate his business trips, making them into mini holidays by asking Lawrence to accompany him. With his mind revived, his body warmed and rested, he ascended the narrow, dark, wooden staircase to the small but comfortable master bedroom.

February 16, 1992

Lawrence was able to finish his business ahead of schedule that week. "I want to change our flight plan," he informed his pilot. "Instead of flying into LaGuardia, I want to go to Logan."

"Yes sir, no problem."

When he arrived in Boston, the weather was brisk and invigorating. Bracing himself against the blast of wind, Lawrence pulled up the collar of his Burberry and walked to Quincy Market to see the new store that had just opened. This was the second shop that had opened in the Boston area. The other shop was on Newbury Street near Suzanne's business. He observed that there always seemed to be people walking, browsing and buying, no matter what time of day, along the heavily traversed marketplace.

He frequently used a service that visited and rated his various establishments, but sometimes he found it interesting to do it himself. He looked like any other businessman as he walked nonchalantly into the store and selected merchandise and let the unwitting salespeople wait on him. Pretending he was a shopper, like anyone else, he tested the clerks to see how courteous, helpful, and knowledgeable they were. He would rate them when he got back to his offices. He had his secretary send a note to the particular counter person, thanking them for their good service. If he was not satisfied with their behavior, he sent a note to that effect and checked up on them at a later time. Lawrence expected top rate, loyal employees, from stock people, salespeople, office employees, up to high management officials.

"May I be of service to you?" a young woman asked. He waited to see what her next move would be.

"Can you tell me something about the fabric of this sweater. I seemed to have left my glasses at my office and I can only wear certain fabrics, since I'm allergic to certain materials."

With a pleasant voice, she read him the list of textiles, asking him other questions, trying to be as cooperative as she could, without seeming pushy. "This sweater is just the right color for your complexion. Feel the softness it's made from the finest material. We have some pants that would match it and if you like, we have other combinations that you might like to see."

After buying a few items he walked out of the store with a broad smile. He looked back with satisfaction at the VanderHyde sign and strolled back to his offices, carrying the packages that he didn't need.

Once there, he wrote a memo about the new store and the delightful salesgirl who had waited on him. Before he realized the time, several hours had gone by.

"Mr. VanDer Hyde, if there isn't anything else you need, would you mind if I left for the day?" a tired Mrs. Lily asked.

"What time is it Mrs. Lily?"

"It's past eight in the evening sir."

"Of course, I became so involved with my paperwork that the time just flew by. I'll see you tomorrow morning, Mrs. Lily. Before you go would you place a call to my Paris office. I'll take it in here."

"Philip, I knew you'd be working at this ungodly hour. How are the new designs coming along? We have approximately two weeks before the large fashion show. Will the new collection be complete and ready?"

"Yes, Mr. VanDer Hyde. That's why I'm working day and night to finish them. You'll be very pleased. Our show will be more spectacular than ever."

"I want you to send the new designs to me as soon as possible. And Philip, be sure there are no leaks to the press before the grand opening. It's imperative that this new line is kept secret." He made a note to get in touch with the jewelry designers and have them coordinate pieces that would complement the clothing designs. The jewelers, long time employees of the VanDer Hyde family, would do the impeccable job they always did. As he walked out of the office, he looked back at the tall, modern, streamlined concrete building, and decided to roam along the streets of Boston. Of all his offices, Boston and New York were his least favorites, structurally.

He missed the architecture and warmth of his European facilities. They had a unique style that was missing in the modern, cold, towering construction of the American offices. If he continued to expand here he would have to buy a home, perhaps one of the old mansions on Commonwealth Avenue. Then he could put his own flavor into the planning and remodeling of this anticipated new project.

He walked along Newbury Street and found himself, unexpectedly in front of the *Metamorphosis Spa.* He was oblivious to the few people who were still walking along the famous street, their conversation and laughter muffled by his speculation and deliberation as he looked inside the spa. The lights were brightly lit and a few patrons were waiting in the lounge, sitting in the beautiful chairs, awaiting their treatments. Suzanne came out of one of the treatment rooms and greeted a customer. She escorted her to the private room and quickly emerged, waiting for the client to ready herself for the facial. She spotted Larry as he walked past.

She rested her hand on his shoulder. "Larry, what a surprise. When did you arrive back in Boston?"

"Suzanne, hello! Only this morning. How are you?"

"Well, thanks. How long are you staying?"

"I'm not sure just yet. Are you free this evening?"

"I'll be through in about an hour and a half. This has been a very busy and long day."

"Would you like a quick bite at one of the restaurants nearby?"

"That sounds great. How about the Ritz?"

"Fine, I'll pick you up at your salon."

Larry was waiting for Suzanne when she finished. They walked along the deserted street and headed to the nearby hotel. Their bodies were in step with one another and Suzanne, aware of his well-toned physique so close to her, tried to avoid physical contact. The maitre de knew Suzanne and escorted them to a quiet table.

"I'm very glad you decided to join me. How have you been and what's been going on in your life?"

Suzanne felt she couldn't tell Larry anything concerning the Pearlman's. Laughing to herself she thought, "Wouldn't that be a hoot, telling Larry about sending my former husband to jail? No, that wouldn't be a wise move."

"Nothing much. I've been very busy at work. I've decided to open an office in Charleston, South Carolina. Have you ever been there?"

"Yes, many years ago."

There was an assured air about him that Suzanne hadn't been aware of before. "Of course, he's a little arrogant. He certainly has a lot to be proud of."

After she told him about her new establishment, he went on to tell her about his desire to move his Boston corporate facility.

"Suzanne, have you ever vacationed in Belgium, the Netherlands or Sweden? There is so much to see and do. You must let me show you Europe, as only a European can."

She asked why he wanted to move. "My main concern is if I spend more time in the States, I want to feel at home here. I've been looking at local real estate and I think I can buy a home on Commonwealth Avenue. The location, where they are now, is very cold and sterile. I'd like to feel as if I'm back home. At my European offices I have my light burning day and evening outside of the building. I have an enormous knight on display. I also have an apartment above each of my offices, so when I work late, I can quickly retire."

"But, let's not talk business any more." After clearing his throat, he sipped his after dinner drink and went on. "Just this once, I'll break my own rule and tell you what effect you have on me. You've awakened a need in me that I haven't felt in many years."

Suzanne felt herself blush. She didn't want Larry to get too personal but waited for him to continue. In a way she enjoyed the compliments bestowed upon her.

"When I mentioned the idea of becoming your financial adviser and helping you take your business public you didn't think it was preposterous. No, you took it under advisement as any good business person would do, thought it over, realized it was a wise thing to do and moved on it. I like a woman of courage and conviction."

"I must admit I sometimes act on instinct. If a situation looks and feels good to me I proceed with my plan of action. I haven't been burnt too many times."

Suzanne found herself talking to him as a friend. "Right now I'm very worried about my parents. I'm an only child and their care, I feel, is my responsibility. The older I become the more I realize how fast life passes us by. You may not understand this because we come from two entirely different worlds. My parents are wonderful people, but they never planned ahead. Don't get me wrong, they aren't irrational or mindless, but they don't want to face reality or what the next step in life is going to be. They're not failures; they just failed to plan. Now no one can really tell what's going to happen in the next few years, but I'd like to do so much for them."

Suzanne continued. "You mentioned Europe. I'd love to take them there, among other places some day. They don't think it's necessary. My parents are still fairly young, and while they can get around on their own two feet, let them see and enjoy the beauty that is out there.

Larry sat quietly, listening to her, admiring the energy she emitted while speaking with much passion. "Don't you think that you might be wrong? You're trying to impose your wishes and desires on your parents. From what you tell me, they seem like agreeable people. Why don't you let them make up their own minds about what they want to do with their lives."

"I suppose you're right. While I was growing up and when I was going through my lean and hard years, they were always there for me. It's just my way of thanking them. They taught me honesty, traditional values and the importance of family."

"I think they got their repayment when they realized what a wonderful daughter they managed to bring up. Look, they have three beautiful, respectful granddaughters, whom you've managed to bring up to be loving and thoughtful women. What else can you ask for in the grand scheme of life?"

"Oh, I know. Yes, I'm very lucky to have wonderful daughters and still have my parents. You know, you hear so many stories today of people who've come from dysfunctional families. It makes me feel grateful that I was raised by loving parents. I'm thankful for that now and for my work. Wouldn't it be awful to work hard at a job you hate? Yes, I do have many things to be grateful for."

"Let your parents do what they want to. They know what makes them happy. Don't be so protective of them."

"Easier said than done," Suzanne smiled.

Reaching across the table, he took her hands in his, "when you smile, you light up the entire room."

Suzanne could feel herself blushing again. "It's getting late, I'd better head for home. I have another busy day ahead of me, as I'm sure you do."

Larry walked Suzanne back to her car and kissed her gently on each cheek.

As much as Suzanne tried to find fault with Larry, she couldn't. All the way home she thought that he came across as a wonderful, likable, person. "Don't forget handsome. But I want only to keep him as a dear friend and business adviser."

Lawrence settled down on his bed. His thoughts were of Suzanne. Invariably, whenever he closed his eyes, her face was in front of him, he found himself thinking of her more and more. All he wanted to do was to protect her and take care of her. He felt as though he was her private knight in shining armor. He felt a devotion to her that he could not explain. "I will be your Percival, Suzanne," he thought as sleep took over.

Chapter Fifteen

Brian and Nancy saw each other at work. Nancy kept her position at the Pearlman's even though her work with the FBI was over. She had fallen in love with Brian, and this was a way for her to be close to him. Nancy looked forward to seeing him every day. Nancy still used the children as an excuse for not being with him more often. She worried about how he would feel about her when she revealed the truth to him. She realized that soon she would have to stop the pretense and hoped he would forgive her dishonesty.

Her life with Peter was a sham. Peter had become completely different from the happy, amiable person that she had met, loved and married years ago. His moodiness was destructive and their lovemaking was a thing of the past. She was biding her time, waiting for the right moment to ask him for a divorce.

A couple of weeks went by and it seemed everyone at the office was sitting on pins and needles. Even the Pearlmans sensed the anxiety that wasn't apparent before. The partners were irritable and were frequently at odds with one another.

Daniel Miller was unable to persuade the bankers to move the money out of the banks. The DEA froze the accounts. The Colombians were furious and were out for revenge.

Daniel, along with Barry Rich and another silent partner, was sitting on a time bomb and didn't know it. They all realized that their money was being held up and that the banking authorities were not cooperating with them. They didn't recognize just how serious their situation was or how desperate the men in Colombia were.

Brian acted as normally as he could when he was in the office and around his partners. The first few days after his meeting with the Federal authorities found him extremely busy. Not used to business espionage, he was both mentally and physically exhausted. Every movement he made had to be orchestrated beforehand.

· He was amazingly cautious, since he could not let anyone find out or become suspicious of his sudden interest and concern about the new real estate holdings. "Hey Barry, would you mind if I used your desk for a few days since you and the Mrs. will be away on vacation?"

"What's wrong with your office?"

"I'm getting mine repainted and my desk refinished. You can't get a desk like that anymore without paying a fortune for it. They just don't make them like they used to."

"Yeah, that's for sure. Okay, I guess so. Just don't mess up the files. Make sure your office and desk are in working order when I get back next week."

"What shit luck," Brian thought to himself as he devised his next plan of action. Now that there was an excuse for him to be using Barry's room he could get into the files without arousing Daniel's suspicion. He often stayed until after midnight.

Looking into business reports and materials, he found details that he had previously failed to notice. He'd overlooked or neglected important itemized acquisitions that would have given him a clue to their illegal deals. "Boy, what a fucking dummy I am. They certainly must have thought me a fool." Gathering up all the information that he was certain would come in handy for the FBI he quickly and efficiently copied all the documents he thought necessary.

The next morning he made the first important phone call. "Mr. Halloran, please. Hi, this is Brian Morse I have some information I think you'll find interesting. When do you want me to drop it by?"

"We don't want to take the chance that you might be followed. Now don't get paranoid on us, it's just a precaution. So instead of coming to Boston, rent a post office box and leave the information in it. Call us later with the number and we'll take it from there."

"That sounds good to me."

"By the way, we'll let you know when to go to the post office again. Your next assignment will be placed in the box. Brian, thanks for cooperating."

Although he was not used to the cloak and dagger scene, it had its exciting moments. In a sick sort of way, it was thrilling, and with trepidation, left him with a feeling of emotional exhilaration. He had to find another clever way to get into Barry and Daniel's offices for his next job without being detected.

Boston, Massachusetts • February 23, 1992

Brian was to have dinner with Nancy at one of their favorite restaurants this evening and wanted to surprise her with a dozen long stemmed red roses. Going out of the office, Daniel asked Brian where he was going. "Just down to the florist to pick up the flowers that I ordered."

"Would you do me a favor and take my car and fill it up with gas. I have a meeting tonight and I don't want to waste time in the evening rush hour traffic. I'll be calling it close as far as time goes, as it is. I'd really appreciate it. Thanks Brian."

Taking the keys from Daniel, Brian didn't mind killing two birds with one stone. With a lighthearted step and thoughts of Nancy's smile, he unlocked and then opened the car door.

He was vaguely aware of office workers rushing out for lunch, and others dashing to pressing appointments. He took no notice of the seedy looking men in the late model car, surreptitiously watching the front door of Mr. Pearlman's establishment. A menacing looking character leaned against the building across the street waiting for the car's owner. Brian was singing his favorite tune as he put the key into the ignition. Nancy's smile was on his mind as he started the car. The explosion was deafening.

With a look of satisfaction, the Colombian gave a subtle signal to the ominous men in the car across from him, then turned and calmly walked away - - whistling.

Shoppers across the street at the Burlington Mall thought first of an earthquake, then that a gas main might have ruptured.

The car exploded. Bright orange flames shot skyward. Acrid smoke billowed as fragments of metal fell to the pavement. People were dumbfounded. Some stood frozen. Others ran in fear, screaming. Two men unwisely approached the car thinking life still remained. The windows were blown away and Brian was choking on blood, his face half-gone. His arm reached out and fell limp with bone protruding through the skin. The hands that had beaten Suzanne were ripped off. He was a ghastly sight as his ravaged body met death. Authorities raced to the scene to disperse the crowd and roped off the area. Those who planted the bomb were well schooled, for the thunderous blast did not reach the adjacent vehicles.

Daniel Miller heard the explosion and was first to the window in the offices above. When he saw that it was his car he got sick to his stomach and vomited on the spot. His body was shaking uncontrollably as hideous thoughts raced through his mind. He didn't know what to do. Should he leave and let people think that he was killed?

Should he run home, take his hidden money and run for his life? He knew that these goons were really after him now.

He was beyond consolation when Barry came up behind him. He jumped as Barry put his hands on his shoulder. "What the fuck happened?"

Through clenched teeth, Daniel almost inaudibly whispered "That fucking bomb was meant for me. I told you we're in big trouble. These guys mean business. They probably think they killed me since it was my car that blew up. I feel like running away and letting them think that they succeeded."

"Well, who the hell was in your car?"

"That potz, Brian. I don't feel sorry for him. He was an asshole. I'm worried about my own ass." He realized that if he hadn't told Brian to buy the gas, the horrendous, tragic figure in the burning car would have been him. He knew that the shit had hit the fan and with shaky legs and hands, he went downstairs to inform the police that the car was his.

Stono Ferry, South Carolina

It was another beautiful day as Suzanne opened her eyes and saw the sun shining through the trees onto the foot of her bed. She loved waking up to a bright and sunny day. With an exaggerated stretch she tensed her taut muscles. After making her morning tea, she tried to decide between shopping or getting in a game of golf before the heat became too oppressive. Reading the local paper an article caught her attention. It was about a young woman who had been murdered by her husband. Chills went through her body as the memories of her own abusive treatment resurfaced. Those feelings never left, they just lay dormant, until a terrible tragedy occurred, triggering the awful pain of insult and injury that Brian inflicted upon her.

The telephone rang, interrupting her thoughts, as she tried to busy herself, by cleaning and straightening up the kitchen.

"Suzanne, Betty. How would you like to join us girls for a game of golf in about an hour?"

"I'd love to. I'll meet you at the greens. Thanks for the invitation. Well, I guess I don't have to deliberate that issue any longer."

The residents from the plantation had responded to Suzanne as their new neighbor with customary southern hospitality. They had taken her in with enthusiasm and showed her all the sights and popular places to shop. She was unaccustomed to such graciousness from new acquaintances.

Suzanne was enjoying herself and found her game going exceptionally well during the first nine holes. On the back nine an unusual sense of anxiety suddenly overcame her. Forcing herself to finish, she thanked the other women and left as soon as she could get away. She tried to ignore the jumpy, on-edge feeling but found it impossible to do so.

To take her mind off her agitation, she went to the local coffee shop and ordered a diet Seven Up. Her hands were shaking visibly as she raised the glass to her mouth. She wondered if a brisk walk by the ocean would help. "Maybe that's what I need to get rid of this uneasiness."

She parked her automobile by the highway and got only a few yards along the shoreline when she abruptly turned and walked back to her car to head home. With apprehension she opened her door and ventured into the great room. The airiness of the atrium with its abundance of flowering plants did not relax her. She put on the stereo and tried to read. A few hours elapsed and, still restless, she filled her hot tub and poured herself a wine cooler.

"This is luxurious," she thought, as she let the hot water and pulsating jets relieve her tension. The phone's ringing confused her for a second. She picked up the receiver located by the large white enameled tub. The disastrous phone call was from Taylor.

"Mom, something terrible has happened." With incomprehensible speech Taylor tried to convey the details over the telephone. Taylor talked in broken half-sentences, and cried so hard that Suzanne couldn't understanding what she was saying. Suzanne had to strain to hear her and make sense of the words.

Suzanne forced Taylor to calm down. Gradually, Taylor got the details out and the pieces of the story fell into place. Suzanne sat down and with a heavy heart wept into the receiver. "Taylor, I'll catch a flight home this evening or as soon as I possibly can. Have the girls stay at my house. I'll meet you there."

Her body felt like lead as she emerged from the sunken tub. A wave of nausea and pangs of guilt engulfed her as she toweled herself dry and steadied herself against the marble vanity. She felt the blood drain from her head as she tried to collect her thoughts and absorb the terrible news she'd just heard.

Suzanne made a reservation on a flight leaving in two hours, then literally threw her belongings into her suitcases. She called Carl Saunders, informing him about her sudden change of plans. She raced to the airport, knowing that he would take care of everything. Suzanne couldn't help thinking that she was the cause of Brian's death. She had to find out more about the circumstances, but she was sure they were somehow related to the money laundering business.

The flight was interminably long. Once on the ground, she got into the waiting limo and explained the situation to the driver who didn't waste any time getting her home to Stoney Brook. Hope and Melanie greeted her as she opened the door. They looked terrible, as if they hadn't stopped crying for hours. They couldn't understand how such a tragedy could have happened. Mrs. Walsh finally persuaded Taylor to lie down in her mother's room. She covered her with an extra quilt and tucked it in around the young woman. Everyone was in shock. The police had already been there and talked to the girls. They left two "plainclothes detectives" to watch the house. Actually, the detectives were two agents Kevin Holloran had sent over.

Mrs. Walsh made them all some hot tea. Suzanne insisted the girls stay at her house. She called Brian's brothers and offered to help with the funeral arrangements. Suzanne wanted to call Nancy, but felt it best to wait until the girls were asleep. She didn't want them to know of Nancy's involvement with Brian.

Suzanne was numb with grief herself. She felt as if she'd put the bomb into the car, ignited it herself, and killed him. As much as she had hated Brian through the years, she'd recently made peace with him in her mind. The hate that was once there was replaced by pity, though, she would never forget or forgive him for what he put her and the children through. Those terrible beatings, insults, violation, all these offenses and more were ingrained in her body and soul. It took many years to get back her self-esteem - - Suzanne had mixed emotions.

She felt it was unfair that he should die in such a tragic way. He had finally found a woman he loved unconditionally and who loved him in return. Thinking how unfair life could be, she tucked the girls in, as she did when they were little. She put her feelings aside, and not allowing the girls, or anyone else for that matter, to see the private conflict she felt. The girls needed her now for support and comfort.

She called Nancy as soon as the girls were asleep. "I know words won't bring him back, I'm truly sorry. How are you doing?"

"As well as can be expected. Peter doesn't understand why I'm so upset. I can't blame him. After all, he has no idea what Brian and I had together."

"Can you come up to Stoney Brook tomorrow? The girls and I want you. I also know you'll need us."

When she finally got to bed herself, Suzanne spent a restless night. Lying in bed, listening to the wind, she made a list of all the matters that she had to attend to. She tossed and turned all night long. Awakening in the morning, she doubted if she got more than three hours sleep. She took a shower to refresh herself and got dressed before the others woke up.

She called Kevin at his home and asked if he'd heard any details about the "accident."

He told her what he knew and promised that Tim would drop by later in the day with whatever information they had. Kevin stressed the need to have agents at the house as a safeguard. Before Mrs. Walsh woke up Suzanne put fresh coffee into the percolator and put hot water up for tea.

The girls looked a little better this morning than they had yesterday. Calmly, she went over the details that they would have to make for the funeral arrangements. The casket would be closed for obvious reasons. She didn't go into detail but told them that it would be closed. Suzanne offered some family pictures for the girls to place around the casket so they could remember him in happier days.

Because of the circumstances surrounding his sudden death, Suzanne thought it best to keep the funeral private for only relatives and close friends of the family. She got in touch with the local funeral home and asked for a non-denominational service. The morning flew by.

It was hard to concentrate as she drove to Stoney Brook. Exhausted as she was from lack of sleep, her mind kept going back to their final weeks of happiness. "I thought I finally had it all. I was looking forward to a long and happy life with Brian." Sighing deeply, anxiety overtook her. "Why did he have to die such a horrible death? It isn't fair, but I should have learned that years ago," she thought to herself as she recalled her early childhood. "Money means shit in the grand scheme of things. You can have all the money in the world, but without love, health, or happiness, you have nothing. I wonder, are you out there, God? I hear Suzanne talk to you often, but if you're there, why do you let so many innocent people suffer?" Wiping the tears on her sleeves, she tried composing herself as she entered the street. "I can't let the girls see me like this. They'd never understand."

Nancy looked like the girls had looked yesterday. They had no idea why she had taken the death of their father as badly as she did. Suzanne hugged Nancy and told her that she blamed herself for the tragedy. As she spoke,

Suzanne broke down and started sobbing uncontrollably. Nancy knew how her best friend was feeling and although she had mixed feelings of anger and sorrow, she held Suzanne and they wept in each other's arms.

When a person is ill the family has time to get used to the idea of their demise. In this case, the tragic accident had occurred so quickly that those who loved him had no time to adjust to Brian's death. The girls were in shock and numb from the grief they felt. Although they had not lived with their father for many years, they did love him.

Hope, who had received the brunt of his anger, had forgiven him years ago. As she grew older she enjoyed his company and spent many leisure hours with him. They talked about many things and she listened to his feelings. Hope loved him and had learned to accept him.

Hope knocked on Suzanne's bedroom door. "Can I come in?"

Sitting on the edge of her mother's bed, Hope broke down once again. "You know, for years, I wished he'd die, especially when I was younger and didn't understand what life was all about. I used to dream and pray that one of my girlfriend's father was my real father because if he weren't my dad, that could be why he hated me so. A real parent wouldn't hit his daughter. Now I'm sorry that I wished him death. I didn't mean it. As I grew older we talked a lot and he did apologize for the way he had treated me. I never told you that did I? Well, he told me about his childhood, and when I was old enough to understand why he did those awful things, I forgave him." Hope started crying again and Suzanne held her close like the young daughter she protected years ago.

Melanie and Taylor had never experienced the hostility that Brian had taken out on their sister, Hope. They dimly remembered their parent's arguments and hostility. Most of their memories of their father were of a fun-loving man. At times they felt sorry for him and worried about his loneliness. They often wished he'd been able to find a woman to love and marry.

For Melanie and Taylor the news of his death was devastating. It never occurred to them that their father could die so young. They were angry with God for taking him the way He did and they didn't want to face the reality of life without their father. Although they didn't see him often, they spoke on the telephone regularly and felt they made his life more pleasurable. Their tears came readily and without shame. The anguish they felt could not be eased.

Suzanne wanted to hold and protect them for the purpose of making everything better. If only she could turn back the clock and undo the horrible tragedy that had befallen Brian. She blamed herself for this fatal calamity. She prayed that in time the girls could accept what happened to their father and not turn their backs on God. "I hope that they never find out that I betrayed him," she told Tim Cassidy that afternoon.

"Suzanne, don't do this to yourself. You're not to blame. Brian was a grown man who knew what he was doing. He shouldn't have gone after the fast buck."

"Or, at least he should have suspected that something illegal was going on," added Kevin. "He was helping us, but he was already in way too deep."

"I'm sorry this happened. But, believe me, this would have caught up with him sooner or later," Tim assured her.

Dallas, Texas

Stephen sat at his office desk, staring at the same piece of equipment for what seemed hours. He still couldn't believe that Brian was dead. "It's awful to think that the bastard got what he deserved. But, who am I to determine what punishment should be given to someone who has dished out such cruelty in his lifetime?"

He decided to wait until after the funeral to visit Suzanne. He was sure she would have to devote all her time, right now, to her daughters. "His unexpected death will, in some way, have a catastrophic impact on those unfortunate girls." He rose from his leather chair and looked out the large picture window not focusing on anything in particular. He realized their relationship could not continue as it was. Yes, he loved Suzanne, but he had to ask himself "is it fair to her to love and be loved by someone who can't give of himself fully?" He yearned to be with her constantly and he wanted to make their union legal. "As long as Lou Anne is alive I know in my heart I can never leave her the way she is now." Facing the reality of his situation, he closed his eyes and gently rubbed them. He was trying to clear the demoniac notions from his consciousness when the telephone's shrill ring startled him.

The day of the funeral was cold, clear and crisp. The service was held at the funeral home as the girls wished. The flowers were placed around the silver and brass casket. Their favorite pictures were placed among the flower arrangements. The mood was somber and melancholy. The girls decided to buy a plot in a nondenominational cemetery. Their father's would be the first of the immediate family to be laid to rest there.

The clergyman said a beautiful prayer as people dipped the shovel into the dirt and quietly placed it on the lowered casket. The girls were now crying softly as they said their final farewell to their father.

As Suzanne placed her shovel of dirt on top of the casket she was surprised to feel tears on her cheeks. "Brian, you made my life one living hell at times, but some good did come out of our marriage - our beautiful daughters." She said a silent prayer. "For their sakes, if I am responsible for your death, I hope you'll forgive me." In all her life she never felt so alone.

They dispensed with the week of mourning and decided to get back to their normal lives as soon as possible. It would be a difficult and trying time, but

Suzanne knew the girls were strong and they would come out of this intact.

Nancy was another matter. She was the only person who knew of their love for each another. ˊ Peter couldn't understand why Nancy was so blue and upset. Even though Brian died, and with him her love, she still planned to divorce Peter.

Suzanne flew back to South Carolina the following week to finish the arrangements on opening the new spa. She had spoken to Stephen and told him about the death of her ex-husband and the girls' reactions. Stephen was as sympathetic and understanding as she'd expected him to be. They made plans to see one another in a few weeks when she visited the Texas salon.

Kevin called Suzanne at her home in the Carolinas and told her that everything was going according to plan. One partner of Morse and Associates had already been arrested for money laundering and drug smuggling. The FBI was close on the heels of the others and was sure to locate them soon. They had obtained a lot more information than they had anticipated with the wiretaps. Even though the dealers moved constantly from location to location, the agents were able to track them through their monitoring. Raids in different cities occurred simultaneously, with the exception of Miami. The people in Miami figured that they were safe and couldn't understand why the other cartels and homes were being shut down. In the high tech game of cat and mouse, the

Justice Department found and froze $60.1 million in assets in five different countries.

Listening to the work that the government was doing made Suzanne feel better. She hoped Brian's death was not in vain. She thought of her last day at the spa on Newbury Street before heading back down to South Carolina and smiled, recalling Mrs. Pearlman. She had come into the spa for her monthly facial. She was able to relax and enjoy the entire massage and treatment this time.

"Suzanne, I'm so happy today. My Harry is feeling much better. But, did you hear about the tragic death of poor Mr. Morse? Did you happen to read about the gangland style bombing that took place just outside of our building? It's a *shunder*, such a young man still. Yet his no good partners are no where to be found. May they rot in hell!"

"My Harry, he's back operating our corporation and it looks as if our sons are now going to come into the firm. It's about time, don't you think? I'm so happy that Harry's health is improving and the boys are willing to learn the "family business."

Concord, Massachusetts

Nancy maneuvered deftly around the rotary and parked in the prison lot. Her eyes, red from crying, were covered with large sunglasses. She joined the others - mothers, fathers, wives, girlfriends, children - who made their way across Elm Street to the prison entrance, through the visitors' gate and up to the second floor of the old brick building.

"How did it come to this?" she wondered as she stood in line to be checked in by the arrogant guard on duty. Humiliated by the frisking, she shook as she waited for her visit with her husband to begin. She had no idea if Peter suspected there was ever someone else, but she had to get this discussion over with. She wanted to get in and out just as quickly as possible.

She moved into the visiting room and chose a cubicle as far away from the guard as possible. She waited for Peter to arrive and sit opposite her from behind the partition.

Peter moved slowly down the stairway and saw his wife in the room below him. "I told her not to come. She knows I don't want her to see me here. Why is she doing this to me?"

As he slipped into the cubicle, partitioned from her, he said "Nancy, God, I don't want you to be exposed to this type of environment."

She took off her dark glasses. "How are you doing?"

He was stunned to see her so thin and embarrassed by the humiliation he could see on her face. Silence hung between them as they looked at each other. It was the first time in a long while that they had been together.

When he didn't answer her, she continued. "Peter we have to talk."

Then he began, "Listen, Nancy, I'm sorry. I know I screwed up - big time, but I'll make this up to you. I promise. When I get out of here, when this is over, we'll begin again. We'll have those children you wanted.

"Peter, it's too late. You know you don't want children. You've said it often enough. I know that now. I do, but it's more than that. We've gone in separate directions. We want different things from life. You know that's true; you must."

Again, he said nothing.

"I've seen my lawyer."

"Nancy, no. Please."

"Peter, don't say anything else right now. This is hard enough for me. Hear me out. I've filed for divorce. I'm here today because I wanted you to hear it from me and not from your lawyer. I'm putting the house on the market. Also, until Suzanne gets things straightened out at the spa, I'm going to take over the day-to-day operation there. She's going to need a lot of help. This whole thing has had a devastating effect on all of us. The girls are a mess. Who knows if the public offering will ever occur now? Maybe I'll like working in the city every day. I'm not sure, but I'm going to give it a try. At the very least, it'll keep my mind occupied."

"Nancy, I need you. I need to know you'll be there for me when I get out. I can't handle it all alone."

"You're going to be here - or somewhere - for a long time and when you do get out, you won't be alone. Alan and your parents will be there for you. And, I'll always be your friend, Peter, but I won't be your wife any more. I can't do it. I'm truly sorry, but this is the way it has to be. I need to be free to do what I want to do with what's left of my life."

She stopped abruptly and stood up. "I'm going to leave now. If you need anything, please let me know. I'll see that you get it."

She took one last look at him. She had a sudden remembrance of the Riviera, Cap-Ferrat, laughter, traffic jams, speeding cars, new friends, and palm groves - - it seemed as if it was another lifetime. Then she turned and brushed quickly past the guards as she left the room, descended the stairs, and went out the prison door and into the sunlight.

Stono Ferry, South Carolina • March 15, 1992

Back in South Carolina, Suzanne walked through her quiet neighborhood to the golf course and visited the stables where the horses grazed on the polo field. The early morning sun glistened on the luxuriant growth that had flourished with the spring season. An alligator swished through the tall grass behind the field and moved across the road where he would lie in wait for his prey.

She sat down on a park bench and reflected on how her life had changed through the years. She thought back to the day she opened her first *Metamorphosis Spa* and how she had changed from an inexperienced, frightened young mother of three, into a powerful and dynamic businesswoman who was in control of her own life and destiny.

A swallowtail butterfly flew out from the bushes near her and landed on her hand. To delay its inevitable flight, Suzanne sat perfectly still and watched its wings fluttering in the light breeze. Reacting to an imperceptible stimulus, the butterfly flew away as suddenly as it had appeared.

She watched a caterpillar crawl up a walnut tree as it sought a home. Secure in its branches, it would first develop into a chrysalis and much later into an adult butterfly. She wondered how beautiful it would be once it emerged from its cocoon.

Just as the hand, held before the eye, can hide the tallest mountain, so the routine of everyday life can keep us from seeing the vast radiance and the secret wonders that fill the world.

Chasidic, 18th Century